SEARCHING *for* PEMBERLEY

MARY LYDON SIMONSEN

sourcebooks
landmark

F SIMONSEN

Published by Sourcebooks Landmark, an imprint of Sourcebooks, Inc.
P.O. Box 4410, Naperville, Illinois 60567-4410
(630) 961-3900
FAX: (630) 961-2168
www.sourcebooks.com

Originally published as Pemberley Remembered in 2007 by TRC Castle Garden
Publishing

Library of Congress Cataloging-in-Publication Data

Simonsen, Mary Lydon.
  [Pemberley remembered]
  Searching for Pemberley / Mary Lydon Simonsen.
    p. cm.
  "Originally published as Pemberley remembered in 2007 by TRC Castle Garden
Publishing" --T.p. verso.
  1. Americans--England--Fiction. 2. Austen, Jane, 1775-1817. Pride and prejudice--
Fiction. 3. England--Fiction. I. Title.
  PS3619.I56287P46 2009
  813'.6--dc22
                              2009035624

Printed and bound in the United States of America.
CHG 10 9 8 7 6 5 4 3 2 1

Dedication

To all of my Irish ancestors who made the voyage to America from Galway, Mayo, and Cork, and to all those who have called Minooka, Pennsylvania, home, including my grandmother, Sarah Sullivan Mahady, and my mother, Hannah Mahady Lydon. You were a hearty breed.

I owe so much to my family who read and reread the manuscript for this work of fiction, including my husband, Paul, my daughters and granddaughter, Meg, Kate, and Kaelyn, my sisters, Betty, Nancy, Kathe, Sally, and Carole. It is a better book because of your suggestions, comments, and encouragement. I couldn't have done it without you.

Cast of Characters

For those who have not read *Pride and Prejudice* or who have not read it recently, please see the Appendix for brief descriptions of the main characters.

Jane Austen's Characters/Characters from *Searching for Pemberley*:
Mr. Bennet/John W. Garrison—Father
Mrs. Bennet/Francine Sims Garrison—Mother
Jane Bennet/Jane Garrison Bingham—Oldest Daughter
Elizabeth Bennet/Elizabeth Garrison Lacey—2nd Daughter
Mary Bennet/Mary Garrison—3rd Daughter
Kitty Bennet/Celia Garrison Stanton—4th Daughter
Lydia Bennet/Lucy Garrison Waggoner Edwards—5th Daughter
George Bingley/George Bingham—Charles's Eldest Brother
Charles Bingley/Charles Bingham—Jane's Love Interest
William Collins/Dr. William Chatterton—Charlotte's Husband
Fitzwilliam Darcy/William Lacey—Elizabeth's Love Interest
Georgiana Darcy/Georgiana Lacey Oldham—Will Lacey's sister
Lady Catherine de Bourgh/Lady Sylvia Desmet—Will Lacey's Aunt

Anne de Bourgh/Anne Desmet—Will Lacey's Cousin
Col. Fitzwilliam/Col. Alexander Devereaux—Will Lacey's Cousin
Col. Foster/Col. Fenton—Waggoner's Colonel
Mr. Gardiner/Mr. Sims—Elizabeth's Uncle
Mrs. Gardiner/Mrs. Sims—Elizabeth's Aunt
Charlotte Lucas/Charlotte Ledger Chatterton—Elizabeth's Friend
George Wickham/George Waggoner—Seducer of Lydia

Longbourn: Bennets End, Hertfordshire
Netherfield Park: Helmsley Hall, Hertfordshire
Pemberley: Montclair, Derbyshire
Rosings Park: Desmet Park, Kent

Chapter 1

MY HOMETOWN IS LITTLE more than a bump in the road between Scranton and Wilkes-Barre in the hard-coal country of eastern Pennsylvania. At the time of the 1929 stock market crash inaugurating the Great Depression, Minooka had already been in its own depression for five years. The lack of work meant that most of the town's young people were reading want ads for jobs in New York, Philadelphia, Baltimore, and Washington.

I was in high school in December 1940 when President Franklin Delano Roosevelt gave his famous "Arsenal of Democracy" radio address to the nation. In that speech, the president committed the industrial might of the United States to defeating fascism in Europe. Because of that commitment, factories that had been idled during the Depression were now running three shifts in an attempt to supply Great Britain with the planes, tanks, artillery, and other war materiel needed to defeat Nazi Germany. It seemed as if every company in America was hiring, and the biggest employer of them all was the United States government.

After the attack on Pearl Harbor and America's entry into the war, what had been a steady stream of job seekers to the nation's capital became a deluge. After graduating from business college in Scranton in June 1944, I headed to Washington to join my two older sisters who had been working in the District since early 1941. Without any experience, I was hired as a clerk typist with the Treasury Department for the princely sum of $1,440 a year. With three paychecks coming in, my sisters and I were able to rent an apartment in a row house near Dupont Circle.

On June 6, 1944, the long-awaited invasion of France had begun, and with the news of the successful landings came the realization that the Allies would win. Finally, on May 8, 1945, America and the world learned that the Germans had officially surrendered. After nearly six years of bloodshed, the war in Europe was over. Now, all resources were being diverted to the Pacific and the defeat of the Empire of Japan.

In August 1945, when the newspapers reported that a B-29 bomber, the "Enola Gay," had dropped an atomic bomb on Hiroshima, no one understood exactly what an atomic bomb was. Then another was dropped on Nagasaki with casualties reported as being in the tens of thousands from just one bomb. Suddenly, the possibility that the fighting might soon end was very real. On a personal level, this meant I might soon be unemployed.

I need not have worried; my job was never in jeopardy. But with the war over, both of my sisters had decided to return to Minooka, which meant I would have to find a place to live. Although I posted a notice on the bulletin board in the lunchroom advertising for a room or roommate, my heart wasn't in it. I was ready for a change, and memories of the heat and humidity of a Washington summer provided the motivation.

A co-worker mentioned that the Army Exchange Service, the agency responsible for providing goods and services to American service personnel, was hiring for positions in Germany because of the large number of servicemen who were stationed in the American occupation zone. I was not ready to go back home, but if avoiding a return to my hometown meant going to Germany, I didn't see how that was much of an improvement.

The war in Europe had been over for more than a year, but the newspapers were full of stories and pictures of a defeated Germany with many cities pounded into powder. The aerial bombing and the fighting on the ground had left many of the structures without windows or walls and with their interiors exposed to passersby. Their occupants, often hungry children, looked out at the photographer with faces full of want and despair. I was depressed from reading about it; how would I feel if I actually lived there?

Notwithstanding all the drawbacks, I went on an interview with the Army Exchange Service. Because AES was so short staffed in Germany, the personnel manager told me that if I agreed to a year's employment in Frankfurt, he would try to get me six months in London. Two weeks later, I sailed for Hamburg and arrived in the former Third Reich in August 1946. As the train pulled into the Frankfurt station, I was met by a scene straight out of Dante's *Inferno*. A huge black hulk of twisted metal was all that was left of the once grand railway station. My first inclination was to get the hell out of Dodge, but instead, I took the bus to the Rhein-Main Air Base, my home for the next year.

Although my co-workers insisted that conditions in Frankfurt had improved since that first year after the war's end, I found it hard to believe when I looked on city block after city block of bombed buildings and piles of rubble or passed Germans on the street who walked with hunched shoulders and downcast eyes. When winter came, it proved to be one of the most brutally cold winters Europe had ever experienced. Rivers were choked with ice, canals froze, rail travel was curtailed, and the coal shortages caused terrible hardships for the Germans. Initially, there was little sympathy for our former enemies, and all contact with the general German population was forbidden. However, by the time I arrived, the non-fraternization policy was a thing of the past, and American servicemen were lining up at military personnel offices to apply for permission to marry German nationals.

After working in Frankfurt for one year, my transfer to London was approved, but because of a reduction in the number of military personnel stationed in Britain, there was no guarantee as to the length of my employment. I was so eager to leave Germany that I agreed and arrived in time to experience late summer in London. Even though the city still showed the extensive damage caused by German bombs, I was more than happy to be in an English-speaking country. I immediately liked England and the English. They were not demonstrative, but in small ways, they showed that they appreciated all the United States had done to help them defeat Germany and Japan.

Every weekend I became a typical American tourist. Riding London's red double-decker buses, I visited the National Gallery, Westminster Abbey, St. Paul's Cathedral, the Tower of London, and all the other popular tourist sites that made London a cultural jewel. I stood in line at the British Museum to see the Elgin Marbles. The friezes from the Parthenon were being displayed for the first time since the beginning of the war when they had been packed up and stored in the Aldwych Piccadilly Underground to keep them safe from German bombs.

After weeks of touring London, I wanted to get out into the countryside, so I asked for suggestions from the girls in my office building who had moved to London from all over the British Isles. As a devoted fan of Jane Austen and *Pride and Prejudice*, I especially wanted to know more about Hertfordshire and Derbyshire, the major settings for the story. Pamela, a Derbyshire native, was also a fan of the book and told me that I should find out if "Montclair," the house where the Darcys had lived, was open to visitors. At first I thought she was "having me on," but then I realized that she was perfectly serious.

"*Pride and Prejudice* is my favorite novel," I told Pamela. "I've read it at least a dozen times, but the characters are fictitious."

"Of course, they're fictitious, but they were based on real people. I grew up in Stepton, which is about five miles from Montclair, or Pemberley, as Jane Austen called it. It's the ancestral home of the Laceys. They're the ones who Jane Austen called the Darcys. If you really love the novel so much, you should at least go to see Montclair." After thinking about it for a minute, Pamela added, "I could go with you. It would give me a chance to see my family."

"Can you walk to Montclair?" I asked doubtfully.

"No, but my brother has a car, and I know how to drive it. I could take you up to the house. Then, we'll stay overnight at my mum's."

Since I had heard that Derbyshire had some of the loveliest countryside in England, I decided to accept Pamela's offer. I needed to take advantage of the mild fall weather because I knew from my experience in Germany, that in two months, the steel gray skies of winter would be the norm. I wrote to the present owners of Montclair, Ellen and Donald Caton, and was given a date and time when the house would be open.

On the train ride to Stepton, I asked Pamela what she knew about the Laceys. "Nothing really. I did know the Australian family, the Pratts, who bought Montclair from the Laceys, because they hosted a harvest festival every August and would have all the village children up to the manor house for games and lemonade and cake. They had a lot of kids known around town as the Pratt brats. Once the kids finished school, everyone was in favor of going back to Australia, so they sold it to the Catons."

Pamela's family lived a short distance from the train station in a red-brick row house, which was covered with the black soot that had accumulated over the decades from the coal-fired engines of the locomotives. On Saturday morning, after finishing a bowl of porridge, Pamela and I headed toward Montclair in her brother's car. I had seen cars like this in my hometown, but they were usually up on blocks and used for parts. Despite all the noises coming from the engine, the car did go forward.

It was a picture-perfect autumn day in Derbyshire when I first saw Montclair. Even though the house was showing its age, with chipped stucco and stonework in need of cleaning, it was a lovely house painted in a beautiful yellow gold, and it glowed in the morning sun. My first glimpse of the mansion was from the top of a gentle rise. The main section was three stories with two wings of two stories and a tower attached to the main section in the rear. It was surrounded by a beautiful park, and a large fountain in front of the drive stood silent.

Pamela and I joined three other couples who were standing at the main entrance, outside the ornate double doors, waiting for the tour to begin. They had also heard that the manor house might have a connection to Fitzwilliam Darcy.

"Welcome to Montclair," Mrs. Caton said while stepping out onto the portico. "I hope you won't be disappointed to learn that this house is owned by Americans. Prior to our purchase in 1937, an Australian couple, Lester and Lynn Pratt, and their family lived here for ten years. Upon taking possession of the property, we immediately started on its restoration, but when the war came, all construction stopped for the duration. Renovations resumed last spring, but as you can imagine, in a country that experienced such extensive bombing, building materials are in short supply."

Pointing to the beautiful but damaged stucco exterior, Mrs. Caton said in a nasal voice revealing her New England roots, "The entire front façade, with its Ionic pilasters and classical pediments, was completed in 1800 and represents the best in Georgian neoclassicism and the Greek Revival.

"Before the Pratts, Montclair was owned by Edward and Sarah Bolton Lacey, and before them, numerous generations of the Lacey family. I suspect that some of you are here because you have heard that this was once the home of Elizabeth Bennet and Fitzwilliam Darcy of *Pride and Prejudice* fame."

As soon as I heard the name, Elizabeth Bennet, my ears perked up. Was it possible that I was actually standing in the home of the real Elizabeth Bennet and Mr. Darcy?

"For those of you not familiar with the novel, it is the story of a wealthy and connected gentleman of the landed gentry who, despite his best efforts to resist, falls in love with the daughter of a gentleman farmer of some means but whose position in society is inferior to his own. In order for the two to finally come together, Mr. Darcy must overcome his pride because of his superior place in society, while Elizabeth must forgive Mr. Darcy's rude behavior from their first meeting at a local dance. I will admit there are many similarities in their stories, and the Laceys may have provided the inspiration for Jane Austen, but that is something each of you will have to decide for yourself." And with that she began her tour.

"A building in one form or another has been on this site since the sixteenth century. However, this particular house was begun in 1704 and expanded to its current size during the reign of George III—the very same king who gave us Americans so much trouble. Most of the interiors of the public rooms were designed by Robert Adam, the most sought-after designer of his day, during the Georgian period in the mid-eighteenth century."

Up to that moment, I had never heard of Robert Adam, but I immediately loved the elegant simplicity of his neoclassical style.

"During the Regency Era, which is broadly defined as the years between 1795 and 1830, work on the interiors continued under the direction of William Lacey and his wife, Elizabeth Garrison Lacey, or Mr. and Mrs. Darcy, if that is your inclination."

We climbed the intricate, double, wrought iron staircase to the first-floor gallery. A photograph propped up in one of several niches showed that two life-sized portraits of William and Elizabeth Lacey from the early 1800s had once been displayed at the top of the staircase. Because the photograph was so faded, it was impossible to know what Mr. Darcy and his "dearest, loveliest Elizabeth" had looked like, except they were very well dressed. When the last of the Laceys sold the house, they had removed all of the family portraits, as well as their art collection, and only empty walls and the shadows of the paintings remained.

Because most of the rooms on the first floor were the private residence of the Catons, we returned to the ground floor, where Mrs. Caton pointed out the "splendid" mural on the wall between the twin staircases, which had been painted by Reed Lacey, the youngest of the last Lacey family to live at Montclair. The floor tile in the painting matched that of the foyer, creating the illusion of a hallway leading to a vine-covered terrace with a beagle puppy sleeping in the corner. We moved on to an extensive library containing books dating from the early sixteenth century, which had remained when the house had been sold. Maybe, this was where Mr. Darcy kicked back after a long day of riding around his estate checking on his tenants. With his wife sitting beside him on the sofa doing needlework, Mr. Darcy would be reading Henry Fielding's *Tom Jones* and laughing at its risqué passages, which he would share with Lizzy.

Crossing the foyer, we moved quickly through the drawing and music rooms, each with its own carved marble fireplace with classical themes, before arriving at the ballroom, which ran the length of the west wing of the house. The room was empty except for the ladders and supplies used by the men who were preparing the walls for replastering.

"In 1941, because of its proximity to the Peak District, the house was requisitioned by the British government as a retreat for officers of the Royal Air Force from Commonwealth countries, but there were also officers from the Free French, Norway, the Netherlands, and Poland, among others, whose countries were occupied by the Germans."

Pamela whispered to me, "I was living in London, but I heard from some of my girlfriends that those airmen did more than rest when they came into Stepton."

Our hostess led us to the terrace at the rear of the house where we were met by the head gardener. Leaning against the balustrades, Mr. Ferguson explained that the grounds had been designed by Humphry Repton, who was considered to be the successor to Capability Brown, the designer of the formal gardens at Blenheim. In a bored monotone, the gardener explained that Repton had also designed the terrace. "You can see his work at Longleat, the home of the Marquis of Bath, in Somerset, or at Cobham Hall in Kent, the estate of the Earls of Darnley, if that means anything to anyone." I had the distinct impression that we were taking Mr. Ferguson away from his work and he didn't appreciate the disruption.

"During the war, the entire garden was turned under and replanted with food crops, such as potatoes, beets, and cabbage, to help in the war effort. As you can see, the upper gardens have been returned to their original purpose as flower gardens, but because of food shortages, we won't be converting the rest of the gardens any time soon. The park at its largest was ten miles around, but the family sold off large parcels and donated others to the National Trust before its sale to its present owners." Putting his finger to his lips, Mr. Ferguson told us the sale was necessary in order to pay the tax man, "but I'm not supposed to tell you that," he said, jerking his head toward the mansion.

The other couples on the tour had quickly walked the gardens and left, convinced that as lovely as the house was, it was not imposing enough to be the storied Pemberley. I found myself wondering if this country house could actually be the home of Fitzwilliam Darcy. Granted, it was very large, but it did not go on endlessly with a series of additions like I had seen at Blenheim, the ancestral estate of the Churchills. After walking down its front lawn, which was being nibbled away by a dozen or more sheep, and seeing all of Montclair from a distance, I found that I agreed with Elizabeth Bennet's reaction upon first seeing Pemberley: "I have never seen a place for which nature had done more or where natural beauty had been so little counteracted by an awkward taste."

While I had been enjoying the gardens, Pamela had returned to the parking area to have a cigarette. Walking down the long drive, I could hear the sound of the carriage wheels and horses' hooves as they made their way up the hill, carrying couples to a night's entertainment. Welcoming them was Elizabeth Darcy, dressed in an elegant but simple ivory-colored Empire dress, while Fitzwilliam Darcy was outfitted in clothing made popular by Beau Brummel: jacket, waistcoat, neckcloth, breeches, and high leather boots.

I found Pamela talking to a man who introduced himself as Donald Caton. "As I have been explaining to your friend, many scholars who have studied Jane Austen's writings believe her model for Pemberley was Chatsworth, the home of the Dukes of Devonshire, and one of the largest estates in the country. When people look at Montclair, they are disappointed because they are expecting Chatsworth." I assured Mr. Caton I was not in the least disappointed.

After a long pause, Mr. Caton said, "You're probably wondering if these stories about the Darcys can possibly be true." Pointing down the hill in the direction of a nearby town, Mr. Caton continued, "There is a couple who lives in the village of Crofton by the name of Crowell. Mr. Crowell and his family have been associated with this estate for generations. He most firmly believes Montclair is Pemberley. You might want to talk to him."

Following Mr. Caton's directions, Pamela and I found where the Crowells lived, just outside the village proper in a lovely home called Crofton Wood, set back from the main road. The front of the house was covered in vines with small yellow flowers, and purple and yellow flowers lined the stone path to their door. A man, whom I assumed to be Mr. Crowell, was standing outside the front door smoking a cigarette.

"Mr. Crowell, you don't know me. I'm Maggie Joyce, but I was wondering if..." But that was as far as I got.

"You're here about the Darcys, right? Don Caton rang me to let me know you might be coming 'round. Come through. Any friend of Jane Austen's is a friend of mine."

Chapter 2

JACK CROWELL WAS A tall man in his mid-fifties with dark graying hair, piercing blue eyes, and the ruddy complexion of someone who enjoyed the outdoors. He explained that coffee was still hard to come by but that he had brewed up some tea.

"I grew up in Stepton," Pamela said while pouring out, "but I'm living in London now. I'd like to move back home at some point, but there are no jobs to be had. So I'll stay in London and type, type, type for the crotchety old solicitor I'm working for. I'm not complaining, though. My boyfriend was demobbed out of the Army six months ago, and the only work he can find is the odd construction job. We can't get married until he finds work, and right now my chances on that score are crap."

Pamela was definitely not shy, and she quickly proved it when she asked Mr. Crowell if the chicken coops we had seen from the road belonged to him. After he acknowledged that they were, she said, "I haven't eaten an egg that came out of the arse of a chicken in a year. All we ever get is that powdered stuff."

After Jack stopped laughing, he told her he would send her home with at least a half dozen eggs. After thanking Mr. Crowell for the eggs, Pamela said she remembered the harvest festivals the Pratts had hosted in late summer.

"That was a tradition of long standing," Mr. Crowell explained. "My father was the butler up at Montclair, and my mother was the housekeeper. We lived below stairs in the senior servants' quarters. We loved it. Great place for my brother and me to run around and explore—lots of nooks and crannies.

"When I was a lad, every August, the Laceys invited the locals up to the house to celebrate 'Harvest Home.' Everyone had a job to do. The two oldest Lacey boys were in charge of games, the daughter told fortunes in one of the smaller marquees, and the youngest son was an artist who would make funny sketches of the children. My brother, Tom, and I would take all the young ones for pony rides around the fountain on a tether. If the wind was blowing, they'd get wet from the spray, and the kiddies would all squeal with delight.

"The largest marquee was where all of the food was served, with roast beef and ham, plum puddings, loaves and loaves of bread, fresh fruit, petit fours, and all the lemonade you could drink. There were about a dozen or so tables out on the lawn, all covered with white linen, and Sir Edward and his wife would walk the grounds making sure that everyone had enough to eat and were enjoying themselves."

After refilling my cup and adding the milk for me, Mr. Crowell asked what I thought of Montclair and if it measured up to Jane Austen's Pemberley. I said that it did, but I also told him that I doubted Jane Austen had used real people for her novels. Certain people may have influenced her writing, but it seemed impossible to me that there was such a person as Mr. Darcy.

Mr. Crowell, who insisted that I call him Jack, said, "It's not my job to convince you, Maggie, but I have a feeling you want to be convinced."

"I would think that if people believed Montclair was actually Pemberley, they would be beating a path to its door."

"You'd be wrong, my dear. Here's what I think," he said, settling back into his chair. "Jane Austen didn't want her identity known. When *Pride and Prejudice* was published, she identified herself only as 'the author of *Sense and Sensibility*.' Originally, her writings were for the entertainment of her family, but they convinced Jane that her stories should be published. She had a decent-sized following before Queen Victoria's reign. However, most Victorians didn't take to her. Silly mother, a lazy father, a fallen sister who wasn't punished. The Victorians would have had the deflowered Lydia dying in the snow on the road to Longbourn. No, they were too serious for someone as lighthearted as Jane.

"People started to rediscover her in the 1900s, but then came The Great War. Ten men from Crofton were killed outright. There's a memorial dedicated to them on the village green." After Jack mentioned the war, there was a long pause before he continued, and I had no doubt that someone he cared about was on that memorial. "The walking wounded, widows, and orphans were everywhere. No one was thinking about Jane's tale of two lovers. Then it was the Depression, and right after that, we were again at war. Not much time for Jane."

"Is there anything to support your idea that the Laceys and Darcys are one and the same?"

"It's more than an idea, Maggie. My family has worked at Montclair longer than anyone can remember. My father's father worked for the Laceys. He had met the Binghams, or the Bingleys, as Jane Austen called them. These stories were all passed down."

But would Jane Austen have written a novel that often ridiculed people who could possibly be identified by their neighbors, for example, Mrs. Bennet, with her fragile nerves and poor judgment?

"Do you know when Jane first wrote the novel?" he asked.

"When she was twenty, so that would be about 1795."

"But it wasn't published until 1813," Jack said, jumping in quickly. "By that time, the Laceys had been married for twenty years! If anyone was trying to figure out if these characters were real, they would have been looking at people in their twenties in 1813. Some of the characters in that book were already dead and buried by the time *Pride and Prejudice* was published."

I was enjoying our conversation so much that I almost forgot about Pamela. She had sat there quietly for a while, but once Jack and I started talking about *Pride and Prejudice*, she started to walk around the room, looking at family pictures. I hoped she wouldn't start opening drawers which, with Pamela, was a possibility. There was so much I wanted to ask Mr. Crowell, but Pamela had promised her brother she would have the car back to him by 7:00.

"Not to worry. If Pamela wants to go on ahead, I can drive you over to Stepton myself. Besides, I'd like you to meet my wife. She's very keen on people who are interested in Elizabeth Bennet's story." After some discussion, I accepted Mr. Crowell's offer, and Pamela left with her six eggs.

Shortly after Pamela drove off, Mrs. Crowell came in carrying groceries. Following a brief conversation with her husband and after handing him her shopping bags, Mrs. Crowell introduced herself. She was a very attractive woman with light brown hair, cut in a short, simple style, which accentuated beautiful dark eyes. She was wearing black slacks and an ivory turtleneck sweater, and after she sat down in a chair across from me, she pulled her long legs back so that she was almost sitting sideways. Obviously, this was someone who had been taught that a lady never crossed her legs.

"On its face, it seems difficult to believe. But I grew up very near to this village, and it has been a part of my family lore for generations." Mrs. Crowell was even more sincere than her husband.

I realized how late it was only when Mrs. Crowell said she was going to start dinner. I was sure I had overstayed my welcome, and I had to get back to Pamela's house.

"You are welcome to stay the night," Mrs. Crowell offered. "We have a guest bedroom with its own bath, and please call me Beth."

Jack jumped in. "I'll ring over to Stepton. You can tell your friend that I'll have you back at her house in time for the evening train to London. No worries."

"I can hardly believe I'm saying this, but I accept."

***

After dinner, the Crowells and I returned to the living room for tea. The remainder of the evening was spent discussing how it was that Jane Austen's Fitzwilliam Darcy, a member of the privileged landed gentry, came to know Charles Bingley, the son of a man who had made his fortune in trade. Jack related the events that led to the lifelong friendship of the real William Lacey and Charles Bingham.

"The head of the Bingham family was George Bingham, a financial genius. Along with his brothers, Richard and James, they owned a large import/export business with warehouses in India and America. When the Revolutionary War broke out, the warehouses in New York, Philadelphia, and Charleston were shuttered. Once the war was over, George sent Richard to America to check on the condition of their properties, and he took Charles with him. But after a year, Richard sent him home. Compared to his colonial friends, who had been educated in England, Charles was coming up short.

"A Mr. Montaigne was hired to tutor Charles in the usual subjects a gentleman of that era would have been expected to know: Latin, French, science, mathematics, and the classics. Socially, George Bingham wanted Charles to be comfortable in any situation, including attendance on the king at the Court of St. James. For that, he turned to William Lacey, Jane Austen's Mr. Darcy."

"The Laceys were an old Norman family, their land grant going back to the twelfth century and the reign of Henry II. Will's father, David Lacey or Old Mr. Darcy as Jane Austen called him, married Anne Devereaux, a pretty young lady from another of the old Norman families.

"When David Lacey died, young Will went over the accounts of the estate with George Bingham, the co-executor of his father's will, and found out that all of his mother's dowry had been spent on the remodeling and expansion of Montclair and that the estate was deeply in debt. Will decided that if he was to maintain the Lacey lifestyle, as well as provide for the proper support of his sister, Georgiana, he had to come up with other ways of making money.

"This is where George Bingham came in," Jack continued. "He had a reputation for helping out some of England's finest but financially stretched families. George and Will worked out a deal. In return for taking Charles under his wing, George Bingham would make the necessary loans to get Will Lacey out of debt as well as provide investment opportunities in the Bingham enterprises. That was the start of Charles and Will's friendship. It was an odd pairing, but it worked because they balanced each other out."

I knew little about the English aristocracy or how one got to be a duke or an earl, but I did know that titles were important. I wondered why the Lacey family did not have one.

Beth chose to answer my question. "Great deference was paid to these old Norman families because of their ancient ties to the monarchy. The Lacey name and land grant were much older than most of those who had been granted earldoms and dukedoms, so the Laceys rested on their ancient Norman laurels."

A combination of the train ride from London, the visit to Montclair, and an overload of information had left me exhausted, and I called an end to the evening. I was shown to a large room that had once been the shared bedroom of their two sons. A dozen pictures of the boys hung on the walls, and more pictures were displayed in a glass case along with their many trophies and ribbons. The evening had been so interesting that, although we had spent eight hours together, I never once thought to ask the Crowells about their children.

Lying in bed, I tried to take it all in, and a lot of what I had been told made sense. It certainly explained how someone from a family as prestigious as the Laceys came to befriend a man whose family had acquired its wealth by trade. But the one question that kept popping up in my mind was, "How on earth did the Crowells know so much about the Bingham and Lacey families?"

Chapter 3

WHEN I CAME DOWNSTAIRS the following morning, Jack and Beth were at church, but Beth had left a note on top of a large manila envelope saying, "I think you'll be interested in this. Help yourself to some tea and whatever is in the icebox, Beth." Inside the envelope was a letter yellow with age.

11 September 1813

Dear Charlotte,

Thank you for your kind letter. My father's health is much improved, so much so that I believe I will be able to return to Canterbury within a fortnight. I long to be back in my own home where I will be safe from Lucy's complaints. Conversation of any length inevitably leads to a discussion of Pride and Prejudice, *Miss Austen's book. I have assured her that no one would recognize her in the character of Lydia. These events took place twenty years ago, and there are very few who remember or care about something that happened at* such a distance in time. She's afraid that Jake will learn the whole of the story if he reads the book. Jake read a work of fiction? When? The farm takes up all his daylight hours, and my nephews' demands on him in the evening do not allow time for anything but smoking his pipe.

I have read the novel and feel there are enough differences in our situations that none would recognize the family. I hardly recognize it myself. Was Elizabeth ever so clever or Jane so perfect? For my part, was I really that tedious a person? As you know, I have never considered myself to be a vocalist, limiting my musical exhibitions to the pianoforte, so the humiliating depiction of Mary Bennet's performance at the Netherfield ball is particularly galling to me. And why did the author choose to disguise only Lucy and Celia's names? If I am to be portrayed so unsympathetically, why was I not given the courtesy of a name change? I will admit that after Henry's death, our mother's occupation of seeing her daughters married consumed most of her thoughts. However, my father could never have married someone as ridiculous as Mrs. Bennet. I think Papa has been dealt with quite harshly as well. The novel is meant to be lighthearted. Therefore, writing about the death of the male heir could not be included. Yet, Papa made his decisions based upon the fact that he did have an heir who would free the family from the entail.

Of course, Lucy's elopement veers most from the truth. As you know, I disagreed with my parents' decision to receive her at their home after embarking on such an escapade. But I think reconciliation would have been impossible if they believed Lucy had knowingly left Brighton with Waggoner without an understanding that they were to be married in Gretna Green *in Scotland, where such marriages take place. Lucy insists to this day that nothing happened between Waggoner and her, as she would not give in to his urges until she was in possession of her wedding clothes. The worst, of course, is Lucy's character living with Waggoner in London for a fortnight without being married!*

I have already wasted too much ink on this subject, but some part of the story is discussed every day. One would have hoped that, with the passage of time and the birth of four children, Lucy would concentrate less on herself and more on others, but that is not the case. The most pleasant part of my stay is visiting with my nieces who, despite the shortcomings of their natural parents, are well-mannered and thoughtful young ladies. Lucy has arranged for Antoinette and Marie to go up to London to stay with Celia for the winter season. She feels their marriage prospects would be much improved being in town. With respect to matchmaking, Lucy is very much her mother's daughter.

Yours in deepest friendship,
Mary Garrison

My mind was racing. I was trying to understand what I had just read, so I reread the letter and then again for a third time. If this was actually a letter written by Mary Garrison to Charlotte, Elizabeth's closest friend, then it contained a wealth of information. Waggoner/Wickham, the young handsome seducer, who had been bribed into marrying Lucy/Lydia, had died, and his widow had remarried Jake the farmer. Celia/Kitty must have married well enough for her sister to believe that by sending her daughters to stay with Celia in London, they would have a better chance of making an advantageous marriage. But why was Mary living with the Collinses in Canterbury?

When Beth returned from church, she found me sitting at the kitchen table rereading the letter yet again.

"Jack stays after church and plays backgammon with the pastor," she explained while removing her hat and gloves. "The house is too quiet for him with our older son, James, living in London with his wife and daughter, and our younger son, Michael, serving in the RAF on Malta. Jack's mother, a perfectly wonderful soul, lived with us until she died two years ago."

Beth asked about my family, and I told her a little bit about my sisters. Katie was a new mother, Annie had joined the Sisters of St. Joseph, a religious order, and Sadie was a recent high school graduate. And then there was Patrick. He was my only brother, but with a brother like Patrick, one was enough. His own grandmother referred to him as "one of the divil's own."

Minooka had its fair share of boys who got into mischief on a regular basis. Patrick was just more creative than most. He had been expelled from the Catholic school we all attended in Scranton and was banned from most homes in town with good reason. When he had led a strike at the high school and gave an interview to a reporter from the Scranton newspaper where my father worked, my parents had finally had enough. He was sent to live with my mother's brother, who ran a bootleg coal operation, and Uncle Bill worked his butt off. Patrick behaved himself for a while, but it took the Navy to really straighten him out.

But I didn't want to talk about my family. I wanted to talk about Mary's letter. "May I ask where you got the letter?"

"Jack's Aunt Margie. She had a keen interest in the Lacey

family history because of their connection to *Pride and Prejudice*. Margie traveled around England, searching for the people and places in the novel. By going through church records, she found the Garrisons, six girls and one boy. The youngest girl had died when she was two and the boy when he was twelve."

Placing a teapot, two cups and saucers, and a plate of biscuits on a tray, Beth gestured for me to follow her into the parlor. She had a way of carrying herself that was almost regal, especially when compared to her husband, who reminded me of a former football player who had taken a hit or two. Their class differences were especially noticeable when they spoke. Beth's accent was definitely upper class, while Jack's was the local Derbyshire dialect.

After pouring the tea into dainty Belleek china cups, Beth explained how it was that the Garrison/Bennet family had managed to evade the entail.

"After George Waggoner's death, Lucy married Jake Edwards. I'm referring to Austen's Wickham and Lydia. I'm not sure if the farm is still owned by the Edwards family, but it was right before the First War. Reluctantly, Mrs. Edwards admitted to Margie that the family was the inspiration for the Bennet family. It wasn't talked up because they didn't particularly like how the Bennets were portrayed in the book. She thought they were either silly or lazy or, in Lucy's case, of low moral character.

"Mrs. Edwards allowed Margie to go up into her attic, where she found the letter from Mary to Charlotte in a portable writing desk, what was known as an escritoire. Fortunately for us, Mary never posted the letter to Charlotte. Mrs. Edwards told Margie to take the whole lot, saying that no one in her family cared about old letters and papers. She seemed to want to be rid of them short of actually throwing them on the fire. Margie got as much history out of Mrs. Edwards as she could, but it wasn't much. She knew that Waggoner's regiment had been transferred to Canada because Lucy had moved back home, which must have been difficult for everyone, but most especially for Mary. The last person in the world she wanted to live with was Lucy, whom she considered to be a fallen woman because of her hurried marriage with Waggoner.

"After Charlotte married William Chatterton, Jane Austen's unctuous Mr. Collins, Mary visited with the Chattertons in Kent. When Lucy took up permanent residence at her parents' home, Mary again visited Charlotte, but she never went home. There is a whole other story about those three living together, but I'll save that for another time."

I thanked Beth for what was clearly an invitation to return. Jack had come home about midway through the story but seemed content to let his wife tell it.

"The reason William Chatterton didn't inherit the estate was simply a matter of Mr. Garrison outliving him. Since the entail stipulated that the heir must be a male, Charlotte could not inherit. After Mr. Garrison's death, the estate passed to the next male descendant in the family, Jane Garrison and Charles Bingham's oldest son. That kept the farm in the Garrison family. Charlotte and Mary eventually returned to the village of Bennets End, the book's Meryton, and lived in a house in the village until their deaths."

Looking at the grandfather clock in their entryway, I thanked the Crowells for sharing what they knew of the Lacey and Bingham families and for their hospitality. I was pleased I had been invited back because we had barely touched the surface of the story, but I also liked Beth and Jack and wanted to see them again.

*****

On the drive to Pamela's house, I asked Jack what it was like growing up at Montclair. "Fantastic! My father's family served as butlers to the Laceys for three generations, and my mother was the housekeeper. By the way, the housekeeper's job in a house of that size has nothing to do with dusting.

"Except for the cooking, my mother and father saw to everything else in order to keep the house running smoothly, including being in charge of all the servants who didn't work for Mrs. Bradshaw, the cook, who had her own little fiefdom downstairs. The Laceys entertained a lot, so my parents' jobs were very demanding. My brother and I were pressed into service when the Laceys had their big affairs. We had our own evening clothes, white gloves and all. We were the cat's meow," he said, winking at me. "We'd help the ladies out of their motor cars or their carriages because some people were still traveling by horse and carriage. When some of the male guests started driving their own cars and not using chauffeurs, we were allowed to park them. That was a big deal in those days.

"The Laceys had four children, three boys and a girl. Along with my brother, Tom, we were all great mates—very close in age. After chores, we played football every day during the summer. The second oldest boy, Matthew, and my brother, Tom, were two of the best footballers I'd ever see."

Arriving at Pamela's house, Jack opened the car door for me. "Beth thought you might want to have something to read on the way back to town." He handed me a large brown envelope.

✳✳✳

On the train ride to London, I told Pamela about my overnight visit with the Crowells and asked her if she believed that the Laceys were the Darcys.

"A lot of people in Stepton believe it, including my mum. I think a lot of it's true, but I've always had a hard time with all the coincidences. You know, Darcy and the evil Wickham being in Meryton at exactly the same time, and Mr. Collins being Darcy's aunt's minister and the Bennets' cousin. Stuff like that. It's just too much. But if you look at the big picture, the two families had enough in common so you think maybe Jane Austen had heard about the Laceys and Garrisons and had used them for the Darcys and Bennets." After listening to Pamela, I felt a bit silly believing any of it. She was absolutely right—too many coincidences.

When I finally settled into bed for the night, I opened the brown envelope. It contained a letter from William Lacey to his cousin, Anne Desmet, who was the novel's Anne de Bourgh. Her mother, Lady Sylvia Desmet, was Jane Austen's overbearing aristocrat, Lady Catherine de Bourgh.

26 March 1792

Dear Anne,

Please be assured that I will send Mr. Oldham for you a week Monday as promised. If your mother has any objection, I will come and bring you to London myself. Georgiana is especially eager for your visit, as she wants you to hear the pieces she has been practicing so diligently.

Bingham has taken a lease on a house in the country and will remain there until such time as he finds a property of sufficient acreage to satisfy his passion for horses and hunting. Hopefully, that will be soon, as there is no reason to linger here. He has already befriended many of the neighbourhood families, and, in turn, he has been visited by every gentleman who has a daughter of marriageable age.

The day after my arrival, Bingham insisted that I attend a local assembly. I was in no humour to do so, as I had just come from a visit with Mrs. Manyard regarding her son. I told the lady that it was impossible for me to continue to pay Roger's gaming debts, and that I had instructed my solicitor to contact the gaming houses he frequents and let it be known that Manyard's debts would no longer be discharged by his client. Up to this point, I had avoided involving my solicitor because I did not wish to revisit this whole unfortunate affair. I do not blame my father for seeking female companionship after my mother's death, but he erred in seeking comfort from Mrs. Manyard, a woman of such low birth. I hope my visit will put an end to any further contact.

At the assembly, Bingham met an attractive young lady, the daughter of a gentleman farmer, who seems to have captivated him. He kept insisting that I dance, but as you know, country dances are much closer to athletic events than to actual dancing, and I had no wish to bound about the room in unfamiliar company. Unfortunately, my comment that the only thing worse than dancing was to be forced into conversation with such company was overheard by the young lady's sister. I considered apologizing but decided that, since I will not be seeing her again, it was of little importance.

Fondly,
Will

If this really was a letter from William Lacey to his cousin, Anne Desmet, then it revealed that Will's father had a mistress, and his son was left to handle the fallout from the relationship! And what was Roger Manyard to Will Lacey? No wonder he was in such a bad mood when he attended the assembly. The letter also showed that, although Will dismissed the insult heard by Elizabeth as being of no importance, he had noticed her.

I could only guess that the reason I had been given this letter was to back up the Crowells' claim that Elizabeth Bennet and Fitzwilliam Darcy were Elizabeth Garrison and William Lacey. What I needed to know was, where did they get the letter?

Chapter 4

WITH SO MANY BUILDINGS destroyed in air raids, housing in London was at a premium. A friend of a friend from my time in Germany had found a place for me to stay with her former neighbors, Mr. and Mrs. Dawkins. The room I rented was a tiny bedroom sitter on the third floor of a terrace house in a working-class neighborhood in north London. My rent included kitchen privileges if I cooked my own food or, if I chose to eat with the family, I was charged for the meals. This was necessary because an austerity program had recently been implemented, which included additional cuts in food rations.

As for bathing, I could have a bath if I gave Mrs. Dawkins enough notice so that she could turn on the hot water. There was a line drawn around the tub to indicate when the maximum allowable height of five inches had been reached—a holdover from the war. When I paid my rent, Mrs. Dawkins totaled up all of my baths and charged me extra for them. As long as I watched out for the wallpaper and carpet, Mrs. Dawkins was a fair if not the friendliest landlady.

More than two years after the war, it wasn't difficult to find evidence of a city that had been bombed night after night during the Blitz and later with V-1 and V-2 rockets. Vacant lots where bombed-out buildings had been cleared were a common sight, especially near St. Paul's, where only the archdeacon's house had miraculously survived, and certain areas were cordoned off because of the instability of the buildings or unexploded bombs. There were shortages of fruit, eggs, meat, and petrol, but as an employee of the Army Exchange Service, I had access to government commodities at the Post Exchange. I shared some of the scarcer items, such as sugar, flour, tea, and coffee, as well as Spam, with Mrs. Dawkins, who doled them out to her neighbors.

After a scorcher of a summer, the arrival of the cooler temperatures had everyone out and about. In Hyde Park, people were lounging in their deck chairs, boys were playing football, moms were pushing prams, and couples were walking hand in hand or lying in the grass.

This was my second autumn away from my family, and even though I was feeling homesick more often now, there were a few reasons why I wanted to stay in England. With the exception of Blenheim, Derbyshire, and a day trip to Hampton Court where Henry VIII had courted Anne Boelyn, I had seen very little of England outside of London. After traveling through the beautiful countryside on the way to Montclair, I wanted to see more. Most importantly, I did not want to go back to the town where I had grown up.

Scranton and the surrounding towns had been in decline since the end of World War I when orders for hard coal had dropped precipitously. When the miners went out on strike in 1928, many mine owners decided to close the mines permanently.

Thousands of miners found themselves without a job and without the skills to do anything else.

My father's job was secure because he worked for the city newspaper. Even though he worked in Scranton, with its sidewalks, street lamps, streetcars, and better schools, my dad chose to live in the town where he had grown up. People from Minooka were known as "Mudtowners" because of our unpaved streets. When I was a child, many families still bathed in tin tubs set up in the kitchen, and there were those, including my Grandma Shea, who continued to use outhouses with a Sears catalog for toilet paper.

Few people owned cars, and you could play tag or shoot marbles in the street, getting out of the way of the occasional huckster. In the summer, hordes of children gathered at the corner of Davis Street and Birney Avenue to play hide-and-seek or dodgeball. The older boys hung out at Walsh's candy store, waiting for the girls to walk by, or flirted with them during Tuesday Night's Devotions at St. Joseph's. It was a wonderful place to be a child as long as you steered clear of the third rail, abandoned mines, and my brother Patrick, but a terrible place to be a working adult. Despite the hardships, many were willing to put up with being underemployed or illegally employed because it was all they knew. But after being away for more than two years, I knew better.

My first letter to the Crowells was to thank them for sharing their knowledge of the Lacey family with me, but I also had a few questions for them. They had told me that Jack's Aunt Margie had found the letter from Mary Garrison to Charlotte when his aunt located the Edwards/Garrison farm, but where had they obtained the letter from Will Lacey to Anne Desmet? Jack Crowell's answers came faster than I could have ever hoped.

12 October 1947

Dear Maggie,

It was really our pleasure to have you here, as you're a delightful young lady. Before the war, I was a railroad engineer in India and Argentina. I came home in 1940 and spent my time during the war supervising crews who were repairing infrastructure damaged by German bombs. I am currently working as a consultant, but at Beth's request, I work only part time, so your interest in the Laceys is a nice diversion for me.

Since we told you some things about Lucy and Waggoner (Lydia and Wickham), we'll start there. As part of the arrangements to get Waggoner to marry Lucy, a commission in the regular army was bought for him by Will Lacey. I suspect that Waggoner had got up to his old tricks (gambling, womanizing, etc.) at his new post near Newcastle because his colonel had him transferred to another regiment that was going to North America.

Antoinette was born in 1794 (the year after the French king and queen lost their heads). Their second daughter, Marie Therese, was born about two years later and, I assume, was named after Marie Antoinette's daughter. Lucy seems to have been fascinated by the French, and at that time, the newspapers were filled with stories describing all the gory details about the Revolution. Some included graphic sketches of aristocrats being guillotined. People ate this stuff up just like people who read about grizzly murders in the tabloids do today.

When Waggoner's regiment was sent to a fort in Kingston, Ontario, Lucy returned home to Bennets End. In one of the boxes found at the Edwards/Garrison farm was a letter from

Waggoner's colonel answering a letter from Lucy. He told her that Waggoner had deserted several months earlier, that he was unable to send any money as he had personally repaid some of Waggoner's debts, and that he had no idea where her husband had gone, but if he was found, he would be brought up on charges for desertion. Lucy was now living in the worst of all worlds. She was married but had no husband.

Richard Bingham, Charles's brother, who ran the American operations, hired an agent to track down Waggoner. He was traced to Louisville, Kentucky, where he had been entertaining the locals by telling them that he was the son of an English lord. Louisville was a rough river town, and with his English accent and fine manners, Waggoner stood out. The agent found Waggoner, except that Waggoner had died a few months earlier of typhoid.

Imagine how Lucy, who was in her early twenties, must have felt. But it worked out all right. It seems that Will arranged for Jake Edwards, the son of his head tenant, to go down to the Garrison farm. He boarded with the Garrisons and, in time, asked Lucy to marry him. I think Mr. Garrison, who was getting up in years, saw this as an opportunity to have someone take over the day-to-day operations of the farm. We'll never know how Lucy felt about Jake, but they did have two sons together.

You asked about when everyone died. At this point, I will tell you that of all the characters in the book, the last one to go was Charles Bingham in 1844, when he was seventy-five. More in the next post.

Jack Crowell (with Beth looking over my shoulder)
35

As interesting as all this information was, the Crowells had not written one word about Will Lacey's letter to Anne Desmet telling of his first appearance in Hertfordshire where he had made such a poor first impression. I would have to ask again.

✳✳✳

I wrote a second letter to the Crowells mentioning that Pamela, who had grown up near Montclair, had doubts about the story, and I cited all of the coincidences she had mentioned. In light of all the hardships the British were still experiencing, my search for Elizabeth Bennet and Mr. Darcy seemed silly. But as a thank you for their hospitality, I put together what everyone called "care packages" and sent them some coffee, tea, and chocolate and other things Americans always seemed to give to people in war-damaged countries.

A second letter arrived the following week from Jack thanking me for my package and saying that they would be sharing the tea and coffee with their closest friends. "However, it's got to be kept a secret that we've got the chocolate. We can't risk a riot in the village." And then Jack got after the real reason for the letter.

8 October 1947

Dear Maggie,

Don't give up on us yet. All those coincidences do look a bit dodgy, but I can explain some of them. Remember sickly Anne Desmet? Will Lacey wrote lots of letters to her.

I'll admit I can't tell you how Mr. Chatterton/Mr. Collins came to Lady Sylvia/Lady Catherine's attention for the position of minister at her parish church, but I do know *she would have insisted on her minister marrying. Since Chatterton would inherit Bennets End one day, it made sense for him to check out his cousins, and it's possible Chatterton put Charles Bingham on to Helmsley Hall/Netherfield Park when Charles was a guest at Desmet Park.*

Waggoner's more of a problem. In the book, it shows that even though Will pays him off after his father's death, he shows up and makes a run at Georgiana Lacey. Will pays him off again to get him away from his sister, but Waggoner shows up in Bennets End where Will just happens to be a guest of Charles Bingham. Coincidence? Did Waggoner come to Bennets End hoping Will Lacey would give him more money in order to get rid of him? And this whole business with the young Lucy Garrison? There's something fishy about it. Of all the girls in Brighton, Waggoner singled out Lucy, a girl he knew to have no fortune of her own, but who did have a sister who was in love with Charles Bingham, Will Lacey's friend. It wasn't as if there was a lack of female entertainment for a man of Waggoner's low tastes because Brighton was a favourite haunt of prostitutes, or what the newspapers euphemistically called 'The Cyprian Corps.'

I agree with you that the world is still turned upside down because of the war, which is why diversions, such as my research, are so important. For a people who have endured so much, a return to normalcy is an essential part of the healing process.

Stay in touch and thanks so much for the Hershey bars. Beth has a real weakness for chocolate.

Jack Crowell

After reading Jack's letter, I was starting to regret my decision to decline the Crowell's invitation to return to Crofton Wood. I certainly had nothing better to do. When I left Germany, I was getting over my first serious romance. I had met Val Sostek at a dance at the USO club in Frankfurt. Val loved to jitterbug, and although I considered myself to be a pretty good dancer, I never came close to wearing out the dance floor like he did. After our relationship heated up, Val began to talk about getting married and going back to Pittsburgh to start a family. After having grown up in a coal town, the thought of raising children in an industrial city was not something I was prepared to do. Even though I cared deeply for Val, when he received his orders to return to the States, I ended the relationship.

Once in London, my co-workers tried to hook me up with other guys—Americans, British, and one Polish officer who had fought in Italy alongside the British. I quickly discovered that the British and Americans had a lot in common. Each thought a date should end in the nearest hotel room. The Polish officer was the only man I went out with more than once, but since it was his hope to return to Warsaw one day, nothing was going to come of it. From what I had seen in the newsreels, I wasn't sure if Warsaw still existed, but if it did, it was in worse shape than Frankfurt.

After thinking about what I would not be doing that weekend, going to Crofton would be a pleasant diversion. I decided to accept the Crowells' offer to return to Derbyshire.

Chapter 5

IN LATE OCTOBER, LOADED down with cigarettes, Spam, Nescafé, Hershey bars, and Hostess cupcakes, I headed to Crofton. For the first time in a week, it was not drizzling or raining, but the weather had turned cold. My room had a radiator in it—the kind that whistled when it came on—but it was not enough to keep out the damp. The room also had a space heater that cost six pence for about thirty minutes of heat. Every night, I huddled in front of it before hopping into bed with my flannel nightgown, long underwear, bed socks, mittens, and hot water bottle.

Jack picked me up in a Jeep he had bought at a surplus auction, and I handed him a pack of Lucky Strikes, which produced a big smile. Weeks earlier, the government had banned importing tobacco from the States. "There's nothing like an American cigarette," he said as he lit his first one.

"I got some very good news yesterday. My younger son, Michael, is coming home from Malta for a few days. The RAF is moving some squadrons back here to England, and Mike is a stowaway on one of the planes. It's only for a few days, but I haven't seen him since James got married, and that's a year and a half now. Mike wants to surprise his mother, so he had someone from the telegraph office hand deliver the telegram to me. I can't wait to see her face."

As we pulled into the drive, the house was in full view. Except for the Norwegian pines, all the trees had lost their leaves, and the fall flowers had been uprooted and disposed of. Beth, who was wearing jodhpurs, was waiting for us at the door.

"Come through," she said, making way for me to pass. "I've got a pot of tea brewing. It will take the chill off." She pointed to the chair nearest the fire, which I gladly accepted since I had not been warm in a week. "One of the hardest things to get used to once we came back to Derbyshire from Asia was the cold and damp. But in England, you keep a stiff upper lip, buy a lot of cardigans, and pretend you aren't cold, especially with the coal shortages."

While the Crowells prepared the tea, I had a look around. This was where Beth and Jack spent most of their time. The furniture faced the fireplace and was arranged in such a way as to best hear the radio, and magazines and engineering journals were on a side table. On the far wall were four beautifully detailed sketches showing the same pastoral scene in each of the seasons with a town in the distance. It reminded me of a view I had seen from the terrace at Montclair. On the mantle was a picture of the older son, his gorgeous wife, and baby daughter on a holiday at the beach. The other picture was of a sergeant in the Royal Air Force. Michael had his mother's dark eyes and slender build but his father's black hair. He was incredibly handsome, and I wondered if he was available. I would find out soon enough.

"I hope you're hungry," Beth said, directing me to the dining room. "I've been saving up my meat coupons for a special occasion." The table was beautifully laid out with Meissen china, silverware with gold edging, and Waterford glasses. On the table was as elegant a meal as you could prepare in post-war England. I complimented her on the beautiful setting, and she told me everything had been handed down to her by her mother, who was from Boston.

When the Crowells learned that I had lived in Washington during the war, they wanted to know how it compared to wartime London. They were surprised to hear that rationing for food and gasoline had been strictly enforced, and that everyone carried around their government-issued coupon books. When my cousin had married in '44, her friends had to donate their food coupons so that we would have enough sugar and flour to bake and frost a wedding cake. The commodity in shortest supply was gasoline, and if your occupation wasn't classified as "essential" to achieving victory, then you were entitled to only four gallons of gas per week. As a result, trains were packed, and if you were actually able to grab a seat, you considered yourself lucky. After eating Hostess cupcakes that had been cut up into little squares, we went into the living room where I was to hear the story of Celia, *Pride and Prejudice's* Kitty Bennet.

"Celia's story is tied up with Caroline Bingham's, Charles's sister," Beth said, getting comfortable in the chair and abandoning the ramrod position from my previous visit. "Unlike the novel, I don't really think Caroline was all that serious about 'securing' Mr. Lacey. In any event, she set her sights on another and ended up with Lord David Upton, who was active in Tory politics.

"With the last name of Joyce, you may be interested in Lord Upton. After the 1798 rebellion in Ireland, he advocated very harsh treatment for the Irish and was instrumental in pushing through the Act of Union between Great Britain and Ireland. He was often in the newspapers, which published his rants on a regular basis."

My grandfather, Michael Joyce, a faithful member of the Ancient Order of Hibernians, was also known to rant, but against the British. One evening when my father was staring into the bottom of his beer glass, he told me that his father had once killed a man in Ireland, and I thought, "Only one?" My grandfather was a tough, mean old man who walked around carrying a six-foot switch that was a foot taller than he was. On occasion, he could be nice, but you always approached him as you would a strange dog. Would he attack or not?

"Upton and Caroline's marriage probably was not a love match, but few marriages of England's upper class were. However, she became a prominent and influential hostess in London and lived in an elegant townhouse in Mayfair. Their opulent lifestyle was made possible because George Bingham's investments continued to make money for all the family.

"At this time, London was flooded with émigrés who had fled the political upheaval in France. As a diehard monarchist, Upton was appalled by the horrors inflicted on the aristocracy by the French Revolutionaries, and his home became a gathering place for these refugees. It was there that Celia met a young Frenchman and fell in love. Everyone would have advised her against continuing this relationship. Because of the increasing violence in France, there was the possibility that the young man would never be able to return to his own country. Since Celia had no money and all of the young man's wealth and property were in France, they had nothing to marry on. Instead, she married Tyndall Stanton, a wealthy businessman, and achieved her own degree of success in society. Celia, who was childless, was devoted to her two nieces, Lucy's daughters, Antoinette and Marie, and introduced them into London society."

At this point, Beth excused herself and went into the kitchen. Jack had been washing the china and glasses, and we could hear his progress.

"Literally, a bull in a china shop," Beth said, returning to the living room. "I should have told him to leave them for me.

"When Celia was in her early thirties, Tyndall died quite suddenly, and she inherited a substantial amount of money, as well as the lease on the London townhouse. After her mourning period, she wed her comte, who was, as fate would have it, a widower. Eventually, Celia, her French lord, and his three children returned to his estate near Limoges. She died when she was about fifty from injuries received in a carriage accident."

I guess I went slack-jawed because Beth said, "You are as surprised as I was when I read her obituary. Because Celia was the widow of Tyndall Stanton, her death notice was published in the London papers. She had converted to Catholicism and was buried in a Catholic church near her estate."

After finishing the dishes, Jack, who had been sitting quietly while Beth continued the story, now jumped at the chance to put in his two cents. "In the nineteenth century, carriage accidents were common. A city is a very noisy place, and runaway horses were a part of urban life. In the country, carriages turned over or broke down when a wheel flew off or an axle broke. They were as dangerous then as cars are now. It was rich people who died or were crippled in these accidents since they were the ones who had the carriages."

"I have seen Celia's portrait," Beth said, taking back the story, "and for all that Jane Austen had to say about Jane's beauty, Celia was just as lovely, with the blonde hair and blue eyes that both Jane and she had inherited from their mother. However, to me, her portrait shows a beautiful woman but one lacking in intelligence. And that, my dear, is all I know of Celia."

I was glad Celia had found happiness with her French lord and that she loved her nieces, but what was even more interesting was how much information Jack and Beth had on Celia. Even allowing for a dedicated Aunt Margie, Beth and Jack knew a lot about her.

With Celia out of the way, I wanted to get to the much more interesting letter from Will Lacey to his cousin, Anne Desmet. "The letter certainly explains his sour mood when he showed up at the dance in Hertfordshire," I said. "Do you know who Mrs. Manyard was?"

"Yes, I do," Beth said. "Her maiden name was Elaine Trench, and she was an actress who performed at the Royal Theatre, Drury Lane. Before marrying Anne Devereaux, David Lacey, whom Jane Austen referred to as Old Mr. Darcy, had a liaison with Miss Trench. She was lowborn but had risen in the ranks as a result of a successful stage career. Their relationship was duly noted in the scandal sheets, which kept everyone up to date on society gossip and who was sleeping with whom, especially if the romance involved the Prince of Wales.

"After Anne Lacey died, David started seeing Elaine again. She was a widow and, as far as I know, only had the one child, Roger Manyard, a dissolute young man. His story puts me in mind of Mr. Wickham."

I was hesitant about asking the next question, but if I didn't get a reasonable explanation as to how the Crowells came to have the letter from Will to his cousin, then any further questions were pointless. "I was wondering where you got the letter," I finally asked.

"When the Pratts moved into Montclair, the Laceys asked if they could continue to use the storage area below stairs. The Pratts are distant relations of the Laceys, and they had no objections. The storage area contained several chests that had belonged to the mother of Edward Lacey, the last Lacey heir to reside at Montclair. In those chests were diaries, letters, accounts, and other personal papers belonging to several generations of Laceys. Before returning to Australia, the Pratts, knowing that Jack's family had been in service at Montclair for generations, left the papers in our care.

"Over the years, we've gone through many of them, but sorting through the lot proved to be a major project. We were able to devote some time to it during the brutally cold winter of 1946–47. Because of freezing temperatures and the difficulty of moving coal along the rivers or even by rail, we were unable to get any coal in Crofton. So we closed up the house, and Jack and I moved in with my cousin in Holland Park. It was a little better in London, but it was a terrible time in England. You had to queue up for everything. And the snow! I can't ever remember having so much snow in one winter. To shake off our post-war blues, Jack and I spent many an afternoon going through those dusty old papers."

The Crowells were making a believer out of me. Whenever I doubted the likelihood of Elizabeth Garrison and William Lacey being Elizabeth Bennet and Fitzwilliam Darcy, they provided reasonable explanations for the events in the book.

At that point, Jack stood up and told his wife he was heading to the Hare and Hound for a pint. "I won't be long," he said, kissing Beth and winking at me.

"Jack just can't sit still. He never could," Beth said as soon as she heard the front door close. "Even with his wonky knee, he still plays football with some of the men from the village."

On our ride from the station when Jack told me Michael was coming home, he had asked me to make sure Beth didn't go to bed early, and when I saw her yawning, I started quizzing her about some of the minor events and characters mentioned in *Pride and Prejudice*. Because Beth was tired, she was giving me very short answers.

"Did Charlotte really have a sister Maria?"

"Yes. I believe Mary Garrison and she were good friends."

"Was there such a person as Mary King?"

"I have no idea."

"Was there a reason for the militia to be encamped near Meryton?"

"I imagine they served the same purpose as our Home Guard did during this last war. But Jack would know that better than I."

I was running out of questions when I heard the Jeep pull into the driveway.

"That didn't take very long," Beth said, looking at the door and waiting for her husband to come in. Instead, the person who stepped over the threshold was Michael.

Beth put both of her hands up to her face and instantly teared up. When she was finally able to move, she went running into her son's arms, and he picked her off the floor and gave her a big hug.

When I had first seen a picture of Michael, I thought no one was that good-looking, but there he was, except he had definitely lost weight. The girls in Minooka would have called him a "dreamboat."

While the reunion continued, I quietly went upstairs. But five minutes later, Beth was knocking on the door, asking me to come down and meet her son. As soon as Michael saw me, he immediately stood up and extended his hand. "It's nice to meet you, Maggie. My parents have been singing your praises in their letters. It's good to have a face to put with their stories."

While Beth went into the kitchen to make coffee, Jack said he was going to have a whiskey, and Michael said, "Make that two," and asked if I would like something. After I hesitated, Jack said, "If you don't have a drink, you'll have to drink Beth's coffee."

"Okay, I'll have a club soda."

Michael smiled at his father's comment and added, "It's probably too late, but I'll warn you, Mom's cooking isn't much better than her coffee."

I must have seemed a little tense because Michael leaned over and said, "You're thinking you shouldn't be here, but my parents speak of you as if you were their daughter, although, I confess, I would have a hard time thinking of you as my sister."

That statement took me by surprise, and I wondered if Michael was flirting with me. Probably not, since he had just met me, and it wouldn't have mattered anyway because he was home for only two days before he had to be at an airfield near London for the flight back to Malta, which was really too bad.

Because they would have so little time together, I told them I was ready to call it a night. Between working that morning and the train ride to Stepton, I really was tired, and I headed to my room before realizing my room was actually Michael's room.

"No worries," he said. "I'll just take the front bedroom, and I'll use the bathroom down here." When his father reminded him that the room was no longer heated, he just laughed. "I need to keep to a Spartan regimen, Dad. The Royal Air Force likes us tough."

The next morning, I was the last one down to breakfast. Although I knew the three Crowells had stayed up late into the night, none of them looked tired. Michael's being home had energized them all.

"Maggie, my parents have told me that you haven't been to the Peak District, and if you don't have anything planned for the day, I'd like to give you a tour." I smiled and nodded. I wasn't about to say "no" to such a good-looking guy.

"You'll need to put on some good walking shoes, and if you have them, a pair of trousers."

I ran back upstairs and changed into slacks and a pair of shoes that were as ugly as they were comfortable, and off we went to White Peak. At home, I was used to riding in clunkers that huffed and puffed to get up to forty miles per hour. But Michael was driving the Aston Martin with the top down as fast as it would go. After we entered the park, he slowed to a crawl so I could see the sights.

"When my brother and I were young, Dad and my mother's Uncle Jeremy, who is a geologist, would take us into the District for all-day outings." Looking out on the Peak's dramatic landscapes, Michael said, "Every time I come here, it looks different."

Because of gasoline rationing, which Jack was exempt from, there were very few cars on the road, although we did pass a charabanc, an open-air motor coach, and horse-drawn wagons filled with tourists. Taking advantage of the lack of traffic, Michael stopped in the middle of the road and pointed out interesting sights, including the numerous caves created because of the area's porous limestone. The Peak had an array of colors that changed every time a cloud passed overhead, creating dramatic views at every turn.

I told Michael that one of the things I missed most from back home was driving a car. My brother had a nice side business of buying dilapidated cars and rebuilding them. He worked on the engines while our cousin, Patty Faherty, did the body work. In case the car broke down, Patrick paid me to drive him to the seller and to follow him home. I loved the independence only a car can give you, and since leaving the States two years earlier, I had not sat in the driver's seat of a car.

Michael pulled into an overlook, put the car into park, and went around to the passenger side. "Change seats with me. You're driving." I was going to protest because this was one expensive car, but I really did want to drive it. So I ran around to the other side. After figuring out how to shift with my left hand, I was off, and it was like driving on a cloud. I had never been behind the wheel of such a fine machine, and before I knew it, I was up to sixty miles per hour, heading for seventy. I drove for about fifteen minutes before pulling over.

"I wish I had a camera. I'd love to send my brother a picture of me sitting behind the wheel of an Aston Martin. He'd be green with envy."

"My parents have one of those Kodak Brownie cameras. I'll take a snapshot of you when we get back to the house if you'll promise to let me have a copy."

I couldn't decide if Michael was flirting with me or if he was just being really, really friendly, but I wasn't complaining.

We headed toward Thor's Cave, a limestone cave with a thirty-foot arch that could be seen for miles from the floor of the Manifold Valley. This natural formation was something I had wanted to see since I had first come to Derbyshire. When we finally pulled over, I watched as two hikers climbed the steep stone steps, and when the steps stopped, they had to claw their way into the opening of the cave. I looked at Michael and shook my head, but he wasn't taking "no" for an answer.

The steps were no problem, but the next bit required that Michael cup his hands as if I was getting on a horse, and then I had to crawl to the cave's mouth. Completely stripped of all dignity, I turned around to watch as Michael got a running start, and using the top step almost as a springboard, he took the last part in one giant leap.

"And there are some who say that once you are out of the Army, you never use the skills you learned in basic training," he said, helping me to my feet.

"You'll have a hard time convincing me that this is the usual way of getting into caves in the District," I said, suspecting that even with the lack of maintenance during the war and tight budgets, it wasn't necessary to crawl around on all fours or have the skills of an acrobat to tour the other caves.

"No, but this gives me a chance to impress you with my athletic prowess," he said, showing off the muscles in his arms.

"And I'm sure I made an impression on you, too."

"Oh, you have." He extended his hand to help me up.

I was shortly to find out that getting into the cave was the easy part. There was a stream running right down the middle of it. As a result, everything was wet. I kept slipping and sliding on the uneven rocks and falling against the steep limestone walls until I finally fell back right onto Michael, and we both went down. He rubbed his hands together as if he was some evil magician and said, "Everything is going according to plan," and I burst out laughing, which didn't help as I continued to grope my way forward. We finally made it to a huge opening that served as a window to the magnificent landscapes of the Peak District, now dressed in its autumn colors.

There was nothing in my experience to compare to the scene before me. I had never been to the American West with its wide open landscapes, and to be a witness to endless miles of rocky crags and lush valleys was a thrill for me. But all the while I was taking in the magnificent views, I felt as if Michael was looking at me and not at the peaks. When I turned around, I finally decided to ask him straight out if he had a girlfriend.

"I am seeing someone who is serving in the Women's RAF on Malta," he said in a tone that was almost sad. "And you? Do you have a boyfriend?"

"Yes," I lied. Michael had a girlfriend, and he was stationed on an island in the Mediterranean that was more than a thousand miles away from England. So it really didn't matter whether or not I had a boyfriend. But on the train ride back to London, I couldn't help but wonder what Michael would have said if I had said, "No."

Chapter 6

THREE WEEKS WENT BY before I was able to return to Crofton Wood. It was Thanksgiving weekend in America, and thinking about my family gathered around a table, eating a turkey with all the trimmings, I was overwhelmed by a sense of being isolated from everything I cared about, and I didn't want to be alone.

While Beth went riding, Jack and I headed toward Chatsworth, the ancestral home of the Dukes of Devonshire. Located near the Peak District, Chatsworth, with its 80,000 acres, was considered to be one of England's great country manors. Looking at the house from a distance, I had to agree that if Jane Austen imagined Mr. Darcy living there, then she certainly had raised him very high indeed. But the scale of the mansion seemed all wrong for Elizabeth Bennet. I think she would have preferred Montclair.

Jack explained that in the early 1900s, when the 8th Duke of Devonshire had died, over a half million pounds in death taxes became due, a phenomenal amount of money. The family had to sell some of their book collection, including four Shakespeare folios, as well as properties from all over the country, to pay the debt, but they had managed to hang on to Chatsworth.

"I'm a Derbyshire man, and I don't mind telling you that some of the most beautiful scenery in England is right here in the Peak District and at Chatsworth. This estate had thousands of visitors even in the eighteenth and nineteenth centuries. Because the Devonshires were involved in politics, they hosted Public Day once a week when they were in residence, and the duke and duchess welcomed the visitors themselves. Some would be invited to stay for dinner, and they would help themselves to the port and get knackered. Georgiana, the Duchess of Devonshire, wrote in her diary about drunks falling down the stairs and relieving themselves in the fireplace. In those days, politics was not for the timid.

"There's an American connection to Chatsworth," Jack said. "William Cavendish, the oldest son of the 10th Duke of Devonshire, or Billy Hartington as he was known to his friends, married an American, Kathleen Kennedy, the daughter of Joseph Kennedy, the Ambassador to the Court of St. James in the late 1930s. The couple hadn't been married but a few months when Billy was killed by a German sniper. I understand her brother, John, is now a congressman from Massachusetts. When their love story hit the front pages, it got a lot of ink, a lot of it nasty, because 'Kick' Kennedy was an American and a Catholic, who was marrying into one of Britain's great titled Protestant families. Oh, what a brouhaha their romance caused! To me, the whole thing was a storm in a teacup. What difference does it make if the two people get on? With all the blood spilled in the wars, people get upset about nonsense like that. Anyway, she's still the Marchioness of Hartington until she remarries.

"The current duke and duchess aren't living here at present, and I haven't heard what their plans are for Chatsworth. Right now, it's occupied by two housemaids, who keep it tidied up with the help of some of their friends. There are more than one hundred rooms in that house, so there's a lot of tidying up to do."

"Did the Laceys socialize with the Devonshires?"

"Yes. In fact, Will Lacey's mother, Anne Devereaux, was a good friend of the most famous Duchess of Devonshire, Georgiana Spencer, and named her daughter after her. I know Elizabeth relied heavily on Her Grace's advice when she became mistress of Montclair. The duchess was several years older than Elizabeth and wrote her letter after letter telling her how to avoid the mistakes she had made when she had first married the duke.

"The next in line was Georgiana's son, Harty Cavendish, the Bachelor Duke. For many years, the duke kept a beautiful mistress named 'Skittles' until she was pushed out by the Duchess of Manchester. Just about the time I was making my appearance in this world, that would be 1891, the Duke of Manchester died, freeing his widow to marry Harty, and she became the Duchess of Devonshire, making her a Double Duchess."

"Did the Duke of Manchester ever find out about their affair?"

"It was never a secret." Looking at my expression, Jack cautioned, "Maggie, when you are that high in society, you make your own rules. The most important ones are that you are always discreet, you don't make a scene when the affair is over, and you never ask for a divorce. Divorces are messy things, and all your dirty laundry ends up in the newspapers. If you break those rules, you are cast out into the wilderness."

I asked Jack if Montclair had visitors like Chatsworth did. "Not like Chatsworth," Jack answered. "It's one of England's great country houses and is chockablock with art, including paintings by Rembrandt, Gainsborough, and Beth's favorite, *The Adoration of the Magi* by Veronese. The cascade fountain alone was a major draw. It was quite a feat of engineering in its day, and as an engineer myself, I agree that it's a mechanical masterpiece, much more interesting than family portraits of well-dressed people with little dogs lying at their masters' feet.

"Now, don't get me wrong. Montclair is a terrific house, and it's had its share of visitors over the years. A lot of people who stopped off in Crofton on their way to the Peak District would come through, and its parkland has always been used by the locals. As long as everyone behaved themselves, the Laceys didn't mind visitors. But with Chatsworth and the spa at Matlock so close, most people bypassed Montclair, excepting people like yourself who went looking for it because they believed the Darcys had lived there."

Because of the late hour, Jack drove me directly to the train station. On the way, I asked him about Will and Elizabeth's children.

"There were four children: twins Christopher and Francine, Laurence, and Phoebe. The impression I got from reading the letters and diaries was that Laurence was a little slow out of the gate. Eventually, he was sent to work in a mercantile house owned by the Binghams in Livorno, Italy, or Leghorn, as the British called it, where Laurence fell in love with a contessa. After they married, I don't know if he put in another day's work for the rest of his life.

"Franny never married and lived at Montclair for all of her life. Her twin brother's first wife died in childbirth, and she ran the house for her brother even after Christopher married a woman who was a first cousin of his deceased wife. They did stuff like that back then. After his second wife's death, Christopher spent most of his time in London and got married for a third time to an actress who loved to entertain. From all accounts, they were happy together.

"The younger girl, Phoebe, made her debut during the Regency Era, when it was a great time to be young. She got into a lot of mischief, and Franny, her older sister, wrote about it in her diary. The one story I remember is that the whole family were in Brussels on the eve of the Battle of Waterloo, and Will was anxious to get everyone back to England. But the Duchess of Richmond was having a ball for the Duke of Wellington, and Phoebe gave her father the slip and went to the ball without him. You need to talk to Violet Alcott, Beth's cousin, who lives in Holland Park in London. Violet and her brother, Geoff, are about the same age as James and Michael, and they spent a lot of time with us when we were all in India together. She's a delightful chatterbox, and I know she wrote a school paper on Franny."

Checking his watch to make sure that I wouldn't miss my train, Jack said, "Next time you come, we'll have to go to Melton Mowbray for a pork pie. I was there the day the town welcomed back the 4th Parachute Brigade. After their big fight at the bridge at Arnhem in Holland in '44, the boys all wanted their pork pies."

By that time, we had arrived at the station. There was still so much that I wanted to know. But there was time. I was sure I would see the Crowells again.

Chapter 7

WITH THE HOLIDAYS APPROACHING, the Crowells invited me to spend Christmas with them at Crofton Wood, but between a hectic work schedule and fighting a cold, I decided to stay in London. However, Jack and Beth continued to write letters to keep up my interest. In the next letter, I was to learn all about Anne Desmet, *Pride and Prejudice's* Miss Anne de Bourgh.

21 December 1947

Dear Maggie,

Jack is insisting I write this letter, accusing me of leaving out important facts from the stories we have told you, especially concerning Anne Desmet and her mother. So under Jack's supervision, I will tie up some loose ends.

The Devereauxs were a wealthy Norman family. Like Anne Devereaux Lacey, Will's mother, Lady Sylvia, received a large dowry when she married Lord Lewis Desmet. There was a considerable age difference between the bride and groom, and it seems that Lord Desmet preferred to spend most of his time in town while Lady Sylvia's preference was to remain in the country at Desmet Park. However, they did get together at least once because Lady Sylvia became pregnant with Anne in her late thirties, and six years after her birth, Lord Desmet died.

Although it was Lady Sylvia's desire that her daughter marry Will Lacey, it was never Anne's. She had been at Montclair when Will's mother had died as a result of a miscarriage about five years after Georgiana was born—probably from septicemia. Because of her poor health, it was Anne's declared intention never to marry. Anne and Will were very fond of each other, and they would often visit in Anne's sitting room after Lady Sylvia retired for the evening. Anne had Will's complete confidence. He not only shared with her his growing interest in Elizabeth Garrison, but her rejection of him. I think you will find the enclosed letter to be quite interesting.

The closing paragraphs of Pride and Prejudice differ greatly from what really happened. If anyone should be congratulated for bringing Elizabeth and Will together, it is Anne Desmet. But that tale is woven into Elizabeth and Will's love story, so we'll hold off on that one.

Jack and I were sorry you did not come to Crofton Wood for Christmas. It would have been our pleasure to introduce you to our son, James, and his family. We received a letter from Michael (and he wishes you happy holidays) in which he said that all eyes are on Germany because of the breakdown in relations between the Western Allies and the Soviet Union. Fortunately, his enlistment ends in November. However, for *the sake of everyone's children, it is imperative that nations find ways to resolve their differences without going to war. For our part, my family has contributed more than their share for King and Country.*

Please write and let us hear of what goes on in town.

Happy Christmas,
Beth

P.S. As a child, my parents took their four children up to London to Harrods during the holidays to do our Christmas shopping so that we could ride the escalator. I remember my mother hesitating because, at that time, women still wore ankle-length dresses. Nervous customers were provided with brandy at the top! Of course, my brothers decided it would be even more fun for them to walk up the down escalator.

I eagerly opened the envelope Beth had enclosed and recognized the stationery and handwriting from Will Lacey's earlier letter to his cousin.

9 April 1792

Dear Anne,
    As mentioned in my last post, Charles Bingham is much taken with Miss Jane Garrison of Bennets End, Hertfordshire. I consider his preference for the lady to be very marked, but as you know, Bingham has often been in love. I am unable to judge how Miss Garrison receives his attentions,

as she is a passive creature. However, her sister, Elizabeth, is Miss Garrison's opposite in every way. The elder sister is fair, with flaxen hair and blue eyes, while Miss Elizabeth has dark brown hair and dark, expressive eyes that show a hint of mischief.

I accompanied Bingham to the home of Miss Garrison's aunt for an evening of cards. I was sitting next to Miss Elizabeth when she said I was very fortunate in that her aunt's house was too small to permit dancing. However, she enquired as to what stratagems I would use in order to avoid conversation, an obvious reference to my remarks, which she had overheard at the assembly. When I told her I chose carefully the people whom I sat next to, she responded by saying I had chosen unwisely, as she loved a good conversation. I noted that she also liked to tease people. 'But never with malice,' she said. I believe my remarks at the assembly wounded her. In my defence, my words were not malicious but were the result of fatigue after a difficult journey.

After a rubber of whist, Miss Elizabeth and I continued our conversation. I found her to be well informed as to national political debates and the events taking place on the continent with particular attention being paid to the anti-monarchial actions of the French National Assembly. Jane Garrison talked with Bingham for most of the evening, choosing not to play cards. There are three other Garrison sisters. The two youngest laughed and talked loudly the whole of the night without correction.

Bingham will remain in Hertfordshire and, no doubt, will continue his attentions to Miss Garrison. He has shown a greater interest in this woman than any other I have witnessed. I look forward to visiting with you in London.

As always,
Will

I loved this letter! Will was falling in love with Elizabeth, but he didn't know it yet. On the other hand, Lucy and Celia's behavior was obviously an irritant for him.

After finishing Will's letter, I reread Beth's letter where she had mentioned that her family had "contributed more than their share for King and Country," and I wondered what she meant.

***

I had planned to spend Christmas Eve listening to the BBC radio broadcast of Charles Dickens's *A Christmas Carol* with the Dawkins's family but was rescued by Leo, my Polish friend, who had been invited to a party by Americans who lived in his building. Because of rationing, Americans were the only ones who could get their hands on scarce food items, and they had always had access to what seemed to be a bottomless supply of booze.

As a rule, I tried to dress simply because many Britons were wearing the same clothes they had worn since the war began in 1939. But this was Christmas, and I wanted to wear the red silk blouse, which complemented my dark hair and blue eyes, that my mother and sisters had sent to me for Christmas. I compromised and wore the blouse with a practical navy blue skirt I had brought from home. I was hoping to meet a nice guy at the party. A handsome man would be just the thing to take the sting out of being alone during the holidays.

Leo was having no trouble attracting a bevy of attractive young women who found his Polish good looks and accent to be irresistible. Up to that point, I hadn't been so lucky until I saw a handsome man across the room. Even though he had a scar on his right cheek, he was very attractive. I was embarrassed when he caught me looking at him, but when he raised his glass to me, I went over and introduced myself after apologizing for staring.

"The scar is actually helpful when you are trying to meet pretty girls." He introduced himself as Rob McAllister from Flagstaff, Arizona. "I was a navigator on a B-17 bomber. When the plane was hit by flak, the Plexiglas on the nose of the plane shattered, and shards went flying. I'm lucky it wasn't worse." He gave that short laugh people use when they are uncomfortable, and after that—nothing.

I'm one of those people who can't stand lulls in a conversation, so I started talking and told him about my job with AES in Germany. I had been able to do some sightseeing since train travel in Europe was so easy once the bombed tracks had been repaired. One of the most accessible destinations was the Black Forest. It was a breathtakingly beautiful ride through mountain passes with postcard villages and thatched, three-story farmhouses paralleling the tracks. On the surface, the villages of the Black Forest appeared to be untouched by the war, but even here, you could not avoid stories about the horrors of war. Troops from North Africa, who had fought with the French army, had gone on a rampage of rape, looting, and murder in those picturesque mountain towns.

After I realized how inappropriate it was to discuss rape and murder with someone I had just met, I tried to cover up my gaffe by asking Rob if he had ever been to Germany, and he said that he had been "over" it many times, but he had never been "to" it.

"Oh, of course, you flew on a bomber," I said. "Well, I lived in Frankfurt for a year, and I can tell you from firsthand experience that you guys did a thorough job."

This was not going well. I had just complimented Rob on bombing a city into rubble.

"Sorry. That came out all wrong." I started to walk away before I could do any more damage, but Rob pulled me back and said, "Don't apologize. We did what had to be done to end the war, but I'm obviously making you nervous. Why?"

He *was* making me nervous. I hadn't felt like this since high school, when I had to sneak around to see my boyfriend, who was Italian and, therefore, unacceptable to my Irish-centric family.

Looking across the room, Rob asked if Leo was my date, and I assured him he was just a friend.

"I'm glad to hear it because I think he's about to leave with the leggy blonde."

As if on cue, Leo looked at me and gestured that he was leaving and was it all right. I gave him the okay sign. I was confident in that large of a group I could find someone to see me to the Underground station, and Rob said he could guarantee it.

***

Rob and I had our first date at an Italian restaurant near the National Gallery and Trafalgar Square. It was your typical Italian restaurant: red and white checkered tablecloths, candle wax dripping down the sides of Chianti bottles, and a waiter in a starched white apron. It could just as easily have been South Scranton as London.

Rob had left England in March 1945 as a captain in the Air Corps and had returned in the spring of '47 as a civilian working for an American corporation based in Atlanta. Smiling, he said, "My second tour of England has been much more pleasant than my first.

"After I returned to the States, I was retrained to teach radar navigation on B-29s at Victorville, California, which was quite a change from England because Victorville is in the Mojave Desert. After I got out of the Air Corps, I applied for a job with TRC, Inc., a company that makes hardware for just about everything. The personnel manager was a veteran of the 8th Air Force and was known to hire Air Corps vets. After six months at the Atlanta headquarters, my roommate and I were transferred to London so we could gain international management experience. Ken and I have been here about nine months, but we don't know how long we'll have the jobs, because they really do want to hire as many British nationals as possible. I'll run with it until they tell me I have to go home."

Rob asked about my two years in Washington. It had been an exciting place to work. I met people from every region of the country, whose customs were so different from mine. My sisters, who had moved to Washington even before the attack on Pearl Harbor, had told me that early in the war, when there was such a demand for clerk typists, they knew of young women who were hired at the train station and taken directly to their jobs. With every desk in every office occupied, temporary buildings had been built all over the city, even on the mall between the Capitol and the Lincoln Memorial. They were ugly but necessary.

The apartment I shared with my sisters had only one bedroom with twin beds and a mattress under each bed. Once word got out from our brother, who was in the Navy, that the Joyce sisters would let anyone from Minooka sleep on their living room floor, it was a rare morning when we didn't have to step over a comatose soldier, sailor, marine, or airman sacked out in our tiny living room. As much as I enjoyed seeing familiar faces, I did not want to date anyone from home. I wasn't willing to risk getting involved with someone who might want to return to Minooka once the war was over. Instead, I went dancing or out to dinner with guys from all over the United States. They were just passing through on their way to Europe or the Pacific, and we had some fun together before they boarded a train that would take them to their next post.

Rob and I had a table at the back of the restaurant, and the owner continued to refill our glasses long after the dishes had been cleared. We sat there for two hours talking about anything and everything. It was the most enjoyable evening I had experienced since I had left the United States, and I did not want it to end. We finally left Lucca's after agreeing that we would see each other again.

Chapter 8

ALTHOUGH ROB AND I lived in different parts of London, he always took me home to Mrs. Dawkins's house. After I started dating Rob, my landlady told me straight out that if I ever had a man above stairs, I would be out on the street on my bum. "I only rent to good girls."

The only place where Rob and I could talk was in the kitchen because the children listened to the radio in the living room, and the front parlor was off-limits. Mrs. Dawkins and her husband, who was rarely seen because he worked the night shift, had two very well-behaved boys, Teddy and Tommy, but they were often in the kitchen looking for a snack or asking Rob a lot of questions about flying in a B-17. As a result, our conversations were constantly interrupted.

Neither Rob nor I had much spare change, so London was the perfect city for two people on a budget because a lot of the major attractions were free. A cheap date might be going to the movies to see *Great Expectations* or *The Big Sleep* followed by dinner at a Lyon's Corner Restaurant. Theater tickets were reasonable, and although the crowds were thinning since the end of the war, dance halls were still popular with young couples swinging to big band music.

After a few weeks of dating, Rob splurged and gave me his own tour of the city as seen through the eyes of a Yank airman, and he hired a cabbie to take us all over London. Rob and three other airmen from his squadron had done the same thing when they first hit town in early 1944. For six shillings apiece, they got the cook's tour.

Rob had the cabbie start near Piccadilly Circus under the enormous Wrigley's gum sign and across from the "Guinness is Good for You" sign. The Rainbow Corner Red Cross Club was often the first stop for GIs on leave and had once welcomed thousands of American servicemen each day.

"In the lobby," Rob began, "was a sign with an arrow pointing toward New York, 3,271 miles to the west, and another to Berlin, 600 miles to the east. It was open twenty-four hours a day with pool tables and pinball machines. It had hot showers, which was a real luxury for some of those guys, because all they ever got were 'cold-water ablutions,' as the Brits called them. A lot of the actresses from the theater district came over and danced with all of the lead foots, and the actors and stagehands served the food. Fred Astaire's sister 'Delly' was married to an English lord and volunteered at the Corner all the time.

"In the basement, there was a place called the Dunker's Den where you could get doughnuts and a decent cup of coffee. They had Coke with ice in it and a hamburger made with Grade-A American beef and someone who knew how to cook it. It had great bands like the Flying Forts and the Hepcats, and some of those couples jitterbugging rocked the joint. There was a huge ballroom on the top floor, and the Red Cross hired hostesses to dance with the men. But there was this unwritten rule that the Rainbow Corner was for enlisted men only. If an officer hung around too long, he'd have a hundred eyes staring him out of the place, so I'd head over to the Red Cross Officer's Club in Knightsbridge.

"All around Piccadilly Circus were the Piccadilly Commandos. One look at those girls, and you understood why the Army made you watch movies about venereal disease. Because everything was blacked out, the girls held flashlights, what they called torches, up to their faces, so you could see what you were getting into. You'd walk by doorways and see the most interesting silhouettes. It was the same thing in Hyde Park. With the blackout, you had to watch out, or you'd plow right into someone guarding an anti-aircraft battery, or step on a couple lying in the grass getting acquainted with each other. I tried to navigate around London with nothing more than a Zippo lighter. The closest I came to getting killed while I was in England was the night I fell down the stairs leading to an Underground station.

"My favorite dance hall was in Covent Garden. This joint wasn't just a hangout for Americans. Every branch of service from every country danced there. The prettiest girl I ever danced with, excluding present company, was a WREN from Wales in navy blue."

At home, women in the military were often the butt of sexual jokes, and the British were no different. "Up with the lark, to bed with a WREN" was the one I had heard about women who had joined the Woman's Royal Naval Service. It was the old story of one bad apple spoiling the reputations of the many women who had served honorably, but there was that occasional girl who went above and beyond the call of duty.

"Another time," Rob said, continuing his story, "a bunch of us took the train into the city, and we met eight girls from the East End, who were in the British Land Army and had been working on farms near Cambridge. The homes of all but one of the girls had been bombed out, and their families were scattered all over London. We went with them to Covent Garden. There wasn't much conversation because I couldn't understand their Cockney accent. But I'm pretty sure a lot of it had to do with sex, and I'm positive I figured out what 'cobblers' meant.

"Everyone on leave in London went to Madame Tussaud's Wax Museum at least once. They had a chamber of horrors and death masks from guillotine victims made during the French Revolution, and because so many Americans went there, they added a bunch of U.S. military brass, including one of Eisenhower saluting. It was so real I saw guys return the salute. The museum had been bombed during the Blitz, and according to the cab driver, 'They found Mary Queen of Scots' head in one place and her arse in another.'

"The Parliament buildings and Big Ben were protected with barbed wire, and all the important buildings had sandbags around them. The moat around the Tower of London had a Victory garden in it, as well as huts for the women in the RAF who operated the barrage balloons.

"Out on the street, there were thousands of servicemen looking for the best show in town. I saw Sikhs wearing turbans, Aussies wearing bush hats, and West Indians, who were as black as the ace of spades, all mixed in with the local residents. The government encouraged the Brits to walk, so there would be more room on the buses for all the servicemen on leave in London."

Rob could have been describing wartime Washington, D.C. Because the hotels were filled to capacity and then some, many of the men simply walked around all day long until they were so tired that they curled up on a bench in Union Station or fell asleep on the stairs leading to the different monuments. When they were awake, they were out looking for action and usually finding it. The newspapers reported that there were enough venereal disease cases in the city to overfill the 30,000-seat Griffith Stadium, and a few of my co-workers found themselves in a family way.

Rob informed me with a straight face that Air Corps officers usually got the best looking girls. "I'm not kidding. We were envied or hated, depending on your point of view, because we were the glamour boys. There was more than one fight between a groundpounder and a flyboy. Because we had triangles on our faces, we were easy to pick out. Above 10,000 feet, you have to go on oxygen, and you might have to stay on it for several hours. Because of the cold air and the sweating, and believe me you can break out into a sweat, even at 25,000 feet, the mask leaves chafe marks around your nose and mouth, making us look like raccoons.

"The British girls figured out pretty quickly that officers had more money to spend, and they'd get to go to nicer places. Remember, the Brits had been at war since '39, and for some girls, this was the best way to get a decent meal. Pat Monaghan, a bombardier and crew mate, and I went into London and hooked up with two swell girls, and we took them to see the play, *The Man Who Came to Dinner*, and then to the Savoy Grill for dinner. The Savoy Hotel was a hangout for American reporters, and one of them interviewed us for the hometown papers. The Savoy had been hit several times during the Blitz, but even so, it was a real classy place.

"Here I was, a guy from Flagstaff, a town of about 20,000 people. Even when the Air Corps was training me, I was stationed in rural areas. Except for a weekend pass in Chicago, I had never been to a big city with clubs, the theater, and girls falling all over you. It was a very strange existence. One day you were dancing at Covent Garden, and the next day you were dropping bombs on Germany."

The cab driver dropped us off in front of Rob's building. His flat was on the top floor of a four-story walk-up, and Ken and he shared a hallway bathroom with the two men living in the opposite flat. Their co-workers had warned them that it was in a dodgy neighborhood, but that was all they could get for the time being. Despite the drawbacks, rooms in London were so scarce that Rob was glad to have it even if it meant spending every spare minute he could out of it.

As soon as we stepped inside the door of the building, Rob informed me that Ken had moved out and that we had the flat all to ourselves. We stood in the foyer facing each other and holding hands. It was understood that if we started going up the stairs, we would make love. What I had to decide was did I love this man, and, more importantly, did he love me. He had never said so.

Rob was trying to help me along because he had unbuttoned my coat and had put his arms around me. If he started kissing me now, it was a done deal. We started kissing.

I was so inexperienced that I didn't know what to do. I was just starting to think I might not be ready for this when I saw that Rob had placed a single red rose on the pillow. There was something so sweet in that gesture that I decided I did want to be with this man. We made love until the early hours of the morning when I had to go back to Mrs. Dawkins's house or risk my "good girl" status. Standing outside my front door, Rob said, "You do know that I love you, don't you?" I hadn't been sure, but now I was. And all was right with the world.

Chapter 9

LETTERS FROM THE CROWELLS came at regular intervals all through the dark of my second Northern European winter. London is located at a latitude that is even farther north than Newfoundland in Canada. It was dark when I went to the office and dark when I left. The combined mixture of fog and coal smoke created an atmosphere right out of a Dickens novel, and the leaden skies and the cold, dreary days were something you had to get used to, or you could find yourself checking sailing dates back to the States.

I felt comfortable enough with the Crowells to share with them that I had fallen in love with a young man from Arizona. I gave them all the particulars: six feet, sandy blonde hair, blue eyes, even tempered, intelligent, and a better conversationalist than Mr. Darcy.

On a rare sunny Saturday morning, Rob and I were sitting in Trafalgar Square feeding the pigeons when he told me about growing up in Flagstaff in Arizona's High Country. If you were heading to the Grand Canyon or traveling the Lincoln Highway between Chicago and Los Angeles, you probably drove by his uncle's Sinclair gas station on Route 66 where he had a part-time job. At home, Rob wore dungarees, boots, and a Stetson, and he could ride a horse and rope a calf. He considered his childhood of growing up in the big-sky country of the American West to be idyllic, with its clean air and mountain backdrops, especially in light of what he had seen and experienced in Europe.

When the war broke out, Rob had joined the Army where his high scores qualified him for the Air Corps. Unlike most other airmen, Rob did not want to be a pilot, and when I asked him why, he said, "The most important factor in the success of a mission, at least the things you can control, is the skill of the pilot and co-pilot. If they screw up, you're dead. Formation flying, when you have hundreds of planes going up at the same time, is an exact science, and there isn't any room for error. I didn't want the responsibility for the lives of nine other guys. I felt the best position for me was as a navigator, and the Army agreed."

In December 1943, Rob was sent to Kearney, Nebraska, to pick up the B-17 he and his crewmates were to fly to England. Stationed at an airfield in Hertfordshire, Rob had flown nineteen missions when his plane was hit by flak over Stuttgart killing the bombardier, his friend, Pat Monaghan. With the navigator's position right behind the bombardier's, metal and plastic fragments from the shattered Plexiglas nose of the plane had torn through Rob's right arm, with pieces of shrapnel flying into his face and shoulder. Tiny bits of metal had to be removed from his eye by a specialist in Oxford, but it healed well enough for him to resume combat status.

"After I got out of the hospital, I figured I'd be assigned to a new crew, but when I reported, the squadron commander told me I had been promoted to captain and that he had cut orders for me to become a lead navigator for the squadron. If that wasn't bad enough, while I was in the hospital, the Air Corps raised the required missions to thirty. So instead of owing Uncle Sam six missions, I owed him eleven. The major said that too many men had completed twenty-five missions and were going home. Losing so many experienced crew members was compromising the effectiveness of the group, and so they had to raise the number of missions to keep experienced airmen flying. Also, because of better fighter support, we weren't as likely to get shot down even though planes from the 91st Bomb Group were getting shot down on a regular basis.

"Flying lead meant it would take a hell of a lot longer for me to finish the last eleven missions because you don't fly as often and because it's so god-damned dangerous. The German fighters often zeroed in on the lead plane trying to kill the pilots, so that it would mess up the whole formation. On one of my early missions, a Messerschmitt didn't pull up soon enough and flew right into the lead ship. I saw the fire, heard the explosion, and then it was gone. Just like that," he said, snapping his fingers, "ten guys were dead—ten guys from my squadron.

"On my next to last mission, I was assigned to a plane flying 'tail-end Charlie,' which is the rear of the low squadron and is as bad, if not worse, than flying lead. That's where the fighters pick you off. Our target was a factory in the Ruhr Valley where we encountered so many fighters that it was like flying through a swarm of bees. We were shot up so badly that we nearly had to bail out in the Channel. Instead, we limped into Kent and made a very rough landing in a turnip field, with a wounded tail gunner and a flight engineer with a broken leg."

For a few minutes, we sat side by side in complete silence. It wouldn't have helped to tell Rob that, before he had even reached England, my cousin, Pat Faherty, had died when his ship was sunk off the East Coast, or to talk about the twenty-five men from Minooka and South Scranton who were killed in Europe and the Pacific. Sharing that information would not have lessened the pain of losing Pat Monaghan and those ten men from his squadron.

As we walked toward the Underground station, Rob took my hand and put it in his overcoat pocket. "Since I'm in such a good mood, and you have asked about my girlfriend in Flagstaff, I'll tell you about Alice." Rob found it amusing that girls always seemed to want to know about old flames, but guys never. As far as men were concerned, once a relationship was over, you were ancient history and about as interesting.

Rob had dated Alice, a waitress who worked in a café near the college, during his last year in school. Before he left for basic training, Alice had started talking about getting married, but Rob had made it clear that marriage was out of the question because just too many things could go wrong, especially when your future included flying bombers over Germany. During his training, he had witnessed a crash where the pilot had just barely gotten off the ground when something went wrong, and the fully-fueled Fortress exploded on impact killing everyone on board. While Rob was in the hospital in England, Alice had written to tell him she was marrying someone else. If their break-up had distressed him in any way, he was hiding it admirably.

While waiting for my train in the Underground station, I asked Rob if he had met anyone while he was in England, and that's when I found out about Millie. The two met at a dance at the airfield sponsored by the Red Cross, and they hit it off right away. Rob told Millie about Alice, and Millie told Rob about her boyfriend, who was in the Royal Navy. They agreed to enjoy each other's company until her boyfriend returned to England. Millie might explain why Rob was not more upset when he got his Dear John letter. He had been stepping out on Alice.

I asked, if Millie had not had a boyfriend, would he have married her, and he said, "No way. Millie was a great girl. She lived in Royston, which was only four miles from the base. I'd ride over on my bike to see her, but that was the extent of it."

What Millie provided more than anything, more than the sex, was female companionship. Rob had tired of listening to men bullshit about their flying experiences. If all the claimed kills of German fighters were true, then there wouldn't have been any Focke Wulfs or Messerschmitts left in the Luftwaffe, and since there was no shortage of fighters when Rob flew, he didn't want to hear it anymore. So a pleasant evening spent with a pretty, young English girl was preferable to a night of pub hopping with guys who drank to mask the fear everyone felt who flew bombers over Germany.

After learning about Alice and Millie, I was left with the impression that Rob liked relationships that didn't require a commitment on his part, which was going to put him at odds with me.

Chapter 10

ROB WAS AMUSED BY my *"Pride and Prejudice* Project," as he called it. As a show of support, he read the novel for the first time. He liked Elizabeth Bennet's character but didn't understand what she saw in Darcy, other than his money and big house. Rob considered Darcy to be a "stiff."

"I have to be honest here because 'disguise of every sort is my abhorrence,'" he said, quoting Mr. Darcy. "Did people actually talk like that?"

Jack and Beth suggested I go to Desmet Park in Kent, the Rosings Park of *Pride and Prejudice*, or if that was not possible, to Bennets End, the village that was the model for Meryton. Because of its easy distance from London, we could see it in a day trip. The next weekend, following Jack's directions, Rob and I set out for Meryton in a car borrowed from one of Rob's co-workers.

When we arrived in Bennets End, my idea was to ask the local postmaster if he knew the Edwards family, but Rob had a better idea and headed straight for the pub. We were directed to the lounge, where they had booths, and ordered two beers.

The man taking our order shouted, "That'll be two beers for the Yanks." And with that, Rob saw his opening and told him that he had been a member of a B-17 crew flying from an airfield right here in Hertfordshire. Other men drifted over to our table and joined in the conversation. From then on, it was like old-home week. Nearly everyone in the pub had seen groups of bombers forming up before heading out on a mission, and if they hadn't seen them, they had heard them or felt the vibrations, which shook buildings to their foundations.

After a few war stories, Rob asked if anyone knew the Edwards family. Joe Carlton was the first and loudest to say he remembered the family from when he was a boy and offered to take us out to the farm. During the ride, Joe said, "It's too bad you didn't come last year when the house was still standing. It survived the war but not the peace."

Rob had driven about a mile from the pub when Joe told him to pull over. Making a wide sweep with his hand, he indicated that all the acreage before us had once belonged to the Edwards family. According to Joe, there had been a large house on the property, so it seemed reasonable to assume that, at one time, the farm had been profitable and had provided a nice living for the family.

"During the war," Joe explained, "this whole area was one big Yank car park: jeeps, armored vehicles, artillery pieces, and trucks as far as the eye could see. Every country road was lined on both sides with steel bays holding artillery shells. Getting ready for the invasion, they were. Even then, the Edwards farmhouse was in terrible shape from years of neglect, but it was good enough for some of the officers, what with our English weather. The rest of the Yanks were living in those freezing Nissen huts, and they were the lucky ones. The ones who come last had to make due living in tents.

"What I remember is that there were two old-maid sisters and their brother living there in the 1930s. The brother had been shot in the head in Flanders. He could do the odd job, but not much more. When he died, they sold out and moved to Bournemouth, I think."

Lighting up the cigarette Rob had offered him, as well as putting one behind his ear, Joe told us we were not the first ones to think this particular town might be Meryton. Maybe, I thought, because the farm was located in Bennets End. That might have been a clue.

Looking off into the distance, Joe said, "The government has bought up 5,000 acres around here, including the Edwards farm and my dad's farm. They're going to build houses for those poor bastards what was bombed out of their homes in London." Joe started to laugh. "When the bigwigs come 'round to let us know what was going to happen, some of the meetings got pretty rough. The farmers don't think it's right for someone from London to tell us they're going to turn our farmland into a town, and there's sod all that can be done about it."

Joe went quiet for a few minutes and then said, "Well, it was bound to happen, us being so close to London. Once people from the city start moving in, it's all over. They come out to the country because it's so beautiful. Everything's terrific until the winds blow the smell of cow shit their way. It's a big surprise to city folk that farms stink." Shaking his head, he added, "Then you have all them soldiers and sailors coming home from the war and getting married. Now, their wives are having babies, and they need a place to live. They've got to live somewhere."

Shrugging his shoulders, he said, "So why not here, is what I say. We can use the jobs."

On the ride back to the village, Joe suggested that we "have a look at the graveyard up to the church. If this is Meryton, then some of them might be buried up there." After Joe "bummed another fag," we dropped him off at the pub.

The cemetery, with its heaving graves and tilted headstones, reminded me of the one in Charles Dickens's *Great Expectations* where Magwitch was hiding when he met Pip. When we saw the size of the graveyard, we were a little discouraged, and our mood was matched by the rain that was just starting to come down. Walking the uneven ground, we quickly glanced at the names on the headstones, some so faded that they looked more like fingerprints than letters.

"I'm going to break a heel," I yelled to Rob, who was on the other side of the cemetery. "That's if I don't sink into the ground first." With the rain getting heavier, I was just about to give up when I saw it.

Henry W. Garrison

1775—1787

Francine Garrison

1750—1810

Thomas H. Garrison

1746—1815

I gave out a whoop, and Rob ran over to see what I had found. He showed the proper enthusiasm for my discovery before pointing out that we were getting drenched and that I was shivering. With my teeth chattering, I told Rob that this backed up a lot of what the Crowells had told me. Holding his coat over my head, he said, "Joe gave me the names of some towns that are better preserved and are probably closer to what people have in mind when they read about Meryton." But with the rain coming down in sheets, we decided to put visiting other villages on the back burner. Instead, we would go to Kent. It seemed unlikely that Rosings Park could have met with the same fate as Longbourn.

***

Rob and I again borrowed a car from a co-worker at TRC and drove into Kent in search of the home of Jane Austen's Lady Catherine de Bourgh. Kent was still quite rural even though it had been at the heart of Britain's defense against the Luftwaffe. RAF pilots flew from airfields in Kent to intercept and destroy the bombers targeting Britain's industrial cities, ports, and airfields, and concrete bases for the anti-aircraft guns could be seen jutting out of green pastures.

We easily found the church and decided to go into the office to see if someone could tell us anything about its history. Mrs. Ives was right out of central casting for a church secretary: late middle age, gray hair tied back in a chignon, and wearing a navy blue dress with embroidered white collar. She needed little encouragement to share what she knew about what was now a Methodist church, but the information she provided didn't help our search at all.

Just as we were about to head for the door, Mrs. Ives said, "Did I mention that before this building was converted for use as the church's office, it was the original parsonage?" Rob and I looked at each other and shook our heads. "If you look past the filing cabinets and desks, you might be able to picture this room as the parlor." I felt my pulse jump because, if that was the case, then we were standing in the very room where William Lacey had made an offer of marriage to Elizabeth Garrison. I asked if there was anything else she knew about the parsonage, and she said, "Oh, yes. Quite a lot."

"The parsonage was built around 1780 on land donated by the Desmet family. After the death of its first pastor, Dr. Augustine Anglum, Lady Sylvia Desmet gave the living to William Chatterton, who had written a monograph on Frederick Cornwallis, Archbishop of Canterbury and a friend of Lady Sylvia's. If the name Cornwallis rings a bell, it's because Frederick was the uncle of Charles Cornwallis, who surrendered the British forces to George Washington in Yorktown and ended the American war of rebellion."

This might explain how Mr. Chatterton (Mr. Collins) came to the attention of Lady Sylvia. After reading the monograph he had written about her friend, Frederick Cornwallis, Lady Sylvia must have contacted Mr. Chatterton.

"Rev. Chatterton lived here until he accepted an appointment to serve at the Old Palace in Canterbury on the staff of the bishop who is the head of the Diocese of Dover."

We thought she was going to keep going, but she stopped. "That's it," she said after realizing we were waiting for more. "Mr. Chatterton was not a Methodist minister but an Anglican vicar, so that's it."

Before leaving, I took one last look at the room where Elizabeth had learned that Will Lacey was in love with her and where he had made her an offer of marriage. I could just picture Will pacing back and forth in front of the fireplace, struggling to find the right words to ask Lizzy to be his wife, and Lizzy, gripping the arms of the chair, getting angrier by the minute at his arrogance and conceit.

"I would have given the guy the finger and told him to take a hike" was Rob's take on Will's proposal to Lizzy.

Mrs. Ives said we were fortunate we were visiting now, as the whole structure was going to be torn down. As with Meryton, another piece of the Garrison/Lacey puzzle was about to disappear, but looking at the condition of the building, it was easy to see why it had to go. There wasn't a plumb wall in the whole parsonage. As a nod to its former benefactress, the building was tilting toward Desmet Park.

"If you are thinking about going to Canterbury, I should tell you that the city was bombed heavily during the Baedeker raids. The cathedral had some damage, but the chapter library and many of the buildings near the cathedral were completely destroyed." Neither Rob nor I had ever heard of the Baedeker raids, so I asked Mrs. Ives if they were a part of the Blitz.

"No, the Blitz was in 1940–41," Mrs. Ives replied. "According to Lord Haw Haw, the British traitor used by the Nazis for their radio broadcasts, the Baedeker raids were in retaliation for the RAF bombing of German cities. Using *Baedeker's Guide to Great Britain*, cities that received three stars in the tourist guide because of their historical importance were bombed by the Luftwaffe. Before Canterbury was bombed in June 1942, Exeter, Bath, and York were also bombed."

After thanking Mrs. Ives for her help, we headed up the hill to Lady Sylvia's manor house.

***

As we entered Desmet Park, we stepped into a huge foyer with vaulted coffered ceilings and black and white tile that could make you dizzy if you looked at it too long. The desk where the information clerk sat looked ridiculously small—almost Lilliputian—in relation to its surroundings. Watching us, the receptionist started laughing. "Everyone has the same reaction. It looks as if my desk was taken from a dollhouse. But that's not the worst of it; it's freezing in here." She pointed to the sweater under her jacket and the space heater at her feet. We asked her if it was possible to view any of the rooms.

"Clive! Clive!" she shouted down the hall. "Lord, he's going deaf." She seemed reluctant to leave her space heater, but finally she stood up and said, "I'll have to go find him." Handing us a small booklet, she told us we could read about the mansion while she went to look for Clive.

Rob flipped through the booklet looking for interesting tidbits. "Desmet Park was built around 1675, shortly after the restoration of the Stuarts to the British throne following Oliver Cromwell's death. Charles II, the new king, needed money, so he sold peerages to commoners for a lot of money, and that's how the first Baron Desmet got the title. The house was built with defensive elements in its design, which accounts for the crenel-lated towers, and it once had a moat. Apparently, Lady Sylvia wanted a house that looked more like a country manor than a fortress, so she filled in the moat and had the fountain in the courtyard built with mosaics and marbles imported from Italy."

After a few minutes, the receptionist returned to the foyer with an older man, whom we assumed to be Clive. "Clive has the time to take you around. He's our handyman, but he gets bored just sitting and waiting for the next pipe to burst. He was asleep back there."

My first impression of our guide was that he was an old pensioner filling in time, but Clive had a spring in his step, despite the weight of the tool belt he wore at all times because of the terrible condition of the building.

Our first stop was what had once been the formal reception room. During the war, Desmet Park had been used as headquarters for an American Army battalion, and as part of its conversion to an operations center, deckboard had been placed over the walls, and maps showing all of the landing beaches on Normandy were still pinned to it. Apparently, the battalion had moved all operations to France when the British troops on Sword Beach had linked up with the American troops on Omaha Beach on June 10th.

"The maps add to the ambience," I whispered to Rob. "From the late military period."

We told Clive of our interest in *Pride and Prejudice* and asked if Desmet Park could possibly be Rosings Park. Looking at the depressing interior, it didn't seem likely. After repeating our question—he was more than a little hard of hearing—Clive shouted, "Look up! At the ceiling! What's wrong with it?"

Rob answered that it was too low and that it didn't fit with the size of the room. "It probably was lowered to install better lighting for its use as a war planning room."

"Right you are! But there's more to it than that." Again pointing to the ceiling, Clive said, "Above that ceiling is a painting by James Thornhill, a contemporary of Laguerre and Verrio, reign of George II. The painting is a mythological allegory, and it takes up the whole bloody ceiling." Clive's little surprise delighted him and us.

"In the 1920s, a fellow named McFadden wrote a tourist book that listed where all the great art was in English and Scottish country houses. He never updated the bloody thing 'cause he's probably dead, but no matter. You can see these tourists with McFadden's book clutched to their bosoms marching up the hill to see the Thornhill." He laughed at the thought. "They get pretty damn mad when they see that ceiling."

Clive explained that Desmet Park was "a disaster waiting to happen" because of the threat of fire from an ancient electrical wiring system. "Even so, the trustees are thinking about putting advertisements in newspapers in the States and Canada. Remember, it has the Thornhill, which is why a lot of people come and have a look at it in the first place." I asked if there were any Devereaux descendants still living, and Clive answered with a quirky smile that made you want to pinch his cheeks. "That line is deader than my granny."

Clive took pride in his knowledge of the house and started to give us a rundown of all of its owners, beginning with the first Lord Desmet. We reminded him that we were looking for a connection between Desmet Park and Rosings Park.

"There's a literary society that meets here once a month, and I've been told by these gray-haired lovelies that Jane Austen visited Kent quite often. Her brother, Edward, was adopted by the wealthy Knight family, and his estate, Godmersham, is less than twenty miles from here, and he had a very large family. Jane could have heard stories about Old Lady Desmet when she was visiting Edward or from her father's cousins because he grew up here in Kent. Legend has it that Lady Sylvia was a real, um, unpleasant lady. I've seen her portrait, and I can tell you she had some beak on her."

While Clive kept talking, we walked through the huge house. There certainly were things to admire: the gorgeous foyer, lead-crystal chandeliers, enormous fireplaces with elegant carvings and tile work, a beautiful staircase with a mahogany handrail, and the unseen Thornhill. But the Yanks had also done a very good job of converting it to a military office building.

"Lady Sylvia died in 1806, and after selling everything right down to the wallpaper, the daughter, Anne Desmet, moved to Bath and lived there until her death in the early 1820s. As far as I can tell, she never once came back here after she sold the house to Jacob Grissom, who made his money by selling gunpowder to the British during the Napoleonic Wars. Today, he'd be tried as a war profiteer; back then, he was a capitalist."

Thanking Clive for the guided tour, we tried to give him a tip, but he refused, explaining that he was very partial to Yanks. "During the war, Kent was overrun with Americans. You couldn't swing a cat without hitting a Yank. Naturally, there were soldiers in every town looking for a little fun. They got into quite a bit of mischief, but they also supported the local shops. You'd see the little ones running down the street after them, shouting, 'Give us some gum, chum.' They also handed out apples and oranges and told the kiddies to take them home to their mums.

"I think about all of those young American boys we seen every day for months, and then 'poof,' they were gone." Looking up to a sky that was threatening rain, he said, "I seen more than one shot-up bomber flying overhead trying to make an emergency landing at one of the RAF airfields nearby."

I think Clive felt that the conversation had become too serious, and an amused look came over his face. "You Yanks helped us in so many ways, including taking the local lovelies out for a good time because our lads were overseas. We'll never forget you. We can't. You left behind dozens of reminders, and they are all about four years old now."

Chapter 11

ON THE DRIVE BACK to London, I asked Rob why he didn't mention that he had been a member of a B-17 crew when Clive talked about the bombers he had seen flying over Kent, especially since Rob had been on a bomber that had crash-landed in Kent

"I think Clive was more of a talker than a listener," he said, and added, "I'm sure he fought in the First War and had plenty of stories of his own."

Rob quickly changed the subject and asked about some of the things that had been going through my mind from the time I had first met the Crowells. "Maggie, from what you've told me about the Crowells, they sound as if they are too intelligent to believe the Darcys are the Laceys unless they have proof. So if this thing is for real, then they have to have all kinds of things—diaries, letters, records."

"Rob, there's a lot we don't know, but for whatever reason, Beth Crowell, and I'm sure Beth is the connection, is not ready to tell us, but I'm absolutely convinced she is leading up to how she is connected to the Lacey family. We'll just have to wait."

Shortly after our visit to Kent, I received another letter from Beth. This time it was about Mary, but also Anne Desmet and Charlotte Chatterton, because their stories were all interconnected.

18 February 1948

Dear Maggie,

I was happy to hear that Rob and you were able to visit Austen's Rosings Park even if you could not see the Thornhill. I can only hope that some conservator will be able to find a way to preserve it because, from what you describe, it is possible that Desmet Park will be torn down for the value of its stone, especially since it appears to be a fire hazard. Every week, I read in the newspaper about manor houses being razed. So many of them were damaged during the war because of their use as barracks, or the costs of maintaining them are so prohibitive that no one can afford them.

It has been a long time since I wrote to you of Mary Garrison because her life was entwined with Charlotte and Anne's, and I was hoping you would be able to visit Kent before I shared with you their strange, but interesting, relationship.

Mary was a friend of Charlotte's younger sister, Maria Ledger. It seems that every time Lucy/Lydia came home to Bennets End, Mary arranged a visit to the parsonage with Maria. When Lucy returned permanently to Bennets End following Waggoner's transfer to Canada, Mary visited Charlotte and never left. You must be asking, why didn't Charlotte or Mr. Chatterton object?

As the wife of the local pastor, Charlotte had many

responsibilities, including visiting the poor and making food baskets for those who were ailing. In addition to these responsibilities, Charlotte acted as her husband's secretary, copying out his weekly sermons and taking dictation for his correspondence and reports to the bishop. Keep in mind that this was the era when people made their own ink and wrote with quill pens, which required constant repair. Anne, recognizing that Mary's stay was open-ended, encouraged Charlotte to have Mary take over many of the less desirable responsibilities of a minister's wife. This allowed Charlotte the time necessary to educate herself in the politics of the church and to learn what was going on in the church hierarchy.

When Lady Sylvia became ill, sometime around 1805, Anne told Charlotte that it was her intention to sell the estate after her mother's death. This is where Charlotte's political acumen bore fruit. She knew of an opening in Canterbury for a position that suited her husband's talents and requested that Anne ask her mother to write a letter to the bishop bringing Mr. Chatterton to his attention. When Lady Sylvia died in 1806, Mr. Chatterton was faced with a difficult choice. In addition to any bequest from Lady Sylvia, Mr. Chatterton, as rector, received an income from a tithe from every farmer or tradesman in his parish. However, Charlotte recognized that without Lady Sylvia's sponsorship, there was no chance for advancement in the church, but there was a possibility for a promotion if he served on the staff of the Suffragan Archbishop of Canterbury.

It turned out to be the correct move. In 1807, Mr. Chatterton, Charlotte, and Mary moved to Canterbury. They had been living in rooms near the Charter House for fifteen years when Mr. Chatterton died suddenly. With his death, the Garrison estate was entailed away from Charlotte because of her sex, and Charlotte and Mary chose to return to Hertfordshire.

I had been reading this letter aloud to Rob when he stopped me. "How does Beth know all this? She's stopped saying this information came through Aunt Margie. She must be related to the Laceys." I nodded and continued.

After her mother's death, Anne Desmet moved to Bath. The city was in its heyday at this time, and she leased a house in a neighbourhood near to the famous Royal Crescent. She brought with her the butler and her nurse, Mrs. Jackson, whom Anne was devoted to, and who spent a good portion of her life caring for Anne. We know she attended concerts and assemblies in Bath, escorted by her cousin, Col. Alexander Devereaux (Col. Fitzwilliam). Col. Devereaux was wounded at the Battle of Waterloo in 1815, and after his release from the Army, he went to live with Anne in Bath. The colonel died in 1819. Anne lived another three years.

I hope her years in Bath were happy ones. She certainly deserved it. Her life demonstrates that even the wealthy can be miserable if they are not nurtured and loved.

Your friend,
Beth

After finishing the letter, I told Rob about the conversation Jack and I had during our drive to Pamela's house. He mentioned that the Laceys had three sons and a daughter, and in Beth's letter recounting her Christmas visit to Harrods, she mentioned her brothers. "I'm positive the daughter is Beth Crowell."

"Why the big secret?" Rob asked.

"I don't know. But there must be something hurtful in this story for her to keep up this pretense." I wouldn't have long to wait before I found out, because Beth and Jack were coming to London.

***

Shortly after receiving the letter regarding Mary, Charlotte, and Anne, the Crowells wrote to let me know they would be visiting London and hoped we could get together for dinner at the Savoy, so they could meet my gentleman friend.

After we were seated in a gorgeous dining room, Beth told us that Jack and she frequently ate out when they moved to London during the winter of 1946–47. "Queuing up for food is unpleasant at the best of times, but with arctic temperatures day after day, I was willing to take advantage of the fact that we didn't need ration coupons to dine in a restaurant. And don't think I didn't feel guilty about doing it," she said emphatically. "Now, it's three years since we defeated Germany, and yet we still have rationing and queuing, and people are still walking around town in drab clothes that have been patched and repatched."

From what I had seen, patched clothing was a minor problem compared to finding enough coal for their homes. All over London, people were still pushing prams they filled up with coal at emergency dumps.

"The lobby of the Savoy was the scene of quite a brouhaha in 1940," Jack said almost gleefully. "The East End, where the docks and warehouses are, took a pounding night after night during the Blitz. The residents didn't think their situation was getting the proper attention, so a crowd of them marched on the Savoy, led by pregnant women and mothers with babes in arms. The marchers closed the restaurant and barricaded themselves in. Some of the group tied themselves to the pillars, while others ran down to the shelters where the hotel kept bunks for the likes of the Duke and Duchess of Kent. It all came to an end when the Savoy's manager wisely ordered tea to be served. That quieted everyone down, and feeling they had made their point, the protestors left."

After dinner, we went into the hotel lobby, where Jack and Rob discussed the war and the engineering jobs Jack had worked on in India, while Beth and I sat on a sofa just out of earshot of the men. She began by asking me the same questions about Rob my mother was asking in her letters, but without the hysteria. There had never been a Protestant in our family. Beth was amused by my mother's phobia of non-Catholics and told me about Kathleen Kennedy, the Marchioness of Hartington, and the widow of the man who would have become the Duke of Devonshire.

"Mrs. Kennedy was so appalled when she learnt her daughter was going to marry a Protestant that she checked herself into a hospital. When she finally agreed to meet with the press, she was wearing a black dress as if she were in mourning. She wasn't impressed by Billy Hartington's title at all, but her father, a son of Irish immigrants, was delighted. In any event, Kick, as she is known, may lose the title because she seems to be on the verge of marriage with Peter Wentworth-Fitzwilliam, the 8th Earl Fitzwilliam. I hope she knows what she is doing. Peter has a reputation for being a player and living in the fast lane."

Beth returned to the topic of Rob and cautioned me against doing anything hasty. I assured Beth in person and my mother by mail that marriage had not even been mentioned. However, I was thinking about it quite often, but what Rob was thinking was less clear. He knew the words to all the most popular songs, but his favorite was a Western, "Don't Fence Me In."

"We have come to London to take care of our granddaughter while James and Angela go off on a brief holiday," Beth said. "I probably won't be able to meet with you again before we go back home, so I thought I'd give you a little bit of Jane and Charles Bingham's story."

Beth started from the point where Charles came into his majority at the age of twenty-one. "As you can imagine, at that time in his life, Charles had no interest in settling down. He wanted to go to dances, meet young ladies, ride horses, and attend the races at Epsom and Ascot. Until such time as he married, Charles was given a yearly allowance sufficient to meet his needs, as long as he stayed out of London's betting parlors. All that changed once he married Jane.

"Charles built a house on property in the southern part of Derbyshire, about thirty miles from Montclair. He really relished this new stage in his life, and to the end of his days, he remained the country squire, riding about his estate and visiting his neighbors. I imagine it gave some shape to his life." Shaking her head, Beth said that Charles Bingham had been kept in perpetual boyhood by his brothers and even Will Lacey.

"Bingham Park is a very large manor house, and only the finest materials were used in its construction. Marble and tile workers were brought to England from Italy, and because this project went on for years, the craftsmen sent for their families.

The Italian community built a small church near Leicester with stunning stained glass windows and mosaics. Unfortunately, the original church is gone. In late 1942, Leicester and the surrounding area were heavily bombed, and one of the casualties was this lovely church."

I knew there were many places of worship that didn't survive the war, the most famous being the fourteenth-century Coventry Cathedral. Numerous churches in London were also destroyed or badly damaged, including several designed by Christopher Wren. However, Wren's greatest creation, St. Paul's Cathedral, survived several close calls, including one in which it was hit with twenty-eight incendiary bombs. One incendiary, penetrating the outer shell of the dome, began to melt the lead, leaving many to believe the cathedral was doomed. Then the miraculous happened; the bomb fell out on to the parapet and failed to explode. One of the war's most famous photographs was of St. Paul's emerging from the smoke of what must have seemed to the people of London to be an entire city on fire. It became a symbol of British resolve to fight through to victory.

Thinking of all the British had suffered, I was glad to return to the Binghams' love story and the nine children that came out of it.

"Charles ran a successful stud farm at Bingham Park and also started a hunting club that still exists. For many years, my parents were subscribers, and I also rode with this club. This was a very important aspect of English society. Members of the British elite visited each other's country estates and went all out running down that little fox. Please keep in mind that foxes were regarded as vermin to be got rid of, much like the coyotes of your American West.

"If I recall correctly, Jane died around 1833, but Charles lived on for another ten years. For all the difficulties they had in their courtship, Charles and Jane's marriage was a great success." And suddenly standing up, Beth said, "I have to go to the loo."

When she returned, Beth wanted to finish up with the Binghams. "The most interesting Bingham was not Charles but his brother, George. He was a financial genius, who helped many of England's elite families who were experiencing financial difficulties, which gave him access to some powerful people. He made a fortune for himself, his family, and his investors from trade with China and India. One of his more lucrative businesses was importing luxury items from France while Britain and France were at war. He believed that trade was a great leveler in society, and since the aristocracy continued to buy these luxuries, he was more than willing to supply them with their perfumes and wines and keep the middle-class shopkeepers employed. You have only to look at the public rooms at Montclair, with all of its French furniture, to see that Will Lacey was of a similar mind. However, George was also an ardent abolitionist, and he left a hefty legacy to the Anti-Slavery Society."

Motioning to her husband, Beth indicated that it was time for them to go back to their room, as they had a little girl to take care of the next day. Beth kissed me on the cheek, and after doing so, handed me a letter and a small parcel bound up with brown paper and string.

"Being married to Jack, a man who spent his whole career working on challenging projects that improved the lives of others, I have always been troubled by Charles Bingham's willingness to live a life so ordinary when he was in a position to do, I don't know—something—anything. But you can draw your own conclusions from the letters."

Chapter 12

AS SOON AS WE parted company, I complimented Rob on making such a good impression with the Crowells. He addressed Jack as "Sir" and Beth as "Ma'am," which, he insisted, was a common courtesy in the western United States.

"Flagstaff is in the West, but it isn't exactly Dodge City or Tombstone. I kept my six-shooter holstered whenever possible," he said, smiling.

Walking to the Underground station, Rob continued, "Oh, by the way, Beth is Elizabeth Lacey, daughter of Sir Edward and Sarah Lacey. Jack told me Beth has a letter for you that will explain all that. They figured you knew."

I had figured it out long ago. I still did not know why Beth felt it necessary to keep this part of her life secret. But whatever her reasons, I was pleased she finally trusted me enough to tell me.

Rob then shared with me some of his conversation with Jack. "Jack and Beth went out to India when their kids were little because he had gotten a job as an engineer with a railroad company. They lived in Calcutta and in these hill towns where the women and children went when the hot weather hit. When the kids turned twelve, they went to a boarding school in Scotland. In '34, heading home to England to take the younger son to school, Jack got sick with malaria while going through the Suez Canal. By the time they got to Marseilles, he had to be taken off the ship. Beth took care of him because she had trained as a nurse's aide, a VAD, which stands for Volunteer Aide something, in the First War.

"Anyway, Jack was really sick, and so they stayed in England for more than a year. When he wasn't working on renovating Crofton Wood, which he pretty much gutted because the building was so old, he worked on the Lacey family history. It was Jack who dug out the boring stuff: estate and church records, real estate transactions, military records, Charles Bingham's journal from when he was building Bingham Park, and so on. The reason Beth and Jack know so much about the Edwards family was because, in the summer of 1913, they went on a motor tour to a lot of the places mentioned in *Pride and Prejudice*, and one of their stops was the Edwards farm. The whole idea of a motor tour was cooked up by Beth's youngest brother, Reed, and the grandmother.

"Beth made her debut in 1912 and had a great time during her first season. But her mother considered it to be a bust because Beth didn't get engaged, which was the whole point of being out in society. She didn't think Beth had given the bachelors enough encouragement, and that she had expressed her opinions too freely. Jack said Lady Lacey didn't mind Beth getting a college education, as long as she didn't actually use it.

"It was the grandmother who suggested that if Beth made a

real effort to land a husband during her second season, she should be rewarded by being allowed to go on this car trip with Reed, who would make sketches of all the places mentioned in *Pride and Prejudice* for his grandmother, who loved the novel.

"Beth was allowed to go because she had caught the eye of this guy named Colin Matheson, who was rich, owned thousands of acres in Ireland, and came from a distinguished Anglo-Irish family. Jack said he was one of the most sought-after bachelors at that time, and Beth's mother was convinced that a proposal would be made during the winter season. It all had to be done on the q.t. If word got out that Beth was driving around the countryside without a chaperone, she would have been 'cut' from society because people would question whether or not she was still a virgin. Beth's dad backed her up, saying that all the society bigwigs would be in the south of France for the rest of the summer, and no one would be the wiser. And it all came off without a hitch.

"Get this. The mother agreed that Beth could go on one condition: that Jack go along, because he had been fixing Sir Edward's cars for a couple of years. This is 1913. Beth's twenty and Jack is twenty-two. Jack said that even though the Laceys treated him well, it never occurred to Lady Lacey that her daughter would be interested in the son of a servant or that Jack would act in any way other than as the son of her butler. It was a good thing Jack did go because the car, a 1912 Rolls Royce, broke down and had flats because of the crappy roads.

"That summer, Beth and Jack fell in love. It was on that trip that they went to Desmet Park and Hertfordshire. They found the Edwards/Garrison farm, and it was the three of them, not Aunt Margie, who talked to Mrs. Edwards. Jack said there's a story that goes with Aunt Margie, but he'd tell us at another time. They found Netherfield Park, which was actually Helmsley Hall, but it had been converted into a private girls' school, and Winchester Cathedral where Austen is buried. Reed made sketches of all these places.

"For Jack, it was the best summer of his life, and he said, 'I was head over heels for Beth, but she would be returning to Newnham College, and I would be going back to The Tech in Manchester. I could hardly believe she was interested in me at all, and I was afraid that once she got back to Cambridge, she'd come to her senses and throw me over. And then the war! My God! No one could have foreseen the bloodbath that was just a year down the road. During the war, I'd think back to that summer with Beth and Reed, and sometimes when I was standing in the mud and muck in France, seeing my mates come back in pieces or not at all, it would keep me from blowing my brains out.'"

Because I pictured Jack Crowell as a tower of strength, I could not imagine him taking his own life. But could I really get my mind around just how awful trench warfare in northern France had been during the First World War, and wasn't it possible that there might be a breaking point, even for a man as strong as Jack?

"Jack also told me that his younger brother, Tom, was killed on the Somme in July 1916. That was all he had to say, and I didn't ask for details."

From the time I had first met Jack, when he had mentioned the town memorial to those killed in The Great War, I knew that someone he cared about was memorialized on the stone monument on the village green. I remembered Jack telling me about

Harvest Home and the two brothers walking the children around the fountain on ponies. His face had lit up at the memory.

My head was bobbing up and down on Rob's shoulder as we rode the Underground to Mrs. Dawkins's house. An occasional grunt reassured Rob that I was listening.

"By the way, I'm having dinner with Jack at the Engineer's Club on Wednesday. He thinks by that time he'll be climbing the walls, being in such a small flat with two females, even if one of them is only a baby."

***

Since Rob would be having dinner with Jack, I decided to make a surprise visit to see Beth and baby Julia. I packed up some sandwiches and coleslaw that Mrs. Dawkins had made, but before heading over to James's flat, I reread the letter Beth had given to me at the Savoy.

3 March 1948

Dear Maggie,

As I am sure you have already guessed, I am Elizabeth Lacey of Montclair. My parents were Sarah Bolton and Edward Lacey, and I had three brothers, Trevor, Matthew, and Reed. They are all gone now, and I am the only Lacey left. First, I must apologize for the untruths I told you, and I hope that you will forgive me. I wanted you to hear the story of my family, but I was not prepared to place myself at the center of it. Jack's been after me ever since your second visit to Crofton Wood to share this information with you.

In my defence, I must say that you were not the first

person to knock on our door asking about the Lacey/Darcy connection. We British like to be close to our poets and authors. We read Wordsworth in the Lake District and the Brontës in Yorkshire. They can also be very demanding. Several asked us to justify their belief that we were related to the Darcys. After that, I cautioned Don Caton about sending just anyone down to the house even if it meant denying Jack an afternoon of talking to the curious about Montclair.

I believe Jack mentioned that my grandmother, Marianne Dickinson Lacey, loved the novel and was captivated by the Lacey connection to it. When she married my grandfather in 1861, Franny Lacey, Will and Elizabeth's older daughter, was living at Montclair, and she had all of these wonderful stories about her parents, which she shared with Grandma. When Grandma's health began to fail, she had the servants gather up everything relating to Elizabeth and Will and had them placed in chests and taken below stairs. The information we have been sharing with you came from diaries, letters, and other papers stored in those chests, and I have enclosed selected entries from Elizabeth's diaries.

Elizabeth and Will Lacey had some wrinkles to iron out in their marriage, but they did succeed and lived full and happy lives. Enjoy!

Fondly,
Beth

Now that the secret was out, I was already thinking of the many questions I would like to ask her. I felt so much of what she wished to keep private was contained in the first paragraph: "I had three brothers... I'm the only Lacey left." Maybe, when Rob saw Jack at the Engineer's Club, he would learn something of the brothers, but I was not going to press Beth.

Chapter 13

WHEN BETH OPENED THE door to the one-bedroom flat, I could tell she was pleased to have company. Behind her, baby Julia was lying on a blanket on the floor surrounded by chewing toys.

"What a pleasant surprise," Beth said. "I am all alone because children as young as Julia are not Jack's strong suit. He prefers them when they're capable of catching a ball. I'll give him his due, though; he did change one dirty nappy. After that, he decided to spend the afternoon at the library."

"Is he looking for anything in particular?" I asked.

"He reads a lot of the old newspapers and regimental histories from the First War. I think he's trying to figure out how things could have gone so badly. Did you know Jack's brother was killed on the Somme?" I told her that I did. "But let us talk of happier times," she quickly added.

As I sat beside Beth on the floor, she took my hand in hers and asked if I had read her letter. "Will you forgive me for not being honest with you?"

"Of course," I said emphatically. "But now that everything is out in the open, I have to say I know more about your great, great grandmother than I do about you and your family. Would 'happier times' include telling me about growing up at Montclair?"

Beth laughed. "You should be a reporter, Maggie. You know how to pursue a story."

Julia was sitting contentedly between my legs gumming a teething ring. She looked a lot like her mother with her tuft of black hair and olive complexion. Looking at this beautiful child, I thought about Capt. James Crowell's good fortune in staying in Angela's village in Italy long enough for them to fall in love. But was it any different than a girl from Minooka, falling in love with a man from Arizona, while living in England?

Beth began by telling me about her parents. Like many people of the British upper class, Edward "Ned" and Sarah Lacey led lives that were very independent of each other.

"Wasn't your father a broker?" I asked.

For a few seconds, Beth put her head back and looked at the ceiling before saying, "Not really. Oh, he had the title, and he'd pop into the office now and then, but he left the running of the office to the professionals. Jack thinks I don't know how little my father actually worked, and I don't want him to know that I know.

"My grandfather, Andrew Lacey, did not like to entertain, so he delegated that job to my father. It was my mother and father who hosted the lawn parties, summer teas, and excursions to the Peak District. It was Papa who was in charge of the shooting parties and who traveled to Scotland to shoot grouse and go salmon fishing. Even though he did all those things, his passion was for motor racing and football. He put together the first organized football club from Crofton. It was made up of boys who worked at the pottery kilns or for the tradespeople and, of course, the boys who worked for us.

"My mother's passion was for horses. Our family often hosted the hunt, which was a very big event and great fun."

"Were Jack and his brother involved in the hunt?"

"It was such a big affair, with so many guests, that everyone had a role. Before the start of the run, there would be lawn meets where the riders would gather to drink and eat and generally get in the mood for the chase. Even though Tom and Jack were not servants, their father insisted they help out, and I'd catch Jack looking at me. I really wanted to stay behind to talk to him, but such a thing 'simply wasn't done.' One of the things that *was* done on these weekends was for husbands and wives to end up in bedrooms with people other than their spouses. Matthew was two years older than I, and Trevor four years. They loved sneaking around to see what went on after my parents retired.

"When I was about thirteen," Beth continued, "my mother took Reed and me to New York, where we lived with my mother's sister for about a year, because my father had a mistress, the widow, Mrs. Lucy Arminster." Looking at my expression and nodding, she said, "The first time Matthew told me my father had spent the night with another woman, I cried until there were no tears left to cry. However, I would subsequently learn my father had more than one affair. The reason my mother went to America wasn't because he was seeing another woman; it was because the relationship with Mrs. Arminster had gotten serious.

"Reed was greatly troubled by the separation and was having bouts of depression. My father was an anchor for my brother. They often traveled together scouting the local football talent and going to auto races. Fortunately, my Aunt Laura and Grandma convinced my parents to reconcile, so we returned to England.

"All of this had a profound effect on me. That's why I was so drawn to Jack. I decided I wanted a man with Jack's qualities, and unlike my father, someone who would be faithful to me. By the time I was eighteen, I had such a crush on him that I couldn't bear to be away from Montclair. I literally threw myself at him when he came home from school one summer. I didn't get the expected response. Jack and I had one of those conversations that stays with you forever. I told him that we were living in the twentieth century, and it shouldn't matter what class a person belonged to in order for them to see each other socially. What Jack said was, 'You're telling me I won't need to use the backstairs anymore. I can just walk around to the front, and when Billy answers the door, tell him I'm paying a social call on Miss Elizabeth. Whose boot do you think will be in my backside first, your mother's or my father's?'

"He was perfectly correct. I later apologized because I wanted him to know I was not some mindless flirt bent on seduction. Even with that, he kept his distance. When my mother asked Jack to serve as our chauffeur for our summer tour, he respectfully declined, and my mother's response confirmed what Jack knew all along. Her requests were actually orders, and she gave him our departure date.

"Of course, Jack thought I had cooked the whole thing up, but it truly was Reed's idea. In fact, when Grandma suggested that Jack be our driver, I said 'no,' because it would only serve to reinforce that I was Miss Elizabeth and he was the butler's son. It started off very badly, with Jack driving and not talking, and Reed and I sitting in the back seat. But little by little, I chipped away at his reserve. When we went to Brighton, we walked along the beach, and he kissed me. After that, we had the best time, bouncing along those horrible country roads.

"Because we had had such a wonderful summer, I had great hopes that Jack and I could find a way to be together, but it didn't happen. Jack went back to Manchester, and I returned to Newnham College. In 1914, the summer before the war, Jack retreated to his earlier position that if his father and my mother learnt of a relationship between us, it would be met with a firestorm. Once again, he pushed off on me, and we saw little of each other.

"When Jack came home for Christmas in 1915 from The Tech, he was polite and friendly, but as for a personal relationship, there seemed to be an unbridgeable chasm between us. Jack had orders to report for basic training in January, and I was afraid I might not see him again. So many of the young men I knew were being killed or maimed. I didn't want anyone but Jack, but Jack didn't want me.

"I invited my old friend, Ginger Bramfield, to dinner on several occasions during the Christmas holiday with one purpose in mind, and that was to make Jack jealous. Ginger had been wounded at Ypres and had lost the use of his right arm, which was why he was available. What a horrible thing to do to that man. But I wanted Jack, and nothing was going to get in my way.

"The evening before Jack left for basic training, I asked him to meet me behind the garages. I told him that I loved him, and I started to cry and sob and generally carry on. He took me in his arms and held me for the longest time, not saying a word, and then he went back to the house. I was twenty-one years old, and my world had fallen apart.

"What I didn't know was that I had an unexpected ally—Jack's mother. One evening, while Ginger was dining with us, Mr. Crowell told everyone downstairs that if things worked out with Ginger, who was the son of a baron, that it would be a good match for me. Later that evening, Jack's mother surprised him by saying she knew he was in love with me. When Jack told her I wanted to get married, she said we should go ahead. You see, the war changed so many things. Tom and Matthew were serving in the Sherwood Foresters, and both would face the same dangers once they went to France. Even though Matthew was an officer, Mrs. Crowell felt that both were giving their all for their country, and in return, their country should treat them equally.

"When Jack came home from basic training, I was living in Sheffield because I was a Red Cross volunteer. My job was to meet the troop trains and make sure the men had something hot to drink—coffee, tea, soup, whatever they wanted—and little finger sandwiches. I was handing out cups of coffee when a man came up behind me and asked if he could have 'a cuppa.' It was Jack. I wanted to fall into his arms, but my supervisor was nearby. I was staying with the Menlo sisters. Mr. and Mrs. Menlo had rescued Jack's mother from an orphanage, and she had grown up with their five daughters. I told Jack to meet me there after my shift ended."

Beth started to laugh. "When Jack came by that evening, he proposed, and what a proposal it was. He said, 'If you still want to get married, we can do it while I'm on leave.' And then he shrugged his shoulders as if to say it didn't matter to him one way or the other. It was not how I had imagined Jack proposing, but I decided to accept it, nonetheless. If I was looking for flowery language, I was marrying the wrong man. We got married three days later in the registrar's office with Mrs. Crowell and her dearest friend, Evangeline Menlo, as witnesses. We spent our wedding night at a hotel across from the train station.

"It was very important that I not get pregnant. The Army provided soldiers with prophylactics by the gross to cut down on venereal disease. Jack had put what were called 'French letters' in his kitbag, and just when everything was getting really hot, he couldn't find his kit. He was walking around the room in the dark, bumping into furniture, saying, 'Oh my God! Where's my kitbag? Where's my kitbag?' It really was funny, and fortunately he found his kit. We made love so often that I thought I'd end up bowlegged."

For once, I didn't blush. I was getting used to Beth's lack of inhibition in sharing her personal stories. At home, no one ever talked about sex. You weren't even supposed to think about it because it was a sin, and it would have to be confessed to our grouchy pastor. There might not be any police in Minooka, but there was Father Lynch. After dark, he walked the streets with a shillelagh, banging the bushes and chasing home any young people out after the curfew. Things like that kept your knees together.

"Even though I transferred to a Red Cross unit in London," Beth continued, "it was very difficult getting the time to see Jack because he had been sent to a camp south of London for additional training. But one evening, Matthew, Tom, Jack, and I all got together for dinner. Tom and Matthew were sailing for France within the week, so we told them we had gotten married. Matthew and Tom jumped up and announced our marriage to everyone in the restaurant and asked if they would join us in a toast. Then the patrons started to come over and congratulate us as if we were old friends. It was wonderful."

I knew almost nothing about Beth's brothers, so I asked her what they were like.

"I got along quite well with Trevor, who had a nice, even disposition. He was very handsome and had a reputation as a lady's man, although I can honestly say that some girls were absolutely shameless in the way they acted around him.

"I have a wonderful niece, Gloria Manning, who lives in the States as a result of a liaison Trevor had with Gloria's mother, who was a serving girl at one of the inns, when he was at Cambridge. If Ellen's pregnancy had become known, Trevor would have been sent down. He would have been forced to leave Cambridge. In order to keep everything quiet, Ellen went to live with my mother's sister in New York where Gloria was born thirty-five years ago. It was very difficult for Ellen to leave her family and England, but she came to believe it was the right decision.

"Matthew was another story. He was all storm and thunder if he didn't get his way. It was not in his nature to lose at anything. His nickname at Glenkill, the school he attended in Scotland, was 'Els,' because he was known to throw elbows when playing rugby. After the war, after word got out about the Battle of the Somme and the complete ineptitude of the British command in ordering that slaughter, Jack and I would talk about how frustrated Matthew must have been knowing that the orders he had been given would not achieve the desired objectives—would not give the British a win. It may sound odd, but Jack and Matthew had dinner together behind the lines in September. Matthew told Jack that there was to be another 'big push,' and that he would not survive it. He was right, of course. His company went over the top on September 26th. He died within a mile of where Tom had been killed in July. Matthew's body was never recovered; he just disappeared."

"Beth, are you saying that your brother was killed at the Somme, as well as Jack's brother?" I had that sick feeling you get in your stomach when you know you're about to get some bad news.

Putting her hand to her head, Beth ran her fingers back and forth along her forehead before saying, "Maggie, I am so sorry. I never told you. Both Trevor and Matthew were killed in France, Trevor in 1915 at Loos, and Matthew a year later almost to the day. I don't like to think about it. I much prefer to picture Matthew, Trevor, and Tom playing football on the lawn below the gardens."

Beth sat quietly for several minutes before continuing. "Every family has its secrets, except we had the money to set things right or to hush them up. At my mother's insistence, we told no one about Reed's depression. By the time he was called up, the ranks were so depleted they had to take everyone who could pass a physical. My father used his influence to see that Reed was not assigned to the infantry, but incidences of favoritism were receiving some very bad press. So there was only so much that could be done to help my brother."

Julia, who had been sleeping quietly next to me, started to stir, and the conversation concerning Reed came to an end. Instead, she talked about her sons. She was very close to both of them and was counting down the days until Michael's discharge from the RAF in November. Her mood improved considerably the more she talked about James and Michael and all the things they had done together, often just the three of them, because Jack was often working.

"It's really a shame, Maggie, that Michael is in Malta because you would have been just perfect for him. I hope Rob appreciates what a special person you are."

"Thank you," I said, smiling at her for the nice compliment. "I know Rob appreciates me, and I know he loves me. It's just that we never talk about getting married. It's as if our relationship is stuck in first gear."

"I wish I could give you some advice because I had the same thing with Jack, but it was only because of the war that we got married."

"I'm sure it will all work out in the end," I said, unconvincingly. "And as far as Michael is concerned, it really doesn't matter, since he already has a girlfriend."

"That's true. But that relationship will never end in marriage." I must have looked puzzled because Beth continued. "I met Audrey, who's about five years older than Michael, at James's wedding, but at the time, they were just friends. She's a charming woman, but when he wrote to say they were seeing each other romantically, Jack and I were surprised because we hadn't seen anything to indicate that a romance was in the offing. And Michael is such a romantic. If Audrey was that special girl, he would have swept her off her feet and carried her to the nearest chaplain. Besides, he asks more questions about you than he writes about her."

Unsure of what to say, I told Beth I would set the table for dinner. But I couldn't help but think about the day Michael and I had spent together at Thor's Cave, and how I had loved every minute of it. But that was before I had fallen in love with Rob. Even so, I was curious as to why Michael was asking questions about me and wondering why I cared.

When Jack returned from the library, he gave me a big bear hug, and after that, there was little opportunity to discuss anything. Every evening, Julia started fussing at just about dinnertime, and she was right on schedule.

With all Beth had told me, I appreciated why she had been so reluctant to discuss her family. Two of her brothers and brother-in-law had been killed in the First World War. Although Beth did not say what had happened to her brother Reed, it was clear that something had gone very wrong.

Chapter 14

THE NEXT DAY AFTER work, I opened the parcel Beth had given to me at the Savoy. The first letter was from Jane, who was in London, to Lizzy in Kent, where she was visiting the newly married Charlotte Chatterton. After the ball at Helmsley Hall, Will Lacey had gone directly to London to talk to George Bingham about his brother's interest in Jane Garrison. Charles was summoned by his older brother and was convinced it was best to end the relationship. At the time she wrote this undated letter, Jane was in Gracechurch Street, trying to mend her broken heart.

> Dear Lizzy,
>
> I have much to acquaint you with. Mr. Bingham came to Uncle Sims's on Monday, as he had just learnt that I was in London. He said nothing of leaving Helmsley Hall so suddenly, but handed me an invitation from his brother George to lunch with him on Wednesday. I was very

apprehensive about meeting the head of the Bingham family, as everyone speaks of him with such deference.

George Bingham is a slightly taller version of Charles but with less hair and spectacles. For all of his wealth, George resides in Cheapside, not more than a mile from Uncle Sims. The house is modest in size compared to his fortune and sensibly furnished. Charles, George, and his wife, Hannah, greeted me warmly, and we had a lovely lunch. George asked me many questions about my family and my interests, all in a very agreeable manner. After the meal, he requested that I join his wife and him in the study. The conversation continued much as before, and then he opened the door and asked for Charles to see me home.

Charles rode with me in the carriage and told me he thought the afternoon had been a great success. A success—to what end? Neither of us knew what to say, so I asked if he had attended the theatre while he was in town. He said that London had lost all attraction for him and that he longed to be in the country. Then, Lizzy, you can't imagine what happened next. The very next day, George Bingham sent word that he would like to visit with me at Uncle's on Friday. I confess I still do not know what to make of his visit, but here is what he said:

'I am a man of few words. I talk openly and honestly so there is no confusion as to what I mean or expect. In short, Miss Garrison, I get to the point. Although Charles's sisters are fond of you, they questioned the wisdom of an association with your family. I might have disregarded their opinions if it were not for the fact that Mr. Lacey had also spoken out against such a union. I need to acquaint you with some facts before you judge him too harshly.

'When Charles was very young, our parents died, and I became the head of the Bingham family enterprises. There were too many demands on my time, and I neglected Charles's upbringing. When he was sixteen, I sent him to America with our brother, Richard, to learn about our business concerns in New York, Philadelphia, and Charleston. In Charleston, his interests were almost exclusively confined to riding, dancing, and hunting. Charles wanted to stay in Charleston, as he found its society to be most agreeable. However, Richard reported that, behind the genteel planter society, the young men engaged in activities that were in conflict with what was expected of a Bingham. Richard sent him home.

'Once back in England, I engaged an excellent tutor for Charles. He did improve under Mr. Montaigne's direction, but before I could be at ease with his entry into society, Charles needed to be guided by someone of impeccable manners and unquestionable morals. Mr. Lacey was such a gentleman. I was acquainted with Mr. Lacey, as I was an executor of the elder Lacey's estate. At my request, he agreed to befriend Charles. The young, well-mannered man you have come to know is largely a product of Mr. Lacey's instruction.

'Now, as to what concerns me with regard to your relationship with my brother, please forgive me, but I must be blunt. I am told your parents have neglected the education and supervision of your younger sisters exactly in the same manner I once neglected Charles's. If not checked, I am sorry to say, they will get into trouble and cause harm to your family. I have also been informed that your mother anticipated an offer of marriage and had acquainted the neighbourhood with this information before the deed was done. That is always unwise.

'I wish you to know that Mr. Lacey spoke most highly of you and your sister Elizabeth. His objections rested exclusively with the behaviour of your mother and younger sisters, as well as your lack of connections. Mr. Lacey comes from a prestigious family, and I hold him in the highest regard. However, if I wanted a pedigree, I would buy a dog.

'When I met my wife, the daughter of my brother's tailor, I recognized in her all the attributes I could hope for in a marriage partner: honesty, integrity, industry, and I cannot emphasize this enough, common sense. I am happy to say that I have observed those very same qualities in you, and my wife concurs. In fact, I have found you to be agreeable in every possible way. My only regret is that I had to say these things to you, but it was important that you know them.

'For all these weeks that Charles has been in London, he has been perfectly miserable. I attribute this to his being deprived of your company. I hope that you understand the importance of the role Charles's wife will play, and for that reason alone, I have acquainted you with my reservations. I am now reassured.'

Lizzy, what am I to think of all this? Am I to anticipate an offer of marriage from Charles? I am flattered that George Bingham has such a high opinion of me, but at the same time, I am mortified by his opinion of our family. Is Charles so in love with me that he will marry me despite all of these objections? And what of Mr. Lacey? If Charles does marry me, will that be the end of their friendship? Please write as soon as you are able.

Love,
Jane

Beth had probably included this letter because it provided a quick study of both Jane and Charles's characters. I didn't think either of them came off very well. Charles appeared to be an immature young man whose main interests were dancing and riding. And Jane! What a docile creature she was, especially considering Charles's shortcomings. After Rob had a chance to read the letter, I asked what he thought about it.

"Whatever went on in Charleston that Charles and the planters' sons got into, George didn't like it one bit. It's pretty obvious that Charles was never going to be allowed to become a partner in the Bingham businesses, so George gave him the money to build a country house that would keep his little brother busy. Basically, Charles was all hat and no cattle."

"I get the feeling that George wanted Jane to be his wife and mother."

"Since Charles never had a mother, maybe that was okay with him. Besides, you told me that the job of the ladies in *Pride and Prejudice* was the 'getting of husbands,' and Jane had got herself a very rich one. She'd have been crazy to have turned him down. Look at it this way, Charles turned out all right. A lot of guys with too much money and time on their hands didn't. After I visited Blenheim, a guy at the village pub told me Randolph Churchill, Winston's father, liked booze and women and died of syphilis, and he was pretty typical of younger sons."

At that point, I told Rob about my visit with Beth. After hearing about Edward Lacey's adulterous affairs and Trevor's illegitimate child, he let out a long whistle. Apparently, social prohibitions were very flexible if you belonged to the gentry or the aristocracy.

We were both so tired that Rob begged off sharing what Jack had told him at the Engineer's Club. Besides, learning about

Beth's brothers had unsettled me. I told him I was still working my way through Beth's latest parcel, so any news from Jack could wait. To the sound of the Dawkins boys giggling, Rob kissed me good night and winked at the two pairs of eyes peeking out of the darkened family room.

As I was going upstairs, Mrs. Dawkins called me into the kitchen and pulled a postcard out of her apron pocket. It was a standard vacation postcard which said, "Greetings from Malta" and showed the capital city of Valletta. On the back, Michael had crossed out "Wish you were here" and had written "Wish I were there. Mike."

"I didn't think you'd want your fellow to see that," Mrs. Dawkins said with her arms crossed over her chest, "so I put it in my pocket."

"Mrs. Dawkins, Mike is the Crowells' son. You know, the family I visit in Crofton. I met him one time when he was home on leave."

Mrs. Dawkins's arms remained crossed.

"He's in the RAF. He's stationed in Malta."

"Then he's not just there on holiday? He won't be coming back here?"

"Eventually, he'll come back here. This is his home, but his enlistment isn't up until the end of this year."

"All right then. That's what I wanted to hear. There's no reason for any girl to have two men in her life at the same time." And she turned off the light and told me she would see me in the morning.

I understood Mrs. Dawkins's concerns. Shortly after I had moved in, I found out about Debbie, the tenant who had immediately preceded me. Debbie had entertained a man above stairs, which Mrs. Dawkins had made very clear would result in the immediate termination of the lease. If that wasn't shocking enough, the man who had been visiting Debbie was not her boyfriend, which would explain why my landlady was unhappy about my receiving a postcard from someone other than Rob.

While I was getting ready for bed, I propped the card up next to my washbasin. It seemed so strange to me. Beth had said that Michael was asking questions about me, but I hadn't heard a word from her son since I had seen him four months earlier at Crofton Wood. After all this time, why now? Did it have anything to do with my telling Beth that my relationship with Rob seemed to have stalled, and the only discussion regarding our future consisted entirely of where we were going on our next date? Had she shared that with Michael? I had no answers, so I put the postcard in my dresser drawer. As Mrs. Dawkins said, there was no reason for a girl to have two men in her life at the same time, and I was already having problems with the one I had.

Chapter 15

AFTER CLIMBING INTO BED, I opened Beth's parcel, which contained several pages of transcriptions from Elizabeth Garrison's diary. In her note, she wrote that she wanted to take me back to the beginning of the story when Mr. Bingham had made his first appearance in Hertfordshire. "You will get a sense of the excitement his arrival caused in a neighbourhood lacking in eligible bachelors."

17 March—While Jane and I were in Mrs. Draper's shop this afternoon, we heard news that a young gentleman has taken a lease on Helmsley Hall. We are told that Mr. Charles Bingham is quite handsome and of good height. He is very fond of horses and is pleased with the fine pastures he finds at HH. We returned home to find this was old news to Papa, as Sir William and he had already met with the subscribers, and all have agreed that the assembly rooms should be opened and a dance held to welcome the gentleman and his party. Mr. Bingham wrote immediately to Sir William, saying he would be honoured to attend the assembly and looked forward to meeting his new neighbours. I wonder what the gentleman will think of our country dances.

The events that took place at the assembly were very close to those described in Jane Austen's novel. Mr. Bingham had a great time, especially with Jane Garrison, Mr. Ashurst was a bore, and the two Bingham sisters tried to keep as much distance from the locals as possible. The only difference was that Mr. Lacey's insult packed even more of a sting: "Mr. Bingham's friend said within my hearing that the only thing worse than dancing with the present company would be the necessity of conversing with them." Ouch!

As in the novel, Jane did have lunch with the Bingham sisters at Helmsley Hall, but that was where any similarities ended. Jane did not get sick, so Lizzy did not have to nurse her sister, and there were no snappy exchanges between Mr. Lacey and Lizzy during Jane's recuperation. But at that lunch, Jane learned who Charles's dour friend was: Mr. William Lacey of Pemberley in Derbyshire.

31 March—Jane found the gentleman to be in much better humour as he commented on how pleasant the local countryside was. Apparently, he has a large estate in the country near Matlock and belongs to one of those ancient Norman families who arrived in England with William the Conqueror. He is very proud, but with his wealth and superior situation in society, I daresay he has a right to be. Jane suspects Mr. Lacey exerts a strong influence on his friend. Of that there can be little doubt.

In addition to Beth's diary transcriptions were undated letters from Will to his cousin Anne.

Dear Anne,

I pay a high price for being Bingham's friend. Each evening, Bingham and I must play cards with Caroline, Louisa, and Ashurst because, if I do not, I must listen to the sisters complain about the lack of society in the country or listen to Ashurst's snoring as he lays sprawled on the sofa.

Bingham's interest in Miss Garrison has grown, and he frequently rides over to Bennets End, the Garrison estate. I advised him that there was no harm in his visits as long as he recognized that Miss Garrison's position in society prevented any serious attachment. He replied that it was comments like these that made him glad he had not been born a Lacey. He said, 'It would require me to limit my circle of friends to those of my exalted rank.' Sometimes Bingham spouts the same egalitarian nonsense we hear coming from France. I asked him if Miss Garrison's ardour matched his own, and he replied that it did not. I believe this shows Miss Garrison to be a woman of good sense who does not encourage the affections of someone who is above her station.

Tomorrow, we are to dine with Sir William Ledger. Caroline and Louisa will not attend, and because of that, I will.

Yours,
Will

The next letter clearly showed that, despite his claims to the contrary, Will was finding it difficult to resist Elizabeth's charms. It also contained the news that Mr. Chatterton had returned to Bennets End with the intention of proposing to one of his cousins.

Dear Anne,

I cannot remember what I wrote that would cause you to believe that, like Bingham, I have become captivated by a Garrison sister. I confess everything to you, so I will tell you Miss Elizabeth has many fine qualities. Her conversation is engaging and, at times, impertinent. At a small private party held at the home of Sir William Ledger, she asked if I often traveled into Kent. I acknowledged that I did, as I wished to visit with my aunt and cousin as often as time and business would allow. She responded: 'I am sure you know that Mr. Chatterton, after receiving his ordination, was provided with a living by your aunt, Lady Sylvia, and I cannot imagine anyone more appreciative of such notice. We have heard such detailed descriptions of Desmet Park that I will never have to actually visit the estate.'

I asked Miss Elizabeth if she was aware that Mr. Chatterton came to dinner at Desmet Park on Thursday afternoons for the purpose of going over that Sunday's sermon with your mother, to which she replied, 'I am not surprised he seeks your aunt's opinion since he holds her in such high esteem.' When I asked if she had heard Mr. Chatterton preach, she said she had, 'but not in church.'

Knowing she was fond of teasing, I mentioned that Lady Sylvia was encouraging Mr. Chatterton to take a wife, as she thought it important for the pastor to set the example of marriage for his parish. Miss Elizabeth turned to me in alarm and asked: 'Has he indicated that this is his purpose in coming into Hertfordshire?' I answered that I thought it likely since he had been much impressed by his Garrison cousins from an earlier visit.

I will be the first to admit I am not as clever as Bingham or Col. Devereaux, who can engage in this type of discourse, and now I was convinced Miss Elizabeth was annoyed by the subject. She sat there silently for several minutes before saying: 'Mr. Chatterton is a good sort of man. From his description of the parsonage, he will be in a position to provide his wife with a comfortable home, and there certainly will be no lack of conversation. Yes, on reflection, I think an offer from such a man should be taken seriously, and why should he not choose from amongst those who have an interest in Bennets End?'

I do not know the lady well enough to say with absolute certainty that she was once again teasing me. Prior to joining Bingham in Hertfordshire, I had met Mr. Chatterton only that one afternoon at Desmet Park, and yet I know a woman as intelligent as she would never entertain an offer of marriage from someone of such meager intellect.

I admit that Miss Elizabeth possesses many fine qualities, but as to the matter of her family, other than her sister Jane, there is little to admire. As soon as I left Miss Elizabeth, her two younger sisters came running into the room, yanked a young man out of his seat, and demanded he dance with them. The quiet sister, I believe her name is Mary, played the pianoforte with a modicum of talent but lacked the proficiency necessary to perform in public. Their mother paid no attention to them, as if this was nothing out of the common, and their father appeared to be amused by it all. Mr. Garrison seems to be a man of sense, but he takes little care of his younger children.

Miss Garrison continues to draw Bingham's attention. I believe she is flattered by his notice, but surely she does not expect something more serious to come of it. Bingham is to host a ball at Helmsley Hall for his neighbours. After that, I shall return permanently to London. Many of my friends are already in town, and my absence has been noted.

Yours,
Will

"Lizzy is intrigued by Will," Beth wrote in her notes, "but I'm convinced she did not entertain any idea of his being attracted to her because of his elevated rank in society. However, you will see from Lizzy's diary entries how much she writes about Mr. Lacey."

8 April—Much to everyone's surprise, Messrs Bingham and Lacey came to dine at Ledger Lodge, and Mr. Lacey chose to sit by me. He is quite handsome, with his black hair and gray/green eyes. Since he sought me out, I thought I should remind him that there was a time when he found such company beneath him. 'If I recall, you do not care for dancing—at least not in Hertfordshire—but what stratagems will you use to avoid conversation?' I thought my directness would drive Mr. Lacey away, but instead he told me he chose very carefully the people whom he sat next to. I cautioned him that he had chosen unwisely, and he accused me of teasing him, which was exactly what I was doing because it is obvious he has had little experience with it. But then he had his revenge by telling me Mr. Chatterton had come to Hertfordshire for the purpose of getting a wife. My discomfort was clear. So that he should not savour his victory too long, I pretended such a proposal should be given serious consideration. Then it was his turn to be alarmed. He thought I should not consider an offer from Mr. Chatterton. What a strange man he is! He looks at me with the most quizzical expression. His face was less difficult to read when Lucy and Celia ran into the room demanding that John Ledger dance with them.

When I remarked that Mr. Chatterton was about to ask me to dance, Mr. Lacey quickly stood up and claimed the dance. He took me by the hand, and I cannot explain it, but I felt something unfamiliar, something that made me uncomfortable. The gentleman is handsome, intelligent, and carries himself with an assurance I have seen in no other man. I am sure he will soon leave for London, as I understand many of his friends are already in town.

Based on this entry, it seemed unlikely that Mr. Chatterton had ever made an offer of marriage to Lizzy. Her comments about the parson were confined to his long-windedness and the length of his visit, but it also included the interesting tidbit that Mr. Chatterton had been invited to dine at Ledger Lodge on two occasions.

In hopes of moving things along for Jane and Bingham, Mrs. Garrison extended an invitation to all the residents of Helmsley Hall to attend a dinner party at Bennets End. After dining at the Garrison home, Will wrote to his cousin summarizing that evening's events. Jack called it an "after action" report, and it was not flattering.

24 April 1792

Dear Anne,

Bingham, Caroline, the Ashursts, and I were invited to dine at Bennets End. Mrs. Garrison, without embarrassment, praised her daughter, Jane, as the most beautiful girl in the county. Served with the second course were additional compliments about her daughter's intelligence, ability to paint tables, embroider, etc., etc., etc. Miss Garrison was deeply embarrassed by this itemization of her abilities, and despite her sister Elizabeth's best efforts to change the subject, her mother continued at every opportunity to add to her long list of her eldest daughter's charms.

As for Mr. Garrison, he is well informed and a very agreeable man. However, he seems to find his wife's undisguised pursuit of Bingham for their daughter to be diverting, and since it provides him with amusement, she is free to chatter on endlessly. The two youngest daughters announced that the militia were now encamped nearby, and it was their hope to meet every officer in the regiment!

Caroline Bingham made no attempt to disguise her contempt for Mrs. Garrison. She points out how the behaviour of the two younger sisters is an embarrassment to her family and anyone associated with them. It is rare that I find myself in agreement with Caroline, but even if you disregard Miss Garrison's inferior position in society, you cannot turn a blind eye to the inappropriate behaviour of the mother and younger sisters.

It became painfully clear as the night wore on that Miss Elizabeth knew what a disastrous impression her family had made on their company. She rarely looked at me, but when she did, it was with embarrassment. I spoke briefly to her and then only to discuss political news from the continent. (She was aware of France's declaration of war against Austria.) She informed me that Mr. Chatterton was dining with the Lucas family, which made me realize the evening could actually have been worse. I hope to convince Bingham to quit Hertfordshire after the ball. I have never felt so ill at ease as I have since coming to Helmsley Hall.

Yours,
Will

P.S. I attended the third bout between Richard Humphries and Daniel Mendoza, as did the Prince of Wales and his retinue. Humphries was no match for Mendoza, and it was all over in fifteen minutes with Mendoza claiming the heavyweight title. As instructed, I placed a bet of one guinea on Humphries for you, but because you are my dear cousin, you may keep your guinea.

I really liked Will's postscript. It showed he had a loving relationship with his cousin and was capable of real tenderness. It almost made up for his obnoxious snobbery.

Also enclosed in the packet was a letter from Will to Anne

written before the ball at Helmsley Hall. It showed just how aware Anne was of her cousin's interest in Miss Elizabeth Garrison.

7 May 1792

Dear Anne,

Once again, you take Mr. Bingham's side. The reservations I indicated in my letter regarding any possible marriage between Bingham and Miss Garrison are just. Your statements are contradictory. You write that these obstacles might prove to be insurmountable if I found myself in such a situation but can be put aside in Bingham's. I take the position that a wrong decision is to be avoided whoever the person is. Is it not because of this type of situation that George Bingham asked me to keep watch over his brother in the first place?

Let me give you an example of Bingham's poor judgment. The militia are encamped outside the village. The senior officers have been invited by Miss Garrison's aunt to her socials. Bingham sees this, and as a result, he invites all the officers to the ball at Helmsley Hall. 'The young ladies must have partners,' he tells me. The invitation includes the junior officers—men about whom he knows nothing. Many of these young officers are new to the regiment, and little is known of them even by their colonel. I cautioned him that after the ball, he might find the silver has gone missing. His solution is to write to his brother and have him send some of his men from London. Of course, it would have been unnecessary if he had thought about the consequences in advance.

I have come to have a high regard for Miss Garrison and Miss Elizabeth. But I have no illusions as to how Miss Garrison would be treated in London society. You had only to listen to the comments made by Caroline after our return from dinner with the Garrisons. After a full hour of attacks on every family member, except Miss Garrison, her quiver was still half full.

I have become acquainted with some of the history of the Garrison family. Apparently, the estate, absent Mr. Garrison producing a son, is entailed away from the Garrisons to the benefit of Mr. Chatterton. This explains his visits to Hertfordshire. If he were to marry one of the daughters, it would solve the Garrisons' problem, if you can view marriage to Mr. Chatterton as a solution to anything. This goes a long way in explaining the mother's behaviour in promoting Miss Garrison so aggressively and why the younger daughters are all out before the elder sisters are married. But by allowing her younger daughters to be out in society without proper instruction, she risks the very thing she seeks. The Garrisons find themselves in an unfortunate position, but as Bingham's friend, I believe my loyalty lies with him. I cannot concern myself with the financial misfortunes of others.

I have asked Bingham to go up to London with me after the ball, but he will not commit. We have already missed the opening of the exhibition at the Royal Academy of Art. I understand that is no hardship for Bingham, but he has also missed the first balls of the season. And you know how Bingham loves to dance! If it were not for this infernal ball, I would already be in London this minute.

Yours,
Will

It was obvious from all the crossed out words that Will was agitated when he wrote this letter. After reading it, I liked Anne Desmet very much. It seemed as if she wanted her cousin to marry for love and to be happy with his choice of wife. On the surface, it appeared that Will was making a real effort not to fall in love, but his actions didn't match his words. He expressed his desire to return to London as soon as possible, but no one was forcing him to stay in the country.

10 May—The ball at HH was truly elegant. I wore my ivory dress and Jane put a wreath of white flowers in my hair and I was very pleased with the result. Many of the younger officers did not know all of the dances, but there were enough men available so that everyone who wished to dance had a partner. I danced all but two dances.

Both Mr. Laceys put in an appearance at the ball. The nice Mr. Lacey requested the second dance. There was little conversation while we waited our turn. After a prolonged silence, the gentleman talked about the weather. I said, 'Mr. Lacey, surely you can do better than that,' and lo and behold, Mr. Lacey smiled and said, 'Actually, Miss Elizabeth, at the moment, that is the best I can do.' At my prompting, we had a pleasant conversation, mostly about his sister, who is in London. Miss Lacey is learning the modern languages and is studying with a piano master. Other than business, this is the reason he travels back and forth to London so frequently. Even though he has all the advantages of elevated rank, I believe him to be a shy man, and despite his superior education, he has little talent for the light conversation one hears at these gatherings. Even so, I must admit I was very glad he had asked me to dance.

The ball had been in progress for about two hours when a group of four officers arrived. One officer, a Mr. Waggoner, had a brief discussion with Mr. Lacey, who was clearly surprised to see him, and his mood altered immediately. I danced with the gentleman, who seemed pleasant enough and is very handsome in his regimentals and well aware of it. Lucy, Celia, and their friends could hardly keep their eyes off of him. He told me he did know Mr. Lacey, as they were both from Derbyshire, but said no more.

The last dance went to Mr. Lacey, who spoke hardly a word. Instead of enjoying the dance, he gave every appearance of being annoyed. Exasperated, I asked him why he gave himself the trouble of dancing when he disliked the amusement so much. He said nothing and left the room. It is impossible to understand this man!

As I waited for our carriage, Mr. Lacey approached me. He led me by the hand to an area under the staircase and said: 'I am returning to London in the morning. I noticed you were talking to George Waggoner. May I advise you to avoid this man and be wary of anything he may say.'

I do not know what to make of this. I also do not know what to make of the fact that, all the while he was talking, he was holding my hand. I am very fond of complex characters, but Mr. Lacey may be too complex, even for me. When he said he was returning to London, did he mean permanently?

There was nothing in Lizzy's diary to indicate that anything was amiss with regard to Jane and Mr. Bingley. When Charles came by to tell Jane he was returning to London, no alarm bells went off. In fact, the big news was not about the ball, or Jane and Charles, but the engagement between Charlotte Ledger and Mr. Chatterton. Just as in the novel, Lizzy was stunned by the announcement, and because her circumstances were similar to her friend's, she was feeling particularly vulnerable about her future. However, she was confident Jane would have no such worries because it was so obvious that Charles was in love with her.

20 May—Mr. Bingham called this morning and told Jane that he has been asked to return to London by his brother, George, whom she knows to be something of a father figure to him. He said he did not know when he would return. Poor Jane! How is she to survive without her Mr. Bingham?

30 May—Is it not always the way? The servants learn everything first. Mrs. Brown tells us the steward at Helmsley Hall has been in town paying all of the bills and informed the butcher that the ladies of the house have returned to London to join their brother. What does all this mean? Jane has not heard from Mr. Bingham, and he is now gone ten days.

4 June—Jane does not think I hear her crying at night. She says Mr. Bingham owes her no explanation for his absence and defends his behaviour saying he made no promises, and I am unfair to reproach him. How is it possible that a man so obviously in love with someone can disappear for two weeks without explanation? His sisters and friend must be behind this.

5 June—We have news from Mr. Glynn, who leased HH to Mr. Bingham, that he has been instructed to cover the furniture and shutter the windows. This means Mr. Bingham has no intention of returning to HH any time soon. I would not have believed him capable of such unkindness.

I agreed with Lizzy. Even though Charles had given into pressure from Will Lacey and his brother, he should have written to Jane to let her know he was leaving Hertfordshire for good. Instead, his lack of consideration left Jane listening for news in the village about Helmsley Hall or checking the post for a letter explaining his absence.

17 June—Everything is now as it was before Mr. Bingham came to Hertfordshire, except that Charlotte and Mr. Chatterton were married today in the parish church. Charlotte has already asked me to visit her in Kent. I agreed to visit but not immediately. I have had enough of Mr. Chatterton and his dissertations for a while. Aunt Sims has written to Jane to come to London. There is so much more to do in town that will divert her mind from other thoughts. When Jane goes to Aunt's house, I will travel with her to London and then on to see Charlotte.

2 July—I have had a most enjoyable stay with Aunt and Uncle Sims, and I believe Jane's mood has much improved. We went to the summer theatre at Haymarket and to a concert at Vauxhall Gardens, which was followed by fireworks. Sir Arthur Morton, a friend of Uncle's, hosted a private ball where Jane and I were asked to dance every dance. Last night, we went with Aunt and Uncle to Ranelagh Gardens and heard Mr. Leonardi, an Italian tenor, sing selections from Don Giovanni. Today's newspapers reported that, after we had left, the Prince of Wales arrived and was seen in the company of Lady Jersey, and that they stayed until dawn. Uncle's man will see me to Kent in two days. With all there is to do in London, I wish I could delay my departure, but Charlotte writes for me to hurry.

These last items from Elizabeth Garrison's diaries, along with the earlier ones that Beth had given to me when she was in London, were all in chronological order. Without the distraction of jumping around in time or from one story to another, what was becoming evident was that Elizabeth Garrison and William Lacey's story was remarkably close to the events in *Pride and Prejudice*. I could not understand how the two stories could be so alike unless the parties knew each other, and if they had, surely Beth would have mentioned it. There had to be a reasonable explanation for all of this. I just couldn't think what it was.

Chapter 16

IN FEBRUARY 1948, THE Communists took over the government in Czechoslovakia, ratcheting up an already strained situation in Europe. Tensions again increased when President Truman refused to give the Soviet Union war reparations from West German industrial plants. Josef Stalin responded by splitting off the Russian occupation zone as a Communist state. It appeared that a conflict was possible between the former allies.

The following month, the Army Exchange Service notified its employees that it would shortly be reducing staff in England and increasing it in Germany. When I told Rob about the announcement, he said he had a feeling he would be hearing from TRC's headquarters in the near future, which would mean he would return to Atlanta and then, possibly, Flagstaff. He often told me he wanted me to see all the great sights that were so near to his home: the Grand Canyon, Petrified Forest, and the red rock country, but marriage was never specifically mentioned.

One drizzly Saturday afternoon, after we had made love, I asked Rob it we had a future beyond our terms of employment in England. After a lengthy silence, he answered, "I'm not sure what I'm supposed to say here." I got dressed and told him I was leaving. Before he could get his pants on, I was down the stairs and out the door. On the way home, I stopped at Boot's Chemist Shop and bought Alka Seltzer. This relationship was starting to affect my digestive system.

Pressure increased at work with the next memo from the AES personnel office. Don Milne, my boss, wanted to give his staff the heads-up and told everyone to assume they would be transferred to Germany. A second option was a ticket on a ship back to the States. Because I worked for Don, I would be able to stay in my job as long as he had his. Even though I had heard from friends that conditions in Germany had improved considerably since those first two dreadful years after the war, I had no intention of going back, especially in light of the current situation with the Soviets. I felt about returning to Germany in the same way that Elizabeth Garrison felt about marrying the reverend, Mr. Chatterton. It wasn't going to happen.

Although my future with Rob was uncertain, his relationship with Mrs. Dawkins was going great guns. Rob's soft-spoken Western drawl had won over my landlady, and the packs of Wrigley's gum he brought the boys didn't hurt, either. As a result, Rob and I were given permission to use the front parlor instead of the kitchen. We had to keep the door open and "mind the carpet," but it was a big improvement over the kitchen table.

We were holding hands on the sofa when Rob told me about his dinner with Jack Crowell at the Engineer's Club. He described the club as a place that would have seemed familiar to President Lincoln. "I've seen caves with more light. There were waiters in there who were probably on staff when Victoria was queen." Victoria had died in 1901.

Rob said their conversation was all over the map. "Let's see here," Rob said, reading from a cheat sheet. "Christopher Lacey, Will Lacey's son, made a fortune in railroads. He donated the property for a railway station near his home, which would become the town of Stepton. By the way, the Lacey Trust still owns ALL of the property under Stepton and collects rent from every business and residence in the town."

"That's similar to what happened in Scranton and Minooka," I said. "The coal companies sold the houses to the miners but kept all the mineral rights. In some cases, they kept right on mining, and a few of the houses near my Grandma Shea's started going down into the mines." That merited a raised eyebrow from Rob.

Scanning his paper, he said enthusiastically, "Oh, you'll like this story. Christopher's son, Andrew, made a fortune in steel, but he also continued to control every aspect of the import/export business his father had built. He and his partners owned textile mills in India, the ships that brought the cargo to Europe, received special rates from the railways, and had controlling interests in several collieries that provided the coal for his trains. In America, that type of operation is considered to be a monopoly, and it's illegal."

"When am I supposed to start liking this story? It sounds like the coal operators who impoverished my grandparents."

"The romantic part's coming," Rob continued. "During the Christmas holidays, Andrew went around to the different offices giving out envelopes with a little something extra in them. The office personnel were allowed to invite their families to a holiday party, and at the Sheffield office, thirty-year-old Andrew met the daughter of his bookkeeper, nineteen-year-old Marianne Dickinson. Apparently, she was one of the great beauties of her time. Andrew was smitten—Jack's word—and they got married and had five children, including Beth's father. It's kind of a Cinderella story," and he started to sing "Isn't It Romantic."

Rob leaned forward so that I could scratch his back and continued to read from his notes. "It was Lady Marianne Lacey who started a tradition of having a Christmas tea for all the servants. They were invited upstairs to join the Laceys in the breakfast room for a catered buffet. Beth and Lady Lacey took turns playing the piano, and the whole gang sang carols. The last time they had it was Christmas 1914. Trevor was killed the following September, so that was the end of that tradition."

"Were you surprised when you found out Beth's brothers had been killed in the war?"

"Not really. We knew about Jack's brother, right? And we knew Beth had brothers she never talked about? I figured the reason for all the secrecy was that the brothers were dead and not in a good way. I'm still not sure what happened to the youngest brother."

"Well, I was stunned when she told me. She looked so sad that I changed the subject to her children. She said she thought Michael and I would make a good couple."

Rob furrowed his brow and looked at me, "I hope you're kidding," he said seriously. I shook my head "no" and asked him to continue.

"We'll get back to you and Michael later." After looking at his notes, he continued. "The next heir to Montclair was Ned Lacey, Beth's father. After university, Ned went to the States and met Beth's mother, Sarah Bolton, at the races at Saratoga where she was spending the summer. Sarah was an expert horsewoman, and Ned was quoted as saying, 'I married her because she had the best seat of any woman I ever knew,' which translates today as 'she had a nice ass.'"

I rolled my eyes and hoped Mrs. Dawkins wasn't close enough to hear him.

"Beth's father was the head of a brokerage house in London," Rob continued. "Jack said not to make too much of Edward Lacey being a broker. It seems that Andrew didn't like to entertain, so that became his son's responsibility. Although Ned hosted shooting parties, he didn't care all that much for shooting. He liked speed, as in racing motor cars, and owned an interest in several. He also owned a Silver Ghost Rolls Royce, which Jack worked on. During the war, Jack drove an ambulance donated by Rolls Royce. Since he had already worked on a Rolls engine, it probably saved him from being assigned to the infantry."

All of this was very interesting, but after being gone for more than four hours, was that all he had learned?

"No, there's a lot more, but it's mostly about the war. Do you really want to hear about it?" I could tell by the change in Rob's voice I probably didn't want to hear anything else.

"No, not now." I wanted to think of it as being Christmas 1914 with Beth playing the piano while her family and all the servants sang carols. It was to be their last Christmas together.

Putting his arm around my shoulders, Rob pulled me close to him and asked, "Now, what's the deal with Michael Crowell?"

Chapter 17

THE WEATHER WAS BEAUTIFUL now that spring had arrived. Rob and I could open the window in his tiny flat, and when there was a breeze, the room was almost bearable. I wanted to talk about something that didn't involve my returning to Minooka or Rob's going to Atlanta. I asked what else Jack had said at the Engineer's Club, and he told me about how Jack and Beth had first gotten together. It would be interesting to hear the story from Jack's point of view.

"This is what Jack said happened. 'I was walking home from the train station after finishing a term at The Tech, and Beth was out riding. Now, Beth and I had been flirting with each other for a while, but when she saw me that day, she jumped off her horse, ran up to me, and threw her arms around my neck. Naturally, I kissed her. This is the hard part to believe; I pushed off on her. This is 1913. It was not possible for the son of a butler, no matter how respected, to have any kind of a relationship with someone of Beth's class.' Jack said he was more afraid of his father finding out than the Laceys. 'My dad would have thrown me off the property. I've no doubt of it.'

"Jack knew he had hurt Beth's feelings, but he wasn't going to embarrass himself by chasing after a girl who was beyond his reach. He tried to get out of being Reed and Beth's chauffeur for that 1913 motor tour, but Lady Lacey told him, 'I wasn't really asking, Jack. The children want to do this, and they can't if they don't have an experienced driver and mechanic.' He said he never felt more like a servant than he did at that moment. He also said, 'That was an example of how the household worked. You did what you were told, when you were told, but it was always put to you in a nice way.'"

While I was listening to Rob, I had been standing near the window in my slip, and he started singing "You Can't Say No to a Soldier." "But I can say 'no' to a civilian. Can we get back to the story?" Did all men think this much about sex?

"After a rough start, they had a blast on that trip. When they finally found the Edwards/Garrison farm, they were sitting in the car just laughing their heads off. Mrs. Edwards came out and asked what they were doing in her drive laughing like school children. Beth explained that they were looking for her ancestors—the ones Jane Austen wrote about in *Pride and Prejudice*, and Mrs. Edwards said, 'Oh, Lord, not another one.' Seems other people had figured it out, too.

"When Beth told Mrs. Edwards she was a blood relation of the Garrisons, she invited them in for tea and said that she had 'never owned to it before. You read that book and you'd think running a farm was like going on a picnic. We work from dawn to dusk here. And Lucy! The one Jane Austen called Lydia. Do you think my husband wants to admit that his great, great, however many greats, had knowledge of a man before they were married?' After lunch, Mrs. Edwards told them to go up to the attic and take whatever they wanted, and they packed up a ton of stuff."

"That was 1913. They didn't get married until 1916. What happened in between?" I asked.

"After the car trip, Jack told Beth that things had to go back to the way they were before the trip because it would have been a disaster for both of them if they were found out. The next summer, Jack was working on a school project in the Highlands, and Beth was back on the marriage circuit. By the end of the 1914 season, Beth's suitors had been narrowed to Ginger Bramfield and Colin Matheson, the Irish guy. Because Beth and Ginger had been friends since they were kids, Jack couldn't see Beth marrying him. He figured she'd end up with Matheson.

"When the war started in 1914, Jack realized if it went on for any length of time he would end up in the Army. He saw it as a way to get away from Montclair and Beth because he was convinced her engagement to Matheson would be announced at Christmas, and it was."

My jaw dropped. At no time, in our many conversations about the obstacles that she and Jack had faced, did Beth mention she had been involved with anyone other than Jack. "What happened? Did she call it off? I wonder if he got killed?"

"Jack didn't say another word about it, but it accounts for all of those missing months. But if Matheson was in the Army, and it's almost guaranteed that he was, then he may have gotten killed. Obviously, we're now into the war years, and with the exception of their marriage, nothing good happened." Looking at me, he said, "Do you want to hear it anyway?"

I nodded. "I care so much about them now that I have to know what happened."

"All right then. The war broke out in August 1914, and in September, some general raised a battalion of London stockbrokers, and Trevor volunteered and ended up serving in the Royal Fusiliers. While he was in training, the regular British army was nearly destroyed in Belgium. From that point on, most of the men who fought on the Western Front were raw recruits who were rushed in to fill the depleted ranks of the professional soldiers. Trevor was wounded at Loos in September 1915. His sergeant got him back behind the British lines, but he died at a clearing station." With a grim face, Rob said, "The British used gas at Loos, but it blew back on their own troops. There is the possibility Trevor was gassed by his own guys.

"When the telegram arrived at Montclair, Mrs. Crowell sent for Jack, who was at school in Manchester, and had him go out to Cambridge. So it was Jack who told Beth that her brother had been killed. He said it was one of the saddest moments of his life. When she came into the visitors' room and saw him, she looked as happy as he'd ever seen her. But then she asked him what he was doing there. Jack said, 'I didn't say anything, but she knew, and the tears just poured out of her.'

"Jack and Beth went to the camp where Matt was training and said Matt wasn't surprised because word had reached the camp of the disaster at Loos. Sir Edward went down to Henley and took Reed out of school, and that was the end of his education. Jack said that was a big mistake. If he had stayed at Henley, Reed probably wouldn't have been called up. But he didn't explain how that would have kept him out of the Army seeing how he was old enough to fight.

"Matt's leadership abilities were obvious from the start, and he was quickly promoted to captain. Tom Crowell served under him, and because Tom and Matt were so close, Jack assumed that Matt would want his brother for his assistant, what the Brits call a batman. But Matt told Jack, 'I've never treated your brother as a servant, and I'm not going to start now.'

"Matt wanted his men to have every advantage possible, so he kept after them to stay in shape and did lots of inspections. He had his men scrounge around farms and villages looking for better food, which he paid for out of his own pocket. Matt was mentioned in dispatches to headquarters, which in the British Army is an official commendation for an act of bravery. It sounds like the guy was a born leader, and he had guts.

"Jack said that people have a misconception about the war, thinking the men were in frontline trenches all of the time. The way it worked was the troops were rotated from the first line of trenches to reserve trenches. After that, they went to the rear for light duty so they could rest up and get ready mentally and physically for the next push. They played football and had cricket matches and went into nearby villages for dinner. In Jack's case, he'd sneak in a visit with Beth.

"The Laceys received conflicting stories about how Matt was killed. Jack thinks he went over the top, was killed by a machine gun, but his body could not be recovered immediately. If it was lying out there in No Man's Land, it probably was hit by artillery shells and blown to bits. This created all kinds of problems for his mother because she got it in her head that Matt had been taken prisoner. But when the Laceys got a letter from the Red Cross, saying they had eyewitness accounts that Matt had in fact been killed, Lady Lacey went into such a deep depression that Sir Edward talked her into going to a sanitarium for a rest. Jack's positive Reed's depression was inherited from his mother.

"Tom Crowell died on July 1, 1916, and is buried at the Heilly Station British Cemetery. He was one of 20,000 killed on the first day of the Battle of the Somme. They went over the top and were mowed down by machine guns. Jack said very little about his brother. He was able to talk about Beth's brothers, but when it came to Tom, he just couldn't do it.

"As for Jack, when the war first broke out, so many men signed up that there was a shortage of skilled workmen. They had to cull the ranks for coal miners, steel workers, engineers, and other highly skilled workers. When Jack went before the registration board, they told him to stay in school because there would be a need for more engineers and mechanics down the line. At The Tech, he and the other engineering students had to practice digging frontline trenches, and the officials invited civilians to go through them so they could get the feel for what 'the boys' were experiencing in France and Belgium, which, of course, was total b.s. because the Tommies were living in filth with rats running everywhere because there was so much death. In January 1916, Jack was called up, and after he had finished his basic training, they got married, and Beth's parents never found out. When Jack went home on leave in 1919, Beth told her mother she was going to marry Jack, and Lady Lacey didn't object. Jack and his brother used to call her the dragon lady, but with all that happened during the war, the fire had gone out of her. Another reason why Lady Lacey didn't pitch a fit was because so many of the men who would have been Beth's suitors had been killed. Those guys tended to go into the Army as line officers, and their casualty rate was disproportionately high. It was Jack's father who had fits.

"This is what Jack told me. 'You have to keep in mind that my father referred to the Laceys as 'our betters.' Servants were downstairs; our betters were upstairs. My father was an intelligent, capable man, but that was his view of the world until the day he died. My mother and Beth had a good relationship, but until the very end of his life, my father just could not relax around Beth. He never addressed her by her name because he didn't know what to call her.'

"Jack and Beth were married at the church in Crofton like it was the first time, but Jack wasn't home for good yet. In France, he was assigned to a Graves Consolidation team. They had to disinter bodies that were scattered all over Northern France and rebury them in these large military cemeteries. If possible, the consolidation team marked the grave for the graves registration team, but a lot of them ended up with headstones that said 'Known Unto God,' including, possibly, Matt Lacey. It was worse than any job he had during the war. He said, 'When you're in war, you know shit's coming down the pike, and you're prepared for it. But once the guns go silent, you come out of that hard shell that's been protecting you. I had terrible nightmares the whole time I was assigned to Graves Consolidation.'

"To be closer to Jack, Beth worked in a French hospital. She spoke French like a native, and they needed all the nurses they could get since the French took even more casualties than the British. After the war, Jack went on to receive his master's degree in engineering, and in the early '20s, he took a job in India building railroad bridges. He was very complimentary about Beth and how she adapted to wherever they were living, especially considering how she was brought up at Montclair. Everything Jack told me was voluntary," Rob said. "I asked him questions about his career, but anything personal, he told me without me asking."

"Did he say anything about the younger brother after the father took him out of school?"

"Yes. Reed was an orderly in a medical unit in Boulogne where the wounded waited for ships back to England. Jack took a belt of scotch and went quiet before finally saying, 'When the Germans broke through our lines in the spring of 1918 near Amiens, every man who could hold a rifle was thrown into the fight, including me and including Reed. We held the line until reinforcements arrived from England, but it was over for the boy. They sent him home to a hospital called Craiglockhart near Edinburgh where he was treated for shell shock.' Jack couldn't continue, so we changed the subject."

After thinking about all Jack had told him, Rob said, "Everyone has their breaking point. The difference is most guys recover over time, but it seems that after Reed went to the front, his mind snapped, and he never came out of it."

Chapter 18

I ARRIVED HOME FROM work one evening to find my land-lady waiting for me inside the front door, and in a voice that clearly showed her disapproval, Mrs. Dawkins informed me that I had a "gentleman caller."

I was carrying a brown bag full of Spam, Lorna Doone cookies, and Wonder Bread for the family. On payday, I tried to bring home something that was either unavailable or in short supply. For the first time in its history, including wartime, Great Britain had found it necessary to ration white flour. After Mrs. Dawkins saw what was in the bag, her attitude softened.

"I'll get a pot of tea going, and I'll bring you in some biscuits. Go see what your visitor wants."

When I opened the sliding door to the family room, I immediately recognized my gentleman caller, even though I had never met him before.

"Maggie, I'm James Crowell." Handing me a large manila envelope, he said, "My mother wanted you to have this, and I decided to hand deliver it. After hearing all about you over the Easter holiday, I thought I should at least introduce myself since we both live in London."

Other than James Crowell being a couple of inches taller than his father, he looked so much like him that I felt as if I was seeing Jack when he was in his twenties.

"Do you have time to stay for tea? My landlady has a pot brewing."

"That would be wonderful. My wife and daughter stayed behind with my parents for another week, and I don't like going home to an empty flat."

Carrying a tray with a teapot and Lorna Doones, Mrs. Dawkins gestured for us to go across the hall to the front parlor. I was being admitted into the holy of holies, and without Rob. After setting the tray down, she offered to "pour out." I was finding this whole scene to be rather funny. It was obvious Mrs. Dawkins was trying to get an idea about who James was and whether Rob had some competition.

"The boys will want to listen to their shows on the wireless, so you can visit in here." Standing behind James, Mrs. Dawkins pointed to her ring finger and then to James, who was wearing a wedding band. I gave her a nod to let her know that James wasn't going to be able to put anything over on me.

"I am so glad to finally get to meet you," I told James. "I've heard so many stories about you and your beautiful wife, and I spent a lovely afternoon with Julia."

James talked for a few minutes about his daughter and how she had started crawling and was getting into everything before the conversation finally worked its way around to a discussion of his childhood in India.

"Mike and I were really small when we went out to India. Like most Anglos, we spent most of our time inside the walls of a compound, including going to school. Everyone had a ridiculous number of servants, but a lot of that had to do with their own rules. We had a cook and an ayah, or nanny, who spoke only Hindi. We also had a bearer, the Indian version of a butler, named Kavi, who taught us martial arts." Taking a sip of his tea, he added, "India was unique. I got to ride on elephants and camels, and we had a mongoose as a pet. But we also had mosquitoes, red ants, and birds that made noises at night that would scare the life out of you.

"Early on, it was fun because there were lots of kids our own age. But that changed because most families sent their kids back to England to go to school when they were eight or nine. My mother refused to believe there was any benefit in sending a child off on their own at so young an age. I think she held us especially close because of losing her brothers in the war, so we didn't go to school in Glenkill in Scotland until we were twelve years old.

"Our tutors were mostly graduates from Oxbridge—Cambridge or Oxford—who came out to India for a bit of an adventure. We went back to England about every other year. The problem for me was going back to India. After spending the summer in the English countryside, it was very difficult to return to the heat, the bugs, and the smells.

"What I liked best was sailing home and going through the Suez Canal. One time when we were at Port Said, we saw a troop ship going back to England. It was a tradition for the soldiers to throw their topees, those tan helmets everyone wears in the tropics, into the water. If it sunk, you would never return to India. If it floated, you'd have to go back. It was a riot to see all the soldiers throwing their helmets into the air and to watch their faces when the blasted things wouldn't sink."

"What did you do when you didn't go back to England?"

"One year, we went on safari in Kenya. We saw elephants, hippos, lions, and lots of other exotics. The whole time we're looking at these animals, we're standing there in the blazing heat, swatting flies. When we got back to England, we went to the London Zoo and saw the same animals without the heat. Now, you could set my brother down in the middle of a desert, and he'd find a way to adapt. Not me. My preferences are pretty girls, football, real ale, and cool weather, in that order."

I remembered Beth telling me that James had actually liked living abroad until he went to school in Scotland when he was twelve. After getting to know the other students, he resented that he had been denied a "normal" British childhood.

"In India, you have to assume that everything is riddled with disease, and everything we drank was made with chlorinated water. When we went to the hill stations during the heat, my mother had to watch the man who milked the cow to make sure he washed his hands. At night, we practically lived under mosquito nets. I was glad when it was time for me to go to school. I'm British and proud of it. I like plain food—meat and potatoes—none of those curried dishes for me."

"I hope you like spaghetti, since you're married to an Italian," I said.

"Actually, I do like it, which is a good thing, because that's all we eat. With the flour shortage, even spaghetti is hard to get. Angela goes to this Italian market in Finsbury, and the owner gives her enough for a few days. He doles it out in small amounts because he wants Angela to come back as often as possible. I went with her one time, and even with me standing right there, the owner was staring her up and down. Cheeky bastard."

"I understand you got married in Italy?"

James nodded his head vigorously. "When Angela comes back to town, we'll have to get together so I can show you our wedding pictures. Everyone in the village came to the party, and we had a blast, especially Mike. All the girls were after him. It's a good thing he brought a lady friend from Malta, or he wouldn't have had a minute to himself.

"Mike's my best mate, but we're complete opposites. He's the man every mother wants her daughter to marry. He was born knowing you're supposed to hold a door open for a lady. I had to be taught those things, which I was in a deportment class that my mother signed us up for one summer. We also had ballroom dance lessons, which we took with our cousins, Geoff and Violet Alcott, and the four of us were tossed out of class for cutting up so much."

"What did your parents say?"

"Dad didn't care at all, and Mum had three brothers, so nothing surprised her. Besides, she's not as prim and proper as you think. When we got older, Mum told us about going back and forth between Boulogne and Folkestone on the hospital ships in the First War, and the Tommies taught her these really vulgar music hall numbers. One time, she started singing one, and we nearly wet our pants we were laughing so hard. Put her and Freddie in the same room, and you've a night's entertainment."

"Who's Freddie?" I asked.

"My God, Freddie! He's the guy who keeps Montclair running. The Pratts brought him from Australia when they moved to England. Mr. Pratt was on the board of a juvenile home, and that's where he found him. Freddie can fix anything. He's even better than my father, but he's far from your typical servant.

"At first, he made Grandpa Crowell crazy, but my grandmother loved him right off. Always said he reminded her of 'my Tom.' After a while, my grandfather saw Freddie's charm, especially since he's a comedian and loves to tell stories and jokes. When the Catons bought Montclair, Freddie was part of the package because he's brilliant at fixing things and saves them a ton of money. He's the one who taught Mike and me to play poker."

"Do you mean he's still there?"

"I just saw him last week when I was in Crofton. Mike and I always visited him when we were between terms. When he's not on maintenance patrol, he's below stairs following the ponies. He has a motor scooter to go into town to place bets at the pub and play darts. The guy's brilliant."

James leaned back into the chair. "My mother told me you'd sit there very quietly, and before I knew it, I'd be telling you my life story."

I laughed and asked him, "What is your life story?"

"I was at Cambridge when I got called up. After basic and officer training, I was assigned to the 8th Army in Italy on the Adriatic side of the Gustav Line. I got there in December of '43, and everyone associated my arrival with terrible things happening, like our being sent to fight with the Americans at Anzio and in front of Monte Cassino. For a short time, I was billeted in a town south of Bologna with a fountain in the center and terraced vineyards—the whole scenic Italian village bit. That's where I met Angela."

The tone of James's voice changed as soon as he mentioned his wife. He started to smile, and it was obvious he was thinking about the first time that they had seen each other.

"I was serving on the staff of the regimental HQ. I was told to go find the mayor, but he wasn't in his office, so I went to the office of the town's notario." James asked if I knew what a notario was, and I shook my head "no." "Neither does anyone else, except it seems that no piece of paper is signed in that town that hasn't passed through his hands. When I got there, Angela was bringing her father his lunch. That's all it took."

"So you're a romantic like your brother?"

James shook his head. "I always thought I'd meet a girl from England at a dance or something like that. But when I saw Angela, I was completely bowled over. That's the difference between Mike and me. I was surprised at how weak at the knees I got; Mike would have been expecting it. That's what happens to a guy who read the Arthurian legends as a kid.

"When the shooting stopped, I went back to see Angela and asked her father for permission to court her. He agreed because, as long as I was in the Army, I could still get my hands on better food. The dating phase lasted five months, and we were always chaperoned, usually by her two widowed aunts, who walked behind us, arm in arm, dressed all in black. Kissing Angela was a challenge; anything more was an impossibility.

"After I got out of the Army, Angela and I were finally allowed to get married. I basically became her father's errand boy, but at least I learnt to speak Italian. Once Angela found out she was pregnant, we thought it best to move to England so the baby would be a British citizen. Italy was and is in terrible shape. Everyone in town had relatives in America sending them food parcels, including Angela and me. When the time came to leave, we practically floated out of the village with all her relatives crying."

James stood up, put on his coat, and pointed to the envelope. "You know that's only a fraction of what my parents have stored away in an upstairs room. I know Dad worked on it during his convalescence, and Mom cataloged everything during the war when she wasn't at the hospital. It probably helped to take her mind off the war, especially since my brother was in Burma fighting Japs."

"And you were in Italy fighting Germans," I quickly added.

"Yeah, but I always thought I was better off than Mike, working on planes in hot, humid, bug-infested Burma. Not only did he have to worry about the Japs, he also had to keep an eye on the locals, who preferred their Jap invaders to us. So much for making the world British." Then he smiled and said, "And Italian girls are much prettier."

Before I let him go, I wanted to ask him one question. "Is your Aunt Margie still living, the one who helped with some of the family research?"

A complete change of expression came over James's face. "I'm sorry," I said quickly. I had said the wrong thing.

"No, no. It's all right. Aunt Margie. My God, I haven't thought about her in years." He looked down and made a circular pattern on the carpet with his foot before saying, "She was married to my Uncle Reed. They had a cabin in Scotland west of Perth." After a long pause, James said, "I've got to go."

While buttoning his overcoat, he said, "My parents are very fond of you, and I think before all is said and done, you'll know more about my family than I do."

***

Shortly after my evening with James Crowell, I stopped by the bookstall near my office building to pick up a newspaper, as I did every day before going to work. On the front page of *The Times* in big black letters was the headline that Lord Fitzwilliam and his companion, Lady Hartington, nee Kathleen Kennedy, had been killed in an airplane crash in France. The couple had been fodder for the tabloids for months, and now they were both dead.

I remembered Jack and Beth talking about Kathleen Kennedy's mother objecting to her marriage to the Duke of Devonshire because he was a Protestant. She must have been horrified when she learned that her daughter had taken up with another titled Protestant who wasn't yet divorced. Now, none of that mattered.

Chapter 19

ROB AND I TRIED to spend as much time together as possible, but occasionally we had to go our separate ways. I had been invited to a bridal shower for Pamela, who was shortly to be not only a bride but a mother. Troy seemed to be a very nice man, but like so many servicemen who had been "demobbed" out of the service, he could not find a job, and now there was a baby on the way.

After returning home from the shower, I heard Rob's unmistakable Western drawl coming from the kitchen. Poking my head around the corner, I saw Rob and Mr. Dawkins sitting at the kitchen table drinking beer. Mr. Dawkins was a World War I veteran, whose hearing had been badly damaged in the war, which was why Rob was shouting. When Mr. Dawkins saw me, he jumped up, patted Rob on the back, and left.

"I didn't mean to chase him," I said after my landlord went upstairs.

"He's embarrassed about his hearing loss. Everything has to be shouted. But Mrs. Dawkins and the boys have gone out to the movies, so I told him there was no one to hear the shouting except me. He was telling me about a village near Rouen in France he came to enjoy for a lot of reasons. He was quick to add he was not married at the time, and Mrs. Dawkins had never heard that particular story."

"Do you have a story like that?" I asked in a teasing way.

"Yep," he said as he pulled me tight against him. "I met this hussy when I was living in London after the war."

I pushed him away and slid into Mr. Dawkins's vacant chair. "Then you had better go look her up."

Jumping up, Rob took me by the hand and led me to the sitting room. Because Rob had worked his way into my landlady's good graces, we were allowed to use the room to go over all the papers Beth had sent to me.

"While you were out, I went to the library. Everyone who is anyone in Britain is listed in a book called *Who's Who*, which includes a short biography listing their titles, honors, and accomplishments. Everyone who was ever knighted or elevated to the peerage is in this book, including Will Lacey, who was knighted by George IV. He also served as a Justice of the Peace, which Mrs. Tobin, the librarian, told me was common practice because he was the Lord of the Manor.

"Will's son, Christopher, was also knighted because he was one of the founders of the Derwent Valley Manufacturing Corporation. Mrs. Tobin said that if you could point to one place in England where the factory system was born, 'for good or ill,' it was in the textile mills in the Derwent Valley in Derbyshire. Chris was a Member of Parliament for a decade from a 'safe' seat under the control of the Duke of Devonshire, and he supported Lord Ashley's 1840 Coal Mines Act, banning women and children from working underground.

"Andrew Lacey, Beth's grandfather, was honored for doing a lot of civic-type things in Stepton, like building a hospital, but the big news there was Andrew was made a baronet. It's a hereditary title between a baron and a knight, but baronets do not have a seat in the House of Lords."

"Which means Beth's father was also a baronet," I said.

"Yes, which made Beth's parents Sir Edward and Lady Lacey. And this is really interesting. Both were honored by George V in 1933 for their work on the War Graves Commission and the creation of the Thiepval War Memorial in Picardy, which is in northern France. There are 72,000 names listed on the Memorial of men who have no known graves. This is just for those killed at the Battle of the Somme, and in addition to honoring his work on the Memorial, Edward Lacey served on the Board of Directors of Craiglockhart Hospital in Edinburgh."

I about jumped out of my chair. "Jack said that Craiglockhart was where Reed went when he was sent home from France, and James told me Reed and his Aunt Margie lived in Scotland after they got married."

"I think Reed was one of those shell-shocked soldiers, and they put him in that hospital. That's why no one talks about him."

"No, that can't be it," I said. "I mean he was at the hospital. We know that. But Reed had to be well enough to get married."

Rob just shrugged his shoulders. "Anyway, I asked the librarian if there was any information on shell-shocked vets, and she said there was a government report commissioned after the war on who served and who didn't serve, and if not, why not."

"Catchy title."

Rob smiled before continuing. "When war was declared, tens of thousands of volunteers showed up, but when the Army gave them their physicals, they found out that many of them, especially those from the cities, were physically unfit because of tuberculosis, chronic skin diseases, malnutrition, etc. This was an ongoing problem. In the last two years, the Army had a difficult time filling its ranks, even with conscription. So if you were a healthy young man, well-nourished because you were rich, and not totally crazy, you almost certainly would have been drafted.

"Mrs. Tobin, who knows everything about everything, said Craiglockhart is famous because two poets, Siegfried Sassoon and Wilfred Owen, both stayed there for a while. Sassoon did some heroic things in France, including single-handedly capturing a German trench, but he also wrote a letter to his commanding officer protesting the war, which was read by a Member of Parliament and published in the press. That took balls to do that. It was then that the Army sent him to Craiglockhart. He wasn't shell-shocked, just crazy enough to tell the truth. Owen met Sassoon at the hospital, and Sassoon was so impressed by his poetry that he gave him an introduction to some heavyweights in the publishing world, but he was killed in France one week before the war ended.

"Mrs. Tobin dug out a newspaper editorial that was published late in the war. It was critical of the way some of the shell-shocked soldiers were being treated. The best these guys could hope for was to be ignored, but many were taunted or even beaten up. There were these women who went around handing out white feathers to men dressed in civilian clothes because they must be cowards, or they would have been in uniform, even though many of them were employed in critical war industries and had legitimate deferments. Keep in mind men were being shot for cowardice in France. England's back was against the wall, and things were getting ugly at home."

I thought about all Rob had said, especially the Battle of the Somme and its tens of thousands of dead. At home, in Minooka, thirteen men from my small town had died in World War I. When the bullets stopped flying, many questioned whether we should have been in France in the first place, and the second-guessing began. What had the United States gotten for its one hundred thousand dead and two hundred thousand wounded? As difficult as it was to deal with so many American deaths, what must it have been like in the villages and cities of Britain and Ireland when the second-guessing began there? What had Britain and Ireland gotten for their one million dead and the loss of a whole generation of young men?

"Oh, by the way," Rob said, interrupting my thoughts, "James called me at work to let me know his father is bringing Angela and the baby back to London, and Jack wanted to know if we would be available for dinner."

"Do you think we should mention this research about Craiglockhart to Jack?" I asked.

"If we can work it into the conversation, but if Reed went over the edge because of his experiences in the war, I don't know if Jack would want to share that with anyone."

"Especially since Reed is not Jack's brother, and Beth has been very careful about not mentioning what happened to him," I reminded him.

***

When we arrived at Lucca's for dinner, we could see that Jack was in a particularly good mood. He had gone on a job interview in Manchester for a full-time position, and he believed it had gone well. If he was hired, he would be a consultant to a major contractor who did construction work in the Midlands. Although he would have to travel, he'd be reasonably close to home.

Jack updated us on the progress being made at Montclair. He found Mrs. Caton to be too snooty for his liking, but he admitted she had excellent taste in decorating. "She's redoing Beth's room as we speak. She's trying to keep it as close to the original colors and wallpaper as possible.

"The first time I was home from France, we stayed in her room. I can't begin to tell you how odd it was to sleep above stairs. Beth and I had been married for three years, which, of course, they didn't know, but when I got into bed with her that first time, it felt more like we were having an affair, except that Beth was six months pregnant. Lying there, I kept waiting for my father to burst into the room and drag me down the stairs. I bloody well couldn't sleep.

"Lady Lacey, Beth's grandmother, tried her best to make me feel at home, and Sir Edward and Lady Lacey invited my parents to have dinner with them because they were Beth's in-laws. My mother did, but my father never would. The only thing he would agree to was lunch in the breakfast room."

I asked Jack about his mother. All I knew about her was that her name was Jenny Moore.

"My mother was an orphan and attended a girls' school in Sheffield run by a Quaker family, the Menlos. They made their money in locomotive engines but were known for their philanthropy. The teachers were former governesses, and their goal was to train these little girls to be future governesses and keep them from falling into poverty. A teacher brought my mother to Mrs. Menlo's attention, so they took her into their home, and Mum was able to stay in school until she was seventeen. When she finished, she was hired by the Menlo School as a teacher.

"When Lady Marianne Lacey decided that Mrs. Philbin, the housekeeper, needed help, she went to the school and was introduced to my mother. Mum had excellent management skills and could speak French and play the piano. After Lady Lacey hired her, she served as under housekeeper for a few years, even after she married my father, but as soon as she got pregnant, she had to resign her position.

"Once it became clear that Mum wasn't going to have any more children, Lady Lacey reinstated her as under housekeeper because Mrs. Philbin was older than Stonehenge and was starting to make mistakes. The head housekeeper has a lot of power downstairs, and Mrs. Philbin wasn't about to give up any of it. It finally came down to Lady Lacey telling Mrs. Philbin, 'Either you agree to work with Mrs. Crowell or you retire.' The old bat had to give in, but she did her best to make my mother's life as unpleasant as possible. Mum put up with that old crank for a couple of years before Mrs. Philbin finally popped her clogs.

"My mother was one of those people you call 'the salt of the earth.' Always went to church, never gossiped, and was fair but firm with the servants. I'd like to tell you my parents fell in love, but it would be a lie. My father had his needs, and my mother wanted children. They went to the Laceys to get their permission to marry, which, in those days, you had to do, and my mother told me they couldn't have been more shocked. I don't think they ever thought of my father as having needs of any kind. My parents got along fine, and if it wasn't love, they certainly respected each other. I never had much luck getting close to my father; Tom did a lot better with him. Now, Mum was different. She could be very strict, but you had some latitude with her."

After reflecting for a bit, Jack added, "I don't want to make it seem like my mother could see into the future, but by the time Tom went to France, England had already lost, I don't know, more than 150,000 men. Everyone knew someone who had lost a family member, including the Laceys. Mum believed she might never see Tom again and got prepared for it. I was in France when they got the news. My dad went to his room and wouldn't come out because he couldn't stop crying. Lady Lacey went down and talked to him. When Matt was killed three months later, Lady Lacey cried on his shoulder. They helped each other to heal.

"I found out about Tom getting killed from my sergeant. I could hardly take it in because I was driving an ambulance at the time, and I was carting off the dead and wounded by the dozens. Remember, he died on the first day of the Battle of the Somme. Tom would have been just one more body. When it finally hit me that my brother was gone, I cried like a baby. Growing up, he was my best mate. We did everything together."

Pushing back on his chair, Jack said, "This is a damn depressing conversation, which is why most of us who survived don't talk about it. So I'm going to change the subject because I have some more good news. James has been offered an accounting job in Sheffield, and Beth is flying high because that means they will be close enough for her to drive to visit them."

Rob ordered a round of drinks to celebrate the Crowells' good news. Before leaving, Jack said, "Now you know Beth wouldn't send me down here without something for you, Maggie," and he handed me a large envelope. "She apologizes for not sending more of Elizabeth's diary, but it's slow going, copying all that out in longhand. When you see the condition of the diary, you'll understand why she has to do that."

Shaking hands with Rob, Jack said he had learned that a bronze plaque commemorating the 91st Bomb Group's contributions to the air war over Germany was being unveiled at Bassingbourn, Rob's former base, on Memorial Day, and he was wondering if Rob would go with him to the ceremony. This request came out of left field and caught both of us by surprise.

"During the war, we'd listen to the wireless for war news, and we'd hear all about America's Mighty Eighth Air Force and its raids over Germany. Of course, we had Bomber Command and Fighter Command, but for sheer size, you couldn't beat the amount of resources that America threw at Hitler. I always wanted to get up close to a bomber, so I checked a few things out and learnt that your old base is having this ceremony."

Jack was waiting for Rob's answer, but what could he say, except "yes"? Rob and Jack agreed to meet at the train station in Royston at 9:00 on Memorial Day, and Beth and I were invited.

Chapter 20

WHEN ROB AND I got off the train from London, Beth and Jack were waiting for us at the Royston station. Beth walked toward me with arms extended, kissed me on both cheeks, and told me how glad she was to see me. Even though the Montclair years were in the distant past, Beth possessed an elegance of style that came straight from England's glory days before the First War. On the other hand, Jack greeted me with a solid handshake and Rob with a slap on the back.

In July 1945, when the Americans had departed, Bassingbourn had been officially returned to the Royal Air Force. The base was little changed from the time Rob had last seen it in September 1944, except that everyone was wearing RAF blue. Rob pointed to the barracks where his quarters had been, a nondescript, two-story, red brick building. "Compared to some guys, we had it good. Bassingbourn was a permanent RAF installation, so it had a lot more going for it than some of the other stations. We had barracks with central heating and not the Nissen huts you'd see in the newsreels. We took a lot of crap from guys stationed at other bases who had potbellied stoves to heat a room with twelve guys living in it. But we all had the mud and the rain and the fog."

Jack pulled up in front of the two-story control tower where a crowd had gathered for the ceremony. Rob looked out at the runways, where hundreds of B-17s had taken to the skies, flying dangerous missions over Germany and occupied Europe. Lined up nose to tail, and in thirty-second intervals, the ten-man crews lifted off and prayed that this would be just one more mission instead of their last mission.

Pointing to the control tower, Rob said, "The ground crew used to stand up there or on the hardstand waiting for the bombers to come back. Of course, they wanted everyone to get back safely, but they'd worry about the other guys once they spotted their own ship."

Jack mentioned that most of the bombers he had seen during the war had German markings on them. "Everyone thinks of London when they think of the Blitz, but any industrial city or port took a hit, and Southampton, Manchester, and Liverpool were all bombed. As soon as the fires were put out, the Home Guard and the fire brigade commanders supervised the clearing of the rubble, and the rebuilding would begin."

"Just like in Germany," Rob said. "We'd have to go back to the same target time and time again, except they used slave labor to clear the rubble."

"Maybe you could tell us what it was like to go out on one of your missions," Jack said.

"After the ceremony, if they let us walk around, I'll tell you what it was like." With that, we joined the group gathered in front of a platform where the speakers were waiting to address the crowd.

We turned our attention to the podium where a number of dignitaries were examining a sketch of a bronze plaque, which would be dedicated at a future date, honoring the five bomb squadrons that had flown 9,591 sorties on 540 missions from this base beginning in September 1942. The Commanding Officer at RAF Bassingbourn introduced an American colonel and a former member of the ground crew of the "Memphis Belle," the most famous B-17 of the war, each remarking on the extraordinary accomplishments of the men of the Army Air Corps, who had taken off from airfields just like Bassingbourn, to take the war to the enemy on his home ground. Col. Hendricks referred to the more than 3,800 graves of American servicemen at Madingley. At one point, Patrick Monaghan had rested in that cemetery before his family had requested that his remains be returned to Omaha.

Jack, Beth, and I saw Rob's growing discomfort as each speaker talked of the heroism of all the air crews who had come to England to help her defeat the greatest enemy ever to confront modern European civilization. As soon as the last speaker had finished, Rob took off his jacket, loosened his tie, and lit a cigarette. Taking a look around the airfield, Rob said, "I can't get you inside a B-17, because all these bombers are British, but..." He hesitated for a long time before saying, "Are you sure you want to hear all about a mission?" We all nodded.

"Okay. Here's how it went. Everything started with the 8th Air Force Headquarters in High Wycombe. They were the ones who decided what the targets were and what groups would fly.

"You checked the alert board to see what aircraft and crews were flying. If your name was on the list, you couldn't leave the base. If you weren't flying, the pilots might use the Links trainer to fly simulated flights, and the navigators would train on a new radar system developed by the RAF. On days off, the whole crew practiced ditching.

"While you were sleeping, the ground crew was going over every inch of your plane, and the ordnance crews were loading the bombs into the bomb bay. Anywhere between 0300 and 0600 hours, a sergeant, a great guy from Kansas, who probably could have sat out the war because of his age, came into our room and said, 'Monaghan, McAllister. You're flying. Breakfast at 0400, briefing at 0430.' Something like that. He'd give you about one minute for this to sink in, and then he'd shine a light in your face. Pat always said the same thing: 'Another day, another dollar,' and then he'd jump down from the top bunk and start getting dressed.

"If you were lucky, your mission would be a milk run to France or Holland, but if it was Berlin or the Ruhr, you'd hear mumblings and groans. The movies showing guys cheering about going to Berlin was b.s., unless they had a death wish.

"You were shown photographs, maps, and diagrams to help you identify the target. When Allied troops were nearby, or if your target was in France or Holland, you had to make visual identification of noted landmarks to make sure you didn't kill friendlies. If you weren't absolutely sure, you went on to your secondary target.

"After that, another officer went over escape and evasion procedures, including where rescue ships were located in the North Sea and the Channel. Before your first mission, in case you had to bail out, you had your picture taken in civilian clothes that a European workman would wear. Hopefully, you would connect with someone from the resistance, and they'd use the pictures to get you false papers. In our escape kits, we had a little compass and a scarf, which was actually a map to help with your escape. Everybody loved those things.

"The navigation officer went over order of takeoff and your position in the group. That's what everyone was waiting to hear. You were known by the name of your pilot, so it would be something like 'Canicatti flying position 3-6.' There were three squadrons to a group: lead, low, and high, with six ships in each squadron and maybe a couple extras in case someone had to drop out."

Crushing his Pall Mall into the runway, Rob continued: "After your briefing, you went to the equipment room to draw your gear: oxygen mask, throat mike, leather helmet, and other stuff all went into the flight bag. Every guy decided how much clothing to wear under his flight suit. The warmest part of the plane is in the Plexiglas nose, or 'the greenhouse,' which is where the bombardier and navigator sit. The gunners have it the worst because they are exposed to freezing temperatures for most of the flight. Your suit has insulated wires that get plugged into the electrical system at your station with a rheostat to control the temperature. You put on rubber boots, fleece flying jacket, your Mae West life preserver, parachute, and flak jacket. A lot of guys grabbed an extra flak jacket to sit on as additional protection for the family jewels.

"A truck came by and picked up the crew and took you to the revetment where your plane was parked. You taxied out onto the runway and waited for the green flare, which told you the mission was on. You waited your turn, and then off you went. Because it took a long time to get hundreds of bombers up in the air at the same time, you had to keep flying around and around while the pilots found their place in the formation.

"Once the plane was over the Channel, the gunners shot off a few rounds to make sure their guns were working. I was always looking for geographical checkpoints to make sure we were on course. I called the flight deck every half hour to let Cosmo and Mick know exactly where we were. When we got up to 10,000 feet, Mick told everyone to go on oxygen and to put on their steel helmets. After that, he'd check on everyone about every fifteen minutes to make sure that no one had conked out because of a lack of oxygen.

"On my first two missions, I flew with an experienced crew, which was standard procedure. I introduced myself to the pilot, but all he said was, 'Do your job.' I didn't understand it at the time, but later on I realized it was because he figured I'd get killed. If he didn't know me, it was one less guy to feel bad about. Keep in mind, this guy is about twenty-one years old, younger than me, but he had the eyes of an old man.

"After the first mission, I felt as if I had aged ten years. I told Pat I didn't see how I could do this twenty-four more times, and he said, 'You won't have to. I hear that the average number of missions for the 91st, our bomb group, is fourteen, and then you're either dead or a prisoner.' Gallows humor. I told him to go...," and then he looked at Beth and said, "take a hike." And everyone started to laugh.

"Early on, because of fuel limitations, we had fighter escort only as far as the German border. After that, we were on our own. The Germans knew exactly where we were because of the bomber stream. Contrails from hundreds of bombers are hard to miss. More often than not, the fighters were waiting for you. When they disappeared, you knew you were heading into flak." Shrugging his shoulders, he said,

"There's not much you can do about flak." It was flak that had killed Pat Monaghan.

"Once the IP or Initial Point had been identified, the lead plane would send out a colored flare to let everyone know we were over the target. At the start of the bomb run, the pilot turned the ship over to the bombardier, who actually flew the plane through the Norden bombsight until after we had dropped our bombs. If a plane got hit, you looked to see if anyone had made it out and counted parachutes. You also had to report on any planes you saw going down or exploding. If a plane went into a spin, centrifugal force often kept the crew pinned inside the plane, and they couldn't get out.

"Back in England, the control tower told you in what order you would land. Priority was given to any ship carrying someone who had been seriously wounded. After that, bombers that had been shot up and might have trouble landing were given priority. From there, you went to interrogation. You're dead tired, but you have to answer all their questions. 'Did you encounter any fighters?' 'Where was flak the heaviest?' 'Did you have a visual on the target?' and so on.

"After flying with Cosmo and Mick, two of the coolest pilots under the worst of circumstances, I didn't want to fly with anyone else. But two other pilots I flew with landed our ship in a turnip field. The wings were so shot up that there was more daylight than not. It was only because of their skill that we made it to land, and we didn't have to ditch. Your chances of surviving a water landing in the English Channel are between slim and none. If by some miracle you manage to get out of the plane, you'd probably freeze to death because of the water temperature.

"Believe it or not, that crash had a happy ending. There were all these girls from the British Land Army, who were working in the fields, and they came over to make sure we were all right. This cute little brunette runs up to the tail gunner and plants a kiss on his cheek. Badger tells the girl that he's going to marry her, and son of a gun if he didn't look her up when he had finished his missions. That's a hell of a way to meet your wife."

With Rob talking about dangerous missions over Nazi Germany, it wasn't the right time to ask about Badger and his bride. But when it was a good time, I wanted to know how Badger knew in a few minutes that this English girl was the right one for him. In five months, Rob hadn't figured it out, or maybe he had.

"Once we got clear of the flak and fighters, we'd tell jokes or start singing. I sang Western ballads, which Cosmo hated, calling it shit kicker's music. His guy was Frank Sinatra. You had to lighten things up, or the pressure could be unbearable.

"That was all there was to it, except you had to do it twenty-five, thirty, or thirty-five times, depending on when you got to England." Taking off his tie, he said, "Let's go into the village and get a beer."

We drove into Royston, which had all of the charm of a small English village, right down to the occasional thatched roof, gray-stone village church, and memorial to those killed in The Great War. We headed to the "Red Cow," Rob's favorite pub during the war. The owner recognized Rob and came over and shook his hand. "The first one's on me," he said, putting his hand on Rob's shoulder. "There's been a bunch of your old gang in here today." Turning his back to me, the owner whispered, "You know that Millie got married?" Rob took my hand and introduced me as "the best thing that ever happened to him."

We ate pub grub—steak and kidney pies—which was a good sign if the pies really had steak in them. After finishing our meal and another round, Jack asked Rob if there was anything else he wanted to do while they were in that part of the country. What Jack was actually asking was, did he want to visit the cemetery at Madingley. Rob thanked him but said he would rather not, and we left it at that.

On the train ride back to London, I thought about something Rob's roommate had once told me. "There were so many ways to die when you flew for the 8th Air Force. Planes exploded on the runway for no apparent reason or collided in the fog during assembly. They crashed on takeoff or were shot out of the sky, sometimes by their own guys. They went down in the Channel and crashed on landing. Flak, fighters, and fog all killed."

I had mixed feelings about our Memorial Day outing. I believe the sacrifices made by others on our behalf should be honored. However, acknowledging those deeds can sometimes be too painful for those who survived while their friends did not. On the train ride home, while Rob slept, I looked at his face and the scar on his cheek and wondered what other scars he had that I would never see.

Chapter 21

FOLLOWING THE MEMORIAL DAY ceremonies at Bassingbourn, I wanted to think pleasant thoughts about love and romance and not about B-17s being shot out of the sky. A dose of romance, eighteenth-century style, was just what I needed. After opening the package I had received from Beth, I read her note, which indicated the enclosed letters were written when Elizabeth was visiting Charlotte Chatterton in Kent.

6 July 1792

Dear Jane,

    Much to my surprise, I find Charlotte to be quite content as the wife of Mr. Chatterton. She is agreeable to all that is expected of a minister's wife and has been well received by his parishioners. With Mr. Chatterton in his study writing sermons and Charlotte content in the parlour, this marriage may prove to be a success. They have a lovely garden and a good view of Desmet Park. I walk in the park every morning, as the weather is perfect for such exercise.

Last evening, I dined at Rosings Park and was introduced to Lady Sylvia Desmet and her daughter Anne. Lady Sylvia wore an elaborate powdered wig, and her gown was the richly embroidered brocade favoured by the Queen and wide enough to hide a litter of kittens. I much prefer the French-styled dresses, which are so popular in town and are truly elegant in their simplicity. Shall I offer Lady Sylvia some of the muslin I bought in London?

Charlotte tells me Her Ladyship is very attentive; I say she is nosy. She asked me a dozen questions before the tea was poured. She has an opinion on everything, and I felt as if I was constantly defending myself. Because of nerves, I was so unsure of my French that I professed ignorance of a language I have studied. For the same reason, I chose not to disclose that our grandmother saw to our education, so we had no need of a governess.

As for the daughter, she is rather pretty but looks as fragile as a porcelain doll and said hardly a word all through dinner. Just as we were leaving, she told me that she liked Charlotte very much and would have said more, but when her mother came near, she stopped talking. Charlotte says we will probably have a visit from Anne tomorrow. She rides by in her phaeton every day when it is warm, so she can get fresh air and get away from her mother, I suspect. I have lost the light and will write more tomorrow.

Anne Desmet did visit Charlotte today and surprised me greatly by saying she already knew about me from letters from her cousin, Mr. Lacey. He told her I possessed *intelligence and great wit, and he was very complimentary of my beauty. I asked her if that was why he had fled Hertfordshire, because he had met an intelligent woman, to which she replied, 'Very possibly.' I do not understand why Mr. Lacey would write to his cousin and tell her I was a beauty, when he had decided at the assembly that I was only tolerable. Anne said he is to come to Kent in a week. At present, he is attending the cricket contests between Oxford and Cambridge. I may meet him in the park on my walks, but other than that, I am sure he will keep to the manor.*

Please write often. Papa gave me money for the post. I want to hear all that is going on in London.

Love,
Lizzy

It was clear from this letter that Anne knew her cousin was already in love with Elizabeth, and because of that, she felt comfortable in telling Lizzy that Will admired her. It must have been Anne who had informed Mr. Darcy that Lizzy was in Kent, and guess who was coming to Desmet Park?

12 July—Mr. Bingham and Mr. Lacey and his cousin have arrived at Desmet Park, and Mr. Bingham has called on Charlotte at the parsonage. When he asked after Jane, I said she was in good health and was ever as she had been, and he said it was the same with him. I am very surprised the gentlemen have come at all. When I was in London, the season was providing an endless succession of breakfasts, balls, dinners, and concerts. We were unable to obtain tickets to the opera because the crowds were so great. It is possible that the lords and ladies have tired of town and have returned to their country estates. As exciting as it was to be in London, the city did stink because of the heat, horses, and overburdened cesspools.

14 July—Mr. Bingham, Col. Devereaux, and Mr. Lacey came to the parsonage today to pay their compliments. Although the colonel is not as handsome as his cousin, his personality has great appeal, and he actually enjoys a good conversation. Mr. Lacey said little other than to ask after my family. He has that distracted look again. Before leaving, he said his aunt had invited us to supper on Friday and is to send her carriage for us. Mr. Chatterton just about fell over himself when he heard the news.

17 July—For the most part, I had a delightful evening. I sat between Col. Devereaux and Mr. Bingham. When I informed Mr. Bingham that Jane was currently in London, visiting with our uncle, he was genuinely pleased to have news of her and said he would call on her when he returned to town. Col. Devereaux is a man of many tastes and is very knowledgeable, especially about events taking place in France, and fears that things will go badly for the king. The only flaw in the evening was when Lady Sylvia insisted, quite emphatically, that I play on the pianoforte. I believe, in an effort to put me at my ease, Mr. Lacey offered to turn the pages and insisted I under-estimated my musical talents. Col. Devereaux joined us,

and wishing to tease the gentleman from Derbyshire just a little, I asked the colonel if he enjoyed conversation more than his cousin did. Mr. Lacey defended himself by saying he has no talent for talking with people not of his acquaintance. Now, in an effort to put him at his ease, I told him that the people of Hertfordshire were eager to engage in conversation with someone of his education and position in life. Then he said, 'You are quite right. If my behaviour has given offence, I apologize. Hopefully, there will be opportunities to make amends.' I did not know how to respond. Mr. Lacey has the most mercurial temperament of anyone I know. If only he would smile more, for he is very attractive when he does, and did I mention his fine legs?

After reading this entry, I couldn't understand how Lizzy failed to recognize that Will Lacey was attracted to her. He repeatedly crossed paths with her while she was out walking in Rosings Park, visited with her at the parsonage, and apologized on more than one occasion for the unfavorable impression he had made when they had first met. And what did Lizzy think he meant when he had said he hoped to have opportunities to make amends in the future? If Lizzy was confused, Charles was less so, because on July 22nd, he left Rosings Park to return to London, no doubt to call on Jane.

23 July—I have met Mr. Lacey three mornings in a row in the park. I am sure he knows when and where I will be walking. I do not understand why he rides just at that time, especially since he does little except to ask after my health and to comment on the weather. Charlotte thinks Mr. Lacey is in love with me. What a ridiculous notion! I assured Charlotte that someone of Mr. Lacey's position in life considers me to be nothing more than a diversion, because he is bored in the country.

25 July—I have had the privilege today of meeting Mr. Lacey's sister, Miss Lacey. She is eighteen or nineteen years old and greatly resembles her brother with her dark hair and gray eyes. Miss Lacey came to Rosings from London. She said she has been in town since Easter and has attended so many balls and dinner parties that she is glad everyone has returned to their country estates. She spoke with great amusement of all the young men who professed their love for her although she had done no more than dance with them. She is well aware that their attentions had more to do with her fortune than her. A Mr. Oldham, a strong, handsome man of about twenty-five years, accompanied Miss Lacey, and it is my understanding the gentleman is her constant companion. I wonder if something happened to Miss Lacey, making it necessary for her brother to employ a man for her protection.

26 July—Mr. Lacey and I had an interesting conversation today while walking in the grove. I said I hoped there was nothing wrong in London to require Mr. Bingham to return so quickly. Mr. Lacey replied that 'Bingham is his own man. He does not require my permission to travel about the country.' I doubted that but said nothing. It was such a beautiful day. I wanted everyone to be happy, even the

dour Mr. Lacey. 'May I ask, sir, what gives you the most pleasure? Is it the theatre, the opera, riding? Your cousin considers you to be an eager dancer when amongst your acquaintances. I am curious as to what you enjoy most.' He misunderstood and thought I was once again rebuking him for his behaviour in Hertfordshire. He answered: 'Miss Elizabeth, I am aware I made a very bad first impression when I came to Hertfordshire. I was in ill humour that day because, on the way to join Bingham, one of the horses threw a shoe, greatly lengthening my journey.' I said that, if his horse losing a shoe had put him in such ill humour, we were fortunate the beast had not broken its leg. Then Mr. Lacey actually laughed out loud. Oh, how handsome he is when he laughs. We continued to walk in the grove, and he said he preferred smaller, private balls rather than large, public ones, and intimate dinner parties of no more than six or seven couples. He recently had the pleasure of seeing Cambridge soundly defeat Oxford at cricket. I know nothing of that sport, but I must admit I was pleased that Mr. Lacey and I were able to engage in a conversation of some length. He can be quite charming.

By this time, we had come to the road to the parsonage, but I wanted to continue our conversation. I told him how honoured I was to have been introduced to his sister, and he freely confessed he is devoted to her and takes pride in the way she performs in public, showing a maturity beyond her years. He then mentioned that Miss Darcy and his cousins intended to play croquet on the lawn tomorrow morning and invited me to join them. Without hesitation, I accepted. What a change has come over me. I thought him to be so *proud and disagreeable, and now I see a different side to the gentleman from Derbyshire.*

27 July—There is yet another side to Mr. Lacey. He is a very serious competitor even when playing croquet with his female relations. Of course, he was the first to strike the final stake, but I finished second. He seemed pleased that I had done so well without actually beating him. I pointed out that the only person I had bested was his sister. Anne is so fragile a creature she provides no competition, and Col. Devereaux deliberately missed, so he would keep pace with her. Mr. Lacey gave me instructions on how to improve my game and insisted we go through the course again. Afterwards, we were enjoying tea on the lawn when Lady Sylvia, with her lady's maid in tow, descended upon the group, and the atmosphere immediately changed. Alas, the conversation turned to me! Lady Sylvia decided I should be introduced to a Mr. Whitman, the local printer, who, according to Her Ladyship, 'will do well enough for you.' Upon hearing this remark, Mr. Lacey walked back to the house, leaving those remaining to amuse his aunt.

Just when it seemed as if Will and Elizabeth were finally getting along, Elizabeth received Jane's letter recounting George Bingham's visit with her in London. Although she was deeply offended by Mr. Bingham's description of her family, it was nothing compared to her anger with Will Lacey when she found out he had gone to London for the very purpose of ending the romance between Charles and Jane.

30 July 1792

Dear Jane,

There is only one interpretation for George Bingham's visit. Charles (May I call him Charles?) has asked for his brother's blessing and permission to marry, and now that George Bingham has met you, he will have it. I would be very surprised if Charles didn't make you an offer very soon. If he doesn't, he is beyond hope. I would not waste one minute of thought on what Mr. Lacey will think of your engagement. If Mr. Lacey chooses to end his friendship because Charles is in love with you, he is not a true friend. On the other hand, if your conscience dictates that you must refuse Charles on account of his friend, then you should do so. But I must warn you that I will thereafter regard you as the greatest of fools.

I do not know how you sat through Mr. Bingham's dissection of our family. How embarrassing to have our weaknesses laid bare. But what did he say that was not true? Until at least one of her daughters is well married, Mama will continue to look at every unattached gentleman as a possible match for one of us, and instead of providing guidance and correction, Papa looks at his wife's inappropriate behaviour as theatre. Celia and Lucy are still young enough to make changes for the better. But these alterations must happen immediately, or it will be too late.

Apparently, Mr. Lacey left the ball at HH and went directly to London. What an arrogant man he is to think he knows what is best for his friend, especially since you now have learnt that Charles has been perfectly miserable since he left Hertfordshire. George Bingham has given Mr. Lacey too much power over Charles. Some guidance is appropriate, but what right does Mr. Lacey have to determine who Charles should or should not marry?

Mr. Lacey has been meeting me on my walks most mornings. I will now alter my schedule so as not to encounter him. I actually thought I saw improvement in his behaviour and attitude here in Kent, but now I know I was wrong. You must write to me immediately upon hearing from Charles, and I know you will hear from him shortly.

Love,
Lizzy

So much in life is timing, and Will Lacey's timing couldn't have been worse. Clearly, he was making an effort to show Lizzy his good side, only to have all of his efforts thrown to the wind because Lizzy had found out about his visit to George Bingham.

3 August—Miss Lacey and Anne Desmet visited the parsonage this morning. Despite Miss Lacey's advantages and station in life, she seems to be a sensible girl, and she plays the pianoforte so beautifully. It is a delight to hear her, even on Charlotte's poor instrument. She is to return to London shortly and will be accompanied by Mr. Oldham. There is a story there, but Charlotte and Anne say nothing about Miss Lacey's guardian. I have successfully avoided her brother, but I will see him at dinner this afternoon. It is Thursday, and we must hear Mr. Chatterton's Sunday sermon. I am seriously considering feigning illness. I am tired of listening to Lady

Sylvia's soliloquies on every subject, no matter how trivial,
and I have no wish to see Mr. Lacey. Uncle Sims has written
that he is sending his man, so that I may return home. If I do
not leave soon, all benefits of the visit will be lost, and I want
to be home when Jane receives her good news.

Lizzy did not dine at Rosings Park that afternoon. Will, who
was probably wondering why he was no longer meeting Lizzy in the
park, must have assumed she was unwell and went to call on her
at the parsonage. His proposal was so insulting that it must have
spilled out of him without any idea of how awful it sounded.

8 August 1792

Dear Jane,

I will return home early next week, but I have news that
cannot wait. After reading your letter regarding the role Mr.
Lacey played in separating Mr. Bingham from you, I was in a
very unpleasant mood, so I told Mr. Chatterton I was unwell
and would not attend the dinner with Lady Sylvia, claiming I
did not want to put Miss Desmet at risk of also becoming ill.

I was sitting in the parlour when the servant announced
Mr. Lacey. I was not pleased to see him, as I felt I could
not forgive him for his interference in his friend's personal
matters and the disservice he had done to you. His behaviour
was very odd, and finally I asked him if there was something
he wished to say to me. To the best of my memory, this is
what followed:

'I have put aside every consideration: your lack of
fortune and connections, the inferior position your family

holds in society, the criticism that will ensue, but I have lost the struggle. I have been unable to repress my feelings.' The speech continued on in this vein, but all I can remember is that whatever it was he was going on about, it was done against his better judgement. At this point, Mr. Lacey stopped speaking, and I told him I did not understand him, and then he continued:

'I love you and have almost from the first moment of our acquaintance. I am now asking for your hand in marriage.'

Jane, you can appreciate the shock I experienced upon hearing his proposal. Mr. Lacey was in love with me! For a second I was quite flattered, but then I thought of the mode of his declaration. I believe this is what I said when I could finally speak.

'I thank you for the honour of your proposal. I appreciate the difficulty of your struggles, and I am sure with the passage of time you will be successful in overcoming those feelings which you found so distressing, and your initial reservations will prevail.'

'May I ask why my offer is rejected with so little consideration?'

'I might ask why you would make an offer of marriage to a woman whom you consider to be unworthy of you. You tell me that in making this offer, you are acting against your better judgement. From your perspective, I would like to know why you would want such a wife, and, more importantly, why would I want a husband who regrets he was unable to overcome his feelings for me? Does such a union have any possibility of success?'

When he had gone, I found I was shaking. I had no

idea he had feelings for me. When Charlotte remarked that Mr. Lacey might be in love with me, I had dismissed it. Just because he had stopped being rude did not mean he was in love. I did notice a change in his demeanor, and I will admit I found him to be very pleasant company on our walks and out on the lawn when we played at croquet, but an offer of marriage never entered my mind.

I am greatly unsettled and look forward to going home. It will be impossible to avoid Mr. Lacey, as he will remain Mr. Bingham's friend. I will need your guidance as how to act when we meet again.

Love,

Lizzy

Before returning to London, Will shared with his cousin the details of what had happened at the parsonage, and because Anne believed Lizzy was perfect for Will, she decided to intervene on his behalf.

10 August 1792

My Dearest Will,

I have visited with Elizabeth and told her I knew of your proposal of marriage. She was much surprised to learn you would tell anyone about the terrible things she had said to you. We went into the garden, and she began to cry. She said she was very flattered by your proposal and would have been more receptive to it but for two things. She had just recently learnt of your visit to George Bingham regarding her sister

Jane. There is no one in the world who is closer to her, and she considers this injury to her sister to be an injury to herself. Secondly, she said she could never be sure that your love would remain constant, since you said that you would have been happier if you had been successful in overcoming your feelings for her.

Elizabeth told me of your walks in the grove and how much she enjoyed your company. She mentioned you had risen in her estimation with each meeting, but then she mentioned how determined you were to keep Charles from her sister, and she again started to cry.

What is to be done? If you love her as ardently as you said last week, then you must start over. Since it is nearly a certainty her sister Jane will shortly become engaged, then you will have ample opportunity to see Elizabeth because you are Charles's closest friend. Show her you harbour no hard feelings because of her rejection and proceed from there. But you must court her, Will. You should not assume she will want to marry you just because of your fortune and position. If that was all she wanted, she would have accepted you at the parsonage. Go to Hertfordshire. Show her you regret the method of your proposal but not the making of it. If Elizabeth did not care for you, she would have shown defiance and not tears when I spoke to her in the garden.

Your devoted cousin,
Anne

After reading this letter, I felt sorrier for Anne than I did for Will. She had encouraged her cousin to stand up and fight for Elizabeth, not to concede defeat, and to go on the offensive. Yet, she was unable to stand up to her mother. Because she lived such a sad, lonely life, she was determined that at least Will would experience a love she would never know.

> *16 August—I have told Jane of Mr. Lacey's proposal, and to my surprise, she was surprised but little. She said his interest in me could not be mistaken, but she did not think he would act because of our different positions in society. She was sorry to hear I had rejected him because of the role he had played in separating Charles from her, saying that, in the end, it was George Bingham's influence that held greater sway. Jane added that it was when Charles saw me in Kent that he made the decision to force the issue with his brother. When George recognized the depth of his brother's feelings, he arranged for the meeting that won his approval for the marriage. Jane asked if I had feelings for Mr. Lacey, and I had to confess that I did. Until the night of his wretched proposal, I did not realize how much I had come to enjoy his company, and thought how terrible a thing it would be if I should never see him again.*

Never see him again? Considering Charles and Jane would shortly announce their wedding plans, and that Will Lacey would almost certainly be asked to stand up for his friend, was there any doubt Will and Lizzy would meet again? Not really. Lizzy wasn't worried about not seeing Mr. Lacey again. She was worried about what would happen when she did.

Chapter 22

ON SEPTEMBER 10, 1792, Charles Bingham married Miss Jane Garrison in the Garrison's parish church. Apparently, it was at the wedding breakfast at Helmsley Hall where Lizzy and Will had their first opportunity to talk since that awful day at the parsonage.

11 September—I was very apprehensive about seeing Mr. Lacey again, but as soon as he saw me, he came over and asked after my health, as he always does. He directed my attention to his sister and Miss Desmet. Mr. Lacey said that, upon leaving Kent, he and his sister had gone to Montclair, as that is the place where his thoughts are clearest. What thoughts were those? Was he thinking of me and his failed proposal? I am sure his cousin acquainted him with our conversation in the garden. I wish I knew what he had said to Anne.

Mr. Lacey asked me to introduce him to Aunt and Uncle Sims, and I mentioned my uncle was in trade and resided on Gracechurch Street. Mr. Lacey said he was often in that part of London, as that is where George Bingham's office is. After we were back at Bennets End, Uncle told me that upon learning we were shortly to visit the Peak District, Mr. Lacey insisted we visit Montclair, and he informed me with great excitement that the estate is mentioned in Walton's The Compleat Angler. *Apparently, there is no greater compliment. I should have nothing to be anxious about, as we have had that dreaded first meeting, and he was so nice to me.*

22 September—I am to go to the Peak District, and Lucy is to go to Brighton as a guest of Col. Fenton and his wife. Papa says nothing can happen to Lucy since she will be under the protection of the colonel. To Papa's amusement, while discussing the militia, Mama told stories of the dances she had attended as a girl when her partners were also handsome officers. With his usual biting wit, Papa said, 'And one of those handsome officers went off to the colonies, where he was promptly dispatched by savages.' To which Mama replied, 'Not killed, dear, but died of dysentery.' I am still uneasy about Lydia, but everyone did have a good laugh.

Lizzy kept up her diary all during her trip. By the time her party had reached Derbyshire, she was thoroughly sick of visiting "great" estates and was looking forward to walking a mountain path. She wrote very little about her upcoming visit to Montclair, and I wondered if it was her way of putting off thinking about her reunion with Will Lacey.

11 October—I will never forget my first view of Montclair. The carriage came over a gentle rise, and there before us was this beautiful mansion all lit up for our arrival. The carriage stopped near a large fountain where we were assisted by servants in livery. I wore the same ivory dress I had worn to the ball at Helmsley Hall. It is the very best dress I own, but it was nothing compared to the finery worn by Georgiana and Anne. For the first time since we met, I heard Anne laugh. She is like a bird set free from her cage. Georgiana played the most beautiful instrument I have ever seen, a recent gift from her brother.

12 October—Georgiana invited us to join her at Montclair while the men went fishing. When they returned, Mr. Lacey suggested we all walk around the lake. Aunt and Uncle declined, and, of course, Anne could not join us. We had gone but five minutes when Georgiana said she thought she should go back to the house to keep Anne company. It was clear she had planned this all along, and I said as much to her brother, who found it amusing. We arrived at a sitting area where you can view the lake and the beautiful countryside. It was there that Mr. Lacey said in a very halting manner: 'When we were in Kent, my proposal, I mean, what I said, was offensive to you, and I wish to apologize.' I asked him if he regretted the proposal or just the manner in which it was delivered. He then laughed and smiled and said, 'I know I am forgiven, Miss Elizabeth, because you tease only your friends.' I told Mr. Lacey he was like a brother to Mr. Bingham, and because of that, we must always be friends. He looked at me very intently and said, 'I would hope we could be more than friends.' We continued our walk in silence, but he extended his arm, and I took it! I went to the inn that night quite pleased with how the day had gone. I will gladly return to this enchanted place. It must be enchanted. Look at the change in Mr. Lacey!

After touring the Peak District, Lizzy returned to Bennets End and almost immediately went to see Jane at Helmsley Hall, where she found her sister quite content in her new role as Mrs. Charles Bingham. When the Lacey party returned from Derbyshire, Jane and Charles hosted their first dinner party.

23 October—Mr. Lacey was most agreeable tonight. He asked about our tour of the Peak and Chatsworth after we left Montclair. As much as I enjoyed the remainder of our holiday, it was nothing to the three days we spent near his estate. Mr. Lacey said it was necessary for Georgiana to go up to London, so she might resume her studies. But more importantly, Lady Sylvia had written to Anne insisting she return to Kent for reasons of her health. What nonsense! Anne has never looked better and told me she spent a good deal of time out of doors on the terrace and frequently walked the gardens while at her cousin's home. I think being free of her mother has actually strengthened her.

Before the Second World War scattered everyone around the country and the globe, young people in my hometown who were dating would see each other, if not every day, at least once a week on Saturday night, so for more than three weeks to pass between Jane's dinner party and the next time Will Lacey was at Helmsley Hall seemed like an eternity to me. On the other hand, once they did get together, Lizzy was able to see Will every day because Jane had asked her sister to stay on at Helmsley Hall because she was feeling unwell.

24 November—Since Mr. Lacey's arrival at HH, we have experienced very fine weather. As a result, Mr. Lacey and I have walked each morning in the park, and I have learnt so much about him and his family. From his description of his mother, it is hard to believe she was the sister of Lady Sylvia, their temperaments being quite the opposite, but Mr. Lacey defended his aunt, who was several years older than his mother and her brother, Viscount Devereaux. She had assumed the role of parent when their own mother had died. However, he admits that being in her company is very trying. He will get no argument from me on that!

25 November—Mr. Lacey informed me he is to return to London and asked if I would walk with him in the park. When we reached the top of a gentle slope, he placed his hat on the bench that is in a recess in the hedge. He then untied my bonnet and placed it on top of his hat. With no resistance from me, he took me in his arms and kissed me. It was not one kiss but many. I stupidly kept my hands at my side, and he took my arms and put them about his neck and kissed me again and told me he loved me. For one of the very few times in my life, I was speechless. That evening, while playing whist, I was unable to concentrate and played so badly that Jane asked if I was unwell. Before retiring, Mr. Lacey stopped me on my way upstairs and kissed me and held me tightly against him. He said if it were not for pressing business in London with George Bingham, nothing could compel him to leave

Hertfordshire. He was gone at first light, and I watched his carriage until it disappeared down the London road.

When I read how Will had removed her bonnet so that he could kiss her, it was as erotic to me as if he had stripped her down to her chemise. At that time, touching an ungloved hand was considered to be sexy, so for Will Lacey to take off her hat so that he might kiss her, well, that got my heart beating.

The next diary entry Beth had copied out was no surprise. The reason Jane was unwell was because she was pregnant. Lizzy noted she had "never seen a man as delighted as Charles was upon hearing that he was to be a father." But Charles and Jane were not the only ones who were jumping with joy.

4 December—I have received a letter from Mr. Lacey professing his love for me. He tells me how he cherishes that moment in the park when we first kissed. It seems Mr. Lacey and I are of similar minds. Whenever I have a spare moment, all I can think about is how he took me in his arms and kissed me. I had never been kissed before, and it made me quite lightheaded. George Bingham and he are to travel to France on business. I do not understand why it is necessary for them to go at this time when there is such violence in Paris and elsewhere in France. There was a report in the newspapers that the Duchess of Devonshire's carriage was attacked near Montpelier. It is best that I do not know where in France they are to go, as I am excessively worried without knowing the particulars.

Unfortunately for Lizzy, Will's visit to France would not be her only worry. The Garrisons were shortly to learn that Lucy had left Brighton with Waggoner. Lucy's stunt could very well have destroyed any chance Lizzy had of receiving a second offer of marriage from Will Lacey. Although I knew the outcome, I really sympathized with Lizzy because she was about to experience great uncertainty, something I was becoming increasingly familiar with.

16 December—Oh what sad news we have had! An express rider came Monday evening from Col. Fenton telling Papa that Lucy had run away with Mr. Waggoner. His men found them in London two days later at a lodging house under an assumed name. Col. Fenton went to London for the purpose of bringing Waggoner back to Brighton for disciplinary action and to restore Lucy to her family, but Lucy would not leave Waggoner! She does not see the harm in what she has done. Lucy is at present with Uncle Sims, and our father left this morning with Charles, who said he was confident his brother James, who is in London while George Bingham is in France, could be of some help. But for so many people to know of our troubles! All we can do now is to wait for news from London.

23 December—At Uncle's insistence, Papa has returned home, as arrangements have been made for Waggoner and Lucy to marry on Wed. in Uncle Sims's church. Papa believes Charles has laid out a good deal of money on his behalf to settle Waggoner's affairs. Since we do not have ready money, Papa has been forced to accept his son-in-law's generosity. Col. Fenton wrote to Papa to say a commission had been purchased for Waggoner in the regular army by a friend, and he is to report to a regiment in the North. Papa will not receive them here, and Mama, realizing Lucy's behaviour could harm the family if the details of her hurried marriage became known, agrees with him. Mama will meet them at the inn at Watford when they travel north. Celia and I will go with her, but Mary refuses.

2 January—We met Lucy and Waggoner at the inn yesterday. Mama has aged ten years since this affair began and said little to Lucy and barely acknowledged Waggoner. I, too, had little to say, but Lucy more than made up for it. I was barely listening when she mentioned that Mr. Lacey had paid for Waggoner's commission. When I asked her why Mr. Lacey should involve himself in her situation, she said he was giving Waggoner his due because he had been denied a living promised to him by Old Mr. Lacey. I made no comment on this slander. I must write to Aunt Sims to find out the reason for Mr. Lacey's involvement in this sordid affair. But there is no one to ask why he did not inform me of his return to England. If Mr. Lacey ever intended to make another offer of marriage, the idea died this week in London.

Elizabeth's aunt's response was on lovely, pale pink, linen stationery, and in her tiny handwriting, Mrs. Sims wrote:

9 January 1793

Dear Elizabeth,

I must rely on your discretion regarding the matter of Lucy and Waggoner because Mr. Lacey did not wish for his role in this affair to become known, especially to your father.

Your uncle has given me his permission to acquaint you with the particulars of the events in London. We are convinced it is because of you that Mr. Lacey became involved.

Col. Fenton delivered Lucy to our doorstep himself. He said Lucy was adamant that she would not leave Waggoner, and the colonel decided it was best to turn the matter over to her family. The poor man could not apologize enough for the unfortunate chain of events. He told us it has caused a rift between him and his wife. Apparently, Mrs. Fenton knew Lucy was expecting a proposal of marriage from Waggoner. The colonel would not have allowed it and would have sent your sister home immediately.

Your uncle was successful in convincing your father to return home where he could be of comfort to his family. He was to be pitied: one minute angry and the next in a state of despair. Under such circumstances, he would not have been helpful with negotiations with Mr. Waggoner, who was quite confident of an advantageous resolution. When your uncle arrived at the solicitor's office, Mr. Lacey and Mr. George Bingham were present. Mr. Bingham was attended by a large man, who sat behind him and said not a word. Waggoner presented his demands to Mr. Bingham, who set the paper aside without looking at it.

George Bingham stated that Waggoner's debts would be discharged in Brighton and Bennets End, a commission would be purchased, including uniforms, and Lucy would receive wedding clothes and an annuity from her father. With that, Mr. Bingham stood up and said that Waggoner would receive no additional money, and there would be no further demands made by him now or at any time in the future. He leaned over the table to get as close as possible to Waggoner and said, 'Bad things happen to bad people, Mr. Waggoner. I strongly urge you to reform and take care of your young wife.' Your uncle said when he stood up, the large man also stood up, and after this very threatening statement, they left. Waggoner said no more. The papers were signed and arrangements made for the wedding.

You asked why Mr. Lacey involved himself in our troubles. One of the reasons given was he felt obligated to do so because, if he had made known Waggoner's true character, this could not have happened. But more importantly, I believe he is in love with you. When he dined with us after all the legal issues were settled, he said not a word about what had happened that day but spoke only of our visit to Derbyshire and his visit to Helmsley Hall. I am sure Mr. Lacey will return to Hertfordshire after there has been time for wounds to heal with one purpose in mind, and that is to see you.

Love,
Aunt Ruth

That was the last of the letters and diary entries, but Beth had also enclosed a note wrapping up the story.

Now for an explanation of how Lady Sylvia came to believe her nephew might make an offer of marriage to Lizzy, which Jane Austen told so dramatically in the novel. Shortly after the problems associated with Lucy's elopement were resolved, Anne traveled with Will Lacey to Helmsley Hall for a visit with Lizzy, Jane, and Charles. Upon her return to Desmet Park, Anne was very complimentary of the hospitality shown to her by the newly married Charles and Jane Bingham. That was when Anne told her mother she might shortly hear news of another marriage—that of her nephew and Elizabeth Garrison.

Lady Sylvia was on the road in a heartbeat. After verbally abusing Lizzy at Bennets End, as Jane Austen wrote about in P&P, she went directly to Helmsley Hall and lashed into her nephew. For once in her life, Lady Sylvia did not get her way. Will rode to Bennets End to apologize for his aunt's behaviour. Instead of breaking up the romance, Will asked Lizzy to marry him right then and there. Shortly thereafter, Elizabeth received a beautiful ruby ring as a symbol of their betrothal. They were married in St. Michael's Church in Crofton on May 20, 1793, and they had their wedding breakfast at Montclair in the company of their friends and family.

I look forward to discussing all of this with you when you are next in Crofton.

Fondly,
Beth

At that moment, I had only one thought, and it was not a pleasant one. As a young girl, the view from my bedroom was of a towering coal breaker bearing down on the town like some industrial monster. Everything in Minooka was covered with a fine layer of soot, and the smell of sulfur permeated the air. A way to escape this bleak landscape was to disappear into other worlds as created by authors like the Brontës, Dickens, Alcott, and Mark Twain. But of all the authors I had ever read, my favorite was Jane Austen. I loved everything she wrote, but I particularly loved *Pride and Prejudice*. I had read it so many times that I had memorized large passages, like an actor would study the lines of a play.

I was willing to accept that Jane Austen had somehow heard of the story that would form the basis of *Pride and Prejudice*. All the letters and family history supported the Crowells' belief that Elizabeth Bennet and Fitzwilliam Darcy were actually Elizabeth Garrison and William Lacey of Montclair in Derbyshire. But how was it possible for the author to know what Elizabeth and Will had said to each other? The only explanation was that Jane Austen had read Elizabeth Garrison's diary, and this seemed to me to be improbable if not impossible. Was Beth in possession of a forged diary that had been written after Jane Austen's novel had been published in 1813?

I told Rob of my concerns, but he doubted the Crowells would be fooled by a forgery. He reminded me that this diary was only one of several. If Elizabeth's handwriting had differed from one journal to the next, it would have been noticed.

"Listen, Maggie, Beth had to have thought about all of these things, too. I suggest you go to Crofton and ask her."

Chapter 23

WHILE ROB WAS AWAY in the North of England on a work assignment, I decided to take a break from too much overtime at the Army Exchange Service. I did go to Crofton but left the parcel at Mrs. Dawkins's house because I wanted to reread all that Beth had sent to me.

After Jack picked me up at the station, we drove up to Montclair, so that I could meet Freddie. Instead of parking next to the fountain, he drove around back to the servants' entrance, and said, "Home, Sweet Home." We walked through a labyrinth until we got to the kitchen area where Freddie was sitting on a stool and reading the sports pages. When we came into the kitchen, he put out his cigar and jumped up to greet us. Jack made the introductions, and I told Freddie I was thrilled to finally meet the real master of Montclair. Freddie, who was short and wiry, gave off a nervous intensity that came at you in waves, and although he had been living in England for more than twenty years, his accent was Australian through and through.

Referring to that day's newspaper, he said, "I was checking yesterday's scores to see how much money I won. I done all right. Do you bet, Maggie?" I said I bought Irish lottery tickets, and he doubled over laughing and slapped the counter. "That's not betting, dear; that's shopping."

After he stopped laughing, he said, "Don Caton and 'her highness' are in London, so why don't you have a look around."

"By myself?"

"Well, I'll have to pat you down when you get back to make sure you didn't pinch nothing, and I'm very thorough." I looked to Jack to see if Freddie was serious, and he just laughed.

"This is the backstairs the junior servants had to use at all times," Jack said as we climbed the staircase. "It leads to the male and female living quarters on the third floor. Before cars, the permanent help had to live on site, but by the late 1920s, it was getting so hard to keep servants, they were allowed to live down in the village. Once things like Hoovers, dishwashers, and washing machines came into use, it wasn't necessary to have so many servants, but by that time, I was long gone."

"But your living area was downstairs?"

"Yes, and the cook's too. The rooms where my family lived are used by Freddie now. All the work the servants used to do, including the cooking, is now hired out. If the Catons were to have a big affair, they would actually rent a butler. If you just felt a shift in the earth, it was my father turning over in his grave."

Jack and I stepped through a door into the main section of the house where Beth's parents had their suite of rooms. Each had their own bedroom, which was the normal arrangement among England's upper class. Jack said the Pratts used only Lady

Lacey's room, "which Mrs. Caton started redecorating as soon as the Pratts reached the end of the driveway."

"Mrs. Caton doesn't hide the fact that she thinks the Pratts had no taste. It's true they were hard on that house, but they were a small part of a big problem. A two-hundred-year-old house needs constant attention. Plaster cracks, wallpaper becomes unglued, chimneys get clogged with soot, drains back up, and that's during peacetime. When the First War came, maintenance fell by the wayside, and it took the Catons and their deep pockets to repair what time and neglect had done."

Jack opened the door to a bedroom adjoining Lady Lacey's. "This used to be Beth's father's room. The sleigh bed and armoire were so large, they left them with the house."

"Beth was very close to her father, wasn't she?" I asked.

"Yes, until Lucy Arminster, his lady friend in London, put in an appearance. Beth and Reed went to live in New York where they stayed with Lady Lacey's sister until their parents ironed out that mess. It would have been disastrous for Reed if his parents had gotten a divorce. But that didn't seem to have occurred to either parent with Lady Lacey storming off to America, and Sir Edward chasing a young woman around town." He shook his head and said, "Let's have a look at Beth's room."

We walked down the hall to Beth's bedroom in the east wing. Mrs. Caton had recently finished refurbishing Beth's room and had been able to locate the original wallpaper pattern, a pale green, with delicate white flowers, and branches with tiny birds sitting on them.

Jack gestured for me to join him on the balcony. Beth's room was on the north side of the house, facing the gardens, and had an extraordinary view of the estate. Between Montclair and Stepton were acres and acres of rolling pastureland, sectioned off with rock walls, and hundreds of fluffy white dots moving around in the distance. It looked just like a scene from a postcard of rural England.

"Reed had the same view from his bedroom, and he painted it every which way from Sunday." This was the scene that had inspired Reed to draw the four sketches hanging in the Crowell's den that I had admired when I first met Beth and Jack. "He was unbelievably talented and could work in any medium. But from the time he came back from America, with the exception of Beth and my brother, Tom, you'd never see an adult face in his drawings. I guess he felt betrayed by the grown-ups in his life."

We walked down the long hallway to the west wing where Jack pointed to door after door. "These rooms were for Trevor and Matt. They had their own bedrooms, bathroom, game room with gramophone, and a kitchen that had originally been part of the nursery and classroom. To say they were overindulged doesn't get there by half." Shaking his head, Jack said, "They were my mates, and I can honestly say they never pulled rank on me or Tom. But the way they lived, with no consequences or responsibilities, was hard to take.

"But having said that, I think both of them would have turned out all right if they had survived the war. When Trevor was working in the brokerage house in London for his father, he told me he realized that it was time to grow up. He wasn't sure what he was going to do, but he knew he was not going to be a broker. He wanted to visit America, which of course, was where Ellen and his daughter were living.

"Matt was the big surprise. He was a good, strong leader, and I think he might have stayed in the Army. The Laceys got lots of letters from the men who served under him, all of them saying what an exceptional officer he was. Matt told me that at his worst, he was a better officer than any of the generals calling the shots. He was right about that."

I had already seen the ground-floor rooms, and there was a padlock on the door to the tower. I assumed it had been closed permanently, but that wasn't the reason why it was locked.

"Sir Edward's brother, Jeremy, has lived there from the time he was a young man, and he rents it from the Catons," Jack said. "When he comes home, he stays in the tower, the bachelor's HQ, he calls it. No one is allowed in there unless Jeremy is with them; even Freddie respects his wishes. You might have a chance to meet him since he's giving a lecture in London in September."

"Mr. Lacey's brother is still alive?" With the exception of one passing reference from Michael, no one had said anything about him.

"He was alive as of the date of the letter he wrote to Beth telling her he was coming to England." Jack was laughing because he didn't understand how I could be so interested in people who were no relation to me.

We went downstairs where Freddie had promised to frisk me. He was bent over with his ear to the radio listening to a broadcast from Russia. "Jack, come here." Pointing to the radio, he said, "That's Moscow I'm listening to. Don't have a bleeding clue what they're saying although I keep hearing the word Berlin." Because of the crackling, Freddie turned the radio off. "I reckon British Intelligence are listening, too, so it's safe for me to take the day off." Looking at me, he said, "I was too young for the first fight and too old for the second, so they made me an air raid warden in the last war. If I saw any Nazi bombers headed our way, I was the one who was supposed to warn the sheep." He jumped off his stool and said, "Would you like a cuppa, dear? I'm just about to have my tea."

Jack told him we had to get back to Crofton, as Beth was expecting us. But Freddie told me to come back and said, "Next time, leave the bodyguard at home, and we'll have some fun."

When we got back to Crofton Wood, Beth was in the kitchen preparing the tea. She asked my opinion of Montclair, and I told her the best view in the whole house was from her bedroom. "Yes, I do miss that," Beth agreed. "There were always sheep in the pastures, and I'd watch the border collies move them from pasture to pasture through the narrow gates in the stone walls." Excusing herself, she told us she would be right back. She returned with a large folder, the kind artists use to carry their drawings. Sitting down on the sofa, she untied the string that was yellow with age, and inside were a dozen sketches drawn by Reed. She pulled out a drawing of the exact view she had just described to me, right down to the collies running through a flock of sheep.

The first sketch had been drawn in the spring, when the sheep had dropped their lambs. There was a man holding a staff moving the sheep from one enclosure to another. You could see enough detail in the hand to know the man was old, but, as Jack had said, Reed chose not to draw his face.

"Here's the same view, painted with watercolors in the spring, but just the pastures." Pulling out a third drawing, Beth said, "and here is a pen and ink drawing of the pastures in winter. Which one do you like best?"

I liked them all. But I was drawn to the winter scene, which showed a stark, snow-covered landscape with broken stone walls and denuded trees. I pointed to the black-and-white drawing, and Beth handed it to me. She explained that she wanted the drawings to go to people she cared about and who appreciated her brother's talents.

After I went to bed that night, the drawing stayed with me. While visiting Venice, I had seen Giorgione's *La Tempesta*, and I had heard an elderly gentleman say that a man's art was a window into his soul. If that was the case, then Reed Lacey's art showed someone who was at ease with nature but who was so distrustful of people that he chose not to draw their faces.

***

On Sunday morning, I was sitting in the pew of St. Michael's Church with Beth and Jack. As a Catholic, I wasn't supposed to participate in a Protestant service in any way, including standing up when everyone else did. But because of my relationship with Rob, I had violated so many of the Church's teachings that I had decided "in for a penny, in for a pound."

Unlike Catholic churches, which have mandatory Sunday attendance and crowded services, St. Michael's was barely halfway full, so it was a good thing Beth's grandmother had bequeathed an annuity to the church to pay the pastor's salary in perpetuity. Rev. Keller's sermon wasn't exactly riveting, and I found myself thinking about the time Michael Crowell and I had toured the Peak District in Beth's Aston Martin. It had been an enjoyable afternoon, followed by dinner with his parents at the Grist Mill, a favorite restaurant of the Crowells.

Between the wars, the owners of the mill had converted it to a restaurant. Cars had made this once-remote spot accessible, and it had become popular with tourists on their way to the Peak District. It was made of solid stone and had massive beams going across the ceiling. Jack explained it was rare to see beams of that length because the Royal Navy took most of them for the masts of their ships "when Britannia ruled the waves."

When we arrived, we were told the restaurant would not open for another three-quarters of an hour. We made a reservation and walked down to the river where picnic benches were scattered under the trees. Sitting at one of the picnic tables, Michael asked what I thought of Montclair.

"It's nice to have a place in the country," I answered. "But it's not Chatsworth."

I started to laugh when I saw his confused expression. "Sorry. I'm kidding." I kept laughing, and so I explained. "In Elizabeth Garrison's diary, she was always commenting on Will Lacey's quizzical expression. He probably looked a lot like you do now. But then he was your ancestor." After he realized I was joking, I answered his question. "Montclair is a jewel, and the grounds are gorgeous. But what I liked best was the mural painted by your Uncle Reed. I felt as if he wanted me to walk out onto the terrace with him."

"The puppy in the mural was Blossom, Reed's beagle," Beth explained. "Blossom's hind legs had nerve damage and were nearly useless, so Tom and Reed made a little cart for her. After that, she got along quite well."

"I'll say she did," Jack said, laughing. "Blossom had free rein in that house, and she banged that cart into every piece of furniture the Laceys owned. I remember Macy, the parlor maid, carried a brown crayon in her pocket to color in the dents on the furniture."

The meal was excellent, but it was the company I enjoyed most. It was obvious how much the Crowells loved being with their son, and with good reason. Michael was gracious, intelligent, and witty. I didn't understand why he was still running around loose.

When Michael mentioned that he was in a relationship with a woman from his station, I lied and said that I was in one, too. After he returned to Malta, I put him out of my mind, and the only direct contact I had with him was an exchange of postcards. But with Rob unwilling to even discuss our future, I could feel the fabric of our relationship beginning to fray. As a result, I was once again thinking about Michael Crowell, and he was helping me along because he had stopped sending postcards and had started writing letters.

The first two were general in nature. He wrote about the long days of serving in a peacetime RAF and about the rebuilding of Malta. The island had been pummeled day after day by the Luftwaffe during the war, and because of their heroism, George VI, in April 1942, had awarded the George Cross on a collective basis to everyone on the island. The second was a visit he and a group of his mates had made to Morocco and its Kasbah. It was in the third letter where he revealed that his relationship with Audrey had ended.

Although Audrey and I never had a definitive conversation about marriage, she believed it was implied, or why else would she be living on an island in the middle of the Mediterranean so far from home? I had no answer, and I felt like a complete heel because I had stayed in a relationship out of habit and because it was convenient. It all ended in a very civilized way with no harsh words exchanged. I have to confess I am a bit of a romantic. I have always hoped that when I met the

girl I wanted to marry, there would be a spark from our first
moment together. That had not happened with Audrey, but I
am positive it will happen.

I knew that Beth was a faithful correspondent and that she kept her son up-to-date on everything that was going on back in England. If those updates included me, then Michael knew that Rob and I were having problems, which might explain why he had enclosed a picture of all four Crowells standing in the ruins of the Acropolis in Athens when he was about ten years old. On the back, he had written, "It's been a while. Don't you think it's about time I went back for a second visit? I don't think you've ever been to Greece, or have you?" Was that an invitation?

That night I had a dream where Michael and I were in bed together, and it was so real that I could almost taste his mouth and feel his weight on top of me. In the morning, I was ashamed of what was happening. I was in love with Rob, but I had been thinking about Michael so much, he was showing up in my dreams in his skivvies.

And did any of this matter? If things did not work out with Rob, I would be long gone by the time Michael was discharged in November because a formal announcement had been made that AES operations were going to be run out of Germany. So there was no point in dreaming about a romance with Michael Crowell. Or so I thought. But events in Berlin were about to change everything.

Chapter 24

AT MY OFFICE, EVERYONE had been on edge waiting for the dreaded memo regarding our reassignments, when events unfolding in Germany turned everything on its head. The Soviet Union had halted all traffic by water and land into or out of the Allied sectors of Berlin. The only remaining access routes into the city were three twenty-mile-wide air corridors across the Russian zone. The Soviets' intention was to take over the three zones of Berlin not under their control. With no Allied traffic coming into Berlin to supply its inhabitants with basic necessities, the Soviet Union would be able to starve Berlin into submission.

On June 26, 1948, the Western Powers responded with the start of the Berlin Airlift. On that day, C-47 cargo planes, flown by the United States Air Force, carried eighty tons of food into Berlin, not nearly enough to provide the minimum daily requirements of Berlin's population, but it would soon be joined by the U. S. Navy and the Royal Air Force. In short order, the United States responded to the Soviet's blockade by making an open-ended commitment to the people of Berlin to supply them with calories and coal, as long as they were willing to stand up to Soviet bullying.

In Britain, tensions that had eased in the three years since the end of the war immediately returned. While events in Berlin were being dissected in Whitehall, the British were having their own discussions in their homes, in the workplace, in pubs, and on the street. "Berlin Airlift," two words that hadn't existed a week earlier, now summarized the greatest threat to peace in Europe since the end of hostilities in May 1945.

In the States, reservists were being called up to augment active-duty personnel now being transferred to Germany. Events moved so quickly that older World War II C-47s that had been flown over the beaches of Normandy were pressed into service. The planes, bearing the white stripes on their wings, which had identified them as "friendly" aircraft during the invasion, were expected to hold down the fort until the larger C-54s could arrive from the States.

One of the pilots in those early days was Greg McAllister, Rob's brother. Greg had received orders assigning him to Great Falls Air Force Base in Montana for retraining on the newer and larger C-54 cargo plane. The Air Force built training facilities that simulated flying conditions over Berlin and runways that replicated the air corridor approach paths into the city.

On his way back to the States, Greg had a scheduled stop in England for refueling and had arranged to see his brother. Rob told me not to look for any great family resemblance. Rob took after his father's side of the family, which included a light-haired, blue-eyed, five-foot-ten Swedish grandmother, while Greg favored his mother's side: solid, muscular, dark hair, brown-eyed German farmers. It seemed the only part of Rob that was actually Scots-Irish was his name. We met Greg at a pub near the air base where his plane was being refueled. If Rob projected an air of being the laid-back cowboy, Greg reminded me of an overwound clock.

"I've got only two hours before I have to fly out of here, but thanks for coming." Looking at me, he said, "If I had a girlfriend as pretty as you, I'd let everyone know, but Rob always did play his cards close to his vest."

I felt as if I had just been slapped in the face. Apparently, no one in his family knew I existed. But I would have to think about that later, as it was clear that something was not right. Under the table, one of Greg's legs was constantly shaking, and he was lighting one cigarette with the burning end of another. Rob understood immediately what was wrong and asked his brother just how bad it was flying into Berlin.

"Really, really bad." Greg told him of the many problems the Allied pilots were facing each day. "We have these very short runways, and you can't make a mistake or you'll crash. You have only one chance to land. If you blow it, you have to return to base and get back in line. You can fly up to three missions a day, and it's hard to think straight." Greg stubbed out his cigarette, but he quickly lit up another one.

"We're flying in tons of coal every day, but it's a real problem. The coal dust gets into the control cables, which makes it difficult to control the airplane. We finally figured out that if we fly with our escape hatches open, the dust gets sucked out the back. But a lot of it still floats in the air, and when you sweat, it sticks to your skin.

"We're flying at 5,000 feet, with the planes stacked five high, and landing every three minutes. The Ruskies jam our radio channels, and when we take off at night, they turn their searchlights on us so that we can't see. But that's not the worst of it. Lately, the YAK fighters have been flying straight at us. The bastards peel off only at the last second, or they sneak up behind you and fly over your wings. They're trying to push us off course so we won't be able to land."

Rob put his hand on his brother's arm to calm him down. The longer he talked, the more rattled he was becoming. "Greg, you've been doing this only for a couple of weeks, so everything's new to you. You're learning how to fly in a tight formation and landing with another plane right on your ass. It takes time to learn those things, and you will." Looking straight into his brother's eyes, Rob said, "Those guys have years of combat experience. I know it's scary as hell to have fighters flying straight at you, but they're not there to kill you, just to scare the crap out of you."

"Well, they're doing a hell of a job." Greg swallowed half of his beer in one go. "Did you ever think you would shit in your pants?" As far as Greg was concerned, I wasn't even there. He needed assurance from his brother that he could do this and that it was normal to be frightened.

"Did I ever think I'd shit in my pants? Hell, yes! Just getting that plane into formation was nerve-wracking. After flying through flak and having German fighters open up on us, you're damn right I was scared. There were times when I couldn't walk I was shaking so badly. I used to think it was just me, but then I'd notice when we went into interrogation to be debriefed, the pilots would head straight for the guy who was handing out shots of whiskey."

"I think it'll be better once I'm trained on the C-54. It's a better plane and can carry more cargo. Some of the C-47s I've flown were shot up over Normandy and have been repaired over and over again. They should be junked."

Apparently, just talking to Rob had been enough to ease the tension, and Greg started to tell us stories about what was now being called "Operation Vittles" by the Americans and "Plain Fare" by the British.

"You should see these Germans go at it. In the time it takes to grab a sandwich and a cup of coffee, they've unloaded the plane and are ready to move on to the next one. And then there are dozens of kids, with their faces pressed up against a chain link fence, watching the show. They're our cheerleading section. They're also in our pockets for candy. One kid told me he doesn't eat the chocolate but uses the Hershey bars for trade. He was about ten years old, and he was smoking!"

After a few more stories, Greg tapped his watch to let us know he had run out of time. He was flying the plane that night to Iceland and then on to Labrador and finally to a base in Nebraska that he hoped would be its final resting place.

***

After retraining on a C-54 in Montana, Greg, along with other squadrons from bases around the world, returned to Germany. Originally, all of the planes flew out of Tempelhof in the American Sector and Gatow in the British Sector, but with additional supplies needed for the upcoming winter, a third airfield was critical. Working around the clock, 20,000 German men, women, and children, under the direction of the Western powers, cleared and built the airfield at Tegel in the French Sector in only sixty days. With the completion of the French runway, the Russians realized the Airlift would continue indefinitely, and on May 12, 1949, the Soviets reopened the land routes into the city.

With assistance from the Air Forces of Australia, South Africa, and New Zealand, and with volunteers from Canada, flights continued through September in order to ensure adequate supplies for the Germans of a free Berlin. This was an incredible achievement for all concerned, but for the British, who were still clearing debris caused by German bombs, it was nothing short of remarkable.

***

On the train to London following our visit with Greg, I asked Rob why he had never mentioned me to his family. I wasn't thrilled with the answer because I learned that Rob had yet another girlfriend in his past. It was beginning to look as if I was just the latest of a string of women who lasted as long as Rob stayed in town.

"When I lived in Atlanta, I dated a girl named Arlene," Rob explained. "I made the mistake of mentioning her in a letter home. The next thing I know, I get a letter from Mom, and it's twenty questions time. I decided that I'd tell them about you when I had something definite to say."

"Do you expect that at any time in the near future you will have something definite to say to them?" I was so hurt, and I could hear it in my voice.

"Maggie, right now everything's up in the air. I'm going hiking in Wales next week with Jake from the office. I'll use the time to plan my next step. Remember, I'm from out West; things move a little slower out there." Taking my hand in his, he said, "Please don't read anything into this business about Arlene. It was never serious."

But I had to know if Rob was serious about me because now there was a deadline. He had been officially notified that his assignment in England would terminate on 30 August 1948, which was only ten weeks away. With the way things were going, it seemed as if Rob would return to Atlanta in September, and I wondered if our relationship would end when we said good-bye on a Liverpool pier.

It all came to a head in Mrs. Dawkins's parlor. After five days of hiking in the mountains of Snowdonia, Rob's big decision was that he was going to pursue an advanced degree in engineering. He would have to move quickly, as all of the schools were overcrowded because of hundreds of thousands of servicemen going to college on the GI Bill of Rights. Nothing was said about our relationship.

I sat perfectly still. I knew if I said anything, I would start crying. As deeply hurt as I was, I was not surprised. I didn't know what Rob McAllister had been like before the war, but his war experiences had left him with a reluctance to make any decision that affected anyone other than himself. Although he had leadership qualities and the intelligence to lead, he abdicated those responsibilities to others. In that way, no one would be hurt, or in the extreme, die because of a decision he had made. It also extended to his personal life in his unwillingness to commit to me.

When I finally found my voice, I told Rob that whatever his plans were, they obviously didn't include me, and there was no point in continuing a relationship because he would be returning to the States in a few weeks. I asked him to show himself out, and I went upstairs. I heard him call out, "What's that supposed to mean?" but I continued up to my room.

From the third floor, I could hear Mrs. Dawkins asking Rob what all the ruckus was about, and then I heard them go into the kitchen. Ten minutes later, Rob was knocking on my door. If I hadn't been so depressed, I would have been in a panic because Rob was above stairs.

Whispering through the door, he said Mrs. Dawkins had said it was okay to come up, but I truly didn't want to talk to him. I came from a hard-drinking town and saw more than my share of unhappy marriages, including my parents'. Early on, I had made a decision that I didn't want to be in a relationship that was anything less than ideal. In this case, the hard truth was that Rob's feelings did not equal mine.

After work on Monday, Rob was waiting for me outside the AES offices, and he asked if I would walk with him to the park. Sitting on a bench in Hyde Park, I looked at the ground littered with fallen petals of some unidentified flower. In another week, they would be replaced by the blooms of midsummer. Rob sat next to me in silence. If he was hoping I would be the first one to speak, he was going to be disappointed. But then I realized he was trying to figure out a way to say what was on his mind. After several minutes, he finally spoke.

"When I returned to the States in March '45, I went to Boca Raton, and a bunch of us would go to the clubs in Miami Beach. As far as the people in Miami were concerned, and the same thing later when I went to Los Angeles, the war was over. Patton was across the Rhine, 300,000 German troops had surrendered, the air war over Germany was winding down, so it was party time. It's true the worst of the fighting was over in Europe, but what about the Pacific? Everyone's dancing while Marines and sailors were dying by the thousands in the battle for Okinawa.

"It was the same thing when I went home on leave. I met guys who had been discharged from the Army, and they had never seen one minute of overseas service. The Army decided it was a waste of money to deploy them even though there were tens of thousands of guys who had seen plenty of combat, who didn't have enough points to go home. Did that make sense?

"I couldn't relax. Everyone was pissing me off. My neighbor tells me he's going crazy because of all the overtime he's putting in for the railroad. I flew three missions in six days, and he's complaining about making overtime. My dad keeps asking, 'What are you going to do with your college education?' I hadn't even been discharged at that point.

"It was worse in Atlanta. By then the war was over in the Pacific, and the newspapers and radio ads were all saying, 'We're looking to the future.' Great. Fine. But what about the guys in the VA hospitals or the families of flyers who were getting letters from the War Department informing them that their son's body had finally been located in a cemetery in Germany, and what did they want to do with the remains? I was angry ninety percent of the time.

"And then I met you," Rob said, turning to face me. "You're living in that tiny attic apartment, sitting in front of a space heater trying to keep from freezing, and sharing rationed food with your landlady. The very first time I saw you, you told me you were wearing the same skirt you had worn for the last four years, but what did I think about your new red blouse? What I thought was, I'm going to take this girl back to my flat and make love to her all night long. I was falling for you even before we got to Mrs. Dawkins's house."

I slid along the bench and sat next to him, taking his hand in mine. I understood why Rob wanted to live in England. The

British were still confronted with daily reminders, not only of what had been won, but also what had been lost. Rob wanted people to remember just how much had been sacrificed.

"Maggie, how can I plan a future with you when I seem incapable of putting together a plan for the next year, no less for a lifetime?"

I could see how unhappy he was, but I had to tell him what was on my mind. "You are hurting because you think the world has moved on when so many people are still suffering. But, Rob, people are not designed to be noble. Our basic instincts are to survive, and part of surviving is standing up, dusting yourself off, and getting on with it. Although I can't stand in your shoes, I understand what you are feeling. I've visited seriously wounded friends at Walter Reed Hospital, and I've been to too many funerals of friends and relatives." Taking a deep breath, I continued, "I love you. But if you are expecting me to wait until all of the hurt has passed, I can't do that, and I won't let you shut me out." Because he was staring at his hands, I couldn't gauge the effect my words were having on him. "What I'm trying to say is, we are in this together or we're not. Either we start a life together, or we say good-bye. That's not a threat. It's just the way it has to be."

I asked him to walk me to the Underground but not to see me home. I told him I loved him and kissed him good-bye, and then I went down into the station alone.

Chapter 25

THE NEXT DAY AFTER work, Mrs. Dawkins knocked on my door, and I was certain she was going to tell me that fights between lovers were not allowed in her house. Instead, she asked if she could have a word with me.

"You and your fellow have had a bit of a dust-up, haven't you?"

"It's not a dust-up, Mrs. Dawkins. It's a breakup. It didn't work out." I was really depressed, and I didn't want to have this conversation.

"Rob's a good man," she told me. "You don't let the good ones get away. There aren't enough of them around."

Because I saw so little of Mr. Dawkins, I couldn't even guess what their marriage was like. I did know that she ate dinner with him every weekday night at 11:00 when he came home from his shift, and because of his hearing loss, she always kept a notepad in her apron pocket to write things down so she wouldn't have to shout at him. Sitting down on the bed, she said, "I'd like to tell you something if you're of a mind to hear it." This was a side of Mrs. Dawkins I hadn't seen, and I couldn't imagine not listening to her.

"Even though my dad had a good job, my mother always rented out this room, your room, for what she called pin money. In 1934, Mr. Dawkins moved in. His wife had died, and he didn't want to live alone. His hearing's quite bad because he was an artilleryman in the First War. He can't tell how loud he's talking, so we always kept paper in the kitchen for us to write each other notes. After he'd been here about a year, he writes me a note, which I'm thinking is how he wants his eggs cooked. But on it says, 'Will you marry me?'" Snapping her fingers, she said, "Just like that. I didn't even know he was interested in me.

"Now, deaf as he is, Mr. Dawkins is not a bad-looking man. He had a decent job, didn't drink, went to church every Sunday, and paid his rent on time. But, I'm thinking, he's twelve years older than me. I was twenty-seven at the time, a very plain girl to be sure, but I hadn't given up all hope of falling in love. But I said 'yes' anyway. Do you know why?" I shook my head. "Because he's a good man, and that's a rare bird for sure. I've never had any regrets, and you've seen how the children run to him when he comes downstairs. I can't give Rob a higher compliment than saying, 'He's a good man,' and you are a kind, sweet girl, and you deserve him. I've seen the way he looks at you. Don't give up on him."

Mrs. Dawkins was not given to displays of emotion, but when she kissed me on the top of my head, it opened a floodgate. She didn't say another word but continued to hand me one Kleenex after another until I could finally stop crying. After that, I went to the nearest pay phone and called Beth. I told her what had happened with Rob, and she asked, "Do you want to come here, or shall I come to London?" I told her that I would prefer to get out of the city.

Beth met me at the Stepton station in her Aston Martin convertible with the top down. Handing me a headscarf, she told me to climb in. "When my father was dying from throat cancer—the cigars got him in the end—he said he was leaving me this car and asked that when I drove it to think of him, and I do every time." Without any detours, we quickly reached the house, and Beth said, "We are quite alone. Jack has gone to Sheffield with Freddie to pick up some hardware for Montclair. So it's just we girls."

Beth had lunch already prepared, and I set the tray down on the coffee table in the living room where we ate bread and butter sandwiches and drank tea. I told Beth what had happened, and afterwards, I had a good cry, not just about Rob, but about being so far from home. I was missing my mother so much that I was ready to book passage to New York as soon as the ship's office opened on Monday.

After listening without interruption, Beth sat quietly for a long while. Finally, it seemed that she had come to a decision, and then she said, "I'm not one to air my personal history unless it will serve some purpose. But Jack had problems, which I compounded, and I don't want Rob and you to fall into the same trap. So if you will allow me, I would like to share some things that may be of help in your understanding Rob.

"When Jack came home from France, he enrolled in a post-graduate program in engineering at Manchester, and he would come home to Montclair on weekends. He was never comfortable living above stairs, and I didn't blame him. It was a damned depressing place in those years right after the war. With Trevor, Matthew, and Tom gone, and Reed in and out of hospitals, a pall fell over the house.

"There was some joy in our lives. James was born in 1920, and Michael arrived in 1922. So we had two young children scampering around the house, but Tom's death was an open wound for Jack. He found it impossible to heal with my mother reminding everyone of what the war had cost her personally."

Beth looked at the clock and said, "It's gone noon, so I'm going to have a Royal Blackla." She poured a whiskey for herself and asked if I would like one. Even though I didn't like the taste of the stuff, I nodded, and Beth made a whiskey and soda for me. "I don't drink all that often, but when I do, I take my whiskey neat."

Returning to the sofa and pulling her legs up under her, Beth continued. "Next thing I know, Jack tells me that he has been offered a job building railway bridges in India. I agreed to go, thinking the job would last for two or three years. Jack worked for the railway company for ten years.

"In '34, he contracted malaria, and we returned to England for about fifteen months. It was a very good time for Jack and me, and the boys were so glad to be with their father. But by the time he was ready to go back to work, there was little work to be found because of the Depression. That's how we ended up in Argentina. A large percentage of the country's railways were controlled by British firms, and they wanted to protect their investments. Because Argentina had also been hit hard economically, the job involved mostly supervising maintenance work.

"Buenos Aires has a large British colony, and I felt as if I was back in England, circa 1910. All the upper-class b.s. I had left behind was alive and well in Argentina. The only person who disliked it more than I did was Jack. I didn't realize how much he hated his job, and he didn't enlighten me. And me? I made a lot of wrong assumptions that very nearly ended our marriage.

"One evening, while attending a company party, Jack's boss, who was three sheets to the wind, came up and slapped him on the back and said, 'Jack's the best. He's the only one who doesn't complain when we send him to some god-awful hellhole. He's even volunteered to go to some of these dumps.' That statement opened my eyes. In India and Argentina, I could rarely visit Jack at his job sites because of disease or unrest or other dangerous situations. Now I believed that Jack had asked for these assignments for the very reason that they were so inaccessible. I was wrong, but that's what I believed at the time."

A look of resolution came over Beth's face. "I decided that if I wasn't wanted, I bloody well could be unwanted in England. At least I would be with my sons. I told Jack that I was returning to England to help his mother care for his father, who was in decline because of heart problems. On the long trip home, all I could think about was what a sham our marriage had been.

"In late 1938, all eyes were on Germany, which, once again, was beating the war drum. For Great Britain, a country that had lost 700,000 men in a war with Germany, there was an underlying panic that it could happen all over again. When Hitler threatened war over the Sudetenland, Britain signed a pact agreeing to the separation of that region from Czechoslovakia, which then became a part of a greater Germany.

"Neville Chamberlain has been vilified for the concessions he made to Hitler at Munich regarding the Sudetenland, but I can tell you he would have been strung up by his toes in Trafalgar Square if he hadn't done just that. People forget that Chamberlain was met by cheering crowds at Heston Airfield when he returned from the Munich conference. The British did not want another war. The French did not want another war. But we were going to get one because now Hitler was talking about Poland.

"Jack was still in Argentina when war was declared in September '39. When he arrived at Crofton Wood shortly before Christmas, I had not seen him for half a year, not since his father's funeral in May. Jack got a job right away because England was rapidly converting civilian plants to military uses. He was even busier in 1940 with the Battle of Britain, trying to repair infrastructure faster than the Germans could bomb it. Then came the Blitz. I saw very little of him in the first half of '41.

"Jack had his own moment of clarity that year. He told me he would be away for weeks at a time because of the extensive damage done to England's industrial cities. I told him I expected that even though nearby Liverpool and Birmingham had been pummeled, it would be absolutely necessary for him to work in Southampton, which was as far away as he could get from Crofton and me. He just stared at me, but he didn't dispute it.

"In late '42, when the wounded started to come back to England from the desert campaigns in North Africa, I was working at a hospital in Sheffield as a nurse's aide, a Volunteer Aide Detachment. In the First War, we had a code of conduct that stated, 'Do your duty loyally; Fear God; Honour the King.' It was a simpler time. We dealt in moral and patriotic absolutes, which is why the country didn't scream bloody murder when 60,000 of our boys died in one battle with nothing to show for it.

"At first, I handed out coffee or tea and sandwiches to returning soldiers at train stations where the waiting rooms had been turned into reception centers, but after Jack went to France, I received extensive medical training at a London hospital and was assigned to the hospital ships sailing between Boulogne and Folkestone. The orderlies walked between double-tiered bunks asking, 'Where in Blighty do you live?' That's what they called

England—Blighty. They wanted to get the men to a hospital closest to their home.

"In February 1917, Jack was wounded when an ammunition storage facility exploded sending shrapnel everywhere. He was sent back to England with an infected arm. I received permission from my head matron to go to him, but only after producing a certificate of marriage. These matrons were tough, very tough, and they didn't tolerate any nonsense or fooling around from their volunteers. They cared so much for their patients, but frankly, until you proved yourself, they didn't give a shit about you."

As serious as the discussion was, I couldn't help thinking how different Beth was from the lady I had met the previous autumn. That Beth would never have said "shit" or drank whiskey "neat." I liked this Beth a lot better.

"After Jack was discharged from hospital, he was given two weeks' leave and two weeks of light duty, but I got only ten days because my time with him when in the hospital was considered to be leave. But it was a wonderful ten days. We went to Lyme Regis in Dorset right on the Channel. You might have read about it in Jane Austen's *Persuasion*. It rained most of the time, but we snuggled in bed or sat in the public room in front of a fire. After Lyme Regis, we'd see each other whenever we could, because I was working, and then he was back to France."

Beth stopped talking and started to rub her arms, as if these memories had brought on a chill of their own. "In April 1917, I was assigned to the hospital in a casino at LeTouquet that had been set up by the Duchess of Westminster. That's where I was when the guns went silent on November 11, 1918."

Suddenly stopping, Beth said, "My God, what a tangent I just went off on." Beth stood up and headed toward the kitchen.

"Let's get some coffee going." After returning with a fresh pot, courtesy of the Army Exchange Service, she continued her story. "What I started to say was that I had a particularly bad week at the hospital in Sheffield. After Freddie picked me up at the Stepton station, he insisted I come back to Montclair for a drink. Remember, at this time, Montclair was being used by the RAF as a retreat. I went into the drawing room, and Freddie introduced me as the 'Mistress of the Manor' to all the officers. I met a captain from the Royal Canadian Air Force."

I closed my eyes because I was afraid of what Beth was about to say.

"Maggie, you may open your eyes. I did not have an affair." I let out a sigh. I cared so much for Jack and Beth I didn't want to think either had been unfaithful. It was upsetting enough to learn their marriage had been so troubled. "But I came pretty close to it. But Peter was married and had a son, and his wife didn't deserve that. He missed his family, and I was very lonely after years of Jack being gone so much. Peter treated me with such kindness. We mostly talked, held hands, went for long walks, and kissed quite a bit, but it lasted all of seven days, and I never saw him again."

Looking at me, Beth asked if I thought less of her because of her flirtation, but after hearing about her life with Jack, I couldn't judge her. "No," I said, "I just wish it had been different."

Beth smiled and then continued, "I believe Freddie said something to Jack. As a result, we had our first serious discussion about our marriage." Beth stopped talking and looked out the window trying to think of the right words to use. "Jack told me that one of the reasons he took the job in India was because it was the only way he could provide for me in the same manner in which I had been brought up at Montclair. If we had stayed in England, he could never have afforded to hire nurses and governesses for the children or maids for me. The hurt I felt went to my very soul. I asked him if he truly believed that having servants was more important to me than having a husband. And what about his sons? They hardly knew him.

"After that, Jack came home more often. He started to tell me things he had kept bottled up inside, like the first time he realized he fancied me. This would be 1909, when I was sixteen years old. We were hosting the Harvest Ball, which was the premier event of the summer, for all of our high-society friends. When our guests arrived, it was Jack and Tom's job to assist the footmen in helping the ladies out of their carriages. Jack escorted Lady Lindsey to the ballroom because she was very old and frail. When he was going back to help the other guests, I was coming down the stairs, and it stopped him in his tracks. My father came over to him and said, 'No harm in looking, Jack, as long as you don't touch.' I'm sure my father meant it as a joke, but Jack took it to mean that no matter how good he was or how high he might rise, I was beyond his reach. That planted the seed that he would never be good enough for me.

"These discussions helped a lot, but there was so much that was simmering under the surface. Then the walls came tumbling down when Michael called. He had joined the Royal Air Force and had been assigned to a bomber base in Lincolnshire as a mechanic. We were so relieved, believing that was where he would serve out the war. However, when he called, he told me that he had orders for Burma. This is in October '44. I was sick to my stomach. By that time, everyone knew how the Japanese fought to the death and what they did to prisoners of war.

"I waited for Jack to come home. I was afraid of how he would react since he was already terribly stressed with James being in Italy. As soon as I told him about Michael, he broke out in a sweat and started to clutch at his throat because he couldn't breathe or swallow. He was having a panic attack. And then he started to rock back and forth, holding his head in his hands, and saying, 'They're going to get my boys.' And he looked right at me and said, 'Just like they got Tom and Trevor and Matt.' And there it was in plain sight, all the pain he had kept to himself for thirty years. When he was able to talk, everything that had been bothering him spilled out. It was true he kept his family at a distance because, in that way, it wouldn't hurt as much when I left him and took the boys with me. He was absolutely convinced I'd see what a 'mug' he was and would look for someone who was brought up like I was.

"Do you see where I'm going with this?" she asked with such concern. "There are as many ways to deal with the horrors of war as there are people. A lot of individuals talk about it and get it out of their system, but some cannot let go. Rob has seen his closest friend die right in front of him and others blown out of the sky. He needs help."

"Is that why Jack suggested we go to Bassingbourn?"

"Yes. He's afraid Rob will take the same wrong path he did. He doesn't want to think of him sitting on the edge of a bed twenty-five years from now crying about the loss of his friends."

"So what do I do?" I asked. Beth had stopped crying, and I had started.

"I'd like for Jack to talk to him. There are no guaranties, but I think at this point, Rob will understand we are concerned for his welfare. If anyone can reach Rob, it will be Jack. He's made that same journey."

***

The following morning, after breakfast, Beth told me Jack wanted to talk to me. I found him at the rear of his property next to the chicken coops, with his foot up on a fence rail, watching a border collie moving a flock of sheep from one pasture to another. It was this very scene that had inspired so many of Reed Lacey's drawings.

"When I was a lad, I could easily spend a part of an afternoon watching those dogs work. They're remarkable animals, incredibly intelligent." After a few minutes, he finally said, "Beth told me you and Rob have hit a rough patch."

I told him about what had happened in London and asked him what he thought.

"To tell you the truth, Maggie, it's more about me than Rob." Looking off into the distance, Jack said, "Beth told you that when I found out that Michael had orders for Burma, I had a panic attack, right?" I simply nodded. "Well, I didn't have a panic attack. I had a nervous breakdown." Switching legs on the fence rail, he continued. "All I could do was sit in my bedroom and look out the window while volunteers from the village worked in our Victory garden. I was supposed to be in Cherbourg working on repairing the harbor facilities, so the Allies could get war materiel to the boys fighting in France. Instead, I was crying on and off all day long with either my mother or Beth wiping my nose.

"It had been building up for quite a while. I knew from news reports that James's regiment was in the thick of it in Italy, but I thought at least my younger son was safe. And then came the call from Michael. After Beth told me about his new orders, I was convinced my boy was going to die in the Burmese jungles.

"Nightmares from the war that I hadn't had in ten, fifteen years came back. Jesus, they all came back," he said, massaging his temples as if that act would block out any unwanted images. "Picking up bodies and having them fall apart in my hands. Stepping on limbs. Being scared shitless during barrages."

Although I could see him only in profile, I knew Jack was fighting back tears. "I would never have believed I could fall apart like that, but I did. Michael came home on leave, and instead of me reassuring him everything would be all right, he reassured me. We went for long walks and talked about everything under the sun. He told me he wanted to be an engineer. He didn't say it, but what he really meant was, if he became an engineer, I would pay more attention to him. After Michael left, I realized that I couldn't help my own boys, but I could help someone else's by getting them what they needed to defeat those Nazi bastards."

Turning to look at me, he said, "Maggie, I've seen a B-17 up close. I know where the bombardier sits and how close he is to the navigator. When the flak hit the nose of Rob's Fortress, it didn't just kill Pat. It blew him to pieces, and Rob had to crawl over his friend's body to get to the switch." Looking at me to see if I understood, he continued, "I'm telling you this because, from conversations I've had with Rob, I don't think he has dealt with what happened over Stuttgart or on the other twenty-nine missions. After the last mission, as far as he was concerned, he had tempted fate thirty times, and he wasn't about to take any more chances. I believe Rob was a cautious man before the war, and his war experiences have only made him more so.

"Rob's just drifting all over the place. If it weren't for you, he wouldn't have any anchor at all. If you and Rob do tie the knot, it's possible he will react much like I did. He'll keep everything buried deep inside, he won't talk about it, and he'll shut you out, just like I shut out Beth." Putting his arm around my shoulder, he said, "If you were my daughter, I'd have this very same conversation with you. But from this point on, if you want my advice, I'll wait for you to ask."

Now it was my turn to stare off into the distance. There wasn't anything Jack had said that I could disagree with. After our trip to Bassingbourn, I was hoping Rob would want to talk, but that hadn't happened. All of this wouldn't have mattered to me if I believed it didn't matter to Rob.

"You don't think we're going to get married. Do you?"

"I don't know," Jack said, shaking his head. "If he ever does open up to you, your support will be very important, but until that time, you're on the sidelines. Unfortunately, there's no way of knowing if he'll even let you in the game."

Chapter 26

WHEN I ARRIVED AT Mrs. Dawkins's house from Crofton on Sunday evening, my landlady handed me a bouquet of flowers that Rob had brought by the house, not knowing I had gone to see Beth and Jack. The card said, "Please be patient with me a little longer. I'm trying to get all of my ducks in a row. I love you, Rob." The expression of "getting his ducks in a row" was one Rob used frequently. What I had come to realize was that Rob had an awful lot of ducks.

On Monday, my boss, Don Milne, called me into his office. Both of us had been waiting for the other shoe to fall regarding our reassignments.

"Maggie, both of us have been granted a reprieve," he said with a big sigh. "I've been notified by Washington that because of what's going on in Berlin, the Air Force is sending three squadrons of B-29s to England, and I've been instructed to hold on to all remaining staff. By the way, we are now officially the Army and Air Force Exchange Service or AAFES." This was terrific news, and I jumped up and gave Don a big hug.

When I met Rob that evening, he didn't know what to say about my extension of employment at AAFES. It was obvious if something didn't happen to change the trajectory of our relationship, Rob would be returning to the States, and I would remain in England.

After thanking Rob for the flowers and note, I told him both of us were invited to Crofton after Beth returned from a visit to Scotland. Beth insisted no sensible person would spend a summer weekend in London if they had a choice. I always enjoyed visiting Derbyshire, but I also needed to return all of the letters Beth had allowed me to read regarding the Lacey/Garrison romance. After rereading all of the letters and Beth's notes, I had more questions than answers, and only Beth could clear things up. Rob agreed to go because he had never been to Crofton, and he really liked the Crowells.

Beth was right about living in London in August. It was bad enough at the office where AAFES had large fans running on high, but my attic bedroom sitter was stifling. Fortunately, London's long days of summer and beautiful parks provided the perfect setting for sharing sandwiches at 8:00 at night. I had not been to Rob's flat since our discussion in Hyde Park. Although I suspected Rob saw the lack of intimacy as punishment, I thought that to continue a physical relationship would give him the false impression that all was well.

Jack met us at the station and took the long way around to Crofton because this was Rob's first trip to Derbyshire. After showing Rob some of the countryside, he drove up to Montclair and pointed out all of the changes the Catons had made on the outside, including a working fountain.

"There's still a shortage of building materials. But I made some phone calls, and I was able to get new pipe for the fountain from a company that sells American surplus. You Yanks left behind enough supplies to build a good-sized town." Pointing his cigarette at the fountain, he said, "As kids, we were allowed to climb in there on hot days and splash around to our hearts' content."

When we arrived at Crofton Wood, Beth had prepared a casual tea that she was serving on the patio. She had just returned from the village, which was humming once again with visitors on their way to the Peak District.

After lunch, I returned the parcel containing all of the letters to Beth, and she asked me if I had any questions. I hesitated for too long, and she noticed I was uncomfortable. She put her arm around me and walked me into the house. "Tell me what's bothering you."

After telling her of my reservations, she said, "You think that the diary may be a forgery. Is that your concern? Well, let me put your mind at ease. It is not a forgery. To the best of my knowledge, the diary has never been outside of Montclair since Elizabeth's death."

"How is it possible that there are so many similarities?"

With a look of total confidence, Beth said, "Maggie, we have discussed every character in that book except one. Can you think who it is?"

I ran through all the cast of characters in my mind before realizing who I had missed: Georgiana Lacey. Beth nodded. "Yes, she's the last piece of the puzzle." I asked Beth if I was finally going to hear about the mysterious Mr. Oldham. "Yes," Beth said. "After this, you will know it all.

"Georgiana Lacey was a talented pianist, and her brother arranged for her to study with a master in London. Because it was necessary for his sister to remain in town, Will Lacey hired a companion for her, a Mrs. Brotherton, but if Georgiana wanted to do anything out of the ordinary, it required his permission. When Georgiana was just about seventeen, she wrote to her brother asking if Mrs. Brotherton and she could go to Weymouth, a popular bathing resort, and indicated in her letter that George Waggoner had offered to accompany them for their protection.

"Now, in Georgiana's defense, she knew nothing bad about Waggoner. What she did know was that he was the son of Montclair's steward and had been mentioned in her father's will. As soon as Will received the letter, he set off for London. After questioning his sister, he learnt that Waggoner had visited the townhouse on more than one occasion, so Will immediately discharged Mrs. Brotherton. We know all of this because Mrs. Brotherton wrote to Will asking to be reinstated. She explained that Georgiana had assured her that Waggoner was a friend of the family. When Waggoner offered to escort them to Weymouth, Mrs. Brotherton insisted that Georgiana write to her brother for permission. They were awaiting his answer when Will arrived at the townhouse in person. Mrs. Brotherton said she had done everything that had been asked of her, and to be discharged in such a manner, was unfair.

"To his credit, Will relented and reinstated her. However, his subsequent action was completely over the top. He wrote to George Bingham, asking if he could hire one of his men. George was a wise man. He knew a young girl wouldn't want to be seen around town with some bewhiskered strongman. Instead, he sent Mr. Oldham, a handsome man in his mid-twenties, who was perfectly capable of protecting Georgiana. As long as Mr. Oldham was with her, Georgiana could travel to Kent or Derbyshire or Bath.

"When Will and Elizabeth married, Georgiana lived with them at Montclair and in London. Georgiana was delighted by her brother's choice of wife and shared the story of Lizzy and Will's romance with a group of women who attended a Bible study at the parsonage led by Charlotte Chatterton. Anne Desmet added what she knew, and I'm sure Mary Garrison told everyone about Lucy's elopement with Waggoner. She probably saw it as a morality tale. But there were two other women in this group, a Miss Knatchbull and a Miss Leigh, both cousins of Jane Austen."

Beth handed me a letter from Will to Anne in which he acknowledged that parts of *Pride and Prejudice* were a retelling of his courtship of Elizabeth Garrison. Will, Elizabeth, and Charlotte all seemed to be pleased with Jane Austen's description of them and the events recorded in the novel.

13 September 1813

Dear Anne,

I was glad to hear that Col. Devereaux was able to be with you for Christmas. When next you see him, ask him why he was not defending us against Monsieur Bonaparte instead of dancing in Bath.

Yes, I have read Miss Austen's novel. As you can imagine, Elizabeth is the most pleased with it, as she appears in the best light. My wife has assured me I am not nearly as boorish as portrayed and that I have improved greatly under her instruction. Jane also admires it, as she is quite happy with how Elizabeth and her husband are described.

Jane's daughter, Miranda, says the novel is talked of everywhere in London and it has prompted a guessing game as to the identities of its characters. Of course, no one thinks to look back twenty years. Once we recognized ourselves in the story, it prompted our own investigation as to how Miss Austen came to know of our affairs. We finally traced the source to my sister. Georgiana admits she is one of the sources and has no regrets for sharing the story with a group of women whom she knew in Kent. She feels she has additional protection because, apparently, you were not only there when these stories were being told but provided some of the information.

I wonder if your little group would have been so willing to share stories if you knew that two of the ladies present were cousins of a talented novelist. I am teasing you because, with the passage of twenty years, who will ever learn the names of the people who inspired the author? Of course, the description of your mother's behaviour is devastating but not undeserved, and more than anyone else, you are the most inaccurately portrayed.

Elizabeth and all the children are well. The only complaint comes from Franny who misses Chris terribly now that he and Laurence have returned to school—one of the disadvantages of being a twin. Georgiana, Nathan, and Stephen were with us during the holidays, and as talented a pianist as Georgiana is, her son outshines her. His fingering is amazing to watch. As for Phoebe, unlike her older sister, she is very sociable and talks of nothing other than her coming out into society. Despite her pleadings, she will have to wait until she is eighteen. Of course, to a sixteen-year-old girl, two years seem an eternity, but you and I know how quickly the years pass. I can hardly believe that it has been twenty years since I took my lovely wife as my bride.

Elizabeth sends her love. We will send word of our arrival date in Bath, as soon as our plans have been finalized.

Your devoted cousin,
Will

"Now that you know it all, you can appreciate what a master storyteller Jane Austen was. She took a moderately interesting story and turned it into a timeless novel."

I must have still looked confused, so she continued: "Let me give you an example of how Miss Austen spun straw into gold. In *Pride and Prejudice*, Darcy comes upon Georgiana just as Wickham has persuaded her to elope with him, and his intervention prevents the ruin of his sister. The truth is that Georgiana never left London and would never have married Waggoner without her brother's consent. I'm sure if Mrs. Brotherton were alive in 1813 and had read *Pride and Prejudice*, she would have been horrified to see her character portrayed as the complicit Mrs. Younge."

"What did happen to Georgiana?" I asked.

"Remember Mr. Oldham? He went to Will and resigned his position as Georgiana's protector. He said if Georgiana had ever been vulnerable to the likes of someone like Waggoner, it had long since passed. Because he had developed an attachment for her that was not appropriate to his job, he had to give up his position, and Will accepted his resignation. But when Georgiana found out about Oldham, she told her brother that she loved him.

"Will wouldn't have been all that surprised because Georgiana had accompanied Lizzy and Will on their honeymoon, which lasted more than a year. When the party returned to England, Georgiana asked that Mr. Oldham be reinstated, and in doing so, she had tipped her hand. After marrying, they lived in London at the Lacey townhouse, and Nathan Oldham started his own, for want of a better term, detective agency."

When Beth finished telling me about the Oldhams, I realized I had heard the stories of all the actors in Jane Austen's novel. The only part of the larger story that had not been told was about Beth's brother Reed, and I would have to accept that. I was thinking about all of this when Beth said: "Maggie, you have been very considerate in not asking personal questions, but if you don't mind, I would like to tell you about my family." Jack came and sat down next to his wife on the sofa, and Rob came and sat on a chair near me.

"Years from now, your generation will divide events into things that happened before Pearl Harbor and those that happened after. The demarcation line for my generation is 1914.

"Christmas of 1913 is one of my most cherished memories. We were all at home for the holidays. The servants came to the breakfast room for our traditional holiday tea, and we had such a good time. Jack and I had fallen in love during our summer auto tour visiting the sites mentioned in *Pride and Prejudice*, and if for no other reason, I am grateful to Jane Austen for writing her novel.

"None of us could possibly have imagined our world would self-destruct in 1914. There had been saber rattling all summer among Britain, France, and Germany. However, when Archduke Ferdinand was assassinated, we didn't know that that event would lead to the ruin of so many lives.

"Trevor enlisted a few weeks after the war started and

was killed at the Battle of Loos in September 1915. Matthew and Tom joined the Sherwood Foresters with many of their friends from the Crofton football club. So many of them were killed on the Somme in 1916, that there was black bunting on almost every door in Crofton. Matthew's remains were never recovered, but he is commemorated on the Wall of Remembrance at Thiepval in France, and Tom is buried in a cemetery nearby.

"My youngest brother, Reed, was not called up after his first physical, but as time went on and England needed more cannon fodder, he was accepted into the Army. He served as an orderly in Boulogne loading stretcher cases onto boats taking them to England. He might have been all right if he had remained an orderly. However, when the Germans broke through the British lines early in 1918, General Haig issued an order that every person must do his duty. Matron told us we would remain at our posts and do ours because, if the Germans weren't stopped in front of Amiens, Britain would lose the war. Reed was in combat for only a short time, but it was enough. He was sent back to England to a mental hospital.

"Reed eventually ended up at Craiglockhart in Scotland. The head of the hospital, W.H.R. Rivers, was a visionary who had taught experimental psychology at Cambridge. In other hospitals, many shell-shock victims were treated with drugs or electroconvulsive therapy, but Dr. Rivers believed the best results might be achieved by talking to these poor souls.

"After Craiglockhart, my parents placed my brother in a private hospital near home, and he improved enough to be discharged to their care. When they brought him home to Montclair, he couldn't stand the sound of so many noises that are part of everyday life. If someone dropped a glass, or he heard a car on the road, he huddled in a corner. But the worst sound was a train whistle. Jack thinks it's because assaults or artillery barrages often started with an officer blowing a whistle. When Reed was unsettled, he would move furniture in front of his bedroom door. And there were relapses."

At this point, Beth stopped talking. She leaned back in her chair, and for a minute or two, she sat quietly. Although it was clearly an effort to continue, she did.

"My Aunt Ginny's in-laws had a hunting lodge west of Perth, and she suggested that my parents see if Reed would do better there. It was very remote, being used only a few times a year for fishing and grouse shooting. The estate was owned in common by the Burdens, and several of the families, including my Aunt Ginny, had their own cabins. She offered her cabin to my parents for Reed's use. The Burdens employed a full-time gillie, Mr. Lachlan, who managed the estate. He and his wife agreed to look after my brother when my parents were not able to be there. Reed did improve, especially after my father returned from Montclair with six of our dogs.

"I had been corresponding with Margie Loftus, the nurse who had been in charge of my training at a London hospital. I asked her for suggestions because she had such a calming effect on the wounded men in her care. Margie was Scots by birth, and she wrote back asking if the family would consider hiring her as Reed's personal nurse. My mother interviewed Margie, who was ten years older than my brother, and came away feeling that Reed would benefit from her experience and care.

"The people in the nearest village were very kind, but in such a conservative society, a woman did not live with a man unless they were married. So, for about a year, Margie lived at the lodge while Reed stayed alone in the cabin. Not the best arrangement. It was Margie who suggested that she and Reed marry. In that way, she could take care of him by herself, allowing my parents to resume some semblance of a normal life. They got married in 1924. By that time, Reed could not have lived without Margie, and he was so happy she wanted to be married to him.

"It was then that my parents gave up Montclair. I had no objections because I was haunted by the memory of my brothers running up and down those staircases or racing in the long gallery. The house had become unbearable for me.

"After Reed's marriage, Jack, the boys, and I went to India and visited whenever we were home. Margie came up with the idea of building a stone-wall enclosure. She hired some local lads from the village to collect the stones. After hundreds of stones had been collected, Reed and Margie began to build the wall, which was only about four-feet high. He believed that as long as he was within the wall, he was safe, even if Margie wasn't with him. This was so important because it allowed Margie to go into the village and to have some time for herself.

"It was such a success that additions were made. They built the wall so that it ran down to a nearby stream. Now Reed could go fishing, which was something he loved to do. After they added a gate, Reed felt comfortable enough to walk down to the road.

"In 1936, Margie was diagnosed with cancer. Reed knew something was wrong, and he told Margie he would now take care of her, which he did to the best of his ability until her death early in '37. By this time, both of my parents were gone, so my Uncle Jeremy stayed with Reed until I could get home from Argentina. I practically got on my knees begging him to come live with us at Crofton Wood, but he told me he was going to stay right where he was. He said, 'Although Margie is gone, this is my home.'

"The boys and I spent most of the summer with him, and James and Michael helped Reed add rocks to his wall. They thought it was a game and great fun. I was supposed to go back to Argentina in September, but I couldn't leave. My gut told me to stay in England. I visited frequently that autumn, and he was doing all right. But once the colder weather came, I again asked him to come to Crofton to stay with Jack's parents and me until spring, as the cabin was absolutely freezing. Reed assured me that he had made arrangements for coal to be delivered from town.

"Mr. Lachlan and I spoke once a week. In November when I called, Mr. Lachlan told me he had good news. When delivering Reed's grocery order, Reed had given him a sketch of a glen on the far side of the stream. In order to make that sketch, Reed had to have gone outside the stone wall. The next week, Reed went out to the glen again. Mr. Lachlan warned him that the weather was getting too cold for him to be out and about on his own. With the shorter days, if he got lost or hurt, he would die from exposure.

"Shortly after his warning, Mr. Lachlan was awakened by Reed's dogs barking. After checking the cabin, he immediately returned to the village and got some of the men to help him look for my brother. It wasn't difficult, as the dogs led them right to him. He had been making sketches of the glen at sunset. He had all of his sketchbooks and pencils with him and a kit containing his lunch and a thermos full of tea."

After trying to control her tears, Beth brought her hands up to her face and started to cry in heartbreaking sobs. Jack said nothing but wrapped his big arms around her. I saw at that moment what Rob so admired about the English after having lived among them during their darkest hours. After a few minutes, Beth took out her handkerchief and dried her tears.

"I know what people think about Reed," Beth said after regaining her composure. "But I don't believe it. He found the courage to go beyond the stone wall, which meant he had at last beaten back the demons that haunted him."

Jack was staring at me, afraid I would say something that should not be said. I went and sat next to Beth, "I don't believe it either," I said, hugging her. "I've always imagined heaven as a place where we exist in God's grace with all those we have loved, so Reed and Margie, your brothers, and your parents are together again." Beth nodded, and Jack looked at me with relief and thanks.

Running her hands over imaginary wrinkles in her skirt, Beth stood and took me by the hand. "Now I would like for you to meet my family and Jack's. I want you to think of them as they were when we were so blest, before that awful war."

On a rear table in the study were numerous family pictures, including a photograph of Jack's parents. If a casting call had gone out for a butler and housekeeper in the early part of the twentieth century, the Crowells would have gotten the parts— stoic, resolute, and capable. There was a picture in a dark brown leather frame of Tom Crowell in his Army uniform. He was even more handsome than his brother, and there was a look about him that let you know he was proud to be serving in the Sherwood Foresters Regiment.

Hanging above Jack's desk was a family portrait painted at Montclair in 1923 of Jack and Beth and their two little boys, who were dressed in sailor suits. On the opposite wall was a portrait of all the Edward Laceys dressed formally for the Christmas holidays. Beth and her mother sat in chairs in elegant evening gowns surrounded by the men of the family. There was a look of command in Lady Lacey's eyes, and Sir Edward Lacey looked every inch the country gentleman. Reed, who was about fourteen at the time, had his hand on his sister's shoulder, a shoulder he had probably leaned on most of his life. Looking at Trevor, there was no doubt why all the girls were after him; he was as handsome as any Hollywood movie star. Matthew had steel gray eyes and a look of absolute determination. It was almost as if he was trying to intimidate the photographer.

After that, Beth showed me a photo of Reed and Margie at their wedding party. Margie was short, with curly brown hair and crystal blue eyes, and Reed, the tallest and thinnest of the Laceys, towered over his new wife. His arms were around Margie, not so much hugging as clinging to her.

In an upstairs room, where Beth and Jack had sorted through all of the many documents, diaries, and letters, was a long table covered with a white linen cloth. On it lay a dozen or more miniatures of all the people I had been reading and hearing about since I had first met the Crowells.

The first two miniatures were of the golden-haired beauty, Jane Garrison, when she was about twenty-five years old, and her husband, Charles Bingham. Except for slightly bulging blue eyes, he was handsome, with curly reddish hair and a very kind look about him.

Mary Bennet was as plain as Jane Austen had described her, with light brown hair pulled back in a severe style, and she wore no jewelry or any ribbons to soften the look. Beth had said that no portrait existed of Lucy, but there were four miniatures of Lucy's children. Antoinette and Marie were light-haired beauties, and the two dark-haired Edwards boys were as stocky as their half-sisters were slender.

Beth was right about Celia. She was beautiful, with her blonde hair encircled by a dark green ribbon and with long curls falling onto her bare shoulders. She must have been newly married to Tyndall Stanton. But I disagreed with Beth when she said her portrait showed a lack of intelligence. When Celia sat for her portrait, she was looking off into the distance to a place where her French lover was.

By this time, I had run out of table and portraits, but where were Lizzy and Will? We walked down the hall to one of the guest bedrooms, and in there, hanging on the wall over a large four-poster bed, were replicas of the portraits of Elizabeth Garrison and William Lacey that had once hung in the gallery at Montclair.

"When Montclair was sold," Jack explained, "the life-sized paintings of Elizabeth Garrison and William Lacey were put into storage. Once we bought this house, I had these smaller portraits painted as a gift for Beth. The Catons sent the originals to London for stretching and repairs, and just last week, they hung them in their original positions at the top of the staircase, and they are now on loan to the Catons."

At long last, before me stood Mr. Fitzwilliam Darcy of Pemberley. William Lacey was a good-looking man, with black hair and grey eyes, and I think if he had been smiling, I would have agreed with Elizabeth that he was the handsomest of men. Hand on hip, Will was dressed in cream-colored breeches, a green coat with a dark waistcoat, and an elaborate neckcloth, just as I had imagined.

And finally, "dearest, loveliest, Elizabeth." The portrait had been painted at the time of her marriage, so she would have been about twenty-two. She had hair as black as her husband's and dark brown eyes with long lashes. Her face was rounder than I had pictured it, but it seemed to add to the look of amusement the artist had captured. Her russet silk dress had a high waist, with the bodice trimmed in gold braid, and little gold tassels hanging from the short sleeves. In her lap was an embroidered lace handkerchief, bearing her initials, EGL. She wore a two-strand pearl necklace and pearl earrings, and on her right hand was a ruby ring.

Miniatures of their four children were on a nearby chest of drawers. All of the children were attractive, but Phoebe was absolutely stunning and looked more like her Aunt Celia than her mother. Jack had said that Phoebe "was a whole other story," and I could see why.

Looking at Elizabeth and Will's portraits, Beth said, "I'm sure we were no more or less interested in our relations than any family who has a famous person amongst their ancestors, but their association with the novel certainly added interest."

After leaving the room for a few minutes, Beth returned with a large book containing sketches of the terrace and gardens at Montclair. "As Mr. Ferguson explained on your tour, the grounds of Montclair were landscaped by Humphry Repton. As part of his presentation, Mr. Repton prepared what was called his 'Red Book' because of the color of its binding. By using overlays, he was able to show the owner the existing view and what it would look like after the work was finished." Looking at me, she said, "I would like you to have it." I had no doubt that the Red Book was very valuable. Surely it should stay with Beth and Jack and be given to their children.

"Maggie, I see what you are thinking, but please do accept it. I have other drawings from Repton and will gladly share them with my children if they should ever show an interest in such things. As for Montclair, I have the best of it in my memory and in my heart." At which point, Jack suggested we adjourn to the Hare and Hound for a pint.

***

When I came down for breakfast the next morning, the house was empty. Jack and Rob had left at dawn to go hiking in the Peak District, and Beth was on her knees working in the garden. Seeing me, Beth said, "Rudyard Kipling said that 'half a proper gardener's work is done upon his knees.' I have to say I agree with him." Wiping the dirt off of her pants, she said, "When the last war came, we quickly learnt how much of our food came from the continent. All of our onions were imported from Brittany, which had been overrun by the Germans. English food is bland enough, but without onions, it's positively tasteless, so you will always find onions in my garden."

Taking off her gloves and satisfied that there was no dirt on her pants, Beth said, "Let's go have some coffee. We'll have to give that instant coffee you brought a go because we are out of the real thing." While I put the kettle on, Beth washed her hands and then sat down at the kitchen table, grinning like the cat who had swallowed the canary.

"The Catons are giving a party to celebrate the reincarnation of Montclair, and Ellen has asked me to co-host. I have been itching to have a party ever since James got married. Having two sons, I knew I was never going to be the mother of the bride, but with James getting married in Italy, I wasn't really the mother of the groom, either. We were completely bowled over by the Paglia family. I was thinking you and Rob could be our special guests. You have become such an important part of our lives; I want everyone to meet you."

After all the Crowells had done for us, it seemed little enough on our part to agree to a party, and I told Beth that was fine. Beth reached over to the kitchen counter where she had a pad of yellow, lined paper that was already full with items for the party. It was then that she told me it would be a catered affair with live music, and formal attire would be optional.

"Formal attire? Whoa! I don't have anything formal." This was already out of my league, and she hadn't even gotten to the yellow pad yet.

"You don't have to worry about a thing," she said reassuringly. "I have at least a half-dozen formal dresses in my closet, and my mother's dressmaker, Mrs. Quayle, lives in Crofton. Although she's up there in years, she can still work a treadle. As for Rob, with some minor alterations, he can wear one of Jack's tuxedos."

Looking at my expression, Beth said, "Maggie, it's a celebration. This is a wonderful time in my life. I have my husband back, my sons are safe, I have a lovely daughter-in-law and a beautiful granddaughter, I've found a wonderful friend in you, Britain's on the mend. I could go on and on."

Taking the cup out of my hand and giving instant coffee a try, Beth said, "Oh, my. It tastes like the ersatz coffee we had during the war. But it will have to do." After taking another sip, she said, "Maybe not. This is worse than my coffee." Both of us started to laugh.

There was another reason that Beth was so pumped up. "Michael is coming home from Malta. I gave him the date for the party, and he was able to get one week's leave."

Michael and Rob together in the same room at the same time? Terrific! Beth was looking at me waiting for an answer. But what could I say except, "When do we go to see Mrs. Quayle?"

Chapter 27

AFTER AN INITIAL CRUNCH at AAFES, where I had been working a lot of overtime, headquarters approved hiring two girls, which eased my workload considerably. Although I would miss the extra money, I was glad to have the shorter workweek. I used my time to go for a long weekend up to Crofton, so I could get ready for the gala.

When I walked into the den, sitting in Beth's chair was Michael. Because he had to catch whatever flight was available from Malta, there was no way to know when he would show up in Crofton until his parents got the call from the Stepton station to pick him up.

"I'm going to make some coffee. Michael brought the real thing from Malta," Beth said with a lilt in her voice. Tomorrow night she would have all her family together, and she was riding high.

He immediately jumped up and shook my hand. "It's good to see you again, Maggie. Are you ready for the big show?"

"Yes, but only because of your mother. I've never been to anything like this."

"Well, when you get right down to it, it's just a dance, except everyone wears nicer clothes." And then he continued, "I'm looking forward to meeting Rob. From what I hear, he sounds like he's a good Joe. Isn't that what Americans say? And he's an American, so that simplifies things. No arguments about where to live."

Jack tried to catch Michael's eye, but not before he had asked if an announcement was to be made at the ball. He had assumed we were getting engaged because we were his parents' special guests.

"No announcement. But Rob will be here tomorrow, so you'll have a chance to meet him."

While waiting for the coffee to perk, Beth said she had planned to serve sandwiches for dinner because she was unsure of what time James would be arriving. "James thought they would be in about 4:00."

"Which means 6:00," Jack added. Angela's tardiness had become a sore point with her father-in-law. Beth had asked Jack to exercise some patience since Angela came from a country where the rhythm was a lot slower, but he wasn't buying it. As far as he was concerned, Angela was living in England, and she had better pick up the pace.

"Forget sandwiches," Michael said, standing up. "Why don't we just go down to the Hare and Hound? We can leave a note and let James know we've gone out."

The Hare and Hound was a typical English country pub. One side had a snooker table and dart board while the other side had a bar and lounge. There was a crowd gathered around the dartboard, and in the middle of it was Freddie, who waved to us with a fistful of darts in one hand and a beer in the other.

After our sandwiches were served, Michael asked his parents about the preparations for the gala. "How are the Catons managing it all without the army of servants?"

"Mrs. Caton has a contract with an agency, and they send her whoever she needs," his father answered. "You'll probably recognize a face or two from Crofton."

"Michael, wait until you see Montclair," his mother added. "The Catons have done a magnificent job in restoring it to the Regency Era. It's absolutely stunning."

"I've always thought that Montclair was beautiful, but, truthfully, I prefer Crofton Wood. It's much more intimate. What do you think, Maggie?"

"Well, I think I'd have to go with Montclair, but only if I don't have to dust it." And everyone laughed. "Actually, in Minooka, I shared a bed with my younger sister, so a step up for me would be having my own bedroom."

"But there are advantages to sharing a bed." After a long pause, he continued. "I mean, your hometown is in the mountains, and it gets cold in the winter, does it not?"

I nodded, but quickly added, "What's the weather like on Malta?"

"Hot and humid."

After that exchange, Michael started to play with his utensils and made a teepee with the forks and spoons. Beth looked at her son with a puzzled expression. Between his remark about sharing a bed and his tableware construction project, it was obvious something was not right.

"I might as well tell you now," he finally said, "my squadron is being sent to Lubeck to help with the Airlift. I won't be going back to Malta. My orders are to go directly to Germany." To which his father said, "Christ."

"Listen, Dad. I'm not crazy about going to Germany either. But the RAF and the Americans have been flying supplies into Berlin around the clock for more than two months now, and I don't see it stopping any time soon. The ground crews have been turning the planes around as fast as safety will allow. With all of these landings and takeoffs, it's rough on the planes, and the air and ground crews are exhausted. There will be accidents if the crews don't get a break. So it makes sense for our squadron to go to Germany instead of just sitting in Malta protecting sea lanes to an empire that really doesn't exist anymore.

"Since I'm due to be discharged in November, I'll be working on the integration of British and Commonwealth crews that are already arriving from Australia, New Zealand, and South Africa." Jack said nothing, so Michael continued, "Six weeks, Dad. That's what we're talking here. Just six weeks before I'm out of the service."

On the drive back to Crofton Wood, no one said anything until we pulled into the driveway. When Jack saw James's car was still not there, he said, "Bloody hell! He never got here. How long does it take a woman to pack a bag for a weekend?"

***

As soon as I came downstairs the following morning, Michael asked if I would like to go for a walk. "The weather's perfect, so my mother has suggested we walk up to the gazebo. It's on the highest point on the Montclair property and provides a spectacular view of the valley."

"You should go, Maggie," Beth said. "You can see all the way to Stepton, with all of its church spires."

Once we stepped outside, Michael turned and said, "Our going for a walk was Mom's idea, and if you'd rather not because of Rob, I understand. But before we go back in, I wanted to thank you for being such a good friend to my mother. As for my father, he told me that he thinks of you as a daughter."

"There is no need to thank me," I said emphatically. "Your parents have been so kind to me from the very start. The first day I met them, they invited me to stay overnight."

"I would have extended the same invitation if I had been home," Michael said, smiling. Every time he smiled, I wondered how a guy who was every girl's dream could still be available.

Without acknowledging what he had said about Rob, I started walking toward Montclair on an old wagon road that ran deep into the property. It was little changed from the time when Beth's father was a boy before the age of the automobile. Deep ruts marked the passage of hundreds of wagons, and there were stiles in the stone walls, just as there had been in the days of Jane Austen when Lizzy used one on her walk to visit Jane at Netherfield.

"To answer your question, I know your relationship with Audrey didn't work out, but if it had, would you have been okay with her going for a walk with another man?"

"I don't know. It's been so long since I fancied myself in love—not since I lived in Australia—that I'm not sure how I would respond. And I take your point. You have reason to be cautious because, if it weren't for Rob, I'd have a run at you myself."

I didn't know what to say, so I kept walking. Although my relationship with Rob was on rocky ground, it seemed wrong to have a flirtation with Michael on one day and to meet Rob at the train station the next.

It was a gentle climb to the top where the gazebo was located in one of the loveliest spots on the property. In one direction, you could see clear across the valley to the boundary of the Peak District and the spires of Stepton's churches from the other. Although the long view was now interrupted by a number of country manors and farmhouses, it was easy to imagine Elizabeth and Will Lacey sitting alone or with their children admiring the view of their slice of Derbyshire.

"Mum told me she and her friends used to stage plays up here when she was a girl. However, while I was still in short pants, the Pratt boys had turned the gazebo into a fort with straw bales as the palisade. Dennis, the youngest Pratt boy, James, and I would have to storm the fort, and the older boys would pelt us with rocks, and on occasion, manure mixed with straw and made into 'shit balls.'" Laughing, he said, "You may hear some awful things said about the Pratts, and everything you hear will be true."

I turned around to face the manor house and its newly restored gardens. Looking at Montclair with the low autumn sun glinting off its windows, I asked Michael if he had any regrets that he had never lived above stairs in the manor house.

"None. When my mother tells stories of growing up there, it's as alien to me as India would be to you. Mum said her parents would often host what they called 'Saturday to Monday' weekends. It was a bit of snobbery because obviously you didn't need to work if you could stay through Monday. Do you know what the guests complained of the most? Boredom. They could ride, play tennis, shoot, go fishing, and yet, with everything there was to do and surrounded by all of this beauty, they were bored. I can't relate to that at all."

We started down the hill toward the village, and we decided to have an early lunch at the inn. When the owner brought the tea and sandwiches over to our table, Michael stood up and gave her a big hug. "My dear boy, where have you been? Your mother says you're stationed in Malta. Are you out of service, or are you just in for the gala at Montclair?" Mrs. Rivers was so happy to see him that she wouldn't let him answer. "Everyone is getting out their best dresses, and because of the war, we're taking them in instead of letting them out." Pulling on her own dress, she said, "I lost a stone during the war, but I've put half of that back on since I'm back in the kitchen. We have a full house every weekend. Even with the rationing, people are finding a way to get here, and that's with Chatsworth closed. If they ever open it again, there won't be a room to be had in the whole county."

Turning to me, she said, "And you and your young man are to be special guests, I'm told." Beth had introduced me to Mrs. Rivers when we had lunch at the inn one afternoon. "You'll be dining with the aristocracy, my dear. I saw Lord and Lady Bramfield and their son yesterday and Sir John Heslip. And if Lady Viola is feeling up to it, you'll have a countess as a guest. But she really is getting on in years." Seeing her husband waving at her, she said, "Oh, he'll be after me for running on with so many customers calling for their tea, but it was lovely to see you."

"Is Lord Bramfield the same person as Ginger Bramfield?" I asked after Mrs. Rivers left.

Michael looked surprised. "How do you know that?"

I didn't think I was telling tales out of school when I told him that his mother had used Ginger to make his father jealous so that he would agree to marry her. This was all news to Michael.

"It must be a family trait. If you want something badly enough, you go after it." After being quiet for a moment, he said, "Look at James and Angela. He stayed in that dusty village in Italy running errands for Angela's father for what, five or six months, before they could marry. He told me he didn't have a beer for three months until a mate brought a case down from Germany. Now that's true love."

I was trying not to compare James's willingness to do whatever it took to win Angela with Rob's decision that marriage should not even be considered until everything was just so.

Arriving back at the house, we could see James's Jaguar, courtesy of the Lacey Trust Fund, in the driveway. Beth had told me at breakfast that Ellen Manning, the mother of Trevor's daughter, as well as Beth's cousins, the Alcotts, were staying at Montclair because there was no room at the inn in Crofton. It was all very exciting. The clans were gathering for a big celebration, and Rob and I would be at the center of it.

Chapter 28

ON THE NIGHT OF the gala, I kept thinking about Elizabeth Bennet and how she felt when she was getting dressed for the ball at Netherfield Hall. She was wearing her favorite ivory-colored dress, and Jane had put a wreath of white flowers in Lizzy's hair. Beth had chosen my gown, a green dress with an accentuated bodice that complemented my dark hair and blue eyes. While Beth was putting up my hair, she told me stories of the Harvest Festival Balls of her youth, and it brought back wonderful memories of her parents and brothers.

Beth, who looked good in gardening clothes, was truly elegant in a simple black dress with a sequined jacket. She wore a beautiful pearl choker, a gift from her father to her mother on their twenty-fifth wedding anniversary. Extending her hand, she showed me the ruby ring Will Lacey had given to Elizabeth Garrison when they had become engaged. She must have fallen out of her chair when she saw that rock.

Once Angela was ready, Beth said we should go downstairs and meet our dates. I thought Rob was very handsome in a suit, but when he met me at the bottom of the stairs in his white tie and tuxedo, I could hardly believe this man was waiting to take Maggie Joyce from Minooka to the ball.

"You look beautiful," I told him, and he laughed and took my hand and kissed it. When we went into the living room, there stood the three Crowell men, who were as handsome a trio as I had ever seen. Putting out his cigarette, Jack said, "Let's get this show on the road, or the guests will be there before us."

All during the war years, the windows at Montclair had been covered with blackout curtains. But not tonight. Driving up to the mansion, I could easily imagine how it appeared to Elizabeth Garrison when she first saw Montclair more than one hundred fifty years earlier. Numerous torches lined the path to the entrance, and men dressed in livery were there to help ladies out of their cars, just as Jack had done forty years earlier. Inside, dozens of candelabra created the warm glow of a late summer's eve, while shadows from the wrought iron staircases cast intricate lace patterns on the walls.

This was to be a night of surprises, but I didn't think there would be a bigger one than the sight of Mrs. Caton, standing in the foyer, straightening Freddie's tie. When Freddie had seen all that Mrs. Caton had done to make Montclair shine, he had gone into the village and borrowed a jacket and tie from the owner of the Hare and Hound. This might possibly be the beginning of a beautiful friendship.

As Beth and I had planned, I asked Jack, James, and Michael to stand with Rob and me at the bottom of the staircase. Beth came down the stairs, just as she had done in 1909, when the sight of her had stopped Jack in his tracks. Their marriage had taken some real blows, but this was true love. He met her at the bottom of the stairs and whispered to her, "My beautiful bride." Both James and Michael nodded their heads, recognizing they were witnessing something very special. The evening was getting off to a very good start.

Beth had cast a wide net when she had sent out her invitations. My first introduction was to Constance Cornwallis-West, the Duchess of Westminster, and her husband, Captain Fitzpatrick Lewes. During The Great War, the Duchess had funded her own hospital in an abandoned casino in Le Toquet, France, and Beth had been a VAD assigned to her hospital. Following on the heels of the Duchess were Lord and Lady Alcott, and their three daughters, Lily, Iris, and Violet, and their spouses, and Miss Lettie Blessing, Beth's former lady's maid, who was dressed in her Sunday best. I met Lord and Lady Bramfield and Ellen Manning and her husband, Scott. Beth had to shout when she introduced me to a cadaverous Viscount Sterling, who looked like Ichabod Crane. He was escorting his beautiful third wife, Althea, who was at least twenty-five years his junior. Rob showed real excitement when he was introduced to Col. Mitchell Armstrong of Bomber Command who flew forty-two missions over Germany.

Rob and I had added a few names to the guest list, and I was so happy to see Rob's flat mate, Ken Burroughs, and my boss, Don Milne, and his date. Don had taken the same train up from London with Pamela and her husband.

"My mum's with the baby, and I'm the only one who can feed her," Pamela said, laughing. "If I stay too long, I'll start leaking, but I wasn't going to miss this for neither love nor money."

Don and Ellen Caton were joined by Don's son, Stephen, an Annapolis graduate, who had been critically wounded when the destroyer, the USS *Hammann*, had been sunk in the Battle of

Midway in June 1942. Mr. Caton had said that when he first saw Stephen at Bethesda Medical Center in Maryland, he thought his son was lost to him, but Stephen had fought back and returned to active duty before the Japanese surrendered in August 1945.

Another surprise was meeting Mrs. Ferguson, the wife of Montclair's grouchy gardener. Mr. Ferguson hadn't married until he was in his forties, and when he did, he shocked the village of Crofton by marrying Linda McDonnell, the daughter of a baronet, who shared his love of gardening. They lived in one of the apartments over the garages so they would be close to the gardens.

I was trying to remember all the stories Beth was telling me as the guests went through the receiving line because I knew that I would never see them again, and I was trying to take a snapshot of each person as they went by.

While the Crowells, the Catons, Rob, and I were meeting the guests, the Crowell sons were under strict instructions from their mother to make sure all the visitors were enjoying themselves. While James Crowell was circulating around the room, pulling at his starched collar all the while, most of the men thought it was their duty to make sure that his wife, who was wearing an ivory sheath that made her look like a Roman goddess, didn't lack for company. Angela's English was limited to a handful of stock phrases, but no one seemed to care.

Another lady who didn't have to worry about a lack of companionship was Eva Greene, Mrs. Caton's stepdaughter from a previous marriage. To use Freddie's word, Eva was a "smasher"—tall, blonde, blue eyes, great figure and smile, and in another century, she most definitely would have had to tuck lace into her bodice. She had most of the men, married or not, lined up to dance with her. But before the evening was over, it was obvious that she definitely had two favorites: Michael and Rob.

Mrs. Caton had asked Jack to say a few words before the ball got under way. In his booming baritone, he thanked his guests for coming. "There are many reasons why we are here tonight, but none of this would have been possible without Don and Ellen Caton." After waiting for the applause to die down, Jack said, "I grew up in this house, and I can honestly say it has never looked more beautiful than it does tonight." Mrs. Caton now had her reward for all of her hard work.

"Another reason is that we are among friends. We've been through a lot together. Britain's not completely recovered, which will be evident once you see the buffet table." Using a voice that was familiar to everyone who had listened to wartime BBC broadcasts, Jack said, "Grow your own vegetables, meats and fats are to be used sparingly, and eat your potatoes in their jackets." Everyone laughed. Even this crowd was familiar with rationing.

"There is a third reason," Jack said looking at me. "Beth and I had the good fortune to meet a young American whose curiosity about Montclair and its history led to a friendship that, I believe, will last a lifetime." And he introduced me, "Miss Maggie Joyce of Minooka, Pennsylvania."

"While in England, it was Maggie's good fortune to meet another American, a former navigator for the 8th Air Force, stationed at Bassingbourn during the war." Turning in Rob's direction, he said, "I'm afraid I'm going to embarrass you." Everyone was looking at Rob, waiting to hear what Jack had to say. "Rob McAllister left his home in Flagstaff, Arizona, and flew thirty missions over Nazi Germany and has the scars to prove it." Everyone burst into applause, and I thought, "There goes my makeup."

"One more thing, and then I'll shut up. I'd like everyone to raise a glass to all of the young people who served us so well in this last war, and I pray to God it is the last. There are too many to mention individually, but we know who you are and what you did. Please be upstanding." And raising his glass, Jack said, "To love, to family, to friends." After everyone emptied their glasses, Jack added, "Cut the ribbon. Let the games begin."

The band's first song, "Sing, Sing, Sing," had everyone on the dance floor and got the night off to a roaring start. Rob and I did a mean jitterbug to "Bugle Call Rag," as did Violet Alcott and Michael Crowell. Apparently, James had been teaching Angela how to swing because she was dancing her heart out. I had only a couple of dances with Rob because there were plenty of young ladies who got in ahead of me, especially Eva Greene. I danced with every man who wasn't in a wheelchair, as well as Freddie, who couldn't dance at all, but that didn't stop him. When the band leader announced the last dance, I looked for Rob, but he was nowhere to be found, nor was Eva. So the last dance, "Always," went to Michael. Instead of taking my hand, he put both of his arms around my waist and pulled me close to him. By that time, I was a little tipsy, and so I put my arms around his neck and laid my head on his chest. And nothing I had ever done seemed as right to me as being in the arms of Michael Crowell. But that last dance would set the stage for all that happened the next day.

***

When I came downstairs the following morning, the house was quiet. I found Rob drinking coffee and reading the newspaper in the garden. "Good morning," I said, still yawning. Rob and I had stayed at Montclair until the last of the guests had left at 3:00 a.m. I was so tired I had fallen asleep on the four-mile trip back to Crofton.

"It's afternoon."

"A little cranky, are we?" I said, taking a chair next to him at the patio table. "Where is everyone?"

"James and Angela left at dawn. Apparently, Julia doesn't travel well, and she was up all night. You just missed Beth, Jack, and Michael. They went up to Montclair to visit with Ellen Manning and the Alcotts. The Catons are having a late lunch for family members."

"Did you have a good time last night?" I asked.

"Yes, I did," Rob said, folding the newspaper. "But now that this shindig is out of the way, we probably should be talking about our next step. I've already booked a berth to New York for September 3rd, but I don't know what your plans are."

For me, this was a shot out of the blue. Rob had not given any indication he was ready to talk about the day after tomorrow, no less our future plans. "Before we start on my plans, may I ask what yours are?"

"Well, I have to go back to Atlanta. I figured I'd give TRC at least a month's notice. I'm not sure they'll need that much time, but it seemed like the right thing to do."

Apparently, step one did not include my going to Atlanta. "And after that?" I asked.

"Flagstaff. I want to spend some time with my family and then go on to California to see if I can get an interview with Boeing. I've heard they're hiring. The problem is, there's no place to live. Every apartment gets snapped up as soon as it's listed. I'll have to check all of these things out."

"And while you're going to all of these places, where am I?" This was the big one, and my heart was pounding because I didn't know what Rob was going to say.

"I assumed that you'd want to go back to Minooka, at least for a while, so that you could be with your family. You've been gone a long time."

"Go back to Minooka?" If only it was that simple. I thought about what would be waiting for me at home: a dying coal town, no jobs, my mean grandfather and alcoholic father, and the deciding factor, my brother, the one who hung my bras out the front window and told his friends when I was "on the rag." "Rob, I am not going back to Minooka until I know when I will be leaving Minooka."

"Is there any other reason why you would rather stay in England?"

I thought of saying something sarcastic about getting so used to post-war austerity that I wouldn't be able to adjust to America's prosperity, but I wanted to know what he meant by "any other reason."

"Maybe it's just me, but where I come from, a man does not flirt with another man's girlfriend when the boyfriend is in the same room."

"If you are referring to Michael Crowell, then I should object to all of the time you spent with Eva Greene. I didn't say anything because it was a party, and after Monday, there's a very good chance I will never see Michael again and you will never see Eva. So this is a non-issue." I should have left it right there, but I didn't. "You know what the issue is? You have plans for you, and you have plans for me. But you don't have any plans for us. And you know why? Because there is no 'us.'"

I had run this whole thing through my mind time and time again. I thought Rob's relationships with women spoke volumes. I thought about Alice in Flagstaff, whom he dumped as soon as he went into the Army, and then I asked him about Arlene in Atlanta, who got the heave-ho when he went overseas.

"Arlene?" Rob looked at me as if I had two heads. "What the hell does Arlene have to do with this?"

"I'm getting to that. How long did the two of you go out?"

"I don't know—three or four months. We enjoyed dancing and going to the movies. That was it."

"I assume the two of you were intimate?" Rob nodded. "And when you told Arlene you were taking a job in England, she was just fine with that. After all, you were just dance partners, right?" Looking at Rob, I said. "I bet she cried her eyes out."

This was getting nasty. I felt like a total bitch, but I kept going. "When you were in the hospital, how often did Millie visit you?" I asked.

"What is your point, Maggie?"

"You told me you and Millie had an understanding that your relationship would last only as long as you were stationed at Bassingbourn because Millie had a boyfriend in the British Navy."

"Yes, that was the agreement. I was not going to get serious with anyone because the odds of surviving twenty-five to thirty missions were not on my side."

"When you were in the hospital, did she visit you once, twice, a dozen times?"

Rob was getting annoyed, but he answered, "I was in two different hospitals. When I was at Bassingbourn, Millie came by most nights. After they decided I needed eye surgery, they sent me to Oxford to a specialist. It was more difficult for Millie to get there because she had to take a train, so I think she came to Oxford only twice."

"Rob, Millie was in love with you."

Now he was very annoyed. "If you're trying to make me feel guilty, it's not going to work. I made it very clear that as soon as I had flown all of my missions, I was hoping to be sent back to the States immediately and alone. That's when she told me she felt the same way because she was 'practically engaged' to this guy Derek."

"Rob, that didn't mean she hadn't fallen in love with you." My tone had softened, but I kept talking. "From what you've told me about Millie, she sounds like a nice girl, who would have been willing to go to see a friend in the hospital almost every night because you were nearby, but I'm having a hard time believing she would take a train to Oxford twice if she didn't have some very strong feelings for you. I know all about train travel during the war. It was like being crammed into a sardine can, smelling of sweat and smoke, and being pressed up against strange men, I had to keep my arms crossed and my knees locked together because of guys sticking their hands where they didn't belong. Millie made the effort because she was in love with you."

Before Rob could answer, a car pulled into the driveway, and our discussion came to an end.

"Maggie, when we get back to London, we'll finish this conversation." Barely controlling his anger, he said, "It's overdue."

Rob and I spent part of an uncomfortable two hours together before Jack drove him back to the train station in Sheffield. I was feeling perfectly miserable about what had been said, but I didn't see what else I could have done. Rob was leaving in three weeks to go back to the States, and I wasn't.

Chapter 29

THE LUNCHEON AT MONTCLAIR was very casual because everyone was still recovering from the previous evening, and its purpose was to allow everyone to relax and talk. Beth's Uncle Jeremy, who apparently hated parties, had come up from London. I had seen pictures of a young Jeremy Lacey, when his hair was black and his face unlined. Years of working outdoors as a geologist had given him the same look as an old tar coming home from the sea. Knowing that Rob was from Arizona, he sought me out immediately and was disappointed when he learned Rob had returned to London. "He escaped, did he?" he said with a smile. "I was hoping to have a discussion with him about his home state."

"I'm sorry he had to leave early," I said. "Something came up." That was the truth. I certainly hadn't planned to have a fight with Rob at Beth's house. "I'm a poor second choice, but I grew up in a small coal town in eastern Pennsylvania."

"What town?" he asked with genuine curiosity.

"Minooka." A lot of people in the Scranton area knew about Minooka because of its interesting characters and bars.

If a man didn't like one bar, he wouldn't have to walk very far to get to one that he did. But outside coal country, it was just another small town no one had ever heard of. "It's just south of Scranton," I answered.

"I've been there."

"You've been to Minooka?" He must be kidding.

"I've always been fascinated by coal because of our family's involvement in local mining operations, and I wrote my senior thesis on the evolution of British mining. As I'm sure you know, Minooka is in the middle of the largest anthracite coal field in the United States. On a summer break from college in 1912, I drove from Carbondale to Mauch Chunk in a battered Tin Lizzy, and I actually spent some time in Minooka because a local geologist took me to a racetrack in town and then for a quaff at a nearby hotel. What I recall is that it was your typical small coal town with unpaved streets."

"Yes, that's Minooka. But it's quite different today. We now have two paved streets." The "hotel" where Jeremy had enjoyed his "quaff" had to be O'Donnell's Hotel and Bar. The "hotel" designation came in handy when prohibition went into effect in 1919. And the "quaff" was almost certainly a Schmidt's Beer, a local favorite brewed in Philadelphia.

Seeing that Jack was headed his way, he said, "I will be in England through the holidays and will divide my time between London and Montclair where I hold court in the tower. I would very much enjoy speaking with you again."

I agreed to meet with him on my next visit, and then responding to a wave from Beth, I headed in her direction. She wanted me to join a conversation she was having with Scott and Ellen Manning and her cousin, Lady Patricia Alcott. That was fine with me because I was deliberately avoiding her son. I was feeling very guilty about how much attention Michael had paid to me at the party and how much I had enjoyed it. Eva Greene was helping me out because, wherever Michael went, Eva was right behind him. But when he finally did break free, he asked me to join him on the terrace.

"I hope you don't mind, but I had to get away from Eva." Glancing over his shoulder to see if we had been followed, he added, "I didn't have this much trouble evading the Japanese in the Burmese jungles."

"I don't mind," I said, "but if I were a guy, I'd be very flattered if a beautiful woman like Eva was interested in me. Freddie called her a smasher, and Rob certainly admired her."

"Eva definitely meets the definition of 'smasher,' but to my mind, there's a lot more that goes into making a girl attractive than a pretty face and a good figure." Looking across the room where his brother and sister-in-law were talking to Violet Alcott, Michael continued, "A sharp wit and a fine mind are more important in the long run."

"Did your girlfriend in Australia meet those criteria?" I had no right to ask that question, but I was a little annoyed by his remark, which was clearly directed at James and Angela.

"Maggie, you are judging me too harshly. Angela is just what James wants in a wife. She grew up in a village where the roles of men and women are clearly defined, and that's fine with James. All I am saying is that type of relationship is not for me. I want a wife who is my equal, not just someone who will keep house and rear children."

"I understand," I said, softening my tone. "It's the same with the Irish. It's only because of the war that things are changing."

Michael seemed relieved by my answer. I didn't want to judge anyone harshly. But in the end, what was important was whether or not the marriage worked, and James's marriage was definitely working. On the other hand, Michael's views of marriage were more in keeping with mine.

"Why didn't your relationship work out with the girl from Australia?" After asking one personal question, I found asking the second to be a lot easier. With everything that had happened in the last three days, I was tired, agitated, and, at that moment, rude.

Pointing to a copse at the far end of the garden, Michael said, "Let's walk down there because it's a long story—one my parents have not heard."

After sitting on one of the benches, Michael began his story. "When I was in Burma, I picked up a parasite, which put me in hospital in Calcutta. At my fighting weight, I'm about 170–175, but I was now 130 lbs. and falling. The doctor said he was going to recommend that I be medically discharged because I was unfit for service. I told my commanding officer that if I went back to England, it would be a terrible burden on my parents. They had lost three brothers between them in the First War, and I did not want them to see me the way I was.

"Before going out to Burma, I went home on leave, only to find that my father was experiencing something akin to a nervous breakdown as a result of my transfer to the China-Burma-India Theater of Operations. I didn't want to go home and possibly be the cause of a relapse. I talked the brass into getting me transferred to Parafield. I went to Australia under the condition that I have monthly weigh-ins, and that my weight had to be maintained between 145 and 150 lbs. That's how I met Abby. I was sitting in an ice cream parlor in Adelaide, and she had watched me drink three malted drinks in a row. We struck up a conversation, and I asked her out. It was the first time I had imagined myself in love, and I fell pretty hard."

I was surprised to hear that Abby had been his first love. It didn't sound right. Michael had come of age during World War II when most of the social norms had gone out the window.

"Abby was your first girlfriend?" I asked in a tone of voice that showed my skepticism.

"Yes. She was my first girlfriend, but not my first—how shall I put this—love affair."

I was sure I was about to hear another story of adultery, and I was right. Someone had told me that, after the war, there were so many divorces on the grounds of adultery that one of the archbishops told the faithful to forgive, forget, and move on.

"When I met Edith, I had never, you know, had sex," Michael said. "She was ten years older than I was. Her husband was in the Navy, and she had a flat. This went on for about six months. She's actually part of the reason I ended up in Burma.

"When I had been called up, I took aptitude tests and qualified for the RAF air cadet program. I wanted to be a pilot, but during my physical, they found I had *aerotitis media*, an inflammation of the middle ear, which meant I would be unable to adjust to pressure at high altitudes. Once it was determined I would not be allowed off the ground, I was sent to the RAF School of Technical Training at Halton, Bucks.

"When it became clear that it was only a matter of time before Germany was defeated, Churchill turned his attention to Asia, for the purpose of preserving as much of the empire as possible. Personnel files were combed to find those who had lived in India and spoke the language. I also showed up in a search for those who had qualified for the cadet's program. They were starting a program in India where I would be trained as a medic and a pilot—something on the order of a bush pilot in Australia. The aircraft were small because they were designed to land and take off on very short runways. Each plane had two pilots who were also trained medics. The men on the ground would call for an evacuation, and we would fly in and get off as quickly as possible, providing medical care in the air. I was asked if I was interested in becoming a part of such a program. I jumped at the chance for several reasons, one of which was ending the relationship with Edith. The longer it went on, the worse I felt about it. Once I got to Burma, God did have his revenge.

"Like I said, I fell pretty hard for Abby, and as a result, I missed all of the signals that the relationship was not going to work out. Abby's father had been critically wounded in the First War and had been receiving one hundred percent disability from the Australian government. Abby's mother had to work to make ends meet, and a good deal of his care fell to Abby. When her dad died sometime during the war, she felt liberated from all the responsibilities she had taken on at such a young age. She was afraid that if she married me, she would end up exchanging one invalid for another.

"In November, my squadron was transferred to Malta. When I got to my new station, I was surprised at how quickly the hurt passed, and I questioned whether I had really been in love. I look at it now as a learning experience, one that will help me recognize the real thing when it comes along."

Michael and I said very little on the way back to the house. But I was thinking about his relationship with Edith. What was a thirty-one-year-old married woman doing with a twenty-one-year-old young man? If God had truly believed that punishment was in order, I felt his wrath should have fallen on Edith not Michael.

Once we were back at the manor house, I told Beth I would like to go back to Crofton Wood. I was physically and emotionally exhausted, and I needed some time to think about all I had said to Rob. The angry tone of the conversation was my fault because I had been giving Rob a free pass during our entire relationship. Instead of dealing with problems as they arose, I had piled on all at one time, and I had come off as mean and petty.

Squeezing my hand, she said, "Yes, of course. Michael will drive you."

I wasn't sure I wanted Michael to be the one to drive me back to Crofton Wood. I was already confused enough about my relationship with Rob. I didn't want to think about anyone else.

"About Rob," Michael said as soon as we walked in the door at Crofton Wood, "I'm pretty sure you two had a dust-up before he left, and I'm afraid I might have been the cause of it." He looked in my direction to see if I agreed, but I said nothing. "I admit I took advantage of Rob being the object of Eva's attention to spend as much time with you as possible. If I did cause you a spot of strife, I apologize."

A spot of strife? I liked that. It sounded a whole better than, "Why don't you want to marry me, Rob?"

"Rob and I had had an argument about a month ago. Some of the issues came up on Sunday morning, and it was neither the time nor place to discuss them. So Rob went back to London." But then I lost it, and tears just poured out of me. In a repeat of the previous evening's last dance, Michael put his arms around me and pulled me to him.

After a moment, I gently pushed him away and said, "I'm sorry. I'm slobbering all over you."

After handing me his handkerchief, he said, "I'll gladly put up with slobber if it means I get to hold you in my arms." He led me to the sofa, and turning to face me, he took my two hands in his.

"My behavior may seem odd to you, but I am working at a disadvantage. I have to leave for Germany tomorrow afternoon, and if I don't do or say the right thing now, there's an excellent chance I will never see you again, and I can't let that happen." After pausing for a moment, he continued, "If you and Rob were engaged, I might not be this aggressive. However, since you are not, I am not inclined to withdraw from the field."

Finally, it was out in the open. Michael had been flirting with me ever since I met him, and I had flirted back. He had written letters to me with a romantic subtext, and despite being deeply involved in a relationship with Rob, I had neither encouraged nor discouraged him. And with this visit, when he took me into his arms, all pretenses had been put aside.

"Maggie, you can't be all that surprised."

"No, I'm not surprised, but I am confused. So much has happened to me in such a short time. Two years ago, I was in love with a guy from Pittsburgh until I realized he actually wanted to live in Pittsburgh, and then I wasn't in love with him anymore. Last Christmas, I met Rob. I thought I had found the man of my dreams—the guy I wanted to marry. There was only one problem; he didn't ask. Now, he's going back to the States. And if history repeats itself, once Rob leaves England, I'll never see him again. If that isn't complicated enough, I spent most of Saturday night flirting with you instead of dancing with the man

I was hoping to marry." Covering my face with my hands, I said, "It's too much."

"Yes, I can see that," Michael said, and he went to the liquor cabinet for a drink. He brought me back a scotch and soda. I was now having my second scotch—same house, different crisis.

"I'm very flattered by what you've said, but I'm completely done in. Can we have breakfast tomorrow at the inn?" Michael agreed and held out his hand to help me up.

"All right, then. I'll see you in the morning" Then he kissed me on the cheek and said he was heading up to Montclair where Freddie was organizing a poker game.

When I got to my room, I plopped down on the bed, fully clothed. I fell into an unsettled sleep with different dreams passing through my mind in quick succession, including one where Michael and Rob were cutting cards to see who would get me. The dream ended before I saw who won.

***

Michael and I walked to the inn in a light drizzle. I loved being out in the rain in the countryside. It wasn't something I was able to do growing up for the same reason I didn't enjoy getting caught in the rain in London. The air in both places was too dirty. There was a good reason why the English carry black umbrellas.

Because we had arrived at the inn when most of the guests had already finished breakfast, we were able to sit by a wood-burning fireplace. Because the family owned their own chicken coops, eggs were plentiful, even if the bacon was limited to one slice. Mrs. Rivers brought over a pot of Earl Grey tea and planted a big kiss on Michael's cheek, believing he was heading back to Malta.

After we finished breakfast, I asked about the poker game. Michael and Mr. Ferguson were the big losers, but he seemed unbothered by his losses. "Lucky at cards, unlucky in love."

We spoke about the gala, the reincarnation of Montclair, the guests, James and Angela, and how she had charmed everyone despite speaking very little English. I talked about everything except what had been said the night before. After our dishes had been cleared, Michael asked, "Is there a point where we can talk about you and not my parents or James and Angela or me?" This comment was out of character. His mother would have accused him of being "peckish," but I knew he had had even less sleep than I did.

Looking at the clock above the fireplace, I said, "It's coming up on 11:00, and you have to leave in a few hours. Your parents will be wondering what you are up to."

Standing up and putting some coins on the table, Michael said, "My parents know exactly what I'm up to."

It was raining harder now, and we had to use our umbrellas. Much to my relief, the rain made it impossible for us to talk. In a couple of hours, Jack would drop me off at the train station and take Michael to an airfield in Hertfordshire where he'd catch a flight to Germany. I needed time to think before I said or did another thing. After shaking out our umbrellas, Michael stopped as if he had something to say to me. I thought that this was his way of saying good-bye, so I offered him my hand. Instead, he put his hands around my waist and pulled me toward him. With his body pressing in on me, he started to kiss me, and for what seemed an eternity, he kept on kissing me, and then he held me tightly against him until I reluctantly pulled away.

I went into the house and immediately went upstairs, telling

Beth that I was soaked and had to change my clothes. Sitting in a chair and looking at the rain pounding against the window, I found I was shaking. I had never felt this lost in my entire life.

When Jack took me to the train station that evening, it was pouring buckets, so he pulled up right in front of the station. Michael hopped out of the car and got my suitcase out of the boot. Once inside, I started to put my hand out but quickly drew it back.

"Don't worry, Maggie. I'm not going to kiss you in public, but correct me if I'm wrong, you did kiss me back."

"I don't know what to say to you, Michael," I said with tears welling up in my eyes.

"You know, Maggie, there's one thing that's bothering me about Rob and you. You've been dating since, when, December? Why hasn't he asked you to marry him? If I were in his shoes, I'd be at the Registrar's Office applying for a marriage license right now." He started to walk away, but then he turned around and said, "I would have married you yesterday."

Chapter 30

SHORTLY AFTER I RETURNED to the city, Rob called me at my office to ask if he could come by Mrs. Dawkins's house, so we could continue the conversation we had started at Crofton Wood. I had a pretty good idea of what was about to happen. If Rob was going to dump me, he would want to do it where I wouldn't be alone.

When Rob arrived, he handed me a single red rose, the same flower he had laid on the pillow the first time we had made love. I took the rose knowing that this time it had an entirely different meaning.

Rob looked exhausted. The long work days required to train his successors were taking their toll on him. Emptying his pockets of several packs of Wrigley's gum he asked if I would give them to the boys. I told him how much Teddy and Tommy would miss his stories about growing up in the Wild West and flying in a bomber, and he nodded.

"About our disagreement in Crofton—maybe you'll understand a little better if I tell you some of the things I have been holding back." Rob's leg started to shake exactly like his brother's had when he had been talking about flying into Berlin. "I know you were very hurt when my brother told you that no one in my family knew about you." After hesitating, he finally said, "It's because you're Catholic. Greg figured it out and mentioned it in a letter to my mother. Next thing I know, I get this letter from Mom asking all of these questions, mostly about your religion. I didn't want to say anything because it makes my mother look bad, and she's really a wonderful woman. But I'd be less than honest if I said she wouldn't be upset if the two of us got married." I actually didn't think badly of Mrs. McAllister since my mother was writing me letters asking why I had become involved with a Protestant. "Rob, I really do understand. My mother's been saying the same things about you."

Rob flashed a brief smile, and then he continued. "That Sunday I went to church with you, I was thinking about how before every mission, Pat and all the other Catholics would kneel in front of the priest. He'd tell them to make a good act of contrition, and then they'd receive communion. By saying that prayer, that act of contrition, Pat told me that he would eventually get into heaven, and it helped him get through the mission. I envied him because I don't have any strong religious beliefs. I figured if I bought the farm, all it meant was that my life had ended when I was twenty-two years old.

"But before we get sidetracked on a discussion about religion, I want to respond to some of the things you said at Beth's. You seem to have the impression that once I got to a new town, I hooked up with a girl, and when I moved on, I dumped her." Opening his hands in front of him, he said, "I'll let you decide."

"I've already told you about Alice. She was very nice, but war or no war, we were never going to get married. It was one of the reasons I was okay with joining the Army. It gave me a way out that didn't hurt her feelings.

"As for Arlene, remember I told you that there was a lot of prejudice in Atlanta? Well, one of those prejudiced people was Arlene. I ended it with her weeks before I left for England. If she was sitting at home crying because of me, too bad."

After telling me about Arlene, his demeanor changed, and he went quiet and closed his eyes. "On the other hand, I have to agree with you about Millie. She was a swell girl with a great sense of humor, and I enjoyed her company a lot. She was one of the people who helped me get through those thirty missions. But we did have the agreement I told you about." Rob started to shake his head because he knew that no matter what had been said between them, Millie had fallen in love.

"When she came to the hospital in Oxford for the second time, I realized that her feelings had changed but mine hadn't. When I got back to Bassingbourn, I told her again that as soon as I flew my thirtieth mission, I was gone. But she said everything was fine. When I went to say good-bye, it got pretty emotional, and I felt like a slug. So I got blind drunk, and when I woke up, I was curled up in a ball in the pub owner's storage room. But I had to get out of Bassingbourn. I didn't want to hear about one more plane crashing or getting shot down.

"When Jack and I went to the Peak District, he talked to me about things that had happened to him during and after the First War. Pretty bad stuff. He wanted me to open up, but all I could manage was to tell him about this dream I have over and over again. On a mission to Cologne, I saw a Fortress from my squadron get hit, and everyone had to bail out. One of the guys who jumped caught his chute on the plane. When he got free, the chute was torn and wouldn't open. I watched as this guy fell to his death from 25,000 feet. It was part of my job—everyone's job—to watch because when you got back to interrogation, you'd have to report on exactly what you saw so they could figure out if the guy was dead or a prisoner. In my dream, I'm the guy, but I never hit the ground. I just keep tumbling through space. I usually wake up in a sweat because I have this weight on my chest, and it makes it difficult to breathe."

After telling me about his dream, Rob took a deep breath and continued, "This past week I've been thinking about you and about everything I should have said or done but didn't. And it's not just you. I should have gone to see Pat Monaghan's family. They wrote me letters inviting me to come visit them because I was Pat's closest friend. When I went back to the States, I was the navigator on a B-17 being delivered to an airfield near Omaha, but I never contacted the Monaghans." Rubbing his temples with his eyes closed, he ended by saying, "That was wrong of me. Once I finish up in Atlanta, I'm going to go to see Pat's family."

"Rob, I'm glad you're going to do that. I think it will do you as much good as it will the Monaghans. It's an important first step."

Nodding in agreement, he said, "Maggie, the one thing I want you to understand, no matter what, is that I love you. When I told you that you were the best thing that had ever happened to me, I meant it. The problem is, I'm not the best thing that ever happened to you, and I'm not going to ask you to put your life on hold while I try to figure out what to do with mine."

I couldn't hold back my tears any longer, and they were streaming down my face. Rob stood up, and I knew there was nothing I could say that would change his mind. I asked if I could see him off when he sailed from Liverpool, but from his expression, I knew that wasn't going to happen. "To be honest with you, Maggie, I don't think I could take it." Opening the door to the foyer, he looked at me for the longest time before saying, "You do know that Michael Crowell is in love with you, don't you?"

"Why are you telling me this?" I said through a flood of tears.

"Because it might be more obvious to me than it is to you."

I turned my back to him because I couldn't bear to watch him walk away. If at that moment the city of London had gone silent, the only sound to be heard would have been that of my heart breaking.

Chapter 31

THE NEXT EVENING, I was lying in bed, with Rob's rose on my chest when Mrs. Dawkins came upstairs to tell me I had a visitor. For a split second, I thought it might be Rob, but she shook her head to let me know that it wasn't. When I saw Beth in Mrs. Dawkins's sitting room, I started to cry as I've never cried before. Beth put her arms around me and tried to comfort me, but I was beyond the reach of even Beth's kindness. Mrs. Dawkins tiptoed into the room and left a box of Kleenex and two cups of tea, but I continued to cry in great gulping sobs.

"From the very beginning, I saw it coming, but I still kept seeing him." In between sobs, I explained, "I have nothing to reproach him about. He never made any promises."

After I had finally stopped crying, Beth told me she was staying at her cousin's house in Holland Park, and she wanted me to come stay with her. I hadn't told my boss that Rob had gone back to the States, but he knew something was wrong when he saw me sitting in front of ringing telephones that I wasn't answering. He encouraged me to take a few days off.

Beth's cousin, Lady Patricia Alcott, welcomed me to her home, but after that, I saw very little of her. She was being very kind by leaving Beth and me alone. We started the next day with a walk through Kensington Gardens. Beth was waiting for me to say something, but I didn't have a clue as to what I was going to do.

"Maggie, I suggest that you not make any decisions as to your future for at least two weeks. Your first inclination might be to return home, but I think that would be a mistake. Your world has greatly expanded since you left Minooka. If you returned, I think you would feel as if everything was pressing in on you.

"I am confident you will be looking at things very differently and in short order. You have been so focused on Rob and how to make him happy, I think you neglected your own happiness. By your own admission, you didn't think your relationship was going to work out, but you stuck by him because he is a decent man. Loyalty is an admirable quality, but it cannot act as a tie that binds you to someone who is not all you deserve. After so many months together, Rob should have been drawing you closer to him. Instead, he kept you at a distance."

"But Jack kept you at a distance."

"Yes, he did, and because of that, our marriage has traveled a very rocky road. It is only in the last few years that we have been able to break down all the barriers that have separated us. But having experienced so much heartache, I don't want the same for you. And there is another reason why you might consider remaining in England. It has something to do with your love of history and *Pride and Prejudice*."

When we got back to the Alcotts', Beth asked me to join her in the morning room. She handed me a box and told me to open it. Removing the lid, I saw that inside were two diaries, and on the cover, in gold, were the embossed initials of Elizabeth Garrison Lacey.

"I've just now got them back from the bookbinder with their beautiful new leather covers. Mr. Selden did a marvelous job, not just on the covers, but on the actual pages themselves. We'll have to wear gloves when we read them, but now we can turn the pages without the risk of them falling apart." Putting her arms around my shoulders, she said, "I'll confess I am using these diaries to entice you to stay in England a while longer because I love you." And she gave me a squeeze. "But there is another reason."

When I had been in Crofton, Beth told me that the expenses for refurbishing and repairing Montclair had run much higher than the Catons had expected, and they were looking for a way for Montclair to help pay for itself.

"They have decided to convert the house into a specialty hotel and market it as the ancestral home of Fitzwilliam Darcy and Elizabeth Bennet. Ellen Caton has asked me to write a history of the Lacey family as it relates to the characters portrayed in *Pride and Prejudice*, and I will need your help because I never learnt how to type."

I actually started to smile. At the time the Crowells had wrapped up the love story of Elizabeth Garrison and William Lacey, Beth had said that "I knew it all." But there was so much I didn't know. What was Elizabeth and Will's courtship like? Where did they go on their honeymoon? What was it like to be the mistress of Montclair? What Beth and Jack had shared with me was only the tip of the iceberg.

When I looked at Beth, she was holding out a pair of white cotton gloves, so I could open the diaries. Putting them on, I flipped to a page near to the end of the first diary. Apparently, the entry was made shortly before Jane was to marry Charles Bingham.

13 September—When Mama came into our room this evening, she was biting her thumb. This is something she does only when she has something unpleasant to say. Jane and I thought we were to hear some bad news, but we were not prepared for what she actually said. 'Lizzy, you may stay and listen. You're of an age so that you can hear this. Jane, you were brought up on a farm, so you've seen things I never saw, having grown up in town.' Jane tried to stop her, but to no avail. 'On your wedding night, it might hurt for a bit, but only the first few times. When they're young, it goes quickly, but you can help it along if you move about a bit. Keep a basin of water and a handcloth near to the bed.' Then she kissed us good night and left. Jane looked at me, and we burst out laughing, and we were still laughing long after we had blown out the candle.

What a wonderful passage! It reminded me of how much pleasure I had gotten from reading *Pride and Prejudice*. I decided to take Beth up on her offer to help organize the Lacey papers. It probably was for the best, and there were so many reasons to stay in England. But was one of them Michael Crowell? I really didn't know, but I had to admit I was curious to find out.

Chapter 32

SHORTLY AFTER ROB SAILED, Lady Patricia Alcott asked if I would like to board with her, rent free. While Britain was at war, the Alcott townhouse had been filled with men who worked with Lord Alcott in the War Office at Whitehall. However, once the war ended, the house had gradually emptied, and now the last boarder, a Canadian liaison officer, was also leaving. Because of London's housing shortage, Lord Alcott was pressing his wife to find replacements.

I had grown very fond of the Mr. and Mrs. Dawkins and their two boys, but just thinking of another cold winter swaddled in layers of clothes in my attic bedroom finally tipped me in the Alcotts' direction. With rental properties so scarce, I was sure Mrs. Dawkins could easily rent my room.

"When your fellow left for America, I said to Mr. Dawkins, if you wanted to move on, I wouldn't stop you. Now you're telling me you can move into a nice room in Holland Park without paying any rent at all. Well, that puts a few quid into your pocket, now doesn't it?" And since she would probably raise the rent with the next tenant, it would put a few, much needed, quid in her pocket as well.

When I asked how much notice she would want, she said, "none." "I'll have someone in there the day after you've gone." It seemed all I needed to do was to pack my bags.

The differences between my room in the Alcott town-house and my bedroom sitter with its plain beige walls and simple metal-framed bed were night and day. There was a double bed with a dark pink canopy and matching drapes and walls covered with the drawings of Beatrix Potter. I was now sharing a room with Peter Rabbit, Jemima Puddleduck, and Timmy Tiptoes.

Looking out the window of my fourth-story window, I wondered how Maggie Joyce of Minooka had ended up living in Holland Park. In the past two years, I had needed to adjust to many different situations, but nothing had prepared me for boarding in a house where a butler answered the door and a cook saw to all of the meals—at least for the Alcotts.

"My husband works long hours," Lady Alcott informed me on my first day, "and frequently takes his meals at his club. My son, Geoff, is currently working in Brussels but could come home at any time. Violet, whom you met at the ball, rents a flat in the mews on the far side of the park and often drops in. The twins, Lily and Iris, live in Surrey. Lily is expecting, so I have been visiting her more frequently. Mrs. Gooding is the cook and pretty much comes and goes because she often has no one to cook for. However, Andrews, the butler, is almost always here, except on his days off." My impression was that I would largely have the house to myself, except when people showed up.

Lady Alcott introduced me to Andrews in the morning room when he brought in the afternoon tea. He was dour, undemonstrative, and not particularly happy to see me.

"If you will be dining in, miss, I would ask that you inform me, so I may tell Cook. If you wish, you may have your meals brought to you on a tray." He nodded, I nodded, and he left.

"Don't worry about Andrews," Lady Alcott said. "It will take him a while to get used to you. The same thing with Mrs. Gooding. However, in short order, you will feel comfortable going below stairs to use the kitchen." Trying to explain her butler's coolness, she continued, "The war has put everyone off his game. No one's sure what his role is, including me. I don't know if things will ever get back to the way they were before the war.

"I hope you will be in tomorrow evening because I have asked Lord Alcott to come home early, so we can have dinner together. I know you were introduced at the ball at Montclair, but I don't think you had time to talk. I don't want your first encounter to be in the upstairs hallway." Pouring out the tea, she let out a little chuckle. "Surely, you remember him. He was the only one wearing an eye patch."

***

Even without the eye patch, Lord Randolph Alcott was an intimidating figure: six-foot-three, two hundred pounds, and a graduate of the Royal Military Academy at Sandhurst. He had been a captain in the Coldstream Guards in 1914 when his battalion came close to being annihilated at the First Battle of Ypres. Three years later, at Passchendaele, a shell fragment had cost him his eye, requiring years of extensive reconstruction by plastic surgeons. In 1922, Lord Alcott, who had been born and raised in India, joined the Indian Civil Service. When Beth and Jack went out to India, the Alcotts were their main link to home.

Beth had filled me in about Rand. "His mother was the daughter of a British Army officer posted to India, and she is as tough as nails. When Mr. Alcott died of dengue fever when Rand was ten, his mother turned him over to a colonel in the British Army. Col. Stirling, who supervised his training, became Rachel's second husband, and he put his stepson through the paces. When Rand went to Sandhurst, he was as hardened as any veteran."

"Is Lord Alcott's mother still in India?"

"No. She lives across the park from her son, with four servants whom she brought with her from India. Once Gandhi's non-violence movement gained traction in the '30s, Rachel said he should be tossed into prison and the key thrown away. When they didn't take her advice, she packed up and left, saying India was 'done.' She's extremely intelligent, but she is also headstrong, abrasive, opinionated, and very often rude."

"Does Lady Alcott get along with her?"

"No one gets along with her. She's just like Jane Austen's Lady Catherine de Bourgh. But she is very wealthy, and there is always the threat of being cut out of her will if she doesn't like you. But I'm sure you will have an opportunity to meet her. There is very little that goes on in this house that she doesn't ferret out, including your holiday to Brighton with Violet. Speaking of Brighton, I'm glad you are going. It's the perfect place to clear your mind, and it will give you an opportunity to visit the place where George Waggoner seduced Lucy Garrison and very nearly cost Lizzy her Mr. Lacey.

***

From the time I arrived in England, I had wanted to visit Brighton and its famous Royal Pavilion, and now it was finally happening. My traveling companion was Violet Alcott Barton. I had met Violet at the Montclair ball, and after returning to London, she had stopped in at Mrs. Dawkins's house to invite me to lunch. Shortly after I moved into her parents' house, Violet popped in to welcome me to the neighborhood.

"This was my bedroom, but don't blame me for the wallpaper," Violet said in a rapid-fire staccato. "My grandmother was very Victorian. It was she who picked it out, and I could never bring myself to take it down. Grandma was also a huge fan of Beatrix Potter. Actually met the lady, which accounts for the bunny and animal prints."

It was Violet's suggestion to go to Brighton because she knew that I was still reeling from my breakup with Rob. When she saw me put a copy of Austen's *Persuasion* in my suitcase, she took it out. "The last thing you need to be reading is the story of a woman who pined for her lover for eight years. Besides, I'm hoping we won't have any time to read."

On the train ride to Brighton, Violet shared some of what she knew about the history of the Lacey family. She had written her senior thesis on Francine Lacey, Will and Lizzy's older daughter, and as part of her research, she had accumulated a lot of information on the family.

"Remember, *Pride and Prejudice* is a novel. Jane Austen was influenced by Will and Elizabeth Lacey's story, but it is in no way a history. Let me give you an example. One thing that was emphasized in the novel was that the Bennet sisters had 'no connections.' That wasn't the case at all. Lizzy's maternal grandfather wasn't some backwater country solicitor, but a man who had retired from a successful London practice. And then there was Lizzy's Aunt Susan, her father's older sister. She had married a baronet and took an interest in Jane. Unfortunately, Aunt Susan did not like Lizzy because she considered her to be 'whimsical,' whatever that means. And then there were Aunt and Uncle Sims, the Gardiners in the book. Mr. Sims was a successful coffee broker and was knighted. Through his connections, Jane and Lizzy would have had ample opportunity to meet some of London's bachelors. But even if they had never married, they would have been able to live in some degree of comfort because of an annuity provided by their Grandfather Sims. They would not have been out on the street selling flowers."

Leaving the grit of London behind, we traveled through the south of England's beautiful rural shires. The green, rolling landscape went on for mile after mile before disappearing into the horizon. But the scenery was familiar to Violet, and so she ignored the lush pastureland, country lanes, and well-sited farmhouses framed by the train windows.

"Thomas Garrison, Lizzy's father, inherited the estate from his uncle, Edward Bennet, which is where the town and the estate got its name. He had been in London, studying for the bar at Lincoln's Inn, when he learned that he had inherited a farm. He moved to Bennets End and never did practice law. Within the year, he married eighteen-year-old Francine Sims, Lizzy's mother.

"When you read Franny's journals," Violet continued, "you'll see she was no fan of *Pride and Prejudice*, mostly because of Austen's portrayal of her grandmother, whom she was very fond of. Other than her concern for her daughters marrying well, Francine Garrison had little resemblance to the novel's empty-headed Mrs. Bennet, and the Laceys and Binghams were frequent visitors to Bennets End.

"On the other hand, Austen was spot on about Lucy being selfish, but Franny also says that her aunt had a wonderful 'almost childlike' sense of fun and took the children to county fairs and staged plays where every child had a part."

Violet talked so fast that it was necessary to hang on to her every word, or I might miss a decade. She was still talking when we pulled into Brighton.

Our hotel, one of dozens facing the sea, was built during the reign of Victoria and had Victorian Age plumbing. I was used to hotels where I had to share a bath and toilet, but because of a "wonky" commode, we had to use the one on the floor above. Although the door to the commode was unmarked, I had no trouble figuring out which one it was because I could clearly see the outline of a man facing the toilet through the frosted glass door, which Violet and I found to be hysterical.

The woman at the registration desk told us the reason the hotel was in such a state of disrepair was because it had been used to billet Australian soldiers during the war. "Ruffians. That's what they were. Nothing less than ruffians."

As soon as we got outside, Violet said, "That hotel hasn't seen a paint brush since Victoria died in 1901. She's blaming the Aussies because they have such a bad reputation." After thinking for a few seconds, she added, laughing, "which they deserved."

We walked the promenade until we found a place to have dinner. After being seated, Violet said emphatically, "After we eat, we're going to go to a pub."

"I'm not one for going to pubs or bars."

"You're not one for doing much," Violet said impatiently. "Brighton has a lot of great pubs and dancehalls, and I think we should go to some of them."

"What about Guy?"

"What about him? Do you mean, can I go out dancing without my husband? Hell yes! Guy has two left feet. If I want to dance, I have to go out with my friends, and I'm not too shy about asking a man to dance with me." Leaning over the table, she continued. "Listen, Maggie, your fellow has gone back to the States, so it's time for you to start meeting other men. I'm not saying you have to let some man get into your knickers, but, truthfully, abstinence is considerably overrated."

"Was there anyone other than Guy? You know what I mean. Was Guy your first…?"

"My first! He wasn't even my fourth. Good Lord, don't look so shocked. I was in London all during the Blitz. We all were, just like the royals. You know that bit about 'The princesses won't leave London without their mother. The Queen won't leave without the King, and the King won't leave.' Same thing with my family. Bombs rained down night after night, killing thousands. At that time, I drove this little lorry with coffee and sandwiches to serve the ARF—the air raid wardens. They were the ones who enforced the blackout, but they also helped rescue people trapped in the rubble. Poor things! I'd have to wrap their hands around the coffee cups because they were just sitting there staring into space. Here I was, twenty-one years old, and I had never been with a man. You probably don't know this, but sex relieves tension. And I was very tense."

"Do you think Guy knows?"

"Knows that I wasn't a virgin? I think it was pretty obvious the first night we spent together. I wasn't exactly lying on my back thinking of England."

"How did you two meet?" Mr. and Mrs. Guy Barton were the most incongruous couple. Violet was tall, dark, and rail-thin, with a posh accent, while her husband was short, fair, and a little on the chubby side. It was comical to listen to their conversations. Guy's working-class background was obvious from the moment he opened his mouth, but Violet loved to listen to him and would often go over and kiss him on the top of his head while he was talking.

"Guy worked in the same building as my father at the War Office. I'd see him when I brought Dad sandwiches and coffee from home. I thought he was cute, but that was it. But then the Germans started with their rockets. The Allied invasion had been successful, so everyone thought that was the end of the bombs. First it was the doodlebugs, which were bad enough, but at least with them, you knew you were safe as long as you could hear them. It was only when the humming stopped that you were in trouble. But you couldn't hear the buzz bombs, and there were more of them. One of the bombs hit down the street from the War Office, and we all ran out to see if we could help. I must have looked terrified because Guy came over, and knowing who I was, whispered in my ear: 'Our troops are forcing the mobile launchers back to the point where London will shortly be out of range.' I think I fell in love with him right then."

While we were out to dinner, our waiter informed us that because the Royal Pavilion was in such a state of disrepair, only visitors accompanied by a tour guide could gain entry.

"Do you happen to know one?" Violet asked, feeling confident that he did.

"My father earns a bit on the side conducting tours, and there isn't anything about Brighton he doesn't know."

Handing the waiter the money for the bill, Violet said, "We'll see your father tomorrow at 9:00 at the main entrance."

***

Our evening of pub-hopping had gone better than I had expected. At the third pub, we hooked up with two sailors on leave, who taught us how to play darts. After Violet explained she was happily married and that I was in mourning, we went dancing, and that was all we did. Jimmy and Lenny saw us back to our hotel, and both of them kissed me on the cheek. However, Lenny pulled me aside and said, "Maggie, you might have taken off your wedding band too soon. I'm not sure you're ready to jump back in the game."

Violet was right. I was acting as if I was in mourning, and I decided that if someone asked me out, I would accept. No more moping around about what might or might not be.

We met our tour guide, Mr. Pendergast, outfitted with a black bowler and, despite a cloudless sky, a black umbrella, at the gates to the Royal Pavilion exactly at 9:00, and he began his spiel immediately. He explained that on the night of November 29, 1940, German bombers appeared in the skies over Brighton, causing extensive damage to the city, but the Pavilion had come through it unscathed.

"According to Lord Haw-Haw, the American who made radio broadcasts for the Nazis, Adolph Hitler intended to make the Royal Pavilion his headquarters once he had successfully invaded England. It seems that information failed to reach the head of the Luftwaffe, Hermann Goering, or he wouldn't have bombed Brighton." That was Mr. Pendergast's idea of a joke, so we laughed, and he looked pleased.

I knew about Lord Haw-Haw, as his real name was William Joyce—hopefully, no relation. Shortly after the war ended, he had been captured by the British, tried for treason, and sentenced to be hung. The death penalty was controversial because Joyce was an American citizen. However, somewhere along the line, he had obtained a British passport, and that provided the British with enough legal cover to carry out the sentence.

We learned the Prince Regent, the future George IV, first came to Brighton, where he rented a farmhouse, so that he could spend time with his favorite companion, Maria Fitzherbert, whom he would secretly marry. Later, the Prince tapped into the enormous wealth of the British Treasury and commissioned Henry Holland, and later John Nash, to design an exotic Oriental palace that one would have expected to find in Constantinople not southern England.

Mr. Pendergast informed us that only the Pavilion's kitchen, banqueting room, and music room were open to view, and even those were in shockingly bad condition. We double-timed it through the building, looking up, down, and all around as if we were plane spotters. Both Violet and I had the impression that part of Mr. Pendergast's fee went to someone inside the Pavilion, who looked the other way while visitors were quickly whisked in and out of the building.

Warned by Mr. Pendergast that we would be moving "apace," we dashed through the Great Kitchen where elaborate banquets had been prepared for guests of the Prince, and on to the music room, which was lit by nine lotus-shaped chandeliers. Our last stop, if it could be called a stop, was the Banqueting Room. Even though it had been stripped by Queen Victoria of its painted canvases depicting Chinese domestic scenes, the elegance of the room remained, and its sheer size was overwhelming.

The tour was supposed to have continued outside, but instead, Violet pulled out a five-pound note. "That was quite invigorating, Mr. Pendergast. Never was so much imparted in so little time," she said, thanking him.

As we walked toward Brighton pier, Violet picked up where our tour guide had left off. "By the way, Jane Austen's Brighton had no resemblance to the Brighton of the Prince Regent. At the time Jane wrote of George Wickham's seduction of Lydia Bennet, it was a popular seaside resort, which was also known for attracting more than its share of prostitutes.

"And speaking of seduction," Violet said, smiling, "why don't we go out on the pier tonight and see what we can do about having the same thing happen to you."

Chapter 33

ONE OF ANDREWS'S MANY responsibilities was to sort the mail, and one way of letting me know that I was not a member of the family was to keep my letters separate from the Alcotts' correspondence. And there, all by its lonesome on the foyer table, was my first letter from Rob since his arrival in Atlanta.

October 14, 1948

Dear Maggie,

Arrived safely in the good old USA. It was smooth sailing once we got clear of the British coast. The British Navy has these buoys all over the place to mark ships that were sunk by German torpedoes. Three years after the war, the Brits are still clearing the approaches to its ports. This guy, who did convoy duty in the North Atlantic, told me that the amount of tonnage that went to the bottom during the war was kept top secret because it might have caused the Brits to "lose heart."

Since neither of us had been here before, after docking

in New York, Frank and I decided to do some sightseeing. We went to the 102nd floor of the Empire State Building and down to the Battery where we could see the Statue of Liberty and Ellis Island. After that, we ate a steak at Jack Dempsey's, which looked huge compared to what I was used to in England. Then we headed to Grand Central Station.

About the disagreement we had at Beth's house, I know I acted like an ass. But before you came downstairs that morning, Michael was telling me how the two of you had gone to the Peak District and had walked down to the village for coffee. Even before I knew about that, I was already pretty steamed because of the way he had come on to you the night before. Thinking about it now, I can't say I blame him. I guess because he had to leave to go to his new station in Germany, he had to go at you head on. As they say, "All's fair in love and war." I just want you to be happy.

Love,

Rob

The following day, I discussed Rob's letter with my boss. Don told me never to go by what a guy said or wrote because "we stink at both." He believed a man's actions spoke louder than words. In that case, it boiled down to the fact that Rob had not asked me to return to the States with him. So that was that—or was it? I would have plenty of time to think about it because that night I came down with the flu. When Beth learned I was sick, she immediately came to Holland Park, bringing her own portable medicine chest as well as some of Reed's drawings from the 1913 road trip.

"I haven't seen these drawings in years. Jeremy had them locked up in the tower." Shaking her head showed that, even after all these years, her uncle's behavior still puzzled her.

Picking up the first sketch, Beth said, "This is the coach inn where we stayed our first night on the road. Many years later, Jack and I stopped there for a drink, and on the wall was a framed drawing Reed had made for the owner all those years ago. The new owner didn't know the story behind it, and when we told him, he asked Jack and me to sign the back of it."

Placing the next drawing on top of the one of the inn, Beth showed me Helmsley Hall, Jane Austen's Netherfield Park, and the home of Charles Bingham and Jane Garrison during the early years of their marriage. It looked nothing like the house I had imagined. The drawing showed a very pretty three-story, red-brick Georgian manor, with one wing and a white porch and white-framed windows, but it wasn't anywhere near as large as I had imagined it. Seeing my expression, Beth said, "It's not as grand as Montclair, but it's a good-sized manor home for the neighborhood."

"But how many people could have attended a ball there?"

"More than you would think. In houses such as this, all of the public rooms were connected, and the furniture was pushed against the walls to make room for the dancers. I don't know if the wing was there at the time Charles leased it, but if it was, the floor plan has a nice flow to it. If you recall, Jane Austen wrote in her novel that the Bennets' neighborhood was made up of about twenty-four families. I would say this house could have accommodated that many couples."

Now that I knew what Helmsley Hall looked like, I understood Will Lacey's objection to Charles's choice of residence.

George Bingham had charged Will with turning his youngest brother into a gentleman, someone who would be received in the finest homes in the country. Will dismissed Helmsley Hall and nearby Bennets End as completely inadequate for his purposes.

I looked at Beth, who was enjoying sharing her brother's work with a friend. Because of Reed's tragic life, too much of his past had been kept in the shadows, and now his sister was bringing it back into the light of day.

The next drawing was of the parsonage that Charlotte Ledger and William Chatterton called home and Jane Austen called Hunsford Lodge. I remembered how thrilled I was when I realized I was standing in the same room where Will Lacey had asked Elizabeth Garrison to marry him. When Rob and I had toured the parsonage, I remembered thinking that Elizabeth Garrison could not have been more in love with Will Lacey than I was with Rob McAllister. That visit seemed like a lifetime ago.

Moving on to the home of Lady Sylvia Desmet, Reed had drawn Desmet Park from a half dozen angles. "When we saw the house, it was being used for storage by the local council, and the courtyard was full of junk. Reed left out the junk and added planters and a working fountain.

"Oh, by the way, I have some information on Desmet Park for you. According to *The Times*, the Thornhill has been sold to an undisclosed buyer. I guess they figured out how to get it off the ceiling. The contents of the house are to be auctioned off the first Saturday in December, and the house itself is to be sold for the value of its stone. The article said it is one of more than one hundred houses that have been torn down since the end of the war because their owners can no longer afford their upkeep."

Here was another piece of the Will Lacey/Elizabeth Garrison love story that was being lost. The Edwards farm, the assembly hall, the parsonage, and now Desmet Park, were all going or gone. The thought of so much of Elizabeth Lacey's personal history disappearing depressed me.

"And here is Brighton where Lydia agreed to an elopement with Mr. Wickham. As you can tell from the number of drawings, Reed loved sketching the royal residence, the gardens, the pier, and the sea. I have a soft spot for Brighton because it was where Jack first told me he loved me."

But that was in 1913. The following year Beth was engaged to Colin Matheson. What had happened in the interim?

Chapter 34

BECAUSE THERE WERE TOO many people on too little land, a lack of housing in London had always been a problem, even for the wealthy. One solution was terrace houses, and this was the style of housing in Holland Park. The Alcotts lived in a five-story, cream-colored stucco townhouse with bay windows and an elevated ground floor with the servants' entrances under the stairs. Even though the townhouses were similar, I found the whole area to be warm and welcoming.

The interior of the house was always as neat as a pin, which was due to the efforts of three women, all from Gibraltar, who descended on the house every Wednesday, and who went through it like whirling dervishes. When I asked Patricia why they were all from Gibraltar, she said, "That's a very interesting story," and she told me a little bit about Holland Park and Kensington during the war.

"In the autumn of 1938, it looked as if Britain would go to war over Hitler's designs on Czechoslovakia, and in anticipation of air raids, Beth, my girls, and I helped dig trenches and fill sand bags in Hyde Park. But because of the Munich Pact with Germany, war was avoided, and everyone broke out the champagne. But 'peace in our time' lasted only one year. In September 1939, we were once again at war with Germany because of its invasion of Poland, and we all went back to digging trenches. We also worked a garden allotment in Holland Park because two dozen War Office workers boarded in this house, sleeping in shifts, and they ate lots of potatoes and vegetables. With most of the servants in uniform or working in war industries, the house was run by Mrs. Redgrave, the housekeeper, Mrs. Bradshaw, and Andrews."

It was hard to picture Lady Patricia Alcott filling sandbags. She was an elegant lady with strawberry-blonde hair, blue eyes, fair complexion, and a lovely figure, who cared a lot about how she looked and the clothes she wore. But according to Beth, her cousin had "steel in her spine" and needed it when Rand had been so badly wounded in the First War. She stuck with him through endless visits to plastic surgeons where his cheek and eye socket were reconstructed. He had been fitted for a glass eye, but the fragile prosthetic broke easily and needed frequent replacements. Eventually, Rand decided to leave the socket empty and to wear a patch.

"I will tell you one story that may give you an idea of the determination of the British to 'carry on.' After war was declared, the government started a metal collection drive. I think you had it in the States where everyone brought in their old pots, pans, and washtubs."

I smiled, thinking about my mother's eagerness to contribute to the war effort. Over the years, an unsightly pile of junk had accumulated in the backyard because my grandfather didn't throw anything away. Mom gladly waved down the truck collecting the scrap metal, and with a clear conscience, rid herself of everything that would stick to a magnet.

"The government decided the wrought iron fences around the parks and some of the most expensive homes in town also needed to come down. This caused a lot of unhappiness because some of the railings were hundreds of years old. The Duke of Bedford flatly refused to allow his to be removed, and a statue of his ancestor in Bedford Square was defaced as a result. But for the most part, down they came, including the iron railings around Kensington Gardens. However, the beautiful gates were saved, and every evening, a park official closed the gates and made his rounds calling, 'All Out.'" Laughing, Patricia said, "Now, keep in mind, the railings are gone. Anyone could walk into the park whenever they wanted to, but it was important to keep up standards and to hold true to tradition.

"As for the ladies from Gibraltar, because of its strategic importance as the gateway to the Mediterranean, the Army decided that the 12,000 civilians living on the peninsula had to be evacuated to England. Although Gibraltans are British subjects, most of them are of Maltese descent and look Italian. When Mussolini brought Italy into the war as an ally of Germany, the Italians had a rough time of it here. That passed, but it was not our finest hour.

"Someone in Whitehall made the decision to place many of these evacuees in two blocks of flats in Kensington near Lancaster Gate, and a few residents complained, saying the Gibraltans were physically, emotionally, and financially ill-suited to be living in Kensington. However, that was a minority view, and the local scout troops integrated hundreds of boys into their ranks. Most evacuees returned to Gibraltar when the war ended, but some stayed on, including the amazing three ladies who clean our house.

"By the way, you may happen upon our former footman, Jim Budd. He does odd jobs around the house. He was captured on Crete and spent nearly four years in a German POW camp. He may seem a bit odd, but he's a good man."

I did happen upon Jim Budd in the pantry where he was stuffing his coat pockets with tins of Spam I had brought from AAFES. His hoarding was a result of his years in the POW camp where he was chronically undernourished, and it was no secret because, on one occasion, Mrs. Gooding asked that I get a tin of sardines out of Jim's bottom drawer. In addition to acting as the on-site repairman, Jim's job included collecting the ration coupons from everyone in the house and waiting in line to buy rationed items. Even on the coldest days, I never heard him complain about the long waits.

Mrs. Gooding was starting to warm up to me, but Andrews was another story. He seemed to bristle whenever I went downstairs, and I didn't know what I had done to offend him. I finally asked Mrs. Gooding. With a cigarette hanging out of her mouth, she said, "It's got nothing to do with you, dear.

"You see, during the war, the male servants went into the military, and because of mandatory national service, the girls were hired on at the factories, making bombs or building airplanes and the like. Even though unemployment is very high right now, most of them don't want to come back into service. It's a dead-end job, you see, so most of the work is hired out." The ash on Mrs. Gooding's cigarette was now an inch long. It was only when tiny flakes started to fall onto her sweater that she finally flicked off the ash. "It's been hard on Mr. Andrews because, before the war, the Alcotts always had guests, and some very important people they were. Lady Patricia says that when they start entertaining again, she's going to hire a caterer." Stabbing the air with her cigarette, Mrs. Gooding said, "Where does that leave me, I ask you? Planning the menus and telling the caterers where everything is, that's where. But I've got nowhere to go. So I'm staying right where I am until they carry me out feet first."

Chapter 35

I HAD BEEN LIVING at the Alcotts for about three weeks when I came home from work to a darkened house. Because of energy conservation, only the light in the foyer was left on. Tonight there was no light in the foyer, but there was one coming from under the door to the morning room. When I opened the door, I didn't see anyone, so I shut the light as I had been instructed to do. Out of the darkness came a voice saying, "If you don't mind."

I was so startled that I let out a very loud, "Jesus, Mary, and Joseph!"

"None of the above," the voice said. "I am, however, Geoff Alcott." Rising from his chair and extending his hand, he asked, "Are you the Canadian or an intruder?"

"Neither," I said, waiting for my heart to stop pounding. "I'm Maggie Joyce. I'm boarding here."

"I apologize for startling you, but no one informed me we had a boarder, even my father, whom I saw three days ago." Looking around, he said, "Where the hell is everyone? Don't we have servants anymore?"

Taking off my coat and hat, I said, "Your father is probably at his club. Your mother is in Surrey with your sister, Lily. Mrs. Gooding is gone for a few days, and it's Andrews's night off. So it's just me, and possibly Jim Budd."

I had been warned about Geoff. According to just about everyone, he was extremely intelligent, loved to argue, and exasperated everyone who came in contact with him—with one exception—his father.

"Ah, an American," he said. "Let's see. You are from somewhere on the East Coast. I attended university in Connecticut, so I know you're not from New England, nor are you from New York City. There's a certain nasal intonation, so I'm going to guess..."

"I can help you out here," I said. When I had first moved to Washington, I had been the butt of numerous jokes because of my nasal accent and my hick colloquialisms. "I'm from eastern Pennsylvania."

"Damn. I was going to say Pennsylvania," he said in a schoolboy voice. "How is it that we are so fortunate as to be graced with your presence?"

"I am a friend of Beth and Jack Crowell's. When the Canadian boarder left, your mother asked if I would like to come and live here. I'm staying in Violet's bedroom."

"The Beatrix Potter suite, as it's known around here," he said, correcting me. Slumping into his chair, Geoff apologized. "Sorry. The Channel crossing was rather nasty."

Geoff had seen my typewriter and asked what I was doing. I explained about the Catons' plans to convert Montclair into a hotel and to market the mansion as the ancestral home of Elizabeth Bennet and Fitzwilliam Darcy. "Mrs. Caton has asked me to write a booklet giving a brief history of the Lacey family, especially its connection to the characters in *Pride and Prejudice*."

"I may be able to help you with your research. While at St. Paul's, I was assigned a history project that required family research. Since Mother was not a saver—if one of her children wished to preserve any of his or her school papers, they had to do it themselves—I have my school reports upstairs. If you can delay your research for tonight, I will give you my papers, and you may go through them tomorrow at your leisure."

After a long day, I was more than ready to let it go for the evening.

"I'll leave the papers on the table in the foyer," Geoff said, standing and stretching. "Please be kind. I was very young when I wrote them."

Geoff did leave the papers, and they were a treasure trove. When I came home from work the next evening, I immediately set to work incorporating his research. I was busily typing when Geoff came up behind me and, once again, startled me. I couldn't decide if he was doing it on purpose or not. I was having flashbacks of growing up with a brother who thought there was nothing funnier than scaring the daylight out of his sisters.

"I am here to make amends," he said and handed me a can of Danish ham. "I have a reputation for being obnoxious, and I certainly lived up to it last night. I smuggled this ham into the country from Belgium, and I am inviting you to join me for dinner."

It was only a one-pound can, but the thought of real ham made my mouth water. Since arriving in England, I had eaten only spiced ham, or Spam, as it was known to millions of servicemen who had been forced to eat it during the war. I was able to get it from AAFES, but I never made the mistake of confusing it with real ham. I offered to set up a tray with cheese and crackers.

A cold front had moved through the city, and the house was chilly in every room, except the study. When I returned from the kitchen, I found Geoff sitting in a chair with his shoes off and his feet in front of a space heater holding a broken key from the ham. Without the key, the can couldn't be opened. I decided a broken key was not going to keep me from eating ham, so I took the can downstairs and went at it with a variety of kitchen utensils until it surrendered. When I came in with a plate of sliced ham, Geoff started clapping.

"May I ask what you were doing in Brussels?"

"In March, the Western European nations signed the Treaty of Brussels establishing a military alliance. Since the United States has all of the money and most of the military materiel, we are now working on an agreement that would bring your country into the alliance. My current role is to deliver papers to the Foreign Office here in London regarding those negotiations." Sighing, he said, "You would think there was no such thing as the telephone, telegraph, or teletype the way I go back and forth across the Channel."

While cutting his ham, Geoff informed me that, in Brussels, the shops were full of every type of commodity and consumer goods. "Shoes, clothing, ham, eggs, bacon—all are plentiful. I don't understand why Britain is still experiencing such privation when Belgium, a country occupied by the Germans, is back to normal. I've seen some very chubby, well-shod Belgians."

"What did you do during the war?"

"I interrogated German prisoners captured during the Battle of the Bulge. But by time I got there, the poor bastards were sitting in groups, waiting—hoping—to be captured. They were more frightened of their fellow Germans than they were of us. The SS had been hanging those whom they considered to be deserters from whatever structure was handy, usually a lamppost or tree, although they tended to shoot the officers. So these war-weary soldiers allowed us to stumble upon them. For some, their uniform was their first pair of long pants. Thirteen- and fourteen-year-old boys. Damn depressing."

All the while Geoff had been talking, he had been making cracker sandwiches of ham and cheese. Pleased with his creation, he asked, "Now, your turn. What did you do during the war? Did Americans have National Service?"

"No. There was nothing like that in the States, but we all tried to do our bit. I moved to Washington in '44 and worked for the Treasury Department, and after the war, I got a job with the Army Exchange Service."

"Boyfriend?"

"In Atlanta, Georgia."

"Is there a reason for such a long-distance romance?"

"Rob's currently working for a company headquartered in Atlanta until December 23rd," I said uncomfortably. "He's not sure what he wants to do after that, so until that time, I've decided to stay here in London."

Geoff tilted his head and looked at me as if he wasn't buying it. Rather than answer any more questions, I asked him about his love life. "I understand you might be pre-engaged." I was repeating a comment his mother had made. Patricia had been considerably annoyed at her son for his failure to take seriously his relationship with the niece of her closest friend.

"That was a joke, but Mother didn't stay around long enough to find that out." After putting his cracker down, he continued. "For some time now, I have been seeing Alberta Eccles. Unlike me, she's a caring and compassionate person. Her parents are in the midst of a nasty divorce, so Bertie runs from her mother's house in Bucks to her father's rooms in London in the fruitless pursuit of trying to salvage her parents' marriage. It is not salvageable! Her mother ran off with her lover to Brazil. Bad decision all around. The British run away to Argentina not Brazil. Once she got to Rio, Mrs. Eccles realized her mistake and returned to England. Bertie blames her mother's behavior on the 'change of life,' and I'm willing to give her the benefit of the doubt. But she must have known she was stepping over the line when she made her affair so public.

"The irony here is Bertie wants her parents to take her advice and 'forgive and forget.' Yet, with everyone in her family telling her the situation is a hopeless mess, she refuses to let it go, because that's advice she doesn't want to hear. By the way, nice job of leading the conversation away from your love life. I suspect all is not well with your chap in Atlanta."

I stood up and excused myself. I was tired from working all day and typing for a few hours each night. But I really wanted to get back to my room and reread a letter I had received from Rob. He was glad to hear I would be living with the Alcotts during the winter months because, "I don't like to think of you curled up in front of that space heater and wearing mittens to bed. Remember how we used to fight off the cold?" Here was another example of Rob flirting with me, but with nothing to back it up, what was the point? He then wrote at length about his brother's role as a pilot flying C-54s into Berlin before getting to the real reason for the letter.

Are Beth and Jack getting any news from Michael? I'm curious about his part in this business. I wonder how long it can go on, especially since flying in conditions in northern Europe in winter can be pretty bad. I know something about that. It's too bad Michael was transferred to Germany. But like he said, he's out in November, so what's that, another three or four weeks? I imagine his first stop will be Crofton to see his parents, and his second stop will be Holland Park. You two seemed to have hit it off. Looking forward to your next letter.

Love,
Rob

I was becoming increasingly frustrated with Rob. It seemed as if he wanted to continue our relationship, or why else would he be writing me letters? But with an ocean between us, how was that supposed to happen? He was definitely trying to figure out if there was something going on between Michael and me, but he knew as much as I did. We had had some passionate moments together before he left for Germany, and I really liked him. But since that time, there had been total silence—that is, until today. When I came home from work, on my section of the foyer table, was a letter from Michael.

Dear Maggie,

I'm not sure if you read my letter to Mom and Dad, but I am now flying back and forth between Lubeck and Berlin repairing aircraft left behind because of maintenance problems. The return flights have been very interesting.

Because of the fuel shortages, children and the elderly are at risk for hypothermia, so we have been flying old people and mothers with small children to the West. The kids seem to get a kick out of flying, but the adults are terrified. I can't blame them because we've had some rough weather, and you can really get bounced around back there. I do what I can to divert their attention. I speak to them in German, and they either start laughing, or it becomes a game trying to figure out what I'm saying.

I'm really looking forward to getting home, but before I do, I wanted to apologize for my behaviour the week of the ball. I came on to you so strongly you must have thought me a total brute. The only excuse I have is that you were the prettiest girl I had met since leaving Australia, and I overreacted. It won't happen again. I appreciate the letters. Please write again.

Mike

After finishing the letter, I thought I should mail it to Rob. In that way, he could see for himself that Michael's second stop after getting home from Germany would not be Holland Park. His interest in me was apparently due to a shortage of good-looking women at his station in Malta. It had been such a short time ago that I had been complaining that my life had become too complicated because two men were interested in me at the same time. That was no longer the case. Problem solved!

Chapter 36

OCTOBER 31ST WAS A glum day for me. The British do not celebrate Halloween, reserving their autumn celebration for November 5th, Guy Fawkes Night, a commemoration of the discovery of a plot to blow up the Houses of Parliament. The British make merry by building bonfires, which are fun, but I missed having little kids come to the door for their trick or treat. In Minooka, where everyone knew everyone else, neighbors demanded a "trick" before they put any goody in your bag. My sisters and I would sing a song, and when we were finished, after accounting for my brother's whereabouts, we held out an old pillowcase and were rewarded with a piece of candy or an apple.

If my mood wasn't gloomy enough, London was experiencing its first major fog of the season. It wasn't the city's famous "pea soup," but it was thick enough to look like a set for a Jack the Ripper movie.

I was hoping someone would be at the house because, for the past two days, I had been all alone. Even Geoff would do, and as it turned out, he would have to. I went into the morning room and plopped down on the chair opposite to him. He offered to give up his chair, which was closer to the fire, but I didn't feel like moving. I hadn't even taken off my coat.

"Have you been in Brussels?" I asked.

"No, worse. I've been closeted in a conference room with Dutch, Belgian, French, British, and American representatives, none of whom speak a common language."

"Americans speak English, Geoff."

"Debatable." I let out a loud sigh. It was going to be one of those nights.

"I went down to see Lily, and as it turns out, my mother *and* father were there. Lily was in false labor, and my mother rang the alarm bell because the baby would be too early. When it comes to Iris or Lily, all that is required is a phone call for my father to rush to their side. There have been royal births with fewer attendants."

I had figured out that when Geoff was in a really bad mood, it usually had something to do with his father. The few times I had seen Rand and Geoff together, the atmosphere had been tense. Geoff, who could rarely keep his mouth shut for more than a few minutes, said almost nothing. There was also a physical change. Geoff abandoned his stooped posture for one that would have passed muster at Sandhurst.

"I don't think it's unusual for a parent to favor children of the opposite sex," I said, yawning. "It certainly was true in my house. If my brother hadn't been under my mother's protection, my father would have killed him."

"It's not a matter of favoritism."

"Then what is it?" I asked, getting my handkerchief out of my purse. For the next four months, because of inadequate heat, my nose would run constantly. There was also the possibility I was getting another cold. And I wasn't alone. Because of a poor diet, many Britons were either sick or getting over being sick.

"I didn't play rugby. I didn't go to Sandhurst. I was never in combat. As far as he's concerned, I don't do manly things. He thinks I'm a twerp."

I didn't know Rand well enough to know what he thought about anything, but Geoff's reasoning seemed all wrong to me. "With all that your father went through after losing his eye, I can't imagine he would have wanted his son to be in combat. I'm sure he thought you were in enough danger where you were."

"Maggie, remember, I was in intelligence. Little danger there."

"Really? I know my classmate, Jimmy Barrett, is buried in Belgium because an artillery shell exploded in a mess tent. He was supposedly behind the front lines and not in danger. Your father saw enough of war to know you could have been killed by an artillery shell or a sniper. Look at the Battle of the Bulge. How many men serving behind the lines were killed or taken prisoner when the Germans broke through?

"Since meeting your father, I've read up on the battle at Passendaele. You'll have a hard time convincing me that your father would want you to go through anything remotely like that. And as for you being a twerp, why don't you stop acting like one? You are intelligent, interesting, and talented, but you act as if life is one big bore." And after blowing my nose, I finished, "And stop slouching."

"You're slouching," was all Geoff said.

"But I'm slouching because I'm cold and tired. You slouch because you're playing defense."

"And your degree is in psychology, I presume?" I could tell he was annoyed.

Standing up, I said, "No, it's simpler than that. Any father who would want to see his son in the thick of battle shouldn't be a father. It's none of my business, but I think you and your father should sit down and talk. You might surprise each other."

Geoff surprised me when he told me to sit down. Without asking, he poured a brandy for me. When I had arrived in England, I had never had a drink of hard liquor. As I took the glass from his hand, I realized how much I had changed.

"Yes, I agree. My father would not wish his experience in battle on anyone's son. However, you haven't seen him when he's talking to someone who has been in combat. Of particular interest to him is the Italian campaign because he was against it."

"So, basically, what you're saying is, your father talks to people who can confirm he was right when he said the Italian campaign shouldn't have been fought at all. It may show him as being proud and lording it over those who got it wrong, but it doesn't show a thirst for blood and guts, especially your blood and guts."

I decided to change the subject in an effort to turn down the temperature. The relationship that was developing between Geoff and me was very much along the lines of the one I had with my brother. We were constantly sparring.

"Why was your father in the European theater anyway considering he was born and raised in India?"

"Dad is deeply attached to India and its people, but he's also a realist. There was no way Britain was going to be able to keep India in the Empire, so he thought we should concentrate on

Germany and let the Indians take care of India, and the same for Burma. It really was the forgotten war, and the CBI was the worst theater in which to fight. If someone received orders for Burma, it was assumed they would be killed, wounded, or sicken or die of disease. Both my father and Jack had severe attacks of malaria while living in India, so they had first-hand experience with the disease part of the equation. When Michael received his orders, well, you can imagine what everyone was thinking. I don't know what happened to Michael in Burma, but it's obvious that something did because he lost more than two stone, and there's something wrong with his left arm."

"Why do you say that?" I asked. I hadn't noticed anything.

"We spent a lot of time together in India. Michael is ambidextrous, but he's always favored his left hand. At dinner, we were always bumping elbows. It was a game we had. Now, he's doing much more with his right hand. It's really obvious in his letters. His handwriting is abominable, and it wasn't when we were in India."

I agreed with Geoff about the handwriting. Considering his education, his penmanship looked as if it was being written by someone who was just learning how to write cursive.

"Other than being in the hospital because of a parasite he had picked up," I said, "Michael hasn't said anything to his parents about being injured or wounded."

"My God, he wouldn't! When Jack learnt that Michael had orders for Burma, he almost fell apart, although I'm not supposed to know about that. He was already worried near to death about James being in the mixer in Italy, but at least Michael was safe at the air base in Lincolnshire. Then the news came about Burma.

"After the Japanese surrender, Michael would have been eligible for home leave. Instead, he went straight from Burma to Australia and from there to Malta. Very suspicious to my mind. Beth and Jack didn't see him until he went to James's wedding in Italy. He was even thinner then than he is now. He tried to put the best face on it, but, my God, you couldn't help but notice the weight loss and the circles under his eyes. Beth was really shaken. Anyway, when the party got going, Michael had a great time, and despite his appearance, his spirits seemed to be in top form. I went up to Crofton Wood last Christmas, and other than being ready to get back to civilian life, he didn't have any complaints."

The same was true of Rob. Before the war, his plans had been to teach math at the local high school, not to navigate a B-17 bomber. Up to that point, I had avoided talking about Rob because of Geoff's wisecracks, but I had since learned how to steer the conversation in such a way that it kept his smart-aleck remarks to a minimum. I summarized Rob's service, his thirty missions over Germany, and his inability to adjust to a peacetime society.

"I'm not sure what you're asking here," Geoff said. "I can't answer for Rob, but if you are asking if Michael is carrying around some terrible burden because of the war, I'm pretty confident in saying 'no.'"

"Why? You hardly ever see him."

"In India, the Crowells had a head servant named Kavi, who instructed us in the martial arts. It involved a lot of kicking and fighting with sticks, but there was also an emphasis on meditation and yoga. James and I loved the fighting part, but we weren't all that keen on meditating. Not so Michael. He wanted to learn everything Kavi could teach him. I don't know if he can still do it, but he was once able to put his legs behind his head. Mike was the calmest chap I've ever known, and a lot of it was due to his training with Kavi. What I'm trying to say is that if something bad happened to him, and there's a good chance something did, then he would have dealt with it head-on." Almost as an afterthought, Geoff added, "As to your relationship with Rob, I'd give it a miss."

"Why?" I asked, surprised.

"First, I don't believe your problems with Rob have very much to do with the war. From the little you've told me, Rob's not acting out of the norm. Most people who have seen horrible things and can't deal with them, do something to blot them out. Usually, it's drink. But I knew one fellow who took up tennis because it kept him busy, and he couldn't concentrate on anything else. He's got a smashing backhand now."

"And secondly?" It was amazing how easily he got off track.

"Let me put it this way, if you were my girlfriend, I wouldn't have returned to the States without you or, if I absolutely had to return to the States, I would have made arrangements for you to follow. He didn't do either of those things. I'd forget about him and concentrate on me."

"You must be joking," I said, laughing.

"Why not? I'm handsome, intelligent, well educated. I have a good job with a promising future. I draw quarterly on a trust fund set up by my Burden grandparents. There's more. Shall I go on?"

"Geoff, I wouldn't be good for you at all," I said in a more serious tone in case he wasn't kidding. "You need a girl who won't put up with your nonsense. Someone like my sister Sadie."

"Is Sadie as pretty as you are?" Geoff acted as if he was really interested.

"Prettier. But she's tough. If it's on her mind, you'll hear about it. She's the only one who ever had the courage to talk back to my grandfather, and he hasn't said a word to her since."

Thinking about my sister, it reminded me of how much I missed all of my family, and with the holidays coming, I was beginning to think it was time to go home. It was too late to get home by Thanksgiving. But if I started making plans immediately, I could give my boss sufficient notice, so that I could be in Minooka by Christmas. The hardest thing would be to leave the Crowells, and now the Alcotts, but without Rob, I was beginning to feel like a woman without a country.

Chapter 37

MY DECISION TO RETURN to the States by Christmas was made easier because I would be flying home. AAFES had contracted with charter airlines to fly dependents and civilian personnel between the United States and its bases in Europe. However, because of the unpredictability of Northern European weather, my boss suggested I pick several departure dates because flights were routinely cancelled due to weather.

There was still the matter of my agreement with Beth and the Catons to write a brief history about the Laceys and Montclair. If I was to honor that commitment, I would have to spend less time with Geoff and more time with Elizabeth Garrison.

8 March—Mr. Lacey, Charles, and Jane came to Bennets End for dinner this evening. After our guests departed, Mama said she could think of no reason for Mr. Lacey's frequent visits to Hertfordshire now that his friend is married, nor does Papa understand why someone of Mr. Lacey's exalted rank was seated at his dinner table. I have mentioned that both

Jane and I believe that Mr. Lacey improves upon further acquaintance, and Papa said it was a good thing, since he is Charles's friend and, as such, 'we are stuck with him.'

11 March—Yesterday afternoon, I had a most unwelcome visitor—Lady Sylvia Desmet. Without any attempt at civility, she told me she had news that her nephew was to make an offer of marriage to me and she had come to make sure no such thing occurred. Her objections to the marriage were so numerous I cannot remember them all, but it was clear that she found me to be unworthy of Mr. Lacey's attentions in every respect, and that he would risk complete estrangement from her if he went forward with such a scheme. She ended by saying that no one in society would receive me, and I would forever be an embarrassment to her nephew and his family. It was impossible to defend myself, as she would not stop talking. Because of infirmities, she walks with a cane, and she kept hitting it against the floor, saying, 'I honoured you with my notice, and this is how you repay me.' She departed for Helmsley Hall with the intention of making Mr. Lacey see what an absolute disaster such an alliance with my family would be. I am crying as I write this, for fear of how Mr. Lacey will respond to such forceful arguments.

12 March—Mr. Lacey arrived at Bennets End early this morning to apologize for his aunt's behavior, and then he drew me to him in a loving embrace. He assured me I had nothing additional to fear from her, as she has severed all bonds between them. His only concern was for Anne.

And then it happened. I am to be Mrs. William David

Lacey. I must quickly put into writing what he said to me, as I do not wish to forget a word of it. 'When I proposed to you last August in Kent, if I had been a wiser and kinder man, you would have accepted my offer, and we would now be man and wife. Your rejection stung, but it provided me with an opportunity to examine my own conduct and the reasons for it. A much humbler man stands before you.'

Having made this confession, he continued with the words I had been waiting to hear. 'Miss Elizabeth, from the beginning of our acquaintance, I have loved you, and I now ask that you accept my proposal of marriage and agree to be my wife.' I was so happy, and we hugged and kissed and laughed until we realized he had not spoken to Papa. I will write tomorrow of his response.

Finally, I had arrived at the diary entry for Will Lacey's proposal to Elizabeth Garrison. I was touched by Will's newfound humility and his willingness to admit that someone, who was not his equal socially, could be his equal in all other things. He was clearly in love with a woman whom he valued for her beauty, wit, and intelligence.

14 March—Oh what an uproar we have caused! The only person more surprised by the announcement of our engagement than Papa was dear Mama. She blurted out, 'But, Lizzy, he is most unpleasant.' When Papa called me into his library, he asked if all the females in our neighbourhood had lost the use of their reason. 'First Charlotte and now you.' It took many minutes to convince him that we had become better acquainted at Helmsley Hall, that I had fallen in love

*with him, and that he was the finest man of my acquaintance.
Given time, I assured Papa that he would come to know
of the gentleman's many attributes. Mr. Lacey, noting
Papa's lack of enthusiasm, told him that it was his intention
to become the best of sons-in-law—'better even than Mr.
Chatterton is to Sir William Ledger,' which he said brought a
smile to Papa's face.*

Geoff was looking over my shoulder trying to read the manuscript, which was something he did when he wanted attention.

"Do you have something on your mind, Geoff?"

"I believe you are going somewhere. You've been typing as if
you are possessed or on a mission, or you would not have avoided
conversation with someone so erudite."

"I am a woman on a mission. I've had these diaries for weeks
now, and yet I haven't even gotten to the wedding, and I'm going
to keep going until I do."

"If you ignore me, I won't tell you about James and Angela's
wedding night."

I turned around and faced him. "Okay. You've got my
attention."

"You have to keep in mind that, during their entire courtship,
James hasn't done anything other than give Angela a chaste kiss.
Around midnight, all of the wedding guests, including Mike and
I, walk with the happy couple through the village to the Paglia
house and keep on going right into their bedroom. Some of the
old ladies throw flower petals on the bed cover, and then we
leave, but we're all right outside the door."

"Are you making this up?"

"Hell, no! I don't have to. James realizes the guests aren't going anywhere, and it's been a long six months, so nothing's going to stop him. While Angela's getting changed, James had to face the wall, and when he turns around, she's standing there in a cotton night gown with full sleeves. He said it was so stiff it could have stood up on its own. But it gets better. Angela gets in bed, fully clothed, and points to the bed cover, which has a hole in it exactly where a shorter man than James might insert a certain object."

"Oh, my God!"

"Exactly. When James figures out what she wants him to do, he goes into a primal mode and pulls the bed cover off the bed."

"And?"

"Apparently, Angela thought it was a great idea, and they had a terrific time even though everyone was just outside the door."

Geoff and I were hysterical. It was ten minutes before I could stop laughing enough to start typing, and Lizzy's diary entry showed that Angela had a lot more fun on her wedding night than Jane did.

17 May—Jane and I have talked about what is expected of a wife. She says the experience can be unpleasant at first, but after that, it seems the body recognizes the sacrifice that is being asked of it and responds appropriately. Her response made me wonder if intimacy can be pleasurable, or is it merely a matter of a wife's duty to her husband?

19 May—Tomorrow I shall become Mrs. William Lacey. How can all of this have happened? To be so in love with one's life partner is a rarity, but such has been my fortune. I am so pleased with my beautiful ivory satin wedding gown and lace veil. My lady's maid, whom I am to call Waite, has been of great help, but I do not know how much I should say to her. Mrs. Hughes, the housekeeper, insists that I must always be discreet or I could embarrass the family, as servants will talk.

According to Elizabeth's brief diary entry on May 20th, Will and his bride had "a merry wedding" with close friends and family in attendance at the church and the wedding breakfast. The food was plentiful, the wine flowed, the musicians played beautifully, and the dancers stepped lively. Everything had gone exactly as Elizabeth had hoped.

26 May—There is so much to write, but I am greatly fatigued, as I have a house full of guests, some of whom have been here near a week. This is the first opportunity I have had to write of the most important event in my life. I hope I can hold forever in my mind the look on Mr. Lacey's face when he first saw me at the church. The pastor at St Michael's received his appointment from the Laceys, and as such, performed the ceremony exactly as directed by his patron. Apparently, Mr. Lacey (whom I am now to call Will, as is his choice) leans toward brevity. The wedding breakfast lasted into the evening when the tables were cleared to make way for more food.

It was well past midnight by the time I went to my bed chamber. All my night clothes had been laid out by Waite, who helped me to get into my silk night gown. After she left, Will came to my chamber and asked if my mother had talked to me. I said that she had, and he was visibly relieved. I found it to be a most curious ritual, but Will was very kind and patient. After five days, I do not make any claim to being a proficient, but it certainly has become less awkward and more pleasurable which, as Will explained, is as it should be. He has been excessively attentive, and after he has fallen asleep, I lie in bed and count my blessings.

A week after their wedding, the couple went to London to make the requisite visits to the social elites who were then in town for the season. The couple seemed to have been given a warm welcome by everyone except Lady Jersey, but because she was the *de facto* leader of the *ton*, her behavior, no matter how offensive, had to be tolerated. But one person was missing, the Duchess of Devonshire.

2 June—We rode past Devonshire House, and I asked if the Duchess was still visiting abroad. I was astounded to learn that Her Grace has been exiled by her husband to the continent for having a child with Charles Grey. She has been gone for more than a year and a half, and while her children remain in England, the Duchess waits in Naples for word from the Duke that she may return. None of this bothers Will, as he has already written to Her Grace at her residence in Naples and has received a response in which she invites us to call as soon as we arrive.

At this point, Geoff coughed to let me know that he was once again being ignored. "Surely, Elizabeth and Will must be grandparents by now with as long as you've been typing."

I was ready to quit for the night anyway, so I asked him what was on his mind.

"You are leaving us. I know you are. So why don't you just tell old Geoff what's going on."

"Do you know what the fourth Thursday of November is in America?" I asked.

After thinking for a minute, he said, "Yes. It's Thanksgiving Day. When I was at Yale, Beth's Aunt Laura was kind enough to invite me to celebrate the holiday at her flat in New York. The table practically bowed from the weight of all that food."

"That's right." I laughed to myself at the thought of skinny Geoff biting into a turkey drumstick.

"Two years ago, I celebrated Thanksgiving in an Army mess hall at an air base. Last year, I had dinner in an office cafeteria, and it looks as if this year may be a repeat of 1947. In our family, Thanksgiving is a big deal. We have tomato juice and fruit cocktail, a turkey, gravy, mashed potatoes, biscuits, bread stuffing, corn, green beans, cranberry sauce, apple and pumpkin pies, all chased down with strong black coffee."

"And you want to spend Thanksgiving with your family," Geoff said sympathetically.

"I know that's not possible, but I'm thinking about how I can get home by Christmas."

"Is this a permanent relocation?"

"It would have to be. I don't have the money to go back and forth across the Atlantic. There's a big part of me that wants to stay in England, but then there's another part that says I'm an American, and it's time to go home. I've been gone for more than two years."

"Does this have something to do with your flyer?"

"If you're asking if I'm going home so I can run Rob to ground in Atlanta, the answer is 'no,'" I said defensively. "Of course, I'll let him know where I am, but I'm not expecting anything to happen."

"And what about Michael?"

"What are you talking about?" I asked too loudly.

"I'll give you credit for being clever by burying your questions about him in more general questions about India or the war. But when I talk about Michael, your interest level goes way up. I know you've had a letter from him recently."

"We had something of a flirtation for a few days before and after the ball at Montclair," I admitted. "But, if you'd like, I can show you the letter I received from him in which he apologized for that very same flirtation, saying he doesn't know what came over him. He assured me there would be no repetition.

"And, yes, I'm interested in him in much the same way I'm interested in you. You don't have any idea how fascinating your life sounds to a girl who grew up looking at the black hulk of a coal breaker. You talk so casually about Paris and Brussels, skiing in the Alps, climbing the Acropolis. These are places I can only dream about, but I'm a very practical working-class girl, who knows when it's time to go home."

"I didn't tell you," Geoff said. "Beth called. She's coming to London next week. She's planning a party and asked if you could help her out. Michael is coming home on the 18th, and the party's for him."

Chapter 38

ALTHOUGH WILL AND ELIZABETH'S honeymoon had nothing to do with Montclair, I did want to spend some time on it. By twentieth century standards, their journey would be exciting, but taking into account the couple had traveled in 1793 in a Europe menaced by French revolutionary armies, their journey was remarkable. After visiting Spa in the Ardennes Forest and touring castles along the Rhine River, they went on to Lausanne on Lake Geneva where they were guests of Edward Gibbon, the historian and author of *The Decline and Fall of the Roman Empire*, at his lakeside home. It was there the couple learned that the Duke of Devonshire had recently sent for his duchess, and the party had immediately set out for England.

After visiting Milan, Verona, and Venice, they settled down for the winter in Florence in a sixteenth-century palazzo fronting the Piazza del Signorini. Inspired by the sights of Florence, Lizzy tried her hand at painting watercolors, with Georgiana as her instructor. However, she was so unhappy with the results, she "donated" all of her canvasses to a fellow Englishman and painter when the party moved on to Rome and Naples.

After an early bout of homesickness, Lizzy eagerly embraced her nomadic existence with her "beloved." Lizzy was a faithful diarist from the time she married Will. Her entries also recorded the intimacies of the newly married couple from the earliest days of their marriage. When Will and Lizzy made love, she made note of it by referring to her husband as "my visitor." Will was a frequent visitor.

The Laceys' stay in Naples was particularly interesting. The Duchess of Devonshire had provided the couple with an introduction to the British Envoy to the Court of Naples, Sir William Hamilton, an amateur vulcanologist, whose beautiful wife was the famous, or infamous, Emma Hamilton, the future mistress of the hero of Trafalgar, Lord Horatio Nelson. I was scanning the pages for interesting entries, when one caught my eye:

14 April—Lady Hamilton never fails to amuse. Tonight, by request of the King, she posed in one of her attitudes as Cleopatra, ending with the Queen of Egypt's death scene. With little more than a few shawls, including one that served as an asp, Lady Hamilton portrayed the grieving queen taking her life after learning that her lover, Mark Antony, was dead. I found myself drawn into her tableau and was deeply touched when at last Cleopatra closed her eyes. However, Will was offended by the suggestive nature of her poses but did not object when I struck a similar pose that evening after we had retired.

I was so glad that Lizzy and Will had married before the Victorian Age. Two generations later, a woman would never have written about the intimacies of marriage, but it was obvious these two lovers complemented each other in so many ways.

I was about to type out the entry regarding Lizzy and Will's journey to Mt. Vesuvius, where Will burnt the soles of his boots on the lava, when the doorbell rang. When I opened the door, I nearly broke Beth's ribs I hugged her so tightly.

"I thought you might be going dotty typing all those diaries, so I decided to come to London for a few days to see how you were getting on," Beth said, putting down her suitcase.

We went into the morning room, and Beth rang for Andrews. Andrews entered the room with a look of disapproval, believing I was the one who had summoned him. When he saw Beth, his whole demeanor changed.

"Andrews, is it possible to have some sandwiches served in here on a tray? Whatever is in the larder will do." This was the Beth I rarely saw, but when I did, it was apparent she had grown up in a household full of servants and was quite comfortable in giving orders.

I told Beth I had come up with an idea that could possibly make everyone happy. A timeline showing events taking place in the lives of the Lacey family, along with transcriptions from Lizzy's diary, would be juxtaposed with quotations from *Pride and Prejudice*.

After thinking for a few minutes, Beth said she liked it, and after finishing the history, she hoped I would continue working on the diary "at my leisure." I didn't say anything about going back to the States.

I told Beth how Lizzy called Will "her visitor" whenever they made love. "They were really and truly in love, just like you and Jack."

Smiling, she said, "I can take a hint. But let's wait for Andrews to bring the sandwiches. He is positively Victorian, and he wouldn't appreciate hearing a discussion of my love life."

Andrews brought in a tray with cucumber sandwiches and coffee. After making sure he was safely out of the room, Beth said, "Actually, at first, it wasn't Jack whom I was attracted to but his brother, who was exactly my age. You've seen pictures of Tom at Crofton Wood, but they don't do him justice. He had these incredible blue eyes and the most engaging smile. He was also a comedian, which made him everyone's favorite.

"When I was about sixteen, Tom had invited me to go to a dance in Stepton. Matthew dropped the two of us and Billy, the footman, off at the dance hall. About an hour later, Jack came in with some friends and asked me to dance. He was most unpleasant." Straightening her skirt, she continued, "He said the local girls had been waiting all week to come to the dance to show off in front of the boys, and then I had walked in and hogged the limelight."

I couldn't help but wince. Apparently, Jack didn't approve of masters and minions mixing.

"I was terribly hurt because the thought had never entered my mind. After I had a few dances with the local boys, Jack offered to take me home. I had no choice because, if I rang the house, they would know what I had got up to. I was really quite intimidated by Mr. Crowell, and I didn't want to have a lecture about above stairs and below stairs not mixing. When I got out of the car, I said to Jack, 'You don't like me very much, do you?' And do you know what he said? 'If anything, I like you too much.' From that time on, I certainly paid more attention to him, but nothing exciting happened until the motor tour."

"I'm surprised your mother let you go."

"No more than I. But I didn't know until later how much maneuvering my grandmother had done behind the scenes. We were a couple of weeks into the trip when we arrived in Brighton. While Reed was busy sketching, Jack and I went for long walks. Finally, he kissed me. There was nothing chaste about these kisses. We just about devoured each other. When we returned to Montclair, he acted as if we hadn't been at each other for weeks. But before I knew it, he was on his way to Manchester, and I was off to Cambridge.

"At our annual Christmas tea, I slipped Jack a note asking him to meet me at an abandoned cottage the following day. I nearly froze waiting for him, but he did come. He was very agitated, and we had a violent argument. He said something to the effect that if we were ever to be together, I would have to be willing to give up Montclair and everything that went with it. I told him I would come into some money of my own from a trust fund when I turned twenty-one the following year. This is what he said to that, 'Christ, would you listen to yourself? Someone who is going to come into some money from a trust fund shouldn't be sneaking around with the butler's son.' And he stormed off.

"After the Lenten term, Jack came home, as he always did, but made no attempt to see me. Then one day my mother sent me to find Clyde, who was not quite normal, but who was capable of exercising the horses. Often, when out on his rides, he'd find a nice shade tree, tie up the horse, and have a lie-down. When I got to the stables, Jack was mucking out the stalls, filling in for one of the grooms. He asked if I was looking for him, and I said 'yes.' And he said, 'What do you want?' And I answered, 'I want you to love me.'

"'I already do. What else do you want?' He said it just like that. 'What else do you want?'

"I told him that I wanted him to marry me, and he dropped his rake and asked, 'Have you gone off your head?' I stood my ground and said, 'No, I'm just in love.'

"I don't know why he finally gave in, but we had a most pleasant afternoon. We met whenever we could, usually at an abandoned cottage at the far end of the property. But then he had to go back to Manchester, and I had to go through the motions of my third season. My mother was nearly in a panic because it was believed if a girl was not married by the third season, something was wrong with her, or why had she not made a match?

"The previous season I had met a handsome and intelligent gentleman named Colin Matheson. He had quite a reputation as a ladies' man, and although I found him to be attractive, I was not going to be one of those who practically swooned when he came into the room. He asked if he could call on me, and not wanting to encourage him because of Jack, I told him I had a very crowded schedule. He didn't like that answer, and he didn't call. When my mother saw him in Paris, he told her what I had said, and she was not amused.

"Because I was in love with Jack, I had to put on this performance of looking for a husband, and so during the 1914 season, I encouraged Colin. Mama was so pleased with the way things were going that she agreed to let me go back to Montclair for a week's rest before getting back into the game for the second half of the season. Of course, the reason I wanted to go back home was because Jack would be at Montclair on summer break.

"Don't let anyone ever tell you that women are the worst gossips. Reed and I returned to Montclair by car with Billy

Hitchens as our driver. Apparently, Billy told Jack about Colin, and when I went to look for him, his mother said he had gone up to the Highlands to work on a school project and would be gone for the rest of the summer. I went up to my room and cried my eyes out. When I returned to London, I agreed that Colin and I would become engaged at Christmastime."

Beth closed her eyes as she tried to retrieve memories from thirty years earlier. "The summer of 1914 was glorious. There was no end to tennis parties and picnics. Colin and I drove down to Henley, where we met some of Reed's friends, and we all went rowing on the Thames. My Aunt Laura, an admirer of Wordsworth, was visiting from New York, and we all went up to the Lake District and Windermere. You could hardly move with all the people strolling about the village. But Aunt Laura and Uncle Cal in New York did not come alone. Without my mother's knowledge, they had brought Ellen Manning and little Gloria with them."

"So Trevor got to see his daughter."

"Yes, he did. Trevor, Ellen, and Gloria spent two weeks at the resort town of Eastbourne. It was Trevor's intention to go to work for my Uncle Cal after the war and to marry Ellen. But you know what happened in France.

"All of that summer, there had been talk about war, and the great powers were mobilizing. But even after Archduke Ferdinand and his wife were assassinated, it seemed impossible that a major war would break out as a result of a death in the Balkans. But Colin was less optimistic." Turning around facing the door, she said, "And I hear someone."

It was Geoff. Beth was pleased to see him, and he put on his best public school manners and asked after the family. Reaching into her purse, she took out a piece of paper. "I've had a letter from Michael." I moved to the sofa, so that Geoff and I could read it together. "I apologize for the handwriting. I don't know what happened there, and he often forgets to date his letters." I thought to myself, so did William Lacey.

Dear Mom, Dad, James, Angela, and Maggie,

This is my first day off since I arrived. It's been ten days of twelve-hour shifts. Lubeck was used by the Luftwaffe as a night fighter base (Junkers 88s for those interested). Because it was a permanent installation on the North Sea, we have some very nice digs. The barracks is a brick building with central heating and is well insulated.

Since my arrival, I have been working on C-47 Dakotas exclusively. The Dakotas' cargo is mostly coal, tobacco, and flour, but one crew delivered the goat mascot for the South Wales Borderer Regiment. The dust from the coal and flour get into everything, and it's a nasty business cleaning everything for the next go-round, but these crews are stellar.

Starting tomorrow, I will be flying in and out of Berlin to work on aircraft that, for one reason or another, were unfit for the return flight. My crew and I will fly in with the parts, fix it, and return to Lubeck. The sergeant major asked if I wanted to go home on a short leave or have the time deducted from the end of my enlistment. I chose the latter because that will get me home on or about November 18th instead of the 25th.

Even though I don't write that often, it doesn't mean you shouldn't. I'm too tired to do anything other than read your letters. It would be a lonely place without them. I love you all.

Mike

"Mike's the last one to be demobbed," Geoff said, "so we'll have to have a grand party welcoming him back to civilian life."

"Will Alberta be joining us?" Beth asked.

"No. Bertie and I have parted company," Geoff said without his usual flippancy. "On the advice of a friend, I ended it because it was basically unworkable."

After several discussions with Geoff about his relationship with Alberta, he had asked for my opinion. I told him that if I was in a relationship that was unworkable, I would rather know about it sooner rather than later. I had started a letter to Rob saying just that, but that letter was on my desk next to one I had received from my mother telling me my Aunt Marie was unwell. Mom did not say I should come home, but knowing how important my aunt was to me, she wanted to let me know that, at my aunt's age, things could go from bad to worse very quickly.

Other than my mother, my grandmother's sister Marie was the most important person in my life. She believed I could do anything I set my mind to. When I wanted to move to Washington after finishing secretarial school, my mother thought I was too shy to work in a big city, but Aunt Marie had encouraged me to go. When I hesitated about going to Germany to work for the Army Exchange Service, she told me if I didn't go, I'd end up marrying a local boy and popping a kid out every other year. She practically pushed me out the door.

"Does your mother know about Alberta?" Beth asked Geoff.

"No. Mother has taken up residence at Lily's house. I think she's exhibiting an overabundance of caution regarding her pregnancy. Yes, she had a miscarriage, but so did you and so did my mother. It does not automatically follow that a miscarriage is a harbinger of future problem pregnancies."

"It's good of you to be so brave about this, Geoff," Beth said, clearly annoyed. Standing up, she added, "I'm very tired, and I need to ring Jack."

After Beth left the room, I told Geoff I didn't know that Beth had a miscarriage.

"It happened in India when Violet and I were staying with Jack and Beth. Beth said she was going to lie down. The next thing I know, she's calling for James to get Ayah and for Michael to bring some towels. When we found her, she was sitting on the bathroom floor with her head on the tub, quietly crying." Standing up, he said, "Excuse me. I need to find Beth."

***

At breakfast, I told Beth that Geoff felt awful about what he had said. I was sticking up for someone who probably didn't deserve it.

"Don't worry, Maggie. Geoff is a very complex character, and I, perhaps more than anyone else, understand why he says the things he does. When he was with Jack and me in India, I was very hard on him. He was ten years old and throwing tantrums, something I never tolerated in my sons when they were toddlers. When he did come around, I found him to be extraordinarily bright and likable.

"Rather than sending Geoff and Violet back to England for schooling, I convinced Patricia to allow the children to stay with me and that I would supervise their education. When Geoff misbehaved, I told him if he didn't straighten up, he would be joining his Burden cousins at Glenkill. That kept him in check."

"Why? What's wrong with Glenkill?"

"Nothing, if it's the right fit, as it was with my boys. These public schools place a great deal of emphasis on games. Geoff is an agile athlete, but he has a slight build, which would have made him a target for bullies. Besides, he's an intellectual with a love for history and the arts. Glenkill was all wrong for him. He managed to get expelled within a month of his arrival."

Beth started to laugh. "He was very clever. He knew that attending religious services was mandatory, but from the beginning, he skipped out on chapel. When he was called before the headmaster, he declared he could not attend chapel because he was agnostic. The school notified Patricia that he could not continue, which is exactly what he wanted in the first place.

"Rand shrugged it off and enrolled Geoff at St. Paul's in London, but Patricia was furious because the Burdens had been one of the founding families of the school. When she told him that every boy in the family had gone to Glenkill for generations, Geoff said..." Beth started to laugh. "He told his mother that generations of Burden males had pissed in the fireplace, 'but we don't do that anymore.'"

I could just picture Geoff standing defiantly before his black-robed headmaster. Geoff was not the big, tall fellow his father was, but he was someone who would stand firm if he believed in something.

"He certainly changes the discussion," I said, declining Beth's offer of sherry.

"Oh, yes. Where was I? It was when Jack and I were having a romp in the stables. We spent as much time pulling hay out of my hair as we did kissing," Beth said, laughing. "But then the war came. All my stories end with 'but then the war came.'"

"My first involvement with the war effort was when our

housemistress at Newnham asked if some of the girls would volunteer to go to the railway station to serve coffee to regiments passing through on their way to the Channel ports. But when we got to the station, the Red Cross had already set everything up. The woman in charge asked if we would be available to help with other things, such as knitting mufflers, and she explained that there were sewing and knitting clubs being organized to teach people how to do those things. All the while I was knitting balaclavas, socks, and mufflers, the British Expeditionary Forces, including Rand, were retreating from Mons in Belgium leaving thousands of dead behind them. Because of censorship, I don't think anyone realized the extent of our losses.

"Our next assignment was to go to a warehouse that had been converted into a hospital. When the wounded arrived, we found they were not British at all, but Belgians. They were exhausted, filthy, and covered with lice, so we threw their uniforms into tubs of boiling water. This experience proved to be quite an eye-opener for me. Let's just say their ideas regarding sanitation and modesty were quite different from mine."

Beth stood up and asked if I had changed my mind about having a sherry, as she was going to have another. Even though it was getting late, and I had to work the next day, I said "yes" because I believed I was finally going to hear about Colin Matheson.

"I have avoided telling you about Colin because, after all of these years, I still find it difficult to talk about him. After Jack pushed off on me, I returned to London, where Colin was waiting. Because of his reputation, I had concerns about whether or not he could be faithful to one woman. I knew from an earlier conversation that he had tired of the whole London social scene. He didn't want to have any more conversations with empty-headed debutantes, and he was tired of being the entertainment for bored wives. But it was only after he had assured me of his fidelity that I agreed to an engagement.

"Over the course of the summer, Colin courted me in royal fashion. There was hardly a day that went by when I didn't get flowers or notes or something that had belonged to his mother. I allowed myself to believe I was in love. Since I couldn't have Jack, the next best thing was Colin. But then the war came. See what I mean?

"Colin had served in the Irish Guards for four years and was considered to be a reserve officer. When war broke out, he was called up immediately. He fought at the First Battle of Ypres with the Guards suffering horrendous casualties. In December, he was given leave to come home so we could become engaged. But before I left Montclair for London, our family had the traditional Christmas tea. I kept looking at Jack, pleading for him to say something, but he didn't.

"Colin was a sensible man, and he thought our wedding should be postponed until after the war. I've often wondered if we would have acted differently if we had known how long the war would last. He returned to Belgium in January and came home for leave in May. With both armies now trapped in static trench warfare, Colin hoped the combatants would negotiate a peace settlement. It was very difficult for him because he had studied in Dresden and had many German friends. He could hardly believe he might be shooting at them.

"I traveled with him to Harwich to see him off. He must have had a premonition about not surviving the war because he gave me his mother's engagement and wedding rings. In his last letter, he wrote that his sector was very quiet. The biggest threats came from infiltrators and snipers and the occasional artillery bombardment each side used to remind the other they were still there.

"Colin was the last in his family, so when the telegram came, it was delivered to my father, whom Colin had listed as next of kin. He had been killed on July 2, 1915, in an artillery barrage. His colonel wrote that his death was immediate, and he did not suffer. I only hope it was true." After pausing to dry her tears, Beth continued, "It's so sad, because Colin had no one to keep his memory alive, so his mother's rings have been in my jewelry box for thirty years.

"I remember crying on and off for days, and would do so again when Trevor was killed that autumn and Tom the following summer. By the time Matthew was killed, there had been so much death on the Somme, that it was a part of daily life. Someone you knew was going to get a telegram from the War Office. By the end of the war, I was barely functioning as a human being. What saved me was my love for Jack, and in the years following the war, my children. You have to move on, or you become a well of sadness."

After hearing about Beth's losses, I started to cry, and I knew it was time for me to go home. I wanted to be with my family, and I explained to Beth about my Aunt Marie.

Beth shook her head and said, "Maggie, please don't. I know I'm being selfish, but this will be the first Christmas since 1940 that I'll have all of my family together, and I consider you to be a part of my family. If you will stay until the new year, I'll pay for an air transport ticket for you to the States." Taking my hands in hers, she asked, "Will you do this for me?"

I loved Beth, but I was having the same tug at my heart as she was. I missed my family terribly. I was even starting to miss my brother. But it was my fear that Aunt Marie would die before I could see her again that was adding urgency to my plans to go home. I agreed to stay as long as I didn't receive any bad news about my aunt. Beth gave me a quick hug and said, "Besides, Michael is coming home, and you wouldn't want to leave before seeing him."

Chapter 39

IN PREPARATION FOR MICHAEL'S party, Beth sent me to an Italian bakery in Finsbury where Angela bought her pasta when she had lived in London. Because Angela was so beautiful, she received extra rations of flour and homemade pasta from an admiring Mr. Giordano. Hopefully, just by mentioning Angela's name, I would get the same results. I did get what I wanted, but so did Mr. Giordano, who managed to brush up against both my backside and my breasts. In case I had to come back for more, I actually thanked him.

When I got home, the first thing I did was to check to see if I had any mail. I wasn't expecting any letters, nor was I expecting to see a RAF hat on the table and a RAF overcoat on the coat rack. I wasn't Sherlock Holmes, but there seemed to be only one explanation—Michael was home early from Germany. I quietly opened the door to the morning room, and there was Michael, stretched out the length of a chair and ottoman, sound asleep. The fire had gone cold, but, apparently, so had Michael, who was softly snoring.

When I arrived in Germany in August 1946, I was a naive, devout Catholic, who believed that sex outside of marriage was not only a mortal sin in the eyes of the Church, but just plain wrong, and that such intimacy had a place only in the bedroom of a married couple. In the subsequent two years, I lost a good deal of my naiveté, and although I faithfully attended Mass, I hadn't received Communion in months because I was guilty of the sin of lust. To make matters worse, I was lusting after two men at the same time, and one of them was asleep in the chair in front of me.

He looked so peaceful, and I wanted to touch his face. Instead, I left a note for Geoff on the foyer table telling him that his cousin was asleep in the morning room, and I went downstairs to find something to eat. I had been eating sardines and crackers for two nights in a row, and it seemed as if I was going to be eating them for a third when I heard Geoff's familiar footsteps. He had bought some Chinese takeaway, which was becoming a mainstay for the two of us.

"Michael's arrival blows Beth's plans for a surprise party all to hell, doesn't it?" Geoff asked.

"Not necessarily," I answered. "Jack and Beth can go with him up to Crofton, and we can plan the party for this weekend. It was going to be tough pulling off a party midweek anyway."

"Do you want a beer?" Geoff asked, as he gazed into the refrigerator.

"Make that two beers," Michael said as he came down the stairs.

Geoff jumped up and shook Michael's hand to the point where he looked like he was working a water pump.

After grabbing a beer, Michael asked, "Were you two planning my surprise party?" Geoff and I looked at each other but said nothing. "I got here at noon, and Mrs. Gooding told me that Maggie had gone to Finsbury to buy flour to bake a cake. So the cake was either for my demob party, or someone is having a birthday."

"Your mother will be so disappointed if you're not surprised," I said.

"I promise to be surprised."

"How's everything going with the Airlift?" Geoff asked.

"They've got this thing running like a well-oiled machine," Michael answered. "A plane lands in Berlin every five minutes. They offload the cargo in a matter of minutes, and if there's nothing wrong with the plane, off it goes back to its home base. The only thing that messes with the system is the weather."

"Don't you find it a bit odd to be doing all this just three years after we were trying to kill them?" Geoff asked.

"Yes," Michael said, nodding his head. "When I got to Lubeck, I was told it had been a night fighter base. We have two German crews working for us. They are well-trained and extremely competent, but I couldn't help but wonder if some of these men had worked on fighters that went after our planes. But you have to get past it. In war, hatred is a valuable tool in keeping you alive. In peacetime, it's a millstone."

Thinking that the conversation had taken a martial turn, I saw it as a chance to make my exit. The last time I had been with Michael, he had been holding me so tightly I could hear his heart beating. I hadn't mentally prepared for his return.

"Good night, gentlemen. I'll let you two catch up. Tomorrow's a work day for me."

As I walked past Michael, he caught me by my arm and said, "Hell, I don't want to catch up with Geoff." Putting his beer down, he said, "Let's go somewhere. There must be a dance club around here that isn't shuttered."

The three of us ended up in a half-empty club with a three-piece band and a piano player who was feeling no pain, but it seemed that neither Geoff nor Michael cared about the quality of the music. While Michael was ordering a round of drinks, Geoff headed straight for a blonde, who was coming out of the ladies' room. After putting three ales down in front of me, Michael offered me a cigarette. I shook my head and told him I didn't smoke.

"You don't smoke, and you drink very little. Do you have any vices?"

"Yes, I swear like a sailor." Michael started to laugh. He had the most beautiful smile. His father told me that he had spent a fortune on braces for Michael, and it had been worth every penny. "My mother always said there were three things a lady never did: smoke in public, chew gum, and cross your legs at the knees. I think she read it in a *Ladies' Home Journal* article."

"Well, it's true that smoking is very bad for you. I'll agree with your mother there. And chewing gum is repulsive, regardless of sex. However, I have to disagree with her about crossing your legs at the knees. In your case, it's just bad advice." It seemed that our flirtation was up and running, and Michael had been home only for a couple of hours.

The band was now playing a piano number that was even worse than the first, but Michael insisted that we dance. Although it wasn't a slow dance, he was acting as if it was and started singing "Always," the song the band had played at Montclair for its last number. I was back in his arms again.

When we returned to our table, two men were sitting there. The more sober one had heard my accent, and he started in on Americans.

"The way I hear it, the British had their thumbs up their arses while America saved the world. Isn't that right, deary?"

There's always a fine line when talking to someone who has had too much to drink. Do you engage in the hopes he will settle down, or do you just walk away? The problem was, he was sitting at our table. I could see Geoff and Michael were not amused and were about to give both of them the boot. I didn't want a barroom brawl, so I decided to walk away and told the boys I was heading home. Michael was out of his chair in a flash. "You can't go home yet."

"Actually, I can. That is possibly the worst band I have ever heard, and I've heard lots of them. I come from a town where every kid thought he was the next Tommy Dorsey. Besides, I have to work in the morning, and I'm tired, but I'd appreciate it if you walked me to the Underground." And we left Geoff behind with the blonde.

Sitting on the bench waiting for the train, Michael asked what I had been doing since our farewell at the train station.

"I'm still with AAFES." I explained about the three B-29 squadrons that were now stationed in England. "But I'm pretty sure I'll be heading home in January."

"Has something caused you to change your mind about going back to your hometown?"

"Yes, my Aunt Marie has been ill for a few weeks now, and she's in her eighties. Besides, I'm beginning to feel as if I'm in limbo here."

"I'm confused as to your plans," he said. "After seeing your family and aunt, are you staying in Minooka? I didn't think that was an option because of the lack of jobs."

Seeing his furrowed brow, I said, "Don't worry. I have cousins strategically placed throughout the country and a sister who lives near New York City."

"I'm probably out of line here, but where is Rob in all of this?"

"Rob's employment with TRC ends on December 23rd. After that, he's going to Omaha to visit with the family of his friend, who was killed on the Stuttgart mission. From there, he goes to Arizona to be with his family, and on to California, where he's going to graduate school at UCLA."

"In school, I was pretty good at geography," Michael said. "It seems to me that while you remain on the East Coast, Rob is moving west."

Just before the train arrived, I had been on the verge of telling him that Rob's whereabouts were of less and less interest to me. But the moment passed.

After we boarded, I asked him what his plans were, hoping to turn the conversation away from Rob and me. "Are you going to The Tech in January?"

"No. I've completely changed my plans. I'm going into medicine."

"Are you talking about the whole nine yards? Are you going to become a doctor?"

"Not sure yet. I've been interested in medicine since I was a boy in India, but I don't just want to practice Western medicine. When I was in hospital in India, Indian troops were segregated from the British troops, mostly because of the diet restrictions of the Moslems and Hindis. I noticed the Indians, who were receiving a combination of Western and Eastern medicine, healed quicker than those who were receiving just Western treatments. Pain management is critical to healing, and Eastern medicine is much better in that area."

Looking at him in a totally different light, I said, "I know you'll be very good at whatever you decide." Michael took my hand and squeezed it and asked what I would be doing that weekend.

"I'm supposed to divert your attention, so that you won't know we're giving you a surprise party.

Laughing, Michael said, "I'm looking forward to being diverted."

***

I was told to keep Michael busy for at least two hours, so we decided to go to the British Museum while Beth got everything ready for the party. Of all the museums and historical points of interest in London, the British Museum was my favorite, mostly because of the Elgin Marbles.

There had been an ongoing debate since the marbles had been removed from Greece in 1806 as to who owned the friezes taken from the Parthenon atop the acropolis in Athens. Britain's position was that they had "rescued" the marbles from centuries of neglect and mutilation by a series of invaders. Greece's position was much more emotional. Britain had looted its artistic patrimony, and they wanted the marbles back.

I was surprised to find Michael firmly on the side of the British and not the Greek underdog, saying that, if the British had not removed the friezes, people hoping to see them *in situ* in Athens would have found little more than fragments lying on the ground. Although I loved being able to view the friezes, the marbles were remnants of Greece's glorious classical past. Surely, something so emblematic of their country should be returned to the Greeks. We decided to enjoy the marbles and let the Greek and British governments fight it out.

The two hours passed quickly, and I told Michael it was

time to go home to meet his adoring fans. The double doors to the dining room were closed, waiting for the honored guest to arrive. When they were opened, everyone broke into applause, and Michael gave a bravura performance of acting surprised. I was looking around the room at all the people who had come to welcome Michael home when I saw Leo and my boss.

"I don't want to seem rude, but what are you doing here?" I asked Don.

"Beth contacted me, figuring that I could come up with a good-sized turkey for the party. She felt it was only fair that if I supplied the bird, I should be invited."

Don was going to say more, when Patricia rang the dinner bell and asked all of her guests to be seated. At a signal from Patricia, Andrews and Jim Budd, who had been waiting behind a screen, began to serve fruit cocktail and tomato juice, which was just what I would have had if I had been at home. After the servants cleared the fruit cups, they entered the room carrying dishes of roast turkey, mashed potatoes, dressing, green beans, biscuits, and something I never expected to see in England—cranberry sauce. It was when the cranberry sauce was placed in front of me that I realized what was happening. Everyone shouted, "Happy Thanksgiving." The party hadn't been for Michael but for me, and I started to cry.

Because it had to have been Geoff who told Beth how much I missed the Thanksgiving holiday, I gave him a big kiss. Michael said from across the table, "Hey, wait a minute. I did more than he did. I kept you busy all morning."

I went around to Michael and kissed him, and he said quietly, "May I have more of that later?"

Chapter 40

WHEN I FIRST MOVED in with the Alcotts, Patricia had said I should feel free to have my friends visit, and my most frequent visitor was Pamela. When we had worked in the same office building, Pamela and I had lunch together almost every day. Since Jack had gotten her husband a job on a construction crew resurfacing roads, Troy was frequently away from their home in Stepton, and she didn't like to be alone. With her son cradled in a carrier, she often came to London, and on one of those visits, she came up with a real nugget.

"After the ball, my mum and I were talking, and that's when she told me my granny had been a scullery maid at Montclair, but only for a short time. Her dad had died, but once her mum remarried, she was able to bring her back home. Anyway, you should come up to Stepton and meet Granny. She could tell you what it was like to work at Montclair around 1900."

As it turned out, I didn't have to go to Stepton because Granny had given Pamela the name of a woman who had also been in service at Montclair and who lived in London. I told Michael about Dottie, and he asked if he could tag along.

Dottie was living with her daughter in a small flat in a South London neighborhood that had miraculously survived the bombings. She was probably in her midsixties, and like many of her generation, was missing most of her teeth. She was very pleased to meet Michael, the grandson of her former mistress, and throughout the afternoon, kept telling him that he should go to Hollywood because he was "better looking than Cary Grant and Clark Gable put together." And to me she said, "And you are quite a looker yourself, with your dark hair and blue eyes and nice figger. You two look just like Tyrone Power and Gene Tierney in *The Razor's Edge*. Did you see that one, Luv? It were the first movie I seen after the war."

I asked her if she minded talking about her time in service. She said her memories from Montclair were good ones, and she had no problem sharing them with us.

"I didn't start out at Montclair but at Turner Hall as a scullery maid when I was thirteen," Dottie began. "My dad was killed in a mine explosion, and my mum couldn't feed all of us—six children—that's how many we were. Two years later, she was gone, too, so there were no going back home for me. Mr. Turner was one of Sir Andrew's right-hand men. He bought some property from the Laceys that were north of Stepton, and the Turners went and built this monster of a house on it.

Taking a deep breath, she said, "It were a horrible, horrible job if ever there were one—sixteen hours a day, scrubbing pots and pans, mopping the kitchen floor over and over, plucking chickens, hauling coal. By the time I was fifteen, I had the hands of an old woman. Your whole life were working and sleeping, working and sleeping. The only time I didn't work was on Sunday mornings, when we all had to go to church with the Turners, and the time my throat swolled up so bad I had to go to hospital, which meant three days of lost pay.

"Mr. Cutter, the butler, who always acted as if he had a broom up his arse, would tell us that servants were supposed to be invisible. Say, I was sweeping the stairs, and by sweeping I mean using a hand brush and going stair by stair on my knees, and Mrs. Turner come by. I was to stay perfectly still and make myself as small as possible until she passed. We were never ever to talk to the family. Not that I would have wanted to. That house wouldn't have lasted one day without the servants, but God forbid the master or mistress should know we were in the house. When I started out at Turner Hall, I cried every night. Poor Ellie, she'd be the scullery maid I shared a bed with, would listen to me cry 'til I fell off to sleep, but she said she done the same thing for the longest time until she seen there weren't nothing she could do about it, so why lose sleep.

"The housekeeper was always getting after the maids 'cause of complaints from them above stairs. I was practically dragged upstairs one day by Mrs. Hallam 'cause she found lint on a stair. You would have thought I had shit on the carpet the way she acted.

"And the cook, Monsieur Rideau! What a nasty piece of work he was, having tantrums, throwing pots and pans, pushing me out of the way. He threw a quail at me once 'cause I missed a feather.

"We had lots of rules. We couldn't leave the property without permission. Family weren't allowed to visit without permission, and if it were found out that a girl had a follower, she would have been sent packing without a character. One of the maids got pregnant, and as soon as it were known, she was put out on the road 'cause it would 'tarnish the family's reputation.' That were a joke 'cause you'd see the young Mr. Turner going into a maid's room at all hours. Only time in my life I was glad that I wasn't good-looking, 'cause he left me alone.

"But then Ellie left and got a job at Montclair, and she got me a job, too. First, I was seen by Mrs. Crowell and then Lady Lacey, Miss Elizabeth's grandmother. She would have been in her fifties at that time, and she was just starting to go gray. She had the most beautiful reddish brown hair, but it were her green eyes that grabbed hold of you. You're not supposed to stare at people, especially your betters, but you couldn't help yourself when Lady Lacey looked at you.

"Anyways, I went in, and Lady Lacey said, 'Please sit down.' Someone above stairs saying 'please' to a servant, that were my first clue this house were different. Then to be asked to sit down—that were the second. I can remember that day like it were yesterday. The day of my freedom from slavery at Turner Hall.

"Lady Lacey said I'd be on probation for six months. If after that time Mrs. Crowell said I was a hard worker and a good girl, I'd be asked to stay on and that I'd have one day off every week. Love a duck! A day off!" Dottie said, nearly jumping out of her chair. "I never had one, so on my first day off, I sat out in the courtyard, not having a clue what to do.

"And then there were the Irish laundry maids. Well, they were a piece of work. Even though they could speak English, they spoke their Irish gibberish. To my mind, the laundry maid's job were worst job in the house for a girl 'cause the lye soaps just eat away at your skin. Those girls weren't the cleanest people, neither. They figgered that they were in water all day, so they didn't need to wash. Mrs. Crowell had to get after them to take a bath and to see to their private parts regular like."

I could see out of the corner of my eye that Michael was finding all of this to be very amusing. I did too, but I was embarrassed that the Irish maids were so dirty.

"Lady Sarah Lacey, your grandmother," she said, pointing at Michael, "was an American and very thrifty. She didn't see no sense in having five or six courses every night when there weren't any guests in the house. Do you now what that means to a scullery? Do you know how many dishes and glasses have to be washed for every course served? It made a big, big difference, especially come the end of the day when you're so tired you can hardly stand. Besides, that whole family had the fidgets, especially Mr. Matthew. He'd always be below stairs looking for Jack or Tom to play football.

"Mr. Trevor were the best-looking boy I ever seen until I set eyes on this beautiful boy right here in front of me," Dottie said with a great big laugh and slapped Michael on his knee. She laughed so hard it brought on a coughing fit. "Fags," she explained, pounding on her chest. "I give 'em up two years ago, but the damage is done.

"Those Lacey boys were always below stairs looking for something to eat, and Mrs. Bradshaw would make 'em sandwiches or heat up the leftovers. Master Reed was my favorite, and Lord could he ever eat! He was always carrying that little beagle with him. That family had more dogs than a city pound, but Blossom were the only dog allowed below stairs 'cause Mrs. Bradshaw wasn't having any fur in her food."

Taking a sip from a glass of water, Dottie said, "I'm surprised you haven't asked about Miss Elizabeth seeing how she's this young man's mother." Michael smiled, knowing I had tried several times to get in a question about Beth.

"Well, your mother, I knew her to be a sweet girl and she'd be prettier than any other girl I ever seen come into that house. She had beautiful long brown hair, and she liked to wear it in a braid. Keep in mind, when I left, Miss Elizabeth was still a girl. After her lessons, she'd come and sit down on the stairs while I was brushing them and talk to me. One time, she asked me if I had a beau. I thought she was a mind reader 'cause I had just started walking out with my Jimmy, who I had met at a dance in Stepton. He come up from Sheffield 'cause he said he'd run through all the girls down there. Cheeky devil.

"Jimmy and me got married in '06, and we moved to London where he got a job on a loading dock at Selfridge's. That were a step up for him. I lost my darling man two years ago. We'd been married for forty years and had six kids together. But you're not here to talk about me. What's your next question?"

"What was it like having Jack and Tom below stairs?"

"At Turner Hall, the housekeeper and butler hardly spoke to each other, so you can imagine my shock when I found out the butler and the housekeeper were married! I'd heard of such things before, but it were after they retired and living in one of the tied cottages on the estate. But Mr. and Mrs. Crowell being married weren't my biggest surprise. When I got there in 1895, there'd be two little boys running around. Well, I never heard of such a thing before or since."

Finally, Michael showed some interest. We had gotten to the part where his father and uncle had come into the story.

"They were good boys. The worst thing they done were run up and down those long halls or kick a ball indoors. Tom could get into mischief now and then, but that just meant that he'd hide under the table in the servants' hall or splash the laundry maids, and the one time he got caught looking up Macy's dress.

"It worked out nicely for the servants 'cause everyone took turns taking the boys outside to play. Getting outside were a big thing for us. I actually looked forward to hauling coal or going to the wood pile 'cause it got me outside where I could at least see the sky.

"I think it were 1922 when Lady Lacey invited me and my family to Harvest Home at Montclair. I hadn't seen her in years and years, and she come over and said, 'Dottie, I'm so glad you could come.' It were like she'd seen me the day before.

"And Miss Elizabeth was there with her older boy scampering around getting into everything. It were a lot of fun to see Jack chasing after him, seeing how we used to chase after Jack. And you, young man," she said, pointing at Michael, "didn't come into this world for another couple of months, but it were plain as day your mum was going to have another baby. So we've already met one time before." Dottie laughed, which caused a coughing fit. "Fags," she said, pounding her chest. "Don't never start smoking."

I asked Dottie if there was anything else she would like to share. After giving it some thought, she said, "I think back to those days, and I can hardly believe how much of our lives were given over to those above stairs. But then I think about those below stairs. They were my family. The footmen were my brothers, and the maids were my sisters. When Jimmy and I started walking out, Mrs. Crowell had the 'birds and bees' talk with me like she were my mum, and Mr. Crowell sat Jimmy down and let him know that there'd be 'consequences' if he didn't treat me right. And we had fun. The lot of us, the junior servants, I mean, would get silly and laugh our fool heads off.

"We've come such a long way from those days when you couldn't walk down the road without getting the housekeeper's permission, and all I can say is, I'm glad that none of my kids ever had to go into service. That would have been hard for me to take."

***

After leaving Dottie's flat, Michael and I went to a fish and chips shop and then to Trafalgar Square to eat. As always, the square was covered in pigeons, all waiting for one of us to drop a crumb. Michael was unperturbed by pigeons hopping on his shoes, but I stomped my feet to get them away from me.

"Well, what did you think?" I asked.

"I agree with Dottie. You are 'quite a looker,' but you're prettier than Gene Tierney. And that were the truth."

"Thanks, Tyrone. That's quite a compliment coming from someone who is better looking than Clark Gable and Cary Grant put together. But what did you think about Dottie?"

"Did you see the thickness of her glasses?" Michael asked. "They looked like shot glasses."

"I meant what did you think about her working at Montclair as a servant?"

"There wasn't all that much that was new for me. Don't forget, my grandparents were servants," Michael said, pulling tiny pieces off of his chips and throwing them to the pigeons. "On rainy days, James and I loved running up and down the backstairs. One time, Dad said, 'Try going up and down those stairs carrying a bucket of coal because that's what the servants had to do.' It was as if a light went on in my head. For the first time, I noticed how the stone was worn in the middle of the steps from all of the times the servants had gone up and down, answering servants' bells or hauling hot water for the master's bath. After that, I'd think about all those servants who did that because they had to—people like Dottie and my grandparents."

Some of what Dottie had shared was also familiar to me. I had plucked my share of chickens, and I had hauled buckets of coal up from the cellar to keep the kitchen fire going. Our family got all of our coal from my uncle's bootleg hole near the cemetery. When Uncle Bill dumped a load in our backyard, my father would string up lights for a "coal-cracking party." All the kids had their own hammers to break the coal into pieces small enough to fit into our stove. By the time we finished, the tips of our fingers were raw from handling the jagged pieces of anthracite, but the next day we would be treated to an ice cream cone at Walsh's.

"It's amazing to me how loyal the servants were, when they were basically second-class citizens. Your Dad told me his father was so angry when he found out your parents were getting married. It was as if he had betrayed the Laceys by presuming to marry into the family."

"Loyalty is usually a good thing," Michael said. "There are times, such as war, when it is what binds a people together, allowing them to do collectively what they could not possibly do individually. But it can also mean that someone, such as my grandfather, would never question anything that was asked of him by 'his betters,' and it can be even trickier in personal relationships."

"For example?" I asked.

"For example, Audrey. I should have ended it sooner, but I had this misguided sense of loyalty because she was such a nice lady. Eventually, I had to let go."

"You seem to be attracted to older women," I said, knowing that Michael had been talking about Rob and me.

"I'm attracted to intelligent women, regardless of age," he answered quickly. "It's true I was often more comfortable with someone who had a few years on me because I was pretty awkward around women."

"Michael, I don't want to give you a big head, but you're handsome, intelligent, witty, well-traveled, and yet when you talk about women, it's like 'Golly, gee. Aw, shucks!'"

"You have to remember I went to an all-boys' school and then to The Tech, which is not co-educational."

"You can't tell me that Manchester didn't have attractive women." I just found it hard to believe that someone as charming and easy to talk to as Michael could be so clumsy around girls, especially in light of the way he was constantly flirting with me.

"Let me tell you a story that will give you an idea of just how backwards I was. When I was at The Tech, James came up from Cambridge for the weekend, and we went to this dance hall. James picked up a girl right away. This girl grabs a friend, and we go back to her house. Her parents aren't home, so she marches James right upstairs. I'm left all alone with Linda, whom I hadn't known thirty minutes earlier. We're sitting there, and she says, 'Well, what would you like to do?' and I said that I'd like some tea. She says, 'Aren't you a laugh,' and starts kissing and pawing me and sticking her tongue in my mouth and in my ear. I managed to get from under her and went back to my room. When James saw me later that night, he called me an idiot, and said, 'She would have done anything you wanted.' And I said, 'All I wanted was for her to keep her tongue out of my mouth.'

I tried not to laugh, but it was impossible. The idea of a guy having to fight off a girl because she was overly aggressive was too funny.

"Sure, it's funny now. But at the time, I felt as if I was being defiled," he said with his million-dollar smile.

"What happened the second year at The Tech?" I asked, still laughing.

"I did a little better than in the first term, but then I got called up. After my basic and advanced training, I ended up in Lincolnshire at a bomber base."

"Where you met Edith?"

"Where I met Edith."

I couldn't stop laughing. I stood up and held out my hand. "Come on, Tyrone. It's time for Gene to see you safely home."

Chapter 41

IN LATE NOVEMBER, A dense fog engulfed most of Western Europe. Airports shut down, ships collided, trains plowed into each other, and cars crashed. With visibility reduced to a matter of feet, people began to carry flashlights when they were out walking.

The fog made me rethink my promise to Beth to stay in England through the holidays. I realized that if I received a telegram with news that my aunt's condition had worsened, it might be impossible, because of the weather, for me to get home in time to see her. I decided to book a seat on the first available flight to the States. I wanted to make sure that I would have one last chance to be with my aunt.

The person in charge of scheduling travel for AAFES employees informed me that, because of the fog, there was now a wait time of at least two weeks for nonessential personnel, and movement on that list could take place only once the fog lifted. A few days after I mentioned my situation to Geoff, I was summoned to Rand's office. Although Rand was always polite to me, I still had the feeling that whenever he addressed me, I was being called on the carpet.

"Maggie, you are not in trouble unless you've done something that I don't know about." I shook my head, and he continued, "Geoff has acquainted me with the state of your aunt's health. Weather permitting, I am returning to Washington on December 15th. I am allowed to travel with one dependent. Are you interested?"

Although December 15th was still ten days off, I would actually have a scheduled departure date. This might be the only way I could get home. I went over and kissed him on the cheek. He smiled for a second before telling me that I would have to make my own way from Washington to Minooka. That would not be a problem because it was something I had done many times during my two years in the District during the war.

Now that I had a better than average chance of leaving on a certain date, I had to finish up the timeline for the history of the Lacey family. That was the easy part. The hard part would be saying good-bye to the Crowells because I wasn't sure if I would be returning to England.

I telephoned Beth and asked if I could come to Crofton Wood on December 11th. She said she would love to have me, but that she and Jack were to attend the wedding of Ginger Bramfield's daughter in Derby on that Saturday. It was the last weekend before I would leave, so I told her I would like to come anyway. I carefully packed up Elizabeth Garrison's diaries and the other letters Beth had given to me, so that I could complete Mrs. Caton's project. I had become so caught up in Elizabeth's story that I felt as if I was parting with a friend. As I traveled north on the train from Euston Station, I noticed that the fog was beginning to lift. If the weatherman was correct, I would be able to leave with Rand on Wednesday.

I had planned to tell the Crowells about my return to the States as soon as I got to Crofton Wood, but with the Bramfield wedding the next day, it didn't seem like the right time to spring my news on them. It would be best to tell them on Sunday, and then head for the train station.

"Mike's been here three days now, and we can't get his nose out of a book," Jack said. "He's always been one to get after something once it's caught his fancy, and it seems that going into medicine has done just that. His mother and I convinced him to get out, so he's down at the Hare and Hound with Freddie."

"We were surprised by his change of profession," Beth added, "but also very pleased. He's certainly intelligent enough, and I know he spent a lot of time with Kavi, our bearer. Many of the servants considered him to be a healer who had cured them of their ailments."

Patting me on my knee, Beth said, "To bed, my dear. I wouldn't be surprised if Michael had something planned for you tomorrow."

***

I got up early to have breakfast with Jack and Beth before they headed to Derby for the Bramfield wedding, and then I went back to bed. My decision to return home had so unsettled me that I was losing sleep over it because there was an excellent chance I would not be coming back. I had this premonition that once I landed in America, I would be sucked into a vortex and deposited in Minooka.

After making the bed, I took Elizabeth Garrison's diaries, the draft of my booklet, and my notes downstairs to the study. I wanted everything to be in order, so Beth could deliver my drafts to Mrs. Caton, who had offered to pay me fifty pounds for my work. I would need that money if I used up the entire eight weeks of leave from AAFES because I would be paid for only the first two weeks.

I hadn't heard Michael come in last night, but I did hear him open the door to the study. "Good afternoon," he said. "I didn't know you were coming, or I wouldn't have gone out last night with Freddie. It wasn't until I saw your coat on the rack that I realized you were here for the weekend."

"It was a spur of the moment thing. London has been so depressing because of the fog."

Although Michael had been discharged three weeks earlier, he was still wearing his Army sweater, and I asked if he was "nervous out of the service." It was a term that had been coined by servicemen who were afraid there would be few jobs available once the American war machine shut down. It never happened; the economy was booming.

Looking at his sweater, he said, "I'm waiting for my separa-tion pay. I got out a few days early because of some imaginative record keeping by my sergeant, but it screwed up my paybook. And I didn't get my demobbed suit either. Once I get the money, I'm buying a whole new wardrobe, and you'll never see this sweater again."

"Your dad says you've had your nose in a book since you got here."

"That's true. I want to be sure I'm on the right path, so I contacted a tutor recommended by the doctor who did my monthly weigh-ins at the Malta station. He was an Army doctor for thirty years and had seen everything, and he provided a lot of guidance."

Looking over my shoulder at Elizabeth's diaries, he said, "Last time we talked, Elizabeth and William had gotten engaged. Did you get to the wedding night yet?" I nodded. Pulling up a chair next to mine, he asked, "Well, how did it go?"

I answered in full blush. "Elizabeth described it as a 'curious ritual,' but then she got the hang of it."

Michael picked up the diary, and it fell open to a page dated 26 March 1793.

I have at last had a letter from Mr. Lacey. He writes he has been unwell and blames the foul London air for his complaints. Georgiana tends to his needs, but he wishes that another was in his chamber ministering to him. He assures me that as soon as he is well enough to ride, and if the weather stays fine, he will be in Hertfordshire at the earliest possible time. My feelings for him are so strong that I lie awake at night and go over in my mind our moments at Helmsley Hall when he first kissed me. I shall never forget the intensity of my feelings when he put his hands around my waist and pulled me to him. I pray that he will return to me soon, as I long for him to place his hands upon me once again.

"That's pretty hot stuff for its time, isn't it? Will Lacey wanting Elizabeth in his bed chamber, and she wanting him to put his hands on her again."

I started to laugh. "She wants his hands around her waist. I'm sure that was exciting enough for someone who had never been kissed before."

"If you think acting out the different parts will help in your research, I am at your disposal." Looking at me intently, he asked, "Why are you blushing? Is it because I'm flirting with you?"

"That's part of it."

"Is there any reason I should stop? Are you spoken for or engaged? Has something changed since I saw you in London?"

"Michael, why did you write that letter when you were in Germany apologizing for flirting with me? You said it wouldn't happen again, but you've done nothing but flirt since you got home." The letter had jarred me. I thought he was letting me know that his interest in me had been a temporary thing and not to expect similar attention when he got back to England.

Michael sat back in his chair and said, "Because I was afraid I had scared you off—that when I got back to England, you would have moved to the States. Do you remember how I closed the letter I sent to my parents? I wrote, 'I love you all.' That was for you."

There was no avoiding it now. I had to tell him I was leaving. "I am going back to the States on December 15th."

Michael pushed back his chair to increase the distance between us. "It's not necessary for you to be so dramatic, Maggie. If you don't want to see me, it doesn't require your putting the Atlantic between us."

I was stung by what he said, and I told him so. "That was unkind. If anything, you would be one of the reasons why I would stay."

"What does that mean?"

"It means that there are so many reasons why I have to go back, but the most important is my Aunt Marie. She's in her eighties and may have only a few more weeks to live. She helped Grandma and my mother time and time again. And I haven't seen my mother and family in more than two years, and I miss them." I felt myself tearing up because I was being pulled in two different directions. I did not want to leave England and Michael, but I had to go home to see my aunt one last time.

"Michael, you would save yourself a lot of heartache if you would find yourself a nice British girl. Not an Australian and not an American."

Michael stood up and pulled me out of my chair and said, "I don't want a nice British girl. I want you." And he started to kiss me, pulling me into him so that I could barely breathe. He kept on kissing me until we had backed onto the sofa, and then he lay on top of me. With each movement, I wanted him more than I had ever wanted anyone or anything in my life. When he sat up and started to unbuckle his belt, I kicked off my shoes and was unhooking my nylons, when he suddenly stopped and pulled me up into a sitting position. I didn't understand why, and I started to cry.

With his arms around me, he said, "Maggie, with all of the things that you have on your mind right now, it would be wrong for me to make love to you." Taking my hands in his, he continued. "You need to go home, but after seeing your aunt and family, you have to decide what it is that you want. If it's Rob, then I'll leave you alone. But if you decide that you want to be with me, I don't want any hesitation on your part—no second guessing—no regrets. I want you to feel about me in the same way that I feel about you. I'm not sharing you with anyone."

We went for a ride to the Peak District. A cold front had brought with it beautiful blue skies but with enough clouds to cast shadows on the rolling terrain. We walked out onto a promontory for the most gorgeous view of the entire district.

We discussed whether he should come to London before I left on Wednesday but decided it would be too obvious why he was there. Before returning to the house, we kissed and hugged, but mostly we talked.

As expected, Beth took the news of my leaving graciously and said I would be with the Crowell family in spirit at Christmastime. Jack said nothing, creating an uncomfortable silence. Finally, Michael suggested we all go down to the Hare and Hound for drinks, but both parents begged off, citing fatigue from the wedding reception.

"Don't worry about Dad, Maggie," Michael said. "He's not the most articulate man. I know he's sorry to see you go; he just doesn't know how to express it."

When I went to my room, there was a note on my desk from Jack, asking if I would join him for breakfast at 7:30.

I'd like to talk to you, so it will be just the two of us. Jack

The change in the weather had brought a biting wind with it, but even so, Jack and I decided to walk to the village. The inn had a fair amount of people eating breakfast in their dining room, but there had been a definite drop-off since the fall colors had faded. After our tea arrived, Jack said, "You know me well enough to know I'm not an emotional man—not on the surface, anyway—but your news, well, it upset me. It's one thing to have your sons go off, but you expect boys to leave."

Jack stopped talking for several minutes and just stared into the fire before saying, "Beth and I had a little girl. We knew from the day she was born that she would—that she would be leaving us. Just one short week. That's all the time we had." Looking at his hand, he said, "She was the smallest baby I ever saw. After losing Tom and Beth's brothers, well, it was too much. I thought

God was punishing me, but last year, when I met you... You see, you're exactly the same age our Jenny would have been."

Jack took a check out of his pocket and slid it across the table. "I called Pan American Airlines, and they told me that was how much a one-way ticket between New York and London costs." The check was for several hundred pounds, and I shook my head.

"Maggie, I grew up in a house where everyone knew their place. Because of that, I always felt boxed in. I was lucky in that Sir Edward saw potential in me and paid my expenses at The Tech. But, you see, it was still his decision." Tapping the check, he continued, "I'm hoping you will use the money to come back to us, but if that's not your choice, then that money is there for you to start out wherever you want. I would have done the same for our Jenny. Please take it."

I had to excuse myself and go to the ladies' room. I was crying for so many reasons. I didn't want to leave the Crowells because they had provided me with love and affection. Beth had done her best to act the part of my mother without usurping her role. But Jack was another story. My father was a man who had been raised in a house where men didn't show affection. The emotional pounding he had taken from his father had left a man who always seemed to be watching his family from a distance. It had literally been years since my dad had hugged me, and the comparison between Jack and my father was breaking my heart.

If that wasn't emotional enough, Jack and I walked down to the World War I memorial on the village green. There were ten names listed on the plaque, including Arnie Ferguson, the older brother of Montclair's gardener; David Rivers, the brother of the owner of the Inn; Trevor and Matthew Lacey; and Michael

Thomas Crowell. I hadn't known that Michael had been named after Jack's brother.

"When Tom was still a lad, there was a footman named Mike below stairs, so everyone took to calling my brother by his middle name. Our Michael is named after Tom, and James is named after me, James Abel Crowell or JAC, Jack."

Puzzled looks greeted us when we got back to the house. Both Michael and Beth could see I had been crying, but neither asked any questions.

The following morning, Michael drove me to the Sheffield Station. Before leaving, I asked that he drop me off at the car park and not go into the station. I had barely recovered from Jack's story, and Beth had lost a gallant effort not to cry. I was already emotionally spent, and I didn't want to start bawling in the station. I was turning into a real crybaby.

As soon as Michael cut the engine, he jumped out, opened my door, and took my luggage to the entrance to the station. "A telegram would be nice once you get to your parents' house."

I nodded. I wasn't trusting my voice. With people milling all around us, I kissed him for as long as decency would allow, and then I went into the station to begin my long journey home.

***

December 15th was a brilliantly clear day at the small airport north of London that was used by the government to ferry its diplomats and officials around the world. On the plane, the seating had all of the bigwigs up front in comfortable chairs with tables. The little people sat in reclining chairs in the rear of the plane which, I was shortly to learn, was where turbulence was felt the most.

The pilot announced over the intercom that our flight plan would take us over Iceland, across the Atlantic to Newfoundland, where we would refuel, and finally down the East Coast of the United States to our final destination at National Airport in Washington. Except for some early queasiness, I did quite well compared to my sea voyage from Philadelphia to Hamburg. I fell asleep over Iceland and didn't awake until we were told we were landing.

During the flight, Rand checked on me every couple of hours but gave no indication he wanted to chat. Once we landed, he said it would be about two hours before we would go on to Washington, and he invited me to go into the terminal for a cup of coffee. On the walls were photos of battles in which Newfoundlanders had fought in The Great War: Arras, Vimy Ridge, Cambrai, Gallipoli. But it was the Battle of Beaumont-Hamel on the Somme that was forever linked with the 1st Newfoundland Regiment. Pointing to a quote by Major General Sir Beauvoir de Lisle, Rand said, "That explains it all."

It was a magnificent display of trained and disciplined valour, and its assault only failed of success because dead men can advance no further.

The regiment went over the top on July 1, 1916, the first day of the Battle of the Somme. When they had time to count their losses, they found that of the eight-hundred men who had gone into battle, fewer than seventy men answered at roll call. In thirty minutes, the regiment had lost ninety percent of its strength. I thought about Tom Crowell, who had also gone over the top on that awful day. It not only took his life, but it changed his brother forever.

***

As soon as we took off, my eyes were glued to the window. I wasn't sure of the distance between Newfoundland and the United States, but I wasn't going to miss seeing any part of the country I had left more than two years earlier. When the pilot announced we had entered the air space of the United States, I had goose bumps. As we traveled down the East Coast, he pointed out the Gaspe Peninsula, Boston, and Providence. From my window, I could see the Statue of Liberty in New York Harbor and the Empire State Building, and after flying over Philadelphia and Baltimore, I could feel the plane losing altitude in preparation for landing.

It was then I caught sight of the Jefferson Memorial and the Tidal Basin. It was in this city that my first venture into the adult world had begun in June 1944. When I had arrived at Union Station on that hot summer day, I didn't know what direction my life would take. Now, I was returning to my home country a different person but still unsure of my future. That had to change. I couldn't continue with such uncertainty. Like Michael had said, it was time to make a decision.

Chapter 42

ST. PATRICK'S DAY MAY be the occasion most Americans associate with the Irish, but it is the wake that comes closest to capturing the emotional complexity of that long-suffering race. Living in isolated homesteads in Ireland, many saw their neighbors only when they had received word that someone had died. Fueled by poteen, a potent home-brewed liquor, the wake took on the celebratory nature of a reunion. If the deceased wasn't one of your loved ones, an Irish wake could provide some of the best entertainment in town, and it certainly was well attended.

As soon as I arrived in Minooka, I immediately went to see my aunt. Although she was in the last days of her life, Aunt Marie greeted me with a feisty, "Jesus, Mary, and Joseph! Now I know I'm dying, if they sent for you." Taking hold of my hand, she said, "Don't look so worried. I've had the last rites twice before, but I'm still alive, and Father Kelly's dead and buried."

It was obvious Aunt Marie wasn't going to leave this world without a fight, but it was a fight she was going to lose. The air in coal towns is hard on everyone's lungs, but most especially on those of miners and ladies from another era, who passed their evenings rocking on front porches while smoking their pipes.

In the last week of her life, my aunt drifted in and out of consciousness. In her lucid moments, she spoke of her childhood on the beautiful shores of Loch Corrib in the west of Ireland, as well as some of the more memorable of the hundreds of her students, including my parents, who had passed through her classroom from the time she had begun teaching in Minooka in 1887. She insisted that her only regret was not returning to Galway, but there was no way that she would have left Minooka with her sister and brother up on the hill in the church cemetery.

The Egan Funeral Home did a nice job with Aunt Marie, and I'm sure she would have been pleased at how good she looked, with curled hair and wearing her best dress, a pale blue A-line, with matching pumps, and a faux diamond brooch given to her at the time of her retirement.

Aunt Marie had died two days earlier, and her open casket was in our parlor for what was to be the first of two days of viewing for family and friends. Three members of the Sodality of Mary, dressed from head to toe in black, had arrived to lead the mourners in the rosary, and Sally Bluegoose, who had once run a hole-in-the-wall, selling whiskey to the miners, started keening. "Wora, wora, wora!" A banshee crying from the hills of Connemara could not have done a better job.

My father, who did not get along with Aunt Marie, nevertheless was busy toasting her memory. While Dad put away another one, my mother was setting out more food for the mourners, all the while trying not to cry because there was just too much to do.

Most of the men were gathered in the parlor, talking politics or telling stories about their days as slate pickers at the breaker or as mule drivers before reaching an age where they were old enough to go underground and work "down in the hole." The women were either helping in the kitchen or were gathered in a circle around the coffin gossiping, but in quiet voices, so as not "to wake the dead."

Along the back wall were the ancient ones, those who still spoke Irish and who punctuated their speech with their clay pipes while enjoying "a drop of the creature." Grandpa Joyce was among the few abstaining because thirty years earlier, at the request of his pastor, he had taken an oath of abstinence. It was too bad Father Loughran hadn't asked him to be nicer to his family.

Through the kitchen window, I could see the perpetual glow from a fire on Downes Mountain fueled by an inexhaustible supply of coal from below. There was nothing that better served as a reminder that I was back in Minooka than the pervasive smell of sulfur that was the signature of every town in the hard-coal country of eastern Pennsylvania.

Patrick had picked me up at the Lackawanna Station, and his first words to me were, "Where's your cowboy? I don't see a ring, and you know what they say, 'It don't mean a thing if you ain't got that ring.'"

"How's your love life, Pat?" I asked, knowing that most mothers wouldn't allow him to darken their doors. Even with a stellar service record in the Navy, including a commendation for bravery when his ship had been torpedoed near Cuba, mothers had long memories when it came to their daughters.

"I don't have one. No one in particular, that is," he said, smiling like the Cheshire cat. "I like to share the wealth."

"In other words, no one will go out with you."

Patrick started to say something when I asked him to stop. "For God's sake, we haven't made it to the city line, and we're already fighting. Can you just give it a rest?" After taking a deep breath, I asked him how Aunt Marie was.

"She's dying."

"Really, Patrick? Thanks for the news bulletin."

"Mom thinks it's only a matter of days."

"How's J.J.?"

John Joseph Mulkerin had come to Minooka from Ireland in the 1870s as a ten-year-old orphan. He had been delivered by an emigrating adult from his village to his father's cousin, Mary Coyne, who "didn't have a pot to pee in." But J.J. was so engaging that the whole town had adopted him. After he got a job as a mailman, he became a hot item because he was employed and he wasn't a miner. But J.J. had eyes only for my Aunt Marie. What on earth would he do without her?

"Aunt Marie's never alone," Patrick continued. "Mom or Aunt Agatha fix her meals every day, and the neighbors are taking turns checking up on her. She wouldn't let J.J. spend the night because it would be 'indacent,'" he said, mimicking Aunt Marie's brogue that had survived her sixty years in America. "At 8:00, he pretends he's leaving, and she pretends he's not in the next room." According to the little man with the big heart, they had been dating for forty years, and he proposed to her every year on her birthday.

"Grandpa's looking forward to seeing you again," Patrick said, smiling. "He just found out where you've been living. He thought you were still in Germany."

When we pulled into the alley behind the house, I was overwhelmed by a flood of memories, especially of my grandmother. All summer long, Grandma would be in the garden checking on her tomatoes and other vegetables to make sure they had ripened to perfection. While Grandma was out in the garden, my mother would be in the kitchen, peeling, slicing, or boiling potatoes, which was what she was doing when I came through the door. I had not seen her since August 1946.

Mom looked much older. Added to the daily stress of living with a husband who drank too much and a father-in-law who raised meanness to an art was the strain of caring for my Aunt Marie. But Mom had an inner strength whose source was her unshakeable faith in her church and her belief that everything happened for a reason, according to God's plan. We had been having a good cry when my Grandpa, sitting in his usual place by the coal stove, woke up.

"I thought you be dead," he said.

In order to keep peace in the house, I needed to come up with a reason why I had been in England, the home of his enemy, for more than a year. But I thought it best to keep it simple. "The U.S. Government gave a lot of money to the British during the war, and there had to be some accountability on how the money had been spent." That was the truth. It just didn't have anything to do with me.

After a long silence, Grandpa finally said, "That be a good thing. Those teeving bastards need watching." And he went back to sleep.

At the end of their workday, Dad and Sadie came home, and my sister grabbed me and spun me around. We had grown up sleeping in the same bed, which provided numerous opportunities to share stories as well as our hopes for the future. As for my dad, he came over and put his arm around my shoulder, and all he said was, "Welcome home, M'acushla."

"Katie and little Jimmy are coming in from Jersey tomorrow to spend time with Aunt Marie," my mother said.

And that brought me back to the reason why I had left England. It also reminded me that I was now on the same continent as Rob. When I sent my telegram to Michael, I would send one to Rob as well letting him know that I was on his side of the Atlantic, and I wondered what, if anything, he would do.

***

After a long evening of catching up with a steady stream of friends and family welcoming me home, I finally went upstairs. Inside the door of my bedroom was a little holy water fountain screwed into the wall above the light switch, and the walls were covered with pictures of the Virgin Mary and the Sacred Heart, which made me realize that I was back under the aegis of Father Lynch. Before I left England, I had gone to confession because I wasn't about to go into the confessional with Father Lynch. Not only would I have to confess that Rob and I had had sex, but I would have to estimate how many times we did it. Sackcloth and ashes would have been too easy a penance for someone who was obviously a loose woman.

The upstairs was heated by grates that opened to the kitchen below. During the night, when the fire in the coal stove had died down, the room was freezing, but for the time being, it was warm enough so that Sadie and I could talk. When I left Minooka in 1944, I was nineteen and Sadie was fifteen. In those four years, Sadie had easily become the prettiest girl in town. Although we shared the same physical characteristics—black hair, blue eyes, and fair skin—Sadie's hair was blacker, her eyes were bigger and bluer, and at five-foot-six, she was four inches taller than I was. If she had a flaw, it was her habit of saying exactly what was on her mind. In the two years I had been overseas, that hadn't changed.

"What happened with Rob?"

Should I tell my little sister that Rob and I were over, and how would I explain Michael? But then I decided to go for it, and I told the story of Michael's waxing and Rob's waning.

"Oh my God! My sister, St. Margaret Mary Joyce, had a flirtation with another guy while she was dating someone else?" Actually, after our time together on the sofa in the study, referring to it as a flirtation was probably no longer accurate, but I wasn't going to tell Sadie that. "Going overseas really did change you. You used to be a real stick in the mud, so this is definitely a change for the better."

✳✳✳

One of the people I had missed the most while I was in Europe was my cousin, Bobby, who owned an Esso gas station with my brother on the main road between Wilkes-Barre and Scranton. Before sitting down in the office, I took out a handkerchief and placed it over the split red-vinyl chair. Bobby opened the vending machine and tossed a bag of M&Ms to me. We were alone, because Patrick was out picking up tires.

"How's your love life?" he asked with his quirky smile that had gotten him out of more than one jam. Obviously, Sadie had told Bobby about Rob and Michael.

"Never mind about my love life. How's yours?"

He answered in almost a whisper. "I'm dating a girl from Southside." That was no big deal because a lot of people from

South Scranton went to St. Joe's, so it was considered to be an extension of Minooka—one with amenities. "Her name is Teresa Mateo." I let out a whoop. Now, this was a big deal. Because of the high position Bobby's father held in local politics, his mother thought she was better than everyone else. Having her son dating an Eye-tie would damage the family's image.

"Do you know who gave me my first kiss?" I asked in the same voice he had used.

"Tommy Gallo." Tommy had been killed on D-Day, June 6, 1944, while climbing the cliffs of Pointe du Hoc in an attempt to knock out a German pillbox. My final letter from Tommy had been dated June 4th. In it, he had talked about how he couldn't wait for the invasion to start because he was tired of being penned up in holding areas with hundreds of guys in miserable weather. He just wanted it to be over, and for him and thousands of other young Americans, it was.

"I saw you getting into his car outside Dugan's Diner. So I asked him if he was seeing you, and he said 'yes,' and then he said, 'All of this baloney about Irish girls dating only Irish boys, and the same deal with Italians, is a load of crap. When I get back, I'm going to take Maggie dancing at the Hotel Casey and to hell with anyone who doesn't like it.'" I brought the conversation back to Teresa Mateo because I didn't want to think about how devastated I was when I had heard that Tommy was gone. He was the only one who could have gotten me to move back to Minooka.

Teresa's family owned a bar on the city line, which was probably where Bobby had met her. She was a beautiful girl: thick black hair and blacker eyes and a very attractive figure. I asked him when he was going to tell his mother. I wanted to know when to leave town.

"Probably on Saturday," Bobby said. "Teresa and I have a wedding to go to. I think her mother has figured it out because I've been eating a lot of spaghetti at the bar, but it's going to be a shot out of the blue for Mom. She'll get over it eventually," he said with a confidence that I doubt he felt. I was happy for him, but I seriously doubted if Mamie Lenahan was going to take this lying down.

Chapter 43

BEFORE LEAVING ENGLAND, I received a letter from Rob saying that Ken and he were heading to Miami Beach where they would spend the Christmas holidays. When my mother told me there was a telephone operator on the line, I couldn't think who would be calling me long-distance. To my surprise, it was Rob.

"Maggie, I just got your letter. How's your aunt?"

I told him that we had buried her two days earlier, but I assured him that she had lived a full and happy life.

"God, Maggie, I can't tell you how good it is to hear your voice. I swear, it's like manna from heaven."

I knew exactly how he felt because just hearing his soft Western drawl was giving me a much-needed boost. But long-distance phone calls were expensive and, in our family, reserved for emergencies. I told Rob his call was costing him a fortune, and he said, "I don't care. You're worth every dime." In that case, if he wanted to talk, I'd oblige, so I asked him how his Christmas holidays had been. He said he didn't want to talk about that. He wanted to talk about "us."

"I'm flying out to Omaha for a visit with the Monaghans, but after that, I'd like to come and see you."

I hadn't been expecting the phone call, and now he wanted to come to Minooka. Feeling very flattered, I told him to come ahead.

Before hanging up, he said, "I couldn't have a better Christmas present than hearing you're back in the States. I love you, and I'll see you soon."

***

Waiting at the station for Rob's train to come in, I wasn't sure how I would feel when I saw him. It had been three months since we had been together in London. But when I caught sight of him, I felt a burst of happiness. He looked so good in his new suit, and living in a state with lots of sunshine certainly agreed with him.

Before December 1941, no one would have hugged and kissed in as public a place as Scranton's Lackawanna Station, but since the war, people were used to returning servicemen kissing their loved ones, so I gave Rob a big hug and kiss.

Walking to the car, he told me he had joined the Air Force Reserves. "I haven't actually reported, but I was able to grab a seat on a flight to an airfield near Philadelphia anyway. As soon as I signed the papers, they told me I could get on any flight that had space available. They're moving planes all over the country, and some are being sold to private contractors. I flew in on a twin-engine job that was used for photo recon that's being sold to a real-estate developer."

I asked Rob if he was hungry, and he said he was starved. "There's no in-flight service on these planes," he said, laughing. After sliding into a rear booth in a West Scranton diner, Rob informed me that he had gone on an interview with Delta Air

Lines in Atlanta for the position of flight engineer. The personnel manager who interviewed him was a former B-17 pilot and liked to hire Air Corps vets.

"I thought you said you didn't like Atlanta." He also said that I would most definitely not like Atlanta, so why was he acting as if this was good news for me?

"I wasn't real keen on the idea of staying in Atlanta, but this guy told me not to make up my mind until I had seen the city from Delta's point of view. Since the war, thousands of servicemen who had been stationed in the South went back to look for jobs. It might be hot in Atlanta, but for some guys, it beats shoveling snow in Des Moines.

"Maggie, this is a great company," he said, placing his hands over mine. "I could support a family on the salary I'd make. They're building houses left and right, and the apartments are air-cooled—the bedrooms, anyway. What better place to kick off your shoes and cool down on a hot summer's night?" I knew he was flirting with me, but I said nothing and just nodded my head. "They have routes from Atlanta to Chicago, Miami, and New Orleans, but that's just the beginning. Why would anyone want to spend four days on a train when you can get on an airplane and be wherever you want in a matter of hours?" Doing a drum roll on the table, he said, "This is big. Really big. The guy even mentioned possible pilot's training for me. Do you know how exciting it would be to fly a plane where your cargo is a group of passengers instead of bombs? I can do this."

His enthusiasm was infectious. Was this what he needed—a challenging but interesting job? It just might be.

"I have a second interview on January 24th. What I'm thinking is that the regional airlines are going to be popping up all over the country. Once I get a few years under my belt, it's possible I could end up flying for an airline in California. How about Phoenix to Los Angeles? And then we could spend some time up in the High Country in Flagstaff."

What did he mean when he said that "we" could spend some time in the High Country? Where was this Rob McAllister when we were together in England?

I was wondering what my grandfather's reaction would be when he heard Rob's last name. He'd want to know if Rob was one of the "teeving Scots who stole all the land in the north of Ireland from the Irish." But after Rob explained that he was mostly German with some Swedish and Scots-Irish thrown into the mix, Grandpa had nothing more to say. It was obvious he was suffering from a case of the "dwindles," and no longer had the energy to argue. Most of his time was spent sleeping in a chair near the stove or in his room.

Once the dishes were washed and dried, Rob, Sadie, and I walked down to Bobby's station where Marty Walsh, Eddie Sullivan, and Joe Mahady were drinking Cokes. The war had been the defining moment in their lives, and more than three years after VJ Day, it was still a frequent topic of conversation. After they had learned that Rob had been a navigator on a B-17, Eddie started in right away.

"You got yourself a flyboy, Maggie," Eddie said. "Cruising up in the clouds while us dopes in the infantry were down in the mud digging foxholes."

Not to be outdone, Marty complained that the Army and the Air Corps had gotten all the glory when it was the Navy and Marines who had beaten the Japs in the Pacific with very little help from the other services. Rob hated this kind of talk. He called them "pissing contests," like little boys who lined up to see whose stream could reach the farthest.

"You're both right. Flying in a B-17 meant taking off in the morning, dropping my load, and coming home to some pretty decent grub and the same bed every night. I always admired the guys in the infantry and armor, and I can tell you, I never even gave the Navy a thought. At least if I had to bail out, I'd hit land."

This seemed to appease Army and Navy, and Rob closed the deal when he offered to buy a round at Judge's. This was the bar where my father had once done most of his drinking, but since the war, the usual crowd was largely made up of friends of mine. The beer mug had been passed to a new generation.

After what seemed like hours, Bobby, Sadie, Rob, and I managed to break loose from the "How I Won the War" group and crossed the street to Bobby's house. Sitting in his front parlor, Bobby told Rob that he had been a pilot on a B-26 Marauder, a medium bomber.

"A plane a day in Tampa Bay," Rob said. "I was glad when they assigned me to the Fortresses."

Bobby slapped his knee. "I was in on those early training flights. I nearly parked one in the bay myself."

Both Rob and Bobby had more than their share of close calls, and because of that, they changed the topic to the Chicago Bears versus the New York Giants. Sadie rolled her eyes and indicated she was leaving. I caught up with her and asked what she thought of Rob.

"Marry him," she said, walking quickly in the cold. "He's handsome, intelligent, and he doesn't live here. He's perfect for you."

I was wondering if Sadie was being facetious when she said: "If you'd give him a chance, you'd probably fall in love with him all over again. If you don't, you'll go back to England, and the only time I'll ever see you is when someone dies."

Sadie was starting to cry—something she rarely did. "I don't think you should go back to England. Forget about that other guy."

***

Rob's visit with the Monaghan family had gone so well that he had been invited back to attend Pat's sister's wedding. Before leaving for the airfield to catch a flight to Omaha, Rob and I went to a nice restaurant near the train station. While waiting for our meals to be served, Rob held my hand the entire time.

"Maggie, I feel I'm finally on the right road. It took much longer than it should have. After Omaha and my interview in Atlanta, I want to come back here. I think it's time that we started planning our future together." He took both of my hands in his and kissed them, which was exactly what Michael had done when he had asked me to come back to him. Rob noticed the change and asked if something was wrong.

"No. Nothing's wrong."

"What do you say? Can I come back?"

"I'd be very hurt if you didn't."

Chapter 44

A FEW DAYS AFTER arriving in Omaha, Rob called to say the city had been slammed with a major snowstorm, and there were no flights out. He mentioned he had a chance to talk to Mr. Monaghan, but he would share that with me when he was back in Minooka in a week. A week? How much snow did Omaha get?

To pick up some extra money, Sadie had arranged for me to work as a temp in her office in downtown Scranton. The job involved phones and typing and little else, which was why the pay was so bad, but I needed money so that I could pay my mother for my room and board.

I was now into my fourth week of leave, and neither of my parents was asking what my plans were. No comments had been made as to how long my visit would last, nor had they asked if Rob had left for good. Apparently, if no one talked about my returning to England or possibly marrying a Protestant, neither of those things would happen. Who knew what was going to happen? I certainly didn't.

It was one of my life's greatest ironies that Patrick was the person who helped me to make my decision. From the moment my brother had picked me up at the station, the two of us had assumed our pre-war roles. He made asinine remarks, and instead of ignoring him, I almost always overreacted. It wasn't until Bobby told me that Patrick had a secret girlfriend, Anna Sokoloski, that I finally had something to hold over his head. The next time he started in on me, I told him I knew about Anna.

"Patrick, I could threaten to tell all your friends about your girlfriend, but I don't want to. In fact, I'd like to meet Anna." I wanted to meet the girl who could overlook my brother's goofiness.

"No one's going to meet her," he said in an angry voice. "She's Polish, and I'm not going to have her be the butt of Polish jokes."

"Are you in love with her?"

"What's it to you?" He was in full defensive mode.

"What's it to me? If you're serious about Anna, she may end up being my sister-in-law, and I think it's unfair of you to keep her under wraps because of your jerky friends."

"You're not going to tell anyone?"

"No. But in return, I want you to show me some respect. I want the two of us to have an adult relationship, and that means you have to grow up."

The conversation immediately bore fruit, so much in fact, that Patrick took me to the tire store where Anna worked so I could meet her. There are two types of Poles: long, lean, and blue-eyed, like Leo, and short, broad, and dark-haired. Anna was the latter and very pretty. She was as short as me, with brown curly hair and gorgeous blue eyes that were almost Oriental, and she had a killer smile. She was also able to lift tires.

We had a nice lunch together at a nearby diner, and Patrick surprised me by the way he acted around her. He held open the door, put his arm around her in the booth, and spoke to her as one adult to another. They looked at each other in a way that left me with no doubt that my brother and Anna had fallen in love, and I suggested that he introduce her to the family.

"That Polish/Irish stuff is a lot of bull, Patrick. She'll get less resistance from Mom than Rob did because she's a Catholic. Invite her to dinner."

At Sunday dinner, Anna received a warm welcome. My father and Sadie didn't seem to care that she was Polish, my grandfather totally ignored her, and my mother was relieved that Patrick had finally found someone to date. After she left, everyone congratulated my brother on finding such a nice girl.

The next day, Patrick asked me to meet him for lunch downtown. Sliding into the diner booth, Patrick immediately got to the point. "Listen, I appreciate how nice you were to Anna, so I'm going to return the favor. You should break up with your flyer."

If this was just another case of Patrick being a jerk, I was going to haul off and punch him, like Sadie did.

"I'm being serious here, Maggie. Because of Anna, I'm seeing things different. You know how, before the war, a bunch of us would go to Avoca for barbecue. No one was dating anyone; we were all just hanging out and putting coins in the jukebox and dancing. That's what you and Rob remind me of—two people hanging out together. Don't get me wrong. I like the guy. But I don't want you to end up with some guy just because he's good-looking and has some dough in his pocket. I want you to be head over heels in love. So I'm telling you straight up; Rob ain't the one."

***

Rob got off the train with a bounce in his step. After giving me a chaste kiss because there was a group of nuns in the station, he asked if there was someplace we could go to talk. We drove to my Aunt Marie's house, which would shortly be J.J.'s house. The kitchen was cold because the morning fire had died down. After stoking the coals, I put a kettle on the burner and asked Rob what he was so eager to talk about.

"Maggie, is there a wedding in our future?"

Rob had said we were going to make plans, but I didn't think he meant that we would start the discussion within minutes of his arrival. After my conversation with Patrick, I had thought long and hard about whether I wanted to spend the rest of my life with Rob. After seeing him following a three-month absence, I was flooded with fond memories of our time together in England, and I was very touched by his efforts to win me back since coming to Minooka. After a long silence, I finally answered, "Rob, I can't."

"That's what I thought you'd say. I think I knew it from the night of the ball at Montclair."

After taking the coffee cup out of my hand, he continued, "I drank way too much that night, and when nature called, I went into the bushes. When I came out, guess who was waiting for me? Eva Greene. And she starts making out with me. It was like I had landed on fly paper. When I finally broke free, I heard the band leader announce that there was one more dance. I wanted it to be with you, but by the time I got into the ballroom, you were dancing with Michael."

"Rob, I looked for you, but I couldn't find you." That was the absolute truth. Michael had been paying a lot of attention to me, but I thought the last dance should be with Rob, if for no other reason than common courtesy—"you danced with the one who brung you."

"I know," he said, nodding his head. "But because of Eva, I got there too late. It gave me a chance to watch the two of you together. From that time on, I was pretty sure it was never going to happen for me and you. But then you threw me a curve when you came back to the States.

"In the few days we've been together, I thought maybe—just maybe—there was still a chance to save this thing. I thought if I told you about my plans you'd see I was ready to make a commit-ment. You were really happy for me, but you weren't happy for us. Like you said in the Crowells' backyard, that's because there is no 'us.'

"It wasn't until I got to Omaha that I put it all together. If I'm wrong here, tell me right now." He looked at me so intently, but I could not say what he wanted to hear. "I didn't think so; I can see it in your face. So now I have something to tell you.

"Going to Omaha was the best thing I could have done. I only wish I had gone three years ago. Everyone from Pat's family wanted to meet me, so they reserved the Knights of Columbus hall. When I saw Pat's photo on one of the tables, I almost bailed, but then I realized that most people were in small groups, laughing and telling stories. The Monaghans were having a party for Pat.

"The next day, Mr. Monaghan told me how excited Pat had been when he found out he was going to flight school. 'When the

Army told Pat his scores were high enough to get into the Air Corps, he was on Cloud Nine. It was the proudest day of his life when they pinned those wings on him. He said it meant that he would never have to work in a meat-packing plant again.'

"The thing that I had been dreading was that his parents would ask me how Pat had died. But all Pat's father said was, 'I can see that something's bothering you. But I want you to know that there's only one reason my son is dead, and that's because a German killed him.'"

I had always suspected that Rob thought he had some role in his friend's death, but I didn't understand how something as random as flak hitting the nose of a bomber could be anyone's fault. Taking his hand in mine, I said, "I'm glad you were able to talk to Pat's dad, and he's exactly right. It's time to let the ugliness of his death go and remember what a fun and funny guy Pat was."

Rob smiled and then continued. "A couple of days before the wedding, the Monaghans had a smaller group over for dinner." Rob hesitated, took a drink of coffee, and then said, "At this get-together, I spent a lot of time talking to Pat's cousin, Peggy. I had met her on my first visit to Omaha. She's one of those people who are very easy to talk to, and we hit it off."

"What do you mean 'you hit if off?' Are you saying you went out with her?"

"Sort of. But that's not the point I'm trying to make here. It was because of Peggy that I realized why I had never asked you to marry me."

"Okay, I'm listening," I said, folding my arms across my chest.

"When we were in England together, I thought about you constantly. From the time I met you at the Christmas party, I believed I had finally found the right girl, but for some reason, I kept hanging back, and I didn't know why. Even when I knew I was hurting you, I still didn't ask you to marry me.

"You are the most curious person I've ever met. Wherever we went in London, you wanted to know everything that had ever happened there. Remember when we went to the cemetery where Elizabeth Garrison's family is buried? You let out a whoop when you found them, as if they were your own family. I didn't give a crap about those people. I got all caught up in it because of you.

"For you, life is an adventure. You want to go places and see things. And as long as you are living overseas, you will continue to do that. I had my adventure. Three years in the Army and thirty missions scratched that itch. I'm ready to settle down, and I think deep down I knew you weren't."

"And how did Peggy help you out?" I was really annoyed. Rob had been gone for ten days, and in that time, he had met a girl who had provided such clarity he had been able to figure everything out.

"She talked about what most women her age want—getting married, buying a house, and having kids. She doesn't care where Elizabeth I is buried or what happened in Regency England."

"You're making it sound as if being interested in people and places isn't a good thing," I answered defensively. "You've seen where I grew up. Of course, I want adventure."

"Do you know what I want?" Rob asked, leaning across the table. "Getting that job at Delta and buying a car. I don't want to tour Europe. I've seen all of Europe that I ever want to see. In a few years, I want to go to the beach in a station wagon with a couple of kids in the back seat. But that's not what you want. You want to walk the streets of Pompeii and climb the Eiffel Tower. And I want you to have it. It's just that you can't have those things with me."

I didn't have a response to that because everything he was saying was true. "Is her name really Peggy?"

"As far as I know. Why?"

"Peggy and Maggie are both short for Margaret."

"That seems about right. Two nice women with the same name."

We said very little on the drive back to the station because I didn't want to start crying.

"Rob, take care of yourself. Don't rush into anything."

"You don't have to worry about that. It'll be a long time before I get over you."

As soon as I got into the car, I started to cry. Rob had been my first true love, and we had some wonderful memories together, and now he was gone forever.

Chapter 45

ALTHOUGH A WEIGHT HAD been lifted from my shoulders, I felt little sense of relief. I was dreading going back to the house because I would have to explain the breakup to my family. What I needed was a few days of quiet, but I wasn't going to get it.

"Where's Rob?" my mother asked while peeling potatoes. "Weren't you supposed to pick him up at the station?"

"He's flying home to see his parents in Arizona. We have decided to stop seeing each other," I said, slumping into a wooden kitchen chair.

My mother, who had a lifetime of experience in navigating bumps, had learned that problems seemed more manageable after drinking a large cup of black coffee, with a splash of whiskey if it involved Patrick. I tried to explain why I had let Rob go, but I was falling short. I finally said, "I just couldn't marry him."

"Then you shouldn't. You absolutely shouldn't," Mom said with a surprising amount of fervor. "Look at me and your father. I was so flattered that a smart, college-educated man was interested in a girl from Miner Hill that I was willing to overlook the drinking and the long silences. We should have left Minooka right after we got married. Get him away from his father and the bars, but I didn't want to leave my mother. So we stayed."

With that opening, I thought this might be a good time to tell her that I was going back to England, but then she said, "While you were at the station, you had a long-distance call from Michael Crowell. He said to let you know he and his parents were thinking about you and to offer the family their condolences for our loss."

"That's it? That's all he said?" I was so agitated that my voice cracked. Whatever thoughts I had had of Rob flew out of my head. The only person I cared about was Michael.

"Well, he asked if you were home, and I told him you were at work, and after that, you had to pick Rob up at the station. Then he said what I told you he said. I didn't rattle on, Maggie. That was a long-distance call from wherever—London—I don't know, and I didn't want to waste his money."

I looked at the clock. It was the middle of the night in England. I'd have to wait until 2:00 in the morning before calling Crofton. I dialed the long-distance operator to find out what I needed to do to place an overseas call. She explained the procedure and told me she would call me back when she had my party on the other line. My mother had been staring at me the whole time I was talking to the operator—not having a clue as to what was going on. When I got off the phone, I tried to explain as best I could what Michael meant to me, but my mother shook her head in total incomprehension.

"You're not thinking this through, Maggie. It is not possible to be in love with one man one day and a different one the next."

Additional explanations were getting me nowhere when Sadie came downstairs and told my mother that she knew about my reservations regarding Rob and my feelings for Michael.

"Mom, it's too late," Sadie explained. "Maggie was already in love with Michael when she got here. She felt bad about letting down someone as nice as Rob, but she knows what she's doing."

"I beg to differ," my mother said angrily. "This shows a lack of seriousness I would never have guessed about you, Maggie."

As much as Mom's words stung, she was not my main problem. What did Michael think when my mother told him that I had a job? That made it sound as if I had made the decision to stay in the States. And what was going through his mind when he heard that Rob had come to Minooka?

At 1:30, I put on a heavy robe and went down to the kitchen to wait for my call to be put through to Crofton. For ninety minutes, I stared at the phone, willing it to ring. The call finally came in at 3:00 a.m. It was Beth.

"Maggie, is there something wrong?" I told her about Michael's call earlier in the day and that I was trying to return his phone call.

"Oh, dear," she said in that clipped English accent that I loved. "He's not here. He's in New York. He must have called you from my Aunt Laura's. Maggie, he went to the States specifically to talk to you."

"I don't understand why he did that. The last thing he said was that he was going to wait in Crofton for me to make a decision. But I'm afraid he got the wrong idea when he called this afternoon. He's probably thinking Rob and I have gotten back together, and it's not true." After a long pause, I said, "Beth, I'm in love with your son."

"Yes, dear. I know," Beth said with a smile in her voice. "I've known since the ball. I was waiting for you to figure it out."

Beth immediately put a plan into action. She would call her Aunt Laura to make sure Michael didn't leave New York. "We have to get you to New York City. Get a pencil and paper, and I'll give you all the particulars."

***

Laura Bolton Winslow was just shy of celebrating her eightieth birthday, but you would never have known it from the spry woman who answered the door of her fifth-floor New York apartment.

"Finally, I get to meet the young woman Beth has been writing to me about for how long now? A year?" she said, gesturing for me to come in.

A colored woman came into the room carrying a coffee tray and smiled broadly when Laura introduced her personal assistant of twelve years, Ruth Johnson. When Laura's husband had died, she had hired Ruth as a maid, but in the intervening years, Ruth had become her friend and companion.

"When Beth called, she left me with specific instructions. I was not to let Michael leave the city until you arrived, but not to let him know that you were coming. So I arranged for him to spend the day with my son-in-law, David Weisman, at Beth Israel Hospital. He'll be home about 6:00, but I won't. Ruth and I are having dinner with my neighbor, Mrs. Kirkpatrick, in Apartment 2B. We won't be home until, let's say, 10:00."

After an enjoyable lunch with Laura, I spent the afternoon resting, bathing, and doing my hair because I had a lot riding on this. I was in the kitchen when I heard Michael come in.

"Hello. Anyone home?"

"I'm in the kitchen," I hollered.

Michael stuck his head around the corner. "Hello." He acted as if he wasn't surprised that I was in his aunt's apartment. "I was expecting to see my Aunt Laura, but this is okay," he said, leaning up against the counter.

"I'm returning your phone call."

"I like the way you return phone calls."

"I thought you said that you would stay in England until you heard from me."

"I didn't think the strategy was working. Besides, I missed you."

"In that case, aren't you going to kiss me?" I asked.

"I would, except I don't think I could stop at kissing. I used up all of my willpower in England."

"Who said you had to?"

Looking around, he said, "Where's Aunt Laura?"

"She's with Mrs. Kirkpatrick, Apartment 2B, and won't be home for three hours—she promised."

Michael came over and kissed me briefly before pulling me into a tight hug. He whispered, "I love you," and for the first time, I was able to tell him how I felt. "I love you, too. Thank you for waiting for me."

Michael reached out to take my hand, and when he did, I remembered what Geoff had said about how Michael was favoring his right hand. With everything that I had gone through with Rob, I needed to know what had happened to him in Burma.

"If you are left-handed, then why are you doing so many things with your right hand?" I asked.

"If this is what passes for sexual banter in the States," he said, completely perplexed, "it's not very effective."

"Geoff said when you two were in India, you always bumped elbows because you were left-handed and he was right-handed."

"Maggie, this is not a question about which hand I favor. What is it you need to know?" Gesturing toward the kitchen table, we both sat down. "If your question is, did I experience some horrendous things during the war, the answer is 'yes.' But if you are asking if I am carrying around some terrible burden, the answer is 'no.' I have had ample time to deal with these things, and I have. I saw what not dealing with the past did to my father.

"As I told you, when I got to India, I was trained as a pilot and a medic. We were responding to a call for an emergency evacuation when we were hit with small-arms fire. It was enough to damage the wing, and we were forced down. Fortunately, the men who had radioed for the med evac were nearby. They established a perimeter while we tried to fix the plane. During the night, our perimeter was breached, and it ended in hand-to-hand fighting. My left shoulder was sliced open by a machete, and it damaged the muscle enough to make certain movements awkward. My range of motion is almost back to normal, but my fine motor skills have been slower to return. Rather than spilling hot coffee on someone, I use my right hand. Now, I do have a magnificent scar on my back." Pulling me onto his lap, he said, "And I would be happy to show it to you."

We went into the guest bedroom, and Michael took off his shirt and undershirt. On his left shoulder was a purple scar that cut across his shoulder blade. I ran my fingers along the scar, and then I started to kiss his back and his neck until he turned around and pushed me onto my back. He slid his hands under my slip and removed my underpants, all the while looking into my eyes, and then he lay on top of me and entered me immediately. At that moment, I wasn't thinking of anything else; I just wanted him to love me forever.

✳✳✳

When Ruth and Laura came in, we were sitting innocently on the couch. We had been talking about Angela and James's wedding night, and Michael said it was a good thing his brother had pulled the covers off the bed because his aim was terrible, and the chances of his hitting the modesty hole dead-on weren't very good.

"I can see that you two have been having a nice talk while we were playing canasta with Mrs. Kirkpatrick, who won every game but the last." Pretending to yawn, she said, "If you don't mind, I would like to retire, and we can visit in the morning. By the way, I'm a very heavy sleeper. I don't hear a thing, and Ruth is the same way."

After I heard the doors close on Laura's and Ruth's doors, I asked Michael if he thought she knew. He laughed, and pointing to my legs, he said, 'You didn't put your stockings back on."

I turned beet red and asked Michael why he hadn't said something.

"About what?" he said, laughing. "Why do you think she left us alone?"

We waited for about ten minutes before returning to the guest bedroom. This time Michael was not in a hurry, and it was different from anything I had ever experienced with Rob. I got to the point where I wanted him more than I had ever wanted anything before, and I wrapped my legs around his and pulled him into me. And, afterwards, I wouldn't release him because I needed to be reassured that someone could love me so much, and it was only with great reluctance that I finally let him go.

After making love, he pulled me onto his chest and asked when I had first known I was in love with him. "I'm not sure," I answered honestly. "I know that as soon as I met you that I liked you a lot. When you came home from Malta, your mother asked you why you had cut your hair so short, and you said, 'So I can do this,' and you combed your hair with your fingers. Then at the Grist Mill, you started flirting with me, and that night I had impure thoughts about you." After I refused to go into more detail, I said, "I knew I was in trouble at the ball, because I had hardly seen Rob all night, and yet it didn't bother me all that much. Shame on me."

"What happened with Rob?"

I told Michael everything about Rob's visit and his comment that he knew Michael was in love with me when he saw us dancing together at Montclair.

"Now, it's your turn," I said.

"I suspected it on the day you fell into my lap at Thor's Cave. I was absolutely sure the night of the ball. By the time we had the last dance, I was in over my head. So Rob was right, when we danced to 'Always,' I was in love with you." Holding me tightly, he asked, "Will you marry me?"

"Yes."

"It's too late to get married today. What about tomorrow?"

I pointed out that we needed a marriage license, and we had to get married in the Church. It was at that point I realized we weren't going to get married anytime soon. There would have to be three weeks of announced banns, and Michael would have to agree to raise any children in the Catholic faith, or a marriage could not take place in the Church. I asked him if this was a problem.

"I was baptized in the Anglican church. However, I grew up in India amid Hindus, Moslems, and Sikhs. I want to have children who are moral and compassionate."

There was also the matter of a courtship. It was wonderful to think that Michael was so in love with me that he wanted us to marry immediately. However, I had to slow the process down. It was true we had known each other for four months, but in those months, we had spent very little time together. Michael suggested the best way to accomplish that was to say good-bye to Aunt Laura and Ruth Johnson and to check into a hotel for a few days.

We chose the Algonquin, and when we weren't making love, I was in the bathroom taking long, hot baths. There was even a shower, and I sat in the tub with the hot water pouring over my head. Michael kept checking on me to make sure I hadn't gone down the drain. But after living overseas for two years, with restrictions on everything because of fuel shortages, I was going to make the most of an unlimited supply of hot water. Finally, Michael climbed into the tub with me saying that it was the only way he was going to get to see me. The experience of having someone who was head over heels in love with me and willing to show it was so wonderful that it had almost a fairy-tale feel to it. But even fairy tales have to come to an end, and after three days, Michael and I boarded a train in Penn Station for our trip to Scranton. The closer we got to Scranton, the higher my anxiety level. How was I ever going to explain what had happened between Michael and me? I didn't think it was going to go well.

Chapter 46

WHEN SADIE, PATRICK, AND my father came home from work, Michael and I were sitting at the kitchen table having coffee. Mom was peeling potatoes and doing her best to ignore me. She had warned me not to go to New York, and I had defied her. All the changes that had happened as a result of the war had passed my mother by. While her daughters had gone to Washington and her son into the Navy, Mom had remained behind in a village that was little different from the one her mother had known in the nineteenth century, and she remained locked into a morality that was as exacting as that of the Victorians. Although she was polite to Michael, she had nothing to say to me.

My father is a man of few words. Instead of asking who Michael was, he sat down in his chair waiting for something to happen. Mom explained that Michael was visiting from England, making it sound as if he had been passing through Scranton and had decided to stop by. We were several minutes into dinner with very little being said, even by Patrick and Sadie, who usually dominated the dinner hour, when Michael finally broke the silence.

"Mr. and Mrs. Joyce, I met your daughter at my parents' home in Derbyshire. It was a brief introduction to a woman whom my parents had come to love as if she were their daughter. But because I was serving in the Royal Air Force, I had to leave to go to my station in Germany. In August, my parents hosted a party, and I was able to get leave. When I saw Maggie again, I realized that I had fallen in love with her. There were complications— another man—but I was not going to be put off for any reason. I was making some headway when she was called home to say good-bye to her Aunt Marie. For the past four weeks, I've been at home in England, pacing the floor, wondering if some unkind fate had intervened and had taken her away from me. I decided to come and find out because this is the woman I want to be my wife." And turning to me, he said, "I have asked Maggie to marry me, and she has accepted."

My mother's mouth dropped open, my father started to scratch his head, and Grandpa came out of his bedroom and said, "Who the hell are you?"

"You must be Mr. Joyce," he said, rising from his chair as if he was addressing a senior officer. "Maggie has told me so much about you, especially your role as a freedom fighter in Ireland. As I'm sure you've guessed from my accent, I'm British, but I'm proud to say that I have a fair share of Irish in me."

"Seafóid," Grandpa said, not believing it for a minute.

"Allow me to translate," my father said, "Garbage, rubbish, nonsense. Take your pick."

"Honestly. It's true, Mr. Joyce. My grandmother's family was from County Meath." After a few minutes of silence, Grandpa said, "County Meath. Bah! Never a callous on the hands of a County Meath man." After saying that, he went back into his bedroom. Michael would settle for his relations being called sissies if it meant that Grandpa wouldn't throw him out of his house.

After Grandpa left, Dad offered his congratulations in a voice that said, "I hope you know what the hell you are doing." My mother said absolutely nothing. I couldn't blame either for their reaction. They had been expecting an announcement that Rob and I were engaged, and instead, I had brought home a different man. Sadie and Patrick made up for my parents' lack of enthusiasm, and my sister, while crying, bear hugged her future brother-in-law. Throughout it all, Michael remained calm and unperturbed. He was probably meditating.

News travels fast in a small town, and by the following afternoon, everyone was talking about my engagement. "It's not the same guy who was at Judge's. It's some English guy nobody knew anything about."

The same day the news was making its way around town, I received two phone calls. One was from Bobby's mother, who demanded that I come to her house and explain myself. There was some unwritten rule that Mamie Lenehan had a right to poke her nose into everybody's business, and for some reason, everyone went along with it. The second call was from Father Lynch, and he wanted to see me in the rectory office.

Sadie said she wished that she could be a fly on the wall in the pastor's office. "I'd love to hear how you're going to explain this."

I decided not to explain it. I didn't go to see Father Lynch, nor did I rush down to Mamie's to make some sort of confession. I had been out of Minooka for four years, and I was not going to run a gauntlet when I hadn't done anything wrong. However, in order to be on the safe side, I called my uncle, Father Shea, whose parish was in a small coal town buried deep in the mountains, but who bought his scotch in Scranton.

Raised jointly by my grandmother and Aunt Marie, John Shea was the cigar-smoking, card-playing type of priest, who had worked among the poor of coal country's mining towns since he had been ordained thirty-five years earlier. In that time, he had shaved his theology down to the two great commandments: Love God and love your neighbor. "Everything else is commentary." He didn't preach; he comforted.

I asked him if I was going to go to hell for defying Father Lynch, and he said, "Don't worry, lass. I'll give Father Lynch a call and get him to back off. As for Mamie Lenehan, she'll have enough to think about when she learns Bobby is dating the Mateo girl."

Michael, who had studied Hinduism, seemed nonplussed by the complexities of the Catholic Church. He left me to sort out the details and went to Judge's for a beer with Patrick. Before leaving, he said, "It'll give you an opportunity to bring your father up to speed on why you are marrying me and not Rob, and while you're at it, see if you can discourage your grandfather from putting me on an IRA hit list."

After Michael left, I knocked on Grandpa's bedroom door and asked if I could come in. He was sitting in the shadows smoking his pipe. When my grandmother had died three years earlier, he had started to spend more and more time in his room. In profile, I could see his expansive chest—one of the signs of emphysema—his reward for forty years of working underground.

"So which one will ye be marrying?" he asked.

"Michael, the one with the black hair," I answered.

Grandpa pointed his pipe at his chest of drawers.

"Go and open Mam's sewing box."

I did what he said, but I didn't know what I was looking for.

"Them silver coins. They washed up on Omey from a Spanish ship. Your Mam's father give 'em to her before we come to America, saying to sell them if need be. Say what ye will, I be putting food on the table even in the worst of times." I picked up five silver coins with irregular edges worn down by time and the sea. "Take them. I'll not be seeing you again."

Before dismissing me, he spoke at length in Irish, but listening to this ancient tongue spoken by a wheezing man with no teeth, I wasn't quite getting what he was saying. But my father, who was sitting near the door, later boiled the speech down to one sentence: "Your mother is not always right."

When I left Grandpa's room, my mother said her brother had called back. "Father Lynch has agreed to let your uncle handle this situation. But Father Shea wants to talk to you tomorrow afternoon here at the house." All of this was said in the dispassionate tone she had been using since my return from New York.

"Mom, do you like Michael?" I asked. I believed if she would only give him a chance, she would see what a kind and decent man I was in love with.

"It doesn't matter what I think. You made that clear when you went to New York. But since you've asked, I'll tell you what I think happened. When you were in England, Rob called it quits on you, so you set your sights on Michael because he's the one who can make sure you get to stay over there."

I have never back talked my mother. She didn't deserve it, and even though what she had said was incredibly hurtful,

I was not going to get into an argument with someone who already had too much pain in her life. I took a dish towel out of the drawer and started to dry the dishes. "What if Michael and I had a lengthy engagement? Would that help put your mind at ease?"

Wiping her hands on her apron, she said, "Remember when Suzie Luzowski wanted to marry that Jewish boy? She told her mother that she would stay a Catholic and he would stay Jewish. But the Jewish priest didn't go for it, saying one was a fish and the other a fowl." She went back to washing the dishes.

Logic was never my mother's strong suit. It was part of the reason why she and Dad had such a strained relationship. He had a university education while my mother had left school in the tenth grade to go to work. His was the world of reasoned debate; hers was all emotion based on an innate sense of what was right. But even for my mother, this argument didn't make sense. Suzie and Seth had gotten married and moved to Philadelphia where he was going to medical school. They had successfully overcome all obstacles, and to the best of my knowledge, were doing well. I decided to leave it alone. Michael was a Protestant, and for someone whose daily life was tied to the Church calendar, it wouldn't have made a bit of difference anyway.

***

After telling Michael about my conversation with my mother, he agreed we needed to hold off on a wedding. "I understand why your mother is upset, but I think if she has an opportunity to see the two of us together, she'll realize how well-suited we are for each other. I'll just have to stay in Minooka for a few weeks."

My first reaction was, "Hell no!" But after calming down, I didn't see any other way to reassure Mom that Michael and I belonged together.

When Father Shea arrived at the house the next morning, I thought he was going to talk to us about laying the foundation for a good Catholic marriage and the importance of bringing the children up in the Church. Instead, he asked Michael about India and the new country of Pakistan. Did Michael think a bloodbath could be avoided between the two countries? As a young priest, my uncle had wanted to be a missionary, and he closely followed international affairs. When Michael took a bathroom break, I hurried after him and told him we needed to get the conversation back on track. Solving Pakistan and India's problems could wait.

"Father, would you like to go for a walk?" I asked in a pleading voice. Although he was my uncle, we were never allowed to call him anything other than Father Shea.

As soon as we got clear of the house, my uncle asked, "Will you be needing to speak to your Uncle John or Father Shea?"

"Both, I think."

We were walking up Birney Avenue to the city line when my uncle asked Michael if he attended church regularly. I thought, "Holy crap!"

"Regularly? No, I don't. When I was in Malta, I occasionally attended chapel. However, there was little opportunity to do so in Germany. Since I've been discharged from the service, I haven't been to church at all." There was nothing defensive about this statement, and I was wondering how my uncle would react to someone who didn't apologize for "not keeping holy the Sabbath day."

"I see," Father said, clearly not pleased with the answer.

"But what I think you are asking me, Father, is if I honor the Creator and his creation, and I most certainly do and plan to continue doing so through medicine."

I looked at my uncle to see if that answer satisfied him. He said nothing, and we kept walking. We were nearly to the city line when he finally said, "Michael, I've worked among miners for most of my adult life. Their occupation of clawing ore out of a mountain is dehumanizing, so they either turn to the Church or they turn to drink. My goal has been to keep them within the arms of the Holy Mother Church because, without it, they descend into a life of alcoholism and abuse. The Church helped my sister to get through the poverty of her childhood and an abusive stepfather. It has comforted her in the loss of a child. It has given her the strength to live in a household with a mean-spirited old man, an alcoholic husband, and a son with the remarkable ability to find trouble where there was none. You, young man, pose a threat to the very thing that has kept her whole.

"Here's what I'm going to do. I'll tell Delia that we spoke at length, and I am convinced your beliefs run deep. I will reassure her that Maggie will continue to attend church." Father looked at me to see if that would be the case, and I nodded eagerly. "I ask that you delay marrying for at least a year because you come from very different backgrounds. If you agree to a year's engagement, I think that it will go a long way to putting my sister's mind at ease. And, Michael, you must understand there is absolutely no divorce in the Catholic Church. Maggie will be your wife in the eyes of the Church until her death."

After crossing into Scranton, my uncle pointed to Mateo's Bar and said, "Now, there is a matter of much greater concern—a possible alliance between Bobby Lenehan and Teresa Mateo. Your difficulties pale in comparison."

Winking at me, my uncle let me know that things would turn out all right. I only hoped that he was right.

Chapter 47

MY UNCLE HAD BARELY reached the safety of his mountain parish before a storm came barreling out of the Midwest hitting the Lackawanna Valley with a foot and a half of snow. After digging out our house, Michael took his shovel and went down to Mamie's where he was bunking out during the Minooka part of our courtship. Bobby had practically begged Michael to stay at his house as a buffer between his mother and him. News of his courtship with Teresa had finally reached his mother, and her reaction had been as expected. A loud, "Hell no!" But Bobby was holding his ground, and Michael's presence was preventing Mamie from killing him.

Michael attended Mass with my family on Sunday. Before beginning his sermon, Father Lynch reminded his congregation that the Catholic Church has closed communion, and that you must be a congregant who is free of the stain of mortal sin in order to receive the sacrament. The part about being a non-Catholic was for Michael; the part about being free of mortal sin was for me.

Since we were the talk of the town, everyone wanted to meet Michael. Because of his British accent, he was something of a curiosity, and he answered even the most embarrassing questions graciously. Mamie proved helpful. In an effort to throw an elbow at Bobby, she was telling all her friends that Michael was everything a mother could possibly want in a son.

Although we had agreed we would not set a wedding date, Michael thought he could garner a lot of goodwill with my cousins and friends if we had an engagement party with an open bar. So we made plans for the big event at the Hotel Casey in downtown Scranton.

The day after the party, Michael and I planned to visit his Aunt Laura before going back to London. I was hoping we could have some private time before returning to England. It seemed to be bothering me more than Michael, and he suggested yoga and meditation.

"I meditated quite a bit when I was in hospital in Burma, and yoga has many benefits. It maximizes flexibility," he said with a big grin. And they say girls are teases.

When we called Beth and Jack to tell them we were going to have an engagement party, they said they wanted to come. Although I warned them about winter weather in the Poconos, they said they would take their chances. When Michael and I arrived at the station to meet the train from New York, sitting on one of the waiting room's wooden benches was Geoff Alcott.

"What are you doing here?" we both asked at the same time.

"I could lie and tell you that I flew in just for the celebration of your engagement, but the truth is that I have been in Washington for the past week. It appears that a North Atlantic alliance between the United States and Western Europe is a reality. The major players have departed, including my father, and have left the subalterns to dot i's and cross t's." Geoff was clearly pleased with the results of months of negotiations. "It is gratifying to see that, on occasion, one's labors bear fruit."

After checking Beth, Jack, and Geoff into the Hotel Casey, we headed to Smith's Diner in South Scranton for lunch. Beth asked how things were going. She was eager to hear how her son had been received.

"Everyone really likes Michael," I said, which surprised neither of his parents.

"Even Grandpa Joyce likes me—somewhat," Michael added. "He told me stories about growing up on Omey Island where two or three men would go out in a curragh and collect seaweed. They'd throw hundreds of pounds of the stuff onto what he called 'rafts' and float them in to shore. The seaweed was used for iodine and potash for pottery. Curraghs are little more than big canoes, so it was quite dangerous."

"My grandfather told you that?" I had never heard that story, but then I realized my grandfather didn't tell stories to anyone other than his card buddies down at the church hall, or when a few old friends stopped in for a cup of tea. I couldn't even eavesdrop because they swapped stories in Irish.

"I'm surprised he's even talking to you," Jack said. "From what I've heard from Maggie, he can't stand the sight or the sound of an Englishman."

I decided not to tell Michael that my grandfather, his new-found friend, had said that listening to his British accent was like having needles stuck in his ears.

"He enjoys telling stories about how the Irish kicked British ass after the first war."

Before anyone got the mistaken impression that my grandfather had opened up a new chapter in British/Irish relations, I told them we would be having a get-together for the two families at Mamie Lenehan's house. I wasn't going to court trouble by having three citizens of his former enemy in his house.

"Michael has been staying at Mamie's," I explained. "She has a larger house than we do, and since Grandpa never leaves the house now, you won't have a chance to meet him."

Jack smiled at me. I was sure that he knew why they would not be meeting my grandfather. "It seems you've had a warmer welcome than you might have expected," Jack said to his son.

"It's been great. I go to Mass with Maggie on Sunday. Father Lynch seems to think I need to be reminded from the pulpit that I am not Catholic. But that's not the best part. After Mass, he told Maggie he hadn't heard her confession since she's been home. I'm sure he suspects some midnight assignation between us."

Michael looked at me as if to say, "If only it were true."

"When you think about it, because he hears confession, he has the goods on everyone in town. Minooka has almost no municipal structure, so Father Lynch is mayor, judge, jury, and the police. It's amazing how much power he has."

"Don't worry about Father Lynch," Jack said. "You'll be out of here soon enough. How are you getting on with Maggie's family?"

"Sadie likes me. And I've lent my services as a mechanic to Patrick and Maggie's cousin Bobby at their gas station, so I'm definitely in their good graces. I went to a local bar with Mr. Joyce to have a few 'shnorts.' He's a quiet man but highly intelligent and knows the newspaper business inside out. When he has a beer or two in him, he'll tell you stories of when he was a breaker boy and mule driver. As for Mrs. Joyce, I'm still trying to win her over. I've rewired the chicken coop, repaired the fencing around her garden, cleaned gutters, and shoveled snow. She acknowledges everything I've done, but..."

The reason Michael couldn't complete the sentence was, despite his best efforts, he had made little headway with my mother. As for me, I had made no headway at all.

"Speaking of Sadie," Geoff said, "when do I get to meet her?"

Michael started to laugh. "Geoff, I'd love to hear a conversation between the two of you. You'd dazzle Sadie with your rapier wit, and she'll respond with a cudgel."

Jack started to tap the table. "Speaking of shnorts, where can we get a drink?"

"Mateo's. It's right across the street," Michael answered. "Bobby is dating their daughter, and Mrs. Lenehan went through the roof when she heard about it. Apparently, the Irish arrived here a generation before the Italians, and they look down on them because of their dark skin and exotic ways. In all seriousness," Michael added, "I think I did a bit of good with Bobby's mother when I told them about James, Angela, and Julia. The past few days I've detected a thawing of relations between Bobby and his mother."

After the men went across the street to the bar, Beth asked, "How are things between your mother and you?"

I didn't know what to say. Mom was still giving me the cold shoulder, believing her obvious displeasure would make me rethink my decision to marry Michael.

"Maggie, you don't have to weigh your words with me. Has she voiced any objections to Michael?"

"No. My mother's problem is not with Michael. It's with me."

"Does her unhappiness have something to do with the fact that Michael is not a Catholic?"

I nodded. "Mom doesn't believe Catholics should marry outside their faith. I could deal with that, but she also thinks I'm promiscuous, and according to her beliefs, I am."

"Maggie, you are not promiscuous. Quite the opposite. Your modesty does you credit." Patting my hand, Beth asked, "Will this affect your decision to return to England?"

"No, it can't. I'm sorry I've made my mother unhappy. Hopefully, over time, that will change."

Beth thought it might be helpful if she talked to Mom, explaining how the relationship between Michael and me had come to be.

"That's fine," I said, "but I'd be surprised if it did any good. That is one lady who can dig in her heels."

***

By the time Beth and Jack had arrived at the Lenehan house to meet my family, everyone knew a great deal about them, including Beth's being the daughter of a baronet. The fact that she was also the wife of a butler's son got less playing time. Mamie wanted to know if she should address Beth as Lady Elizabeth, and I explained that Beth's only title was Mrs. Jack Crowell.

Beth was as charming as she could be. She didn't react when Uncle Mike, who was missing all but his thumb and forefinger on his right hand, shook her hand very much the way a lobster would. She admired Uncle Joe's shrapnel scar from World War I that ran just below his ribs, and she pretended to be impressed when Mamie pointed out that, as the wife of a prominent Democrat, she entertained so much that she had to special order extra leaves from Philadelphia for her dining room table. When introduced to J.J., she offered her condolences for his loss of my

Aunt Marie and later spent a generous amount of time listening to the story of their unmarried life together.

Jack made an excellent impression as someone who didn't stand on ceremony, and since many of the young men were earning a living in highway construction, Jack shared some stories of building railway bridges in India while listening to the difficulties of paving roads on the steep inclines of the Pocono Mountains. With my father, Jack discussed the one American baseball game he had seen during the First War. The Yanks had invited the British to an exhibition game of their national pastime, and Jack readily conceded that baseball was a lot less boring than cricket. Dad took the opportunity to boast of all of the local talent that had come out of our little town, including Steve O'Neill and his brothers, Chick Shorten, and Mike McNally, all of whom had gone on to play in the majors.

Michael had already worked himself into the fabric of the town and walked about the room with confidence. He ended up sitting next to a toothless Sally Bluegoose, who showed up at every social event. Sally, who earned money for her keening, took her pipe out of her mouth and gave Michael and Jack an on-the-spot demonstration, which was the only time during the evening when Beth looked rattled. Without missing a beat, Jack told Sally it reminded him of "the night birds in India that scared the tar out of my boys when they were little." He said that he could understand why her services were so sought after, which delighted Sally.

And then there was Geoff. There were good reasons why women loved Geoff, and he demonstrated it with my Aunt Agatha. She was the worker bee of the family, preferring to stay in the background, washing dishes, replenishing the food, making coffee. But Geoff had wandered into the kitchen while she was doing the dishes and had picked up a dish towel. In short order, he had her talking about her children and Aunt Marie. He also won praise from Sadie: "I don't get him, but he's cute."

Whenever Mom got really dressed up, she always wore her favorite navy blue dress with tiny red flowers, and she had gone to the expense of buying a matching hat and shoes. Tonight, she was wearing one of her older Sunday dresses. The Crowells didn't know any better, but I understood Mom was sending a clear message that she was unhappy with me. Before the end of the evening, Beth asked Mom if they could possibly have lunch together—just the two of them. My mother agreed and suggested they go to her sister's house.

The next morning, I delivered a bag full of groceries to my aunt's house. Aunt Agatha had never recovered from the night when her husband went out to buy a pack of cigarettes and kept walking, leaving her to raise four children on her own. Uncle Leo's desertion had condemned his family to a life of poverty. My mother had chosen Aunt Agatha's house because she wanted Beth to know: "You are not like us, and we are not like you."

As instructed, I returned an hour later to pick them up. As soon as I saw the two women come through the battered screen door, I knew that Beth had gotten nowhere. The mood in the car was so strained that I knew I was in for it when I got home. After walking through our kitchen door, Mom immediately slipped on her apron in an effortless exercise repeated thousands of times during her lifetime. Within a minute, she was washing and peeling potatoes for dinner. One by one, I transferred the potatoes from the sink to the cutting board and waited for what proved to be an explosion.

"Do what you want. I don't care. If you are willing to turn away from your faith, your upbringing, everything you've been taught just so you can live in England and have a rich husband, go ahead."

"Why are you saying I've turned away from my faith? I go to Mass; I receive Communion. And Michael is not rich. Besides, he will be going to school for years, and I'll have to keep working as long as he's in school. And, believe me, we won't be living in the lap of luxury in England because it's as if the country is still on a wartime footing. Beth and Jack and Michael all carry ration books because there are still shortages of just about everything, including bread and fruit and gasoline. It's worse than anything we had during the war."

Mom stopped peeling potatoes and looked at me and shook her head. "Maggie, you and Michael are so different, just like your father and I were different. He was so smart, and I always hoped it wouldn't matter, but it did. I'm afraid the same thing is going to happen to you. Look at where you come from, and then look at his mother. She grew up in that big house with servants. I left school at sixteen to go to work, and I changed linen at the Heidelberg Inn during the summer. I *was* a servant."

"Mom, Michael's grandparents were servants, too, and you don't know Beth. She's had so much heartache in her life. The reasons were different, but Jack kept her at a distance, just like Dad did to you. Her baby daughter died, just like Bridgit did. She lost two brothers in the war, and a third nearly went insane.

"It's true Beth and you are from very different backgrounds, but your values are exactly the same. There is nothing more important to Beth than her family. She has raised two fine sons, pretty much on her own, and she is the moral center of her family, just like you are for ours. Mom, you've always been my guiding light, and that's not going to change, no matter where I live."

"I hope for your sake you're right, Maggie." After squeezing my hand, she went back to peeling potatoes.

Chapter 48

THE EVENING BEFORE THE engagement party, Michael presented me with a beautiful diamond ring in an antique setting. "It has a bit of history to go along with it. A friend of my mother's, who was killed in the First War, left it in her care, and knowing how sentimental you are, she thought you might like it. If not, there are plenty of jewelry stores in New York and London."

I told him that I would gladly wear it. Colin Matheson's ring had finally found a home.

At the party, while Beth mingled comfortably among all of my family and friends, Jack sat down with Father Shea and my father. He wanted to get to know Dad, and by "chatting him up," it also cut down on the number of trips he took to the bar.

Despite her reservations, Mom was a gracious host to her British visitors. I didn't want to get my hopes up, but she was wearing her navy blue dress with the tiny red flowers. I could only hope that was a small step toward reconciliation. One of the best sights of the evening was my Aunt Agatha wearing a brand new, store-bought dress. Where on earth had she gotten the money to buy a new frock? And I looked at Geoff, and he gave me a sly smile.

Geoff was absolutely captivated by Sadie. When she asked him what it was like to work for the Foreign Legion, he answered in typical Geoff fashion: "I have not offered my services to the Foreign Legion. I am, however, a civil servant of the British Government working in the Foreign Office, and I would be more than happy to explain the differences to you."

Having the party with an open bar turned out to be a stroke of genius. By the end of the evening, everyone was toasting the Crowells' health, and some broke into an unintelligible "Knees Up Mother Brown," a popular WWII song in Britain.

I danced until I could no longer keep my shoes on, and it was nearly 1:00 when the lead singer announced that there would be one more dance. We had requested "Always." It was that song that Michael and I had been dancing to when we had fallen in love at Montclair. Everyone looked for their best girl or guy. Patrick danced cheek to cheek with Anna while Bobby and Teresa kept some space between them because Mamie was watching their every move.

As Michael and I danced, I thought about the long journey that I had traveled to arrive at this place and the people I had met along the way. With the exception of my family, it was Jack and Beth who had the greatest impact on my life, and I was looking forward to becoming a part of their family. In order to do that, I had to leave behind family and friends and the town that had helped to shape the person I had become. It was my intention to take with me the best of all those whom I had known and loved. But the next part of my life's journey lay in England with Michael.

Of all those whom I needed to thank, there was one person who was not there. I owed a debt of gratitude to Jane Austen and her tale of two lovers. After all, it was Jane who had led me to Michael.

The End

Appendix:
Dramatis Personae

Mr. Bennet (Mr. Garrison)—A gentleman farmer and the father of five daughters. Because of an entail placed on the estate, Longbourn will be inherited by his closest male relative, the Rev. William Collins. Elizabeth, his second oldest daughter, is his favorite.

Mrs. Bennet (Mrs. Garrison)—Acutely aware that her husband's death will mean that the family will have to vacate Longbourn, Mrs. Bennet becomes obsessed with marrying her daughters off to the first eligible bachelor. A silly woman, her interference proves embarrassing at best, and in the case of her daughter, Jane, and the eligible and wealthy Mr. Bingley, nearly fatal.

Jane Bennet (Jane Garrison Bingham)—The eldest Bennet daughter and the prettiest. A kind, sweet creature, she is agreeable in every situation and sees good in everyone. This results in her misjudging Charles Bingley's sisters, who are determined to keep her away from their brother, Charles. She is viewed as the family's savior because she is the one most likely to make an advantageous marriage.

Elizabeth Bennet (Elizabeth Garrison Lacey)—An attractive, intelligent, and witty young woman. Despite her precarious situation because of the entail, "Lizzy" is determined not to marry unless she falls in love. Offended by Mr. Darcy's rude behavior when he first comes to Meryton, she refuses his offer of marriage when he tells her he has had to put aside his own objections to marrying her because of her inferior position in society. However, when she later meets Darcy at Pemberley, his estate in Derbyshire, she recognizes he has changed and is now a man worthy of her love.

Mary Bennet (Mary Garrison)—The middle daughter, a sanctimonious scold, who thinks she is morally superior to everyone around her.

Kitty Bennet (Celia Stanton Garrison)—An empty-headed girl of seventeen, who follows her younger sister, Lydia, in her pursuit of a good time, which includes flirting with the officers quartered near Meryton.

Lydia Bennet (Lucy Garrison Waggoner Edwards)—The black sheep of the family. This sixteen-year-old flirt runs away with the cad, Mr. Wickham. This action has the potential to harm the marriage prospects of her four sisters because no respectable man would want to have anything to do with the Bennet family. Lydia is rescued by Mr. Darcy, who arranges for her marriage and purchases an army commission for Wickham.

Henry Bennet* (Henry Garrison)—The Bennets' only son, who died when he was twelve. Without a male heir, the Bennet estate will be entailed away to the benefit of Mr. Collins because it cannot be inherited by a female.

Caroline Bingley and Louisa Hurst (Caroline Bingham Upton and Louisa Bingham Ashurst)—Charles's conniving sisters, who attempt to sabotage Jane and Charles's romance. Caroline wants to get her brother back to London as quickly as possible because she has noticed that his friend, Mr. Darcy, is attracted to Elizabeth Bennet, and she wants Darcy for herself.

Charles Bingley (Charles Bingham)—Darcy's friend, whose family made their fortune in trade. Although he holds an inferior position in society to Darcy, his amiability wins him many friends and the love of Jane Bennet. He is convinced by his sisters and friend that Jane is not in love with him.

George Bingham*—Charles's eldest brother and the head of the large Bingham family. His success in business is the source of the family's wealth. As a result, he exerts a strong influence on all of his siblings. Richard and James Bingham are also Charles's older brothers.

Mr. William Collins (William Chatterton)—Described as one of literature's greatest bores, he is to inherit the Bennet estate upon Mr. Bennet's death. Supremely obnoxious, he goes to Longbourn with the intention of marrying one of the Bennet daughters. After he is told that Jane will shortly be engaged, he turns his attention to Lizzy, who finds him to be ridiculous. Over the objections of her hysterical mother, she refuses his offer of marriage. He quickly recovers and proposes to Lizzy's closest friend, Charlotte Lucas.

Fitzwilliam Darcy (William Lacey)—Born to privilege and status, this wealthy son of the landed gentry offends Elizabeth when they first meet at an assembly in Meryton because he believes himself to be superior to everyone there. It is only when Lizzy rejects his offer of marriage that he takes a long hard look

---

*These characters do not appear in Jane Austen's *Pride and Prejudice*.

at his actions and realizes he did not behave like a gentleman. A chastened Darcy renews his attentions to Lizzy, resolves Lydia and Wickham's problem, and informs his friend, Charles Bingley, that he was wrong about Jane Bennet and that they should marry. Lizzy recognizes the changes in Mr. Darcy and accepts his second proposal.

Georgiana Darcy (Georgiana Lacey)—The much younger sister of Mr. Darcy, who becomes the target of George Wickham in his effort to secure her fortune, but Darcy was able to prevent an elopement.

Anne de Bourgh (Anne Desmet)—The sickly daughter of Lady Catherine, who is supposed to marry Mr. Darcy because it was the wish of both their mothers.

Lady Catherine de Bourgh (Lady Sylvia Desmet)—Mr. Darcy's overbearing aristocratic aunt, who interferes in everyone's affairs. When she learns her nephew is possibly engaged to Elizabeth Bennet, she hops in her carriage and heads for Longbourn with the intention of preventing such an ill-advised proposal.

Col. Fitzwilliam (Col. Alexander Devereaux)—Mr. Darcy's cousin and the younger son of an earl. Elizabeth is mildly attracted to him, but because he must marry a woman of fortune, nothing can come of it.

Charlotte Lucas (Charlotte Ledger)—Lizzy's best friend and a sensible, plain-looking girl who knows she must marry or become a burden to her family. When Lizzy rejects Mr. Collins, he proposes to Charlotte, who recognizes that he is not the most intelligent man in England but one who will be able to provide her with a good home.

George Wickham (George Waggoner)—The son of Old Mr. Darcy's steward, he takes advantage of the old man's affections to secure enough money to purchase a living in the military, the church, or the law, and immediately squanders it. He attempts to elope with Georgiana, Darcy's much younger sister, because of her fortune. Darcy thought he was rid of Wickham after he had paid him off, but he shows up in Meryton and has a flirtation with Lizzy. When the militia removes to Brighton, he seduces Lydia Bennet, who is visiting with his colonel's wife.

Acknowledgments

I would like to thank my aunts, Patricia Lydon, Miriam Rothbauer, and Ann Snyder, as well as Dr. Joseph Lydon, the sage of Minooka, who provided numerous stories that are included in this book. I am also indebted to all of the World War II airmen of the 8th Air Force, who published their memoirs on the Internet, and to all of those who participated in Britain's World War II Oral History Project. You have done history and me a great service.

About the Author

Mary Lydon Simonsen has combined her love of history and the novels of Jane Austen in her first novel, which explores universal truths about love and conflict that cross generations and oceans. The author lives in Peoria and Flagstaff, Arizona.

Mr. Darcy Takes a Wife

LINDA BERDOLL

"Wild, bawdy, and utterly enjoyable...Austenites who enjoy the many continuations of her novels will find much to love about this wild ride of a sequel." —*Booklist*

Hold on to your bonnets!

Every woman wants to be Elizabeth Bennet Darcy—beautiful, gracious, universally admired, strong, daring, and outspoken—a thoroughly modern woman in crinolines. And every women will fall madly in love with Mr. Darcy—tall, dark and handsome, a nobleman and a heartthrob whose virility is matched only by his utter devotion to his wife...

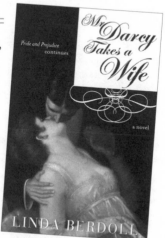

"Masterfully aligns Jane Austen's characters, taking us further into their lives and intrigue. Linda Berdoll, I am in awe...The regular Jane Austen community is in an uproar over this scandalous enlightenment."
—*Pop Syndicate*

What Readers Say:

"I thoroughly enjoyed this book, once my eyes stopped popping and I readjusted my lower jaw."

"Shocking and lusty... I loved every minute of it."

"Lizzy and Darcy like never before!"

978-1-4022-0273-5
$16.95 US/ $19.99 CAN/ £9.99 UK

Loving Mr. Darcy: Journeys Beyond Pemberley
SHARON LATHAN

"A romance that transcends time." —*The Romance Studio*

Darcy and Elizabeth embark on the journey of a lifetime

Six months into his marriage to Elizabeth Bennet, Darcy is still head over heels in love, and each day offers more opportunities to surprise and delight his beloved bride. Elizabeth has adapted to being the Mistress of Pemberley, charming everyone she meets and handling her duties with grace and poise. Just when it seems life can't get any better, Elizabeth gets the most wonderful news. The lovers leave the serenity of Pemberley, traveling through the sumptuous landscape of Regency England, experiencing the lavish sights, sounds, and tastes around them. With each day come new discoveries as they become further entwined, body and soul.

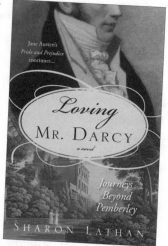

What readers are saying:

"Darcy's passion for love and life with Lizzy is brought to the forefront and captured beautifully."

"Sharon Lathan is a wonderful writer... I believe that Jane Austen herself would love this story as much as I did."

"The historical backdrop of the book is unbelievable—I actually felt like I could see all the places where the Darcys traveled."

"Truly captures the heart of Darcy & Elizabeth! Very well written and totally hot!"

978-1-4022-1741-8 • $14.99 US/ $18.99 CAN/ £7.99 UK

Mr. and Mrs. Fitzwilliam Darcy: Two Shall Become One
SHARON LATHAN

"Highly entertaining... I felt fully immersed in the time period. Well done!" —*Romance Reader at Heart*

A fascinating portrait of a timeless, consuming love

It's Darcy and Elizabeth's wedding day, and the journey is just beginning as Jane Austen's beloved *Pride and Prejudice* characters embark on the greatest adventure of all: marriage and a life together filled with surprising passion, tender self-discovery, and the simple joys of every day.

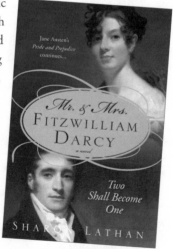

As their love story unfolds in this most romantic of Jane Austen sequels, Darcy and Elizabeth each reveal to the other how their relationship blossomed from misunderstanding to perfect understanding and harmony, and a marriage filled with romance, sensuality and the beauty of a deep, abiding love.

What readers are saying:

"This journey is truly amazing."

"What a wonderful beginning to this truly beautiful marriage."

"Could not stop reading."

"So beautifully written...making me feel as though I was in the room with Lizzy and Darcy...and sharing in all of the touching moments between."

978-1-4022-1523-0 • $14.99 US/ $15.99 CAN/ £7.99 UK

Mr. Darcy's Diary
AMANDA GRANGE

"A gift to a new generation of Darcy fans
and a treat for existing fans as well." —AUSTENBLOG

The only place Darcy could share his innermost feelings...

...was in the private pages of his diary. Torn between his sense of duty to his family name and his growing passion for Elizabeth Bennet, all he can do is struggle not to fall in love. A skillful and graceful imagining of the hero's point of view in one of the most beloved and enduring love stories of all time.

What readers are saying:

"A delicious treat for all Austen addicts."

"Amanda Grange knows her subject...I ended up reading the entire book in one sitting."

"Brilliant, you could almost hear Darcy's voice...I was so sad when it came to an end. I loved the visions she gave us of their married life."

"Amanda Grange has perfectly captured all of Jane Austen's clever wit and social observations to make *Mr. Darcy's Diary* a must read for any fan."

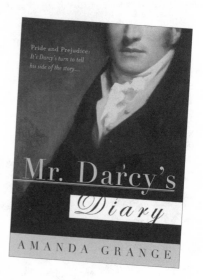

978-1-4022-0876-8 • $14.95 US/ $19.95 CAN/ £7.99 UK

The Ladies of Longbourn

The acclaimed **Pride and Prejudice** *sequel series*

The Pemberley Chronicles: Book 4

REBECCA ANN COLLINS

"Interesting stories, enduring themes, gentle humour,
and lively dialogue." —*Book News*

A complex and charming young woman of the Victorian age, tested to the limits of her endurance

The bestselling *Pemberley Chronicles* series continues the saga of the Darcys and Bingleys from Jane Austen's *Pride and Prejudice* and introduces imaginative new characters.

Anne-Marie Bradshaw is the granddaughter of Charles and Jane Bingley. Her father now owns Longbourn, the Bennet's estate in Hertfordshire. A young widow after a loveless marriage, Anne-Marie and her stepmother Anna, together with Charlotte Collins, widow of the unctuous Mr. Collins, are the Ladies of Longbourn. These smart, independent women challenge the conventional roles of women in the Victorian era, while they search for ways to build their own lasting legacies in an ever-changing world.

Jane Austen's original characters—Darcy, Elizabeth, Bingley, and Jane—anchor a dramatic story full of wit and compassion.

"A masterpiece that reaches the heart."

—BEVERLEY WONG, AUTHOR OF *Pride & Prejudice Prudence*

978-1-4022-1219-2 • $14.95 US/ $15.99 CAN/ £7.99 UK

Eliza's Daughter

A Sequel to *Jane Austen's* Sense and Sensibility

JOAN AIKEN

"Others may try, but nobody comes close to Aiken in writing sequels to Jane Austen." —*Publishers Weekly*

A young woman longing for adventure and an artistic life...

Because she's an illegitimate child, Eliza is raised in the rural backwater with very little supervision. An intelligent, creative, and free-spirited heroine, unfettered by the strictures of her time, she makes friends with poets William Wordsworth and Samuel Coleridge, finds her way to London, and eventually travels the world, all the while seeking to solve the mystery of her parentage. With fierce determination and irrepressible spirits, Eliza carves out a life full of adventure and artistic endeavor.

"Aiken's story is rich with humor, and her language is compelling. Readers captivated with Elinor and Marianne Dashwood in *Sense and Sensibility* will thoroughly enjoy Aiken's crystal gazing, but so will those unacquainted with Austen." —*Booklist*

"...innovative storyteller Aiken again pays tribute to Jane Austen in a cheerful spinoff of *Sense and Sensibility*." —*Kirkus Reviews*

978-1-4022-1288-8 • $14.95 US/ $15.99 CAN

MR. DARCY, VAMPYRE
PRIDE AND PREJUDICE CONTINUES...
AMANDA GRANGE

"A seductively gothic tale..." —Romance Buy the Book

A test of love that will take them to hell and back...

My dearest Jane,

My hand is trembling as I write this letter. My nerves are in tatters and I am so altered that I believe you would not recognise me. The past two months have been a nightmarish whirl of strange and disturbing circumstances, and the future...

Jane, I am afraid.

It was all so different a few short months ago. When I awoke on my wedding morning, I thought myself the happiest woman alive...

"Amanda Grange has crafted a clever homage to the Gothic novels that Jane Austen so enjoyed." —*AustenBlog*

"Compelling, heartbreaking, and triumphant all at once."
—*Bloody Bad Books*

978-1-4022-3697-6
$14.99 US/$18.99 CAN/£7.99 UK

"The romance and mystery in this story melded together perfectly... a real page-turner." —*Night Owl Romance*

"Mr. Darcy makes an inordinately attractive vampire.... *Mr. Darcy, Vampyre* delights lovers of Jane Austen that are looking for more." —*Armchair Interviews*

Mr. Fitzwilliam Darcy:

THE LAST MAN IN THE WORLD

A *Pride and Prejudice* Variation

ABIGAIL REYNOLDS

What if Elizabeth had accepted Mr. Darcy the first time he asked?

In Jane Austen's *Pride and Prejudice*, Elizabeth Bennet tells the proud Mr. Fitzwilliam Darcy that she wouldn't marry him if he were the last man in the world. But what if circumstances conspired to make her accept Darcy the first time he proposes? In this installment of Abigail Reynolds' acclaimed *Pride and Prejudice* Variations, Elizabeth agrees to marry Darcy against her better judgment, setting off a chain of events that nearly brings disaster to them both. Ultimately, Darcy and Elizabeth will have to work together on their tumultuous and passionate journey to make a success of their ill-timed marriage.

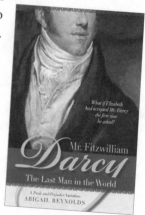

What readers are saying:

"A highly original story, immensely satisfying."

"Anyone who loves the story of Darcy and Elizabeth will love this variation."

"I was hooked from page one."

"A refreshing new look at what might have happened if…"

"Another good book to curl up with… I never wanted to put it down…"

978-1-4022-2947-3
$14.99 US/$18.99 CAN/£7.99 UK

THE OTHER MR. DARCY

PRIDE AND PREJUDICE CONTINUES...

MONICA FAIRVIEW

""A lovely story... a joy to read."
—*Bookishly Attentive*

Unpredictable courtships appear to run in the Darcy family...

When Caroline Bingley collapses to the floor and sobs at Mr. Darcy's wedding, imagine her humiliation when she discovers that a stranger has witnessed her emotional display. Miss Bingley, understandably, resents this gentleman very much, even if he is Mr. Darcy's American cousin. Mr. Robert Darcy is as charming as Mr. Fitzwilliam Darcy is proud, and he is stunned to find a beautiful young woman weeping brokenheartedly at his cousin's wedding. Such depth of love, he thinks, is rare and precious. For him, it's love at first sight...

"An intriguing concept...
a delightful ride in the park."
—*AustenProse*

978-1-4022-2513-0
$14.99 US/$18.99 CAN/£7.99 UK

The Plight of the Darcy Brothers
A TALE OF THE DARCYS & THE BINGLEYS

MARSHA ALTMAN

*"A charming tale of family and intrigue,
along with a deft bit of comedy."* —Publishers Weekly

Once again, it falls to Mr. Darcy to prevent a dreadful scandal...

Darcy and Elizabeth set off posthaste for the Continent to clear one of the Bennet sisters' reputation (this time it's Mary). But their madcap journey leads them to discover that the Darcy family has even deeper, darker secrets to hide. Meanwhile, back at Pemberley, the hapless Bingleys try to manage two unruly toddlers, and the ever-dastardly George Wickham arrives, determined to seize the Darcy fortune once and for all. Full of surprises, this lively *Pride and Prejudice* sequel plunges the Darcys and the Bingleys into a most delightful adventure.

"Ms. Altman takes Austen's beloved characters and makes them her own lovely results."
—*Once Upon A Romance*

with

978-1-4022-2429-4
$14.99 US/$18.99 CAN/£7.99 UK

"Humorous, dramatic, romantic, and touching—all things I love in a Jane Austen sequel." —*Grace's Book Blog*

"Another rollicking fine adventure with the Darcys and Bingleys...ridiculously fun reading." —*Bookfoolery & Babble*

WILLOUGHBY'S RETURN
JANE AUSTEN'S SENSE AND SENSIBILITY CONTINUES

JANE ODIWE

"A tale of almost irresistible temptation."

A lost love returns, rekindling forgotten passions...

When Marianne Dashwood marries Colonel Brandon, she puts her heartbreak over dashing scoundrel John Willoughby behind her. Three years later, Willoughby's return throws Marianne into a tizzy of painful memories and exquisite feelings of uncertainty. Willoughby is as charming, as roguish, and as much in love with her as ever. And the timing couldn't be worse—with Colonel Brandon away and Willoughby determined to win her back...

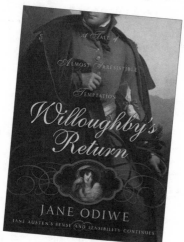

Praise for Lydia Bennet's story:

"A breathtaking Regency romp!" —Diana Birchall, author of *Mrs. Darcy's Dilemma*

"An absolute delight." —*Historical Novels Review*

"Odiwe emulates Austen's famous wit, and manages to give Lydia a happily-ever-after ending worthy of any Regency romance heroine." —*Booklist*

"Odiwe pays nice homage to Austen's stylings and endears the reader to the formerly secondary character, spoiled and impulsive Lydia Bennet." —*Publishers Weekly*

978-1-4022-2267-2
$14.99 US/$18.99 CAN/£7.99 UK

Darcy and Anne
Pride and Prejudice continues…

JUDITH BROCKLEHURST

"A beautiful tale." —*A Bibliophile's Bookshelf*

Without his help, she'll never be free…

Anne de Bourgh has never had a chance to figure out what she wants
for herself, until a fortuitous accident on the way to Pemberley separates
Anne from her formidable mother. With her stalwart cousin Fitzwilliam
Darcy and his lively wife Elizabeth on her side, she begins to feel she
might be able to spread her wings. But Lady Catherine's pride and
determination to find Anne a suitable husband threaten to overwhelm
Anne's newfound freedom and budding
sense of self. And without Darcy's help, Anne
will never have a chance to find true love…

"Brocklehurst transports you to another
place and time." —*A Journey of Books*

"A charming book… It is lovely to see
Anne's character blossom and fall in
love." —*Once Upon a Romance*

"The twists and turns, as Anne tries to weave a
path of happiness for herself, are subtle and
enjoyable, and the much-loved characters of
Pemberley remain true to form."
—*A Bibliophile's Bookshelf*

978-1-4022-2438-6
$12.99 US/$15.99 CAN/£6.99 UK

"A fun, truly fresh take on many of Austen's beloved characters."
—*Write Meg*